FATE OF THE JEDI

OUTCAST

D0734131

FATE OF THE JEDI

OUTCAST

AARON ALLSTON

BALLANTINE BOOKS • NEW YORK

Star Wars: Fate of the Jedi: Outcast is a work of fiction. Names, places, and incidents either are products of the author's imagination or are used fictitiously.

2010 Del Rey Mass Market Edition

Copyright © 2009 by Lucasfilm Ltd. & ® or ™ where indicated. All Rights Reserved. Used Under Authorization.

Excerpt from *Star Wars: Fate of the Jedi: Omen* copyright © 2009 by Lucasfilm Ltd. & ® or ™ where indicated. All Rights Reserved. Used Under Authorization.

Published in the United States by Del Rey, an imprint of The Random House Publishing Group, a division of Random House, Inc., New York.

DEL REY is a registered trademark and the Del Rey colophon is a trademark of Random House, Inc.

Originally published in hardcover in the United States by Del Rey, an imprint of The Random House Publishing Group, a division of Random House, Inc., in 2009.

This book contains an excerpt from *Star Wars: Fate of the Jedi: Omen* by Christie Golden. Available from Del Rey.

ISBN 978-0-345-50907-9

Printed in the United States of America

www.starwars.com
www.delreybooks.com

9 8 7 6 5 4 3 2 1

Acknowledgments

Thanks go to:

Troy Denning and Christie Golden, partners in a writing wing trio;

Shelly Shapiro, Sue Rostoni, Keith Clayton, and Leland Chee, the best lariat suppliers any goat rodeo could ask for;

And my agent, Russell Galen.

THE STAR WARS NOVELS TIMELINE

Dramatis Personae

Ben Skywalker; Jedi Knight (human male)

Corran Horn; Jedi Master (human male)

Han Solo; Captain, *Millennium Falcon* (human male)

Jagged Fel; Head of State, Imperial Remnant (human male)

Jaina Solo; Jedi Knight (human female)

Kenth Hamner; Jedi Master (human male)

Leia Organa Solo; Jedi Knight (human female)

Luke Skywalker; Jedi Grand Master (human male)

Mirax Horn; businesswoman (human female)

Natasi Daala; Chief of State, Galactic Alliance (human female)

Valin Horn; Jedi Knight (human male)

The darkness was eternal, all-powerful, unchangeable.

She stared into it, unblinking and unafraid. She was determined that it would not claim her. She had resisted it these many years. She would resist it forever, never despairing.

It was unchangeable, but change would take place. The Force said so.

Chapter One

ONE BY ONE, THE STARS OVERHEAD BEGAN TO DISAPPEAR, swallowed by some enormous darkness interposing itself from above and behind the shuttle. Sharply pointed at its most forward position, broadening behind, the flood of blackness advanced, blotting out more and more of the unblinking starfield, until darkness was all there was to see.

Then, all across the length and breadth of the ominous shape, lights came on—blue and white running lights, tiny red hatch and security lights, sudden glows from within transparisteel viewports, one large rectangular whiteness limned by atmosphere shields. The lights showed the vast triangle to be the underside of an Imperial Star Destroyer, painted black, forbidding a moment ago, now comparatively cheerful in its proper running configuration. It was the *Gilad Pellaeon,* newly arrived from the Imperial Remnant, and its officers clearly knew how to put on a show.

Jaina Solo, sitting with the others in the dimly lit passenger compartment of the government VIP shuttle, watched the entire display through the overhead transparisteel canopy and laughed out loud.

The Bothan in the sumptuously padded chair next to

hers gave her a curious look. His mottled red and tan fur twitched, either from suppressed irritation or embarrassment at Jaina's outburst. "What do you find so amusing?"

"Oh, both the obviousness of it and the skill with which it was performed. It's so very, *You used to think of us as dark and scary, but now we're just your stylish allies.*" Jaina lowered her voice so that her next comment would not carry to the passengers in the seats behind. "The press will love it. That image will play on the holonews broadcasts constantly. Mark my words."

"Was that little show a Jagged Fel detail?"

Jaina tilted her head, considering. "I don't know. He could have come up with it, but he usually doesn't spend his time planning displays or events. When he does, though, they're usually pretty . . . effective."

The shuttle rose toward the *Gilad Pellaeon*'s main landing bay. In moments, it was through the square atmosphere barrier shield and drifting sideways to land on the deck nearby. The landing place was clearly marked—hundreds of beings, most wearing gray Imperial uniforms or the distinctive white armor of the Imperial stormtrooper, waited in the bay, and the one circular spot where none stood was just the right size for the Galactic Alliance shuttle.

The passengers rose as the shuttle settled into place. The Bothan smoothed his tunic, a cheerful blue decorated with a golden sliver pattern suggesting claws. "Time to go to work. You won't let me get killed, will you?"

Jaina let her eyes widen. "Is that what I was supposed to be doing here?" she asked in droll tones. "I should have brought my lightsaber."

The Bothan offered a long-suffering sigh and turned toward the exit.

They descended the shuttle's boarding ramp. With no

duties required of her other than to keep alert and be the Jedi face at this preliminary meeting, Jaina was able to stand back and observe. She was struck with the unreality of it all. The niece and daughter of three of the most famous enemies of the Empire during the First Galactic Civil War of a few decades earlier, she was now witness to events that might bring the Galactic Empire—or Imperial Remnant, as it was called everywhere outside its own borders—into the Galactic Alliance on a lasting basis.

And at the center of the plan was the man, flanked by Imperial officers, who now approached the Bothan. Slightly under average size, though towering well above Jaina's diminutive height, he was dark-haired, with a trim beard and mustache that gave him a rakish look, and was handsome in a way that became more pronounced when he glowered. A scar on his forehead ran up into his hairline and seemed to continue as a lock of white hair from that point. He wore expensive but subdued black civilian garments, neck-to-toe, that would be inconspicuous anywhere on Coruscant but stood out in sharp relief to the gray and white uniforms, white armor, and colorful Alliance clothes surrounding him.

He had one moment to glance at Jaina. The look probably appeared neutral to onlookers, but for her it carried just a twinkle of humor, a touch of exasperation that the two of them had to put up with all these delays. Then an Alliance functionary, notable for his blandness, made introductions: "Imperial Head of State the most honorable Jagged Fel, may I present Senator Tiurrg Drey'lye of Bothawui, head of the Senate Unification Preparations Committee."

Jagged Fel took the Senator's hand. "I'm pleased to be working with you."

"And delighted to meet *you*. Chief of State Daala

sends her compliments and looks forward to meeting you when you make planetfall."

Jag nodded. "And now, I believe, protocol insists that we open a bottle or a dozen of wine and make some preliminary discussion of security, introduction protocols, and so on."

"Fortunately about the wine, and regrettably about everything else, you are correct."

At the end of two full standard hours—Jaina knew from regular, surreptitious consultations of her chrono—Jag was able to convince the Senator and his retinue to accept a tour of the *Gilad Pellaeon*. He was also able to request a private consultation with the sole representative of the Jedi Order present. Moments later, the gray-walled conference room was empty of everyone but Jag and Jaina.

Jag glanced toward the door. "Security seal, access limited to Jagged Fel and Jedi Jaina Solo, voice identification, activate." The door hissed in response as it sealed. Then Jag returned his attention to Jaina.

She let an expression of anger and accusation cross her face. "You're not fooling anyone, Fel. You're planning for an Imperial invasion of Alliance space."

Jag nodded. "I've been planning it for quite a while. Come here."

She moved to him, settled into his lap, and was suddenly but not unexpectedly caught in his embrace. They kissed urgently, hungrily.

Finally Jaina drew back and smiled at him. "This isn't going to be a routine part of your consultations with every Jedi."

"Uh, no. That would cause some trouble here and at home. But I actually *do* have business with the Jedi that does not involve the Galactic Alliance, at least not initially."

"What sort of business?"

"Whether or not the Galactic Empire joins with the Galactic Alliance, I think there ought to be an official Jedi presence in the Empire. A second Temple, a branch, an offshoot, whatever. Providing advice and insight to the Head of State."

"And protection?"

He shrugged. "Less of an issue. I'm doing all right. Two years in this position and not dead yet."

"Emperor Palpatine went nearly twenty-five years."

"I guess that makes him my hero."

Jaina snorted. "Don't even say that in jest . . . Jag, if the Remnant doesn't join the Alliance, I'm not sure the Jedi *can* have a presence without Alliance approval."

"The Order still keeps its training facility for youngsters in Hapan space. And the Hapans haven't rejoined."

"You sound annoyed. The Hapans still giving you trouble?"

"Let's not talk about *that*."

"Besides, moving the school back to Alliance space is just a matter of time, logistics, and finances; there's no question that it will happen. On the other hand, it's very likely that the government would withhold approval for a Jedi branch in the Remnant, just out of spite, if the Remnant doesn't join."

"Well, there's such a thing as an *unofficial* presence. And there's such a thing as rival schools, schismatic branches, and places for former Jedi to go when they can't be at the Temple."

Jaina smiled again, but now there was suspicion in her expression. "You just want to have this so *I'll* be assigned to come to the Remnant and set it up."

"That's a motive, but not the only one. Remember, to the Moffs and to a lot of the Imperial population, the Jedi have been bogeymen since Palpatine died. At the

very least, I don't want them to be inappropriately
afraid of the woman I'm in love with."

Jaina was silent for a moment. "Have we talked
enough politics?"

"I think so."

"Good."

HORN FAMILY QUARTERS,
KALLAD'S DREAM VACATION HOSTEL,
CORUSCANT

Yawning, hair tousled, clad in a blue dressing robe,
Valin Horn knew that he did not look anything like an
experienced Jedi Knight. He looked like an unshaven,
unkempt bachelor, which he also was. But here, in these
rented quarters, there would be only family to see him—
at least until he had breakfast, shaved, and dressed.

The Horns did not live here, of course. His mother,
Mirax, was the anchor for the immediate family. Manager of a variety of interlinked businesses—trading, in-
terplanetary finances, gambling and recreation, and, if
rumors were true, still a little smuggling here and
there—she maintained her home and business address
on Corellia. Corran, her husband and Valin's father, was
a Jedi Master, much of his life spent on missions away
from the family, but his true home was where his heart
resided, wherever Mirax lived. Valin and his sister, Jysella, also Jedi, lived wherever their missions sent them,
and also counted Mirax as the center of the family.

Now Mirax had rented temporary quarters on Coruscant so the family could collect on one of its rare occasions, this time for the Unification Summit, where she
and Corran would separately give depositions on the re-
lationships among the Confederation states, the Imperial Remnant, and the Galactic Alliance as they related

to trade and Jedi activities. Mirax had insisted that Valin and Jysella leave their Temple quarters and stay with their parents while these events were taking place, and few forces in the galaxy could stand before her decision—Luke Skywalker certainly knew better than to try.

Moving from the refresher toward the kitchen and dining nook, Valin brushed a lock of brown hair out of his eyes and grinned. Much as he might put up a public show of protest—the independent young man who did not need parents to direct his actions or tell him where to sleep—he hardly minded. It was good to see family. And both Corran and Mirax were better cooks than the ones at the Jedi Temple.

There was no sound of conversation from the kitchen, but there was some clattering of pans, so at least one of his parents must still be on hand. As he stepped from the hallway into the dining nook, Valin saw that it was his mother, her back to him as she worked at the stove. He pulled a chair from the table and sat. "Good morning."

"A joke, so early?" Mirax did not turn to face him, but her tone was cheerful. "No morning is good. I come light-years from Corellia to be with my family, and what happens? I have to keep Jedi hours to see them. Don't you know that I'm an executive? And a lazy one?"

"I forgot." Valin took a deep breath, sampling the smells of breakfast. His mother was making hotcakes Corellian-style, nerf sausage links on the side, and caf was brewing. For a moment, Valin was transported back to his childhood, to the family breakfasts that had been somewhat more common before the Yuuzhan Vong came, before Valin and Jysella had started down the Jedi path. "Where are Dad and Sella?"

"Your father is out getting some back-door information from other Jedi Masters for his deposition." Mirax pulled a plate from a cabinet and began sliding hotcakes and links onto it. "Your sister left early and wouldn't say what she was doing, which I assume either means it's Jedi business I can't know about or that she's seeing some man she doesn't *want* me to know about."

"Or both."

"Or both." Mirax turned and moved over to put the plate down before him. She set utensils beside it.

The plate was heaped high with food, and Valin recoiled from it in mock horror. "Stang, Mom, you're feeding your son, not a squadron of Gamorreans." Then he caught sight of his mother's face and he was suddenly no longer in a joking mood.

This wasn't his mother.

Oh, the woman had Mirax's features. She had the round face that admirers had called "cute" far more often than "beautiful," much to Mirax's chagrin. She had Mirax's generous, curving lips that smiled so readily and expressively, and Mirax's bright, lively brown eyes. She had Mirax's hair, a glossy black with flecks of gray, worn shoulder-length to fit readily under a pilot's helmet, even though she piloted far less often these days. She was Mirax to every freckle and dimple.

But she was not Mirax.

The woman, whoever she was, caught sight of Valin's confusion. "Something wrong?"

"Uh, no." Stunned, Valin looked down at his plate.

He had to think—logically, correctly, and *fast*. He might be in grave danger right now, though the Force currently gave him no indication of imminent attack. The true Mirax, wherever she was, might be in serious trouble or worse. Valin tried in vain to slow his heart rate and speed up his thinking processes.

Fact: Mirax had been here but had been replaced by an imposter. Presumably the real Mirax was gone; Valin could not sense anyone but himself and the imposter in the immediate vicinity. The imposter had remained behind for some reason that had to relate to Valin, Jysella, or Corran. It couldn't have been to capture Valin, as she could have done that with drugs or other methods while he slept, so the food was probably not drugged.

Under Not-Mirax's concerned gaze, he took a tentative bite of sausage and turned a reassuring smile he didn't feel toward her.

Fact: Creating an imposter this perfect must have taken a fortune in money, an incredible amount of research, and a volunteer willing to let her features be permanently carved into the likeness of another's. Or perhaps this was a clone, raised and trained for the purpose of simulating Mirax. Or maybe she was a droid, one of the very expensive, very rare human replica droids. Or maybe a shape-shifter. Whichever, the simulation was nearly perfect. Valin hadn't recognized the deception until . . .

Until *what*? What had tipped him off? He took another bite, not registering the sausage's taste or temperature, and maintained the face-hurting smile as he tried to recall the detail that had alerted him that this wasn't his mother.

He couldn't figure it out. It was just an instant realization, too fleeting to remember, too overwhelming to reject.

Would Corran be able to see through the deception? Would Jysella? Surely, they had to be able to. But what if they couldn't? Valin would accuse this woman and be thought insane.

Were Corran and Jysella even still at liberty? Still *alive*? At this moment, the Not-Mirax's colleagues could be spiriting the two of them away with the true Mirax. Or Corran and Jysella could be lying, bleeding, at the bottom of an access shaft, their lives draining away.

Valin couldn't think straight. The situation was too overwhelming, the mystery too deep, and the only person here who knew the answers was the one who wore the face of his mother.

He stood, sending his chair clattering backward, and fixed the false Mirax with a hard look. "Just a moment." He dashed to his room.

His lightsaber was still where he'd left it, on the nightstand beside his bed. He snatched it up and gave it a near-instantaneous examination. Battery power was still optimal; there was no sign that it had been tampered with.

He returned to the dining room with the weapon in his hand. Not-Mirax, clearly confused and beginning to look a little alarmed, stood by the stove, staring at him.

Valin ignited the lightsaber, its *snap-hiss* of activation startlingly loud, and held the point of the gleaming energy blade against the food on his plate. Hotcakes shriveled and blackened from contact with the weapon's plasma. Valin gave Not-Mirax an approving nod. "Flesh does the same thing under the same conditions, you know."

"Valin, what's *wrong*?"

"You may address me as Jedi Horn. You don't have the right to use my personal name." Valin swung the lightsaber around in a practice form, allowing the blade to come within a few centimeters of the glow rod fixture overhead, the wall, the dining table, and the woman with his mother's face. "You probably know from your research that the Jedi don't worry much about amputations."

Not-Mirax shrank back away from him, both hands on the stove edge behind her. "What?"

"We know that a severed limb can readily be replaced by a prosthetic that looks identical to the real thing. Prosthetics offer sensation and do everything flesh can. They're ideal substitutes in every way, except for requiring maintenance. So we don't feel too badly when we have to cut the arm or leg off a very bad person. But I assure you, that very bad person remembers the pain forever."

"Valin, I'm going to call your father now." Not-Mirax sidled toward the blue bantha-hide carrybag she had left on a side table.

Valin positioned the tip of his lightsaber directly beneath her chin. At the distance of half a centimeter, its containing force field kept her from feeling any heat from the blade, but a slight twitch on Valin's part could maim or kill her instantly. She froze.

"No, you're not. You know what you're going to do instead?"

Not-Mirax's voice wavered. "What?"

"You're going to *tell me what you've done with my mother!*" The last several words emerged as a bellow, driven by fear and anger. Valin knew that he looked as angry as he sounded; he could feel blood reddening his face, could even see redness begin to suffuse everything in his vision.

"Boy, put the blade down." Those were not the woman's words. They came from behind. Valin spun, bringing his blade up into a defensive position.

In the doorway stood a man, middle-aged, clean-shaven, his hair graying from brown. He was of below-average height, his eyes a startling green. He wore the brown robes of a Jedi. His hands were on his belt, his own lightsaber still dangling from it.

He was Valin's father, Jedi Master Corran Horn. But he wasn't, any more than the woman behind Valin was Mirax Horn.

Valin felt a wave of despair wash over him. *Both* parents replaced. Odds were growing that the real Corran and Mirax were already dead.

Yet Valin's voice was soft when he spoke. "They may

have made you a virtual double for my father. But they can't have given you his expertise with the lightsaber."

"You don't want to do what you're thinking about, son."

"When I cut you in half, that's all the proof anyone will ever need that you're not the real Corran Horn."

Valin lunged.

Chapter Two

Valin swung his blade in a lightning-quick circle, low backward to high forward, a move that would cut the imposter in two vertically.

The Not-Corran's lightsaber blade was suddenly alive and raised horizontally, blocking his blow. Like the real Corran's, it shone silver. Perhaps the man had seized the real Corran's weapon; it certainly looked identical. Valin felt his heart sink further.

He threw a series of short slashes at Not-Corran's head, left shoulder, and left side, but his opponent blocked each one with minimal arm motion, with little effort. Then the imposter's brown boot was slamming into Valin's chest, hurtling him backward and to his right. Valin crashed down painfully atop the water-filled sink, his ribs bruising against the faucet, his right buttock shattering soaking dishes. Disoriented, he spun his blade in a defensive circle. But Not-Corran did not immediately follow up; instead, he was shouting, "Mirax, *out now,*" and the woman impersonating his mother was leaving the room at a dead run, tears and a bewildered, pained expression on her face.

Valin heaved himself off the sink, his rear end wet, and landed on his feet. He pointed his blade at Not-Corran, an informal salute of grudging respect. "You've studied. Where?"

"Put the blade away, boy. I don't know what you're

seeing or feeling, but we can get people in here whom you trust. We can even get Luke Skywalker here."

"Sure, I'll happily give you time to call your reinforcements. Tactically, that's a good solution for me."

"*You* make the calls, then."

Valin paused as if hesitating but took that moment to assess his options.

Not-Corran was at least as good a swordsman as Valin, and Not-Mirax was clearly off calling in more help. Soon enough, Valin would be overmatched.

To Valin's right were the sink and stove, cabinets above, wall behind. To the left was a wall between him and the living room; against it stood a sideboard and the small table where Mirax's carrybag rested. Ahead was the only path out of this chamber, and Not-Corran was in the way.

Well, that was all right. In rental quarters like these, lightly constructed for ease of remodeling and for the sake of cheapness, Valin didn't need a door.

He darted to the left and boosted his speed with a touch of the Force. He aimed for the open spot between table and sideboard, and the wall there was suddenly wreckage filling the air with white powder, falling away from him in pieces, barely registering as an impact against Valin's body; it gave way as readily as a flimsi barrier would to a normal man.

Now he was in the main living chamber. Ahead was a sofa; in the wall behind it was a large picture viewport with a real waterfall cascading by a few meters beyond. To the right was the door out and another window beside it—

Also to the right was a blur, Not-Corran in Force-speeded motion, paralleling him, now between him and the door.

Valin didn't alter his trajectory. He dived forward into the viewport, counting on the minimal-expense construction of this property to mean that the transparisteel there was thin, or that the mountings holding it into the wall were not the stoutest . . .

He was right on both counts. Again he barely felt the impact as he punched through the viewport. The thin transparisteel folded around him. Together they hurtled into sunlight, through the waterfall downpour, and into open air beyond.

Valin exerted himself, throwing the oversized sheet of transparent foil away, and dropped into what looked like a bottomless city canyon bordered on two sides by soaring, gaudily decorated banks of skytowers.

This was a vacationers' district, the vast lengths of skyrises occupied mostly by hostels, restaurants, spas, and other businesses catering to travelers and celebrants from all over Coruscant and the Alliance. The gap separating this bank of skytowers from the one facing it was about thirty meters wide, farther than his leap would carry him, but there were multiple streams of speeder traffic above and below. As he dropped, he took note of a blue-and-yellow-striped speeder approaching below; he twisted, angling toward it, and he came down on the hood of the vehicle, landing in a deep crouch.

The front end of the speeder dipped precipitously under the force of his impact. The pilot was an Ortolan, rotund and blue-skinned, his broad ears and snout suddenly being snapped back by the wind; Valin saw the pilot's eyes open wide. The repulsorlift of the speeder shrieked under the sudden demand imposed by Valin's landing. It tried to bring the speeder's nose back up.

It succeeded, and as it did, Valin sprang up and forward, leaping as far as the opposite traffic lane. There he came down atop a long bus, which did not budge under his landing. Valin flipped forward again, somersaulting, and this time landed on the deck of an open-air tourist conveyance that was beginning to fill up with vacationers boarding via a short ramp from the adjacent hostel patio. The vacationers started with surprise at the sudden appearance of a drenched, insufficiently clothed Jedi with a live lightsaber in his hand.

Valin couldn't keep anger and a little panic out of his voice. "I need a comlink, *quick*." He held out his hand.

The few seconds that followed crawled like an eternity but gave Valin time to think, to wonder. The vacationers and tourists boarding this vehicle were, to all outward appearance, ordinary beings of the middle class. Most of them were dressed in garments far more colorful, revealing, or both than they would ever wear at home. They seemed normal, but how many of them, too, might be imposters? He had no sense whatsoever of the scale of this deception.

One of them, a beautiful red-skinned Twi'lek woman, finished struggling to unclip something from her white halter top. She extended the object toward Valin, her hand open. It was a comlink. He reached for it.

Not-Corran thumped shoulders-first into the deck and rolled to his feet four meters from Valin. His own lightsaber was in his hand but unlit. His voice, raised so all on the vehicle could hear, sounded sad, pained. "Everybody stand back. This man is . . . not well. I'll handle this."

Valin gestured at Not-Corran. "*You're* not well. You're conspiring against the Jedi Order, and you should know that's a dangerous, usually fatal mistake."

He called on inner resources, on memories of scores of battles endured and won. He let those memories fill him and push out the panic and anguish he'd been feeling. New calmness quieting and deepening his voice, he said, "All right. Your decision. Your fate. I'm just going to cut my way through you and then go find out who's behind this." Again he sprang at the man who was not his father.

This time no concern for self-preservation affected his tactics. He went completely on the offensive, his sole goal to cut down Not-Corran. He threw blow after blow with stuttered-laser speed, backing Not-Corran up against the vehicle rail, then down the ramp to the hostel's patio restaurant beyond. Restaurant patrons scattered, leaving tables loaded with half-finished meals, drinks, and bags.

Not-Corran did not take advantage of a couple of openings Valin's tactics offered him. Valin felt a surge of optimism. Not-Corran's adherence to the true Corran's loyalties clearly meant he would not cut Valin down. Valin did not feel the same consideration toward his enemy.

And though Valin was tiring, Not-Corran had it worse: the older man was beginning to sweat.

Not-Corran backflipped to the far side of a round white table made of light durasteel. As he landed, he kicked the table toward Valin. Valin ignored the dishes and food hurtling toward him; he slashed at the table itself, cleaving it in two. Had he possessed the full range of Jedi powers, he could have swept it aside with an exertion of telekinesis, but like his father he was deficient in that ability.

Not-Corran now stood five meters away, breathing heavily, his blade at a single-handed, downward defensive angle.

Valin gave him a look of grudging admiration. "You know, to exhibit all the Jedi skills but refrain from using telekinesis so that you can maintain the impersonation shows a lot of dedication. Too bad it won't get you anything. Too bad you have to die."

"Boy, this has *got* to end." Not-Corran threw up his free hand as if finally to make a telekinetic attack. Valin hesitated, not sure which way to jump. Then he realized something bad.

Not-Corran hadn't used any Force power, but had, through his gesture, frozen Valin in place just for an instant. Valin felt a sensation of imminent danger.

Then it hit him, a blow from behind, a shock felt by every part of his body. His knees gave way. He fell forward, his vision graying.

But before he lost consciousness completely, he saw, beyond the railing of the patio, a hovering airspeeder—his mother's speeder, with Not-Mirax standing in the driver's seat, her military-grade blaster pistol in her hands aimed at him. Tears streamed from her eyes as if to mimic the artificial waterfall that framed her from thirty meters beyond.

SENATE BUILDING, CORUSCANT

Luke Skywalker found it amazing that there was a chamber this large in the Senate Building he had never seen. It was six stories in height, and broad and deep enough to hold two thousand spectators. The permanent bench seating was filled almost to capacity, late arrivals moving along the aisles and peering anxiously to find open spots. At the head of the chamber stood an enormous dais with two cloth-draped tables, swivel seats set up behind them, and a lectern between them. On the carpeted floor before the dais were round tables with chairs placed to face the front of the room. It was much like an oversized courtroom set up for a panel of judges, but more informal in its arrangement, and far less somber in its decorative style: the carpets and padding on the bench seats and backs were of soothing blues and purples; the walls were off-white with Galactic Alliance symbols painted large upon them; and the furniture up front was an unthreatening tan-gold.

And Luke had never seen the place before. Had it always been here? Were there many more such chambers in this gargantuan building?

The dais tables were fully occupied, and the male Bothan sitting in the most central chair, his red and tan fur rippling with the consequence of the moment, nodded to an aide who had just whispered to him. The Bothan stood and took the lectern beside his seat. "Only forty-five minutes late," he said, his amplified voice booming across the chamber. "Not bad for a Galactic Alliance event, yes?"

His remark drew a faint laugh from the crowd. Encouraged, he continued, "I am Senator Tiurrg Drey'lye, chair of the Unification Preparations Committee, and the organizer of this event. Over the next several days, in both private and public sessions, we will be examining the relationship between the Galactic Alliance, the states of the Confederation, the Galactic Empire, and individual planet-states with the aim of restoring our great planetary union to levels of strength and security equaling, even surpassing, those it enjoyed before the recent war."

Ben, Luke's sixteen-year-old son, sat to Luke's left. Redheaded, athletic, he was dressed in the black tunic and pants that were his trademark whenever Jedi dress was not absolutely called for. Now he frowned, curious. "What about the Hapans? They were invited."

Luke gestured for Ben to lower his voice, though the remark had not been loud enough to carry beyond the Jedi table. "They were invited, but they were invited *incorrectly,* so they didn't come."

"Huh?"

The Bothan's renewed speech checked Luke's reply for a moment. "This morning, we'll be hearing opening remarks from some of the session organizers and speakers offering a sense of what we hope to accomplish . . ."

Luke tuned him out and turned toward Ben. "The Hapans were issued an invitation, but its language suggested very faintly that their presence was less critical than that of the Remnant and the Confederation. They couldn't agree to attend without appearing to accept a lower status than the others. So, knowing that there will be later Unification Summits where they can be the stars, they claimed a prior commitment."

Ben frowned. "Why was the invitation worded that way? Was it an accident?"

Leia Organa Solo, Luke's sister, sitting to Luke's right, looked toward father and son. A slightly graying dark-haired, diminutive woman dressed in brown Jedi robes, she currently blended in with her company, but as a former Chief of State of the New Republic, she could have dressed to be the equal of the most extravagant politician present and not been ill thought of because of it.

She offered Ben a knowing smile. "No written invitation sent to an important leader has accidents like that in it. Of course, the Alliance diplomatic corps claims that no insult was intended. They claim 'Regrettable misinterpretation of figures of speech,' which subtly puts the blame on the Hapans for being touchy."

"I still don't understand why the Alliance wouldn't want them here for this," Ben pressed.

Luke shrugged. "Actually, I don't have any idea."

Leia nodded toward the dais, gesturing at the table to the right, to the Bothan's left. "They don't want to dilute the Imperial presence or to interfere with Imperial cooperation."

Startled, Luke gave the table another look.

Galactic Alliance Chief of State Natasi Daala sat at the end of the table. A woman of late middle years, she had copper-colored hair and lovely features made less appealing by her rigid, military bearing. She wore a white admiral's uniform with broad swaths of service medals across the tunic. A onetime protégée of the Empire's Grand Moff Wilhuff Tarkin—and uncharitably assumed by many to have achieved her military rank because she was also his lover—she had been leader of the Galactic Alliance for two years and had done a fine, measured job of restoring the union's economies and networks of political alliances, which had been shattered by the recent war.

To her right sat Jagged Fel, the young Head of State of the Imperial Remnant. Raised among the Chiss, proven in battle as a combat pilot in the Yuuzhan Vong War, he was a reluctant leader who had shown himself to be adept at keeping the Imperial Moffs in line and in managing difficult Imperial–Hapan relations.

To Jag's right, immediately beside the still-droning Bothan, was Turr Phennir, Supreme Military Commander of the Confederation. He was the closest that loose alliance of planets had to an overall leader. Pale, aristocratic, with a scar reaching from the middle of his left cheek to the left corner of his mouth, he, like Fel, was a former combat pilot. The reputation he'd earned early in his career for classic Imperial backstabbing politics and combat savagery had changed over the years to one of pragmatism and honorable service.

And until now, Luke had given no conscious thought to the fact that these three, the most eminent politicians on Coruscant at this moment, were all Imperials. That realization struck him like a bucket of icy water. He had fought the Imperials for decades, had played a role in the defeat of every one of their major operations during that time, and here they were, in charge of . . . everything.

Leia glanced at Luke, amused. "I felt that."

"I didn't put it together before now. I've been thinking of the three of them as *themselves,* not as Imperials. The fate of the galaxy is, all of a sudden, in the hands of *Imperials.*"

"Yes."

"When did it strike *you*?"

"Two years ago, when Daala and Fel took their posts within a short time of each other."

"You didn't mention it to me."

She shrugged. "There was nothing I could do about it. Or *should* do about it. The symbolism of them all being Imperials in one way or another is nothing compared with the question of who they are inside. I mean, the Rebellion was largely made up of former Imperials. Crix Madine. Mon Mothma. Jan Dodonna. I'm a former Imperial Senator."

"True. And all three leaders up at that table are honorable people."

"Yes. But that doesn't mean they want what we want. Or that they can see the consequences of their decisions the way we can." Leia's smile became distinctly ironic. "I bet Palpatine's ghost is laughing at us right now."

Luke forced himself to relax. He had, over the years, become convinced that in the absence of Palpatine and his immediate successors such as Ysane Isard and Sate Pestage, what it meant to be an Imperial had changed. The Moffs, sector governors, tended to be as scheming and self-serving as they were forty years earlier, but the military, an even more potent force in the Remnant, was largely populated by men and women who simply preferred a more orderly, more governed society than that found in the Alliance. The Empire was no longer a symbol of tyranny or of planetary genocide.

But the strangeness of the situation did not leave Luke. He took a look around his table to see if the others present were similarly affected.

Kyp Durron faced the dais and wore an expression suggesting that he was somewhere else, maintaining a false show of interest that was nothing but polite veneer. Jaina, as beautiful as her mother, Leia, but even more dangerous, concentrated on those at the dais, especially Jag Fel. Han Solo, lanky, weathered, and vital, sitting to the right of Leia, wore his traditional vest and trousers, the latter decorated with the Corellian Bloodstripes, his informal mode of dress in defiance of event protocols; he stared in heavy-lidded disinterest at the speaker. Kam and Tionne Solusar, no visible sign left of the savage mutilations they had survived during the recent war, ignored the Bothan's speech and whispered between themselves.

And the Horns—

Luke blinked. Where *were* Corran and Mirax? They'd be testifying before separate panels later today and had announced they would be present at these opening ceremonies. Luke grinned sourly to himself. Corran Horn was a loyal ally and would stand beside him in the face of any danger, but he was obviously canny enough to avoid the threat of death by boredom.

Two hours later, those who had been sitting at the Jedi table moved out in a knot from the Senate Building into the sunlight shining on the plaza outside. Immediately Luke felt heat from the sun soaking into his dark Grand Master garments.

Han stretched, resulting in a series of popping noises from his arms and shoulders. "I think I died a couple of times during the speeches." His voice was a grumble. "Leia kept poking me and starting my heart again. Some sort of dark side Force technique, I bet."

Leia smirked and gave his ribs a two-fingered jab. "Like that?"

Han shrank away. "Ow. And yes. And I think maybe you should have let me stay dead. Because I just know there are more speeches to come, and I have to be at some of them."

Leia gave him a look that was both disapproving and

amused. "It wasn't that bad. Neither the pokes nor the speeches."

Luke grinned and brought out his comlink. It, like all comlinks taken into the ceremonial hall, had been switched off as a courtesy to the event. Now he switched it on. Immediately it beeped multiple times, indicating that he had several messages to listen to, several calls to return.

Jaina's was doing the same thing. She grimaced. "Busy day to come."

Luke felt it first, a ripple in the Force, not exactly of menace but of disquiet. He looked around the plaza, seeing the ostentatiously dressed members of the crowd continuing to stream out from the Senate Building. Speeder traffic confined itself to its proper travel lanes some distance away—

No, that wasn't quite true. Four night-blue personnel transport speeders, traveling in a tight chain and at moderate speed just above pedestrian head height, were moving toward this building entrance. This was not an unusual sight in the government districts of Coruscant; troops were often moved in to offer security at an event. But such movements usually took place before the event began, not after it ended.

The other Masters present felt the disquiet and became more alert, but made no outward sign. Then Jaina noticed. She put her hand on her lightsaber.

"Ben." Luke kept his voice low. "Drop back, blend with the crowd. Call Nawara Ven."

Ben glanced around and spotted the transports. His jaw tightened. He looked as though he wanted to argue, but he simply stopped in place, disappearing from among the other Jedi as they continued to move forward. He drew out his comlink and thumbed it on.

The four personnel carriers broke formation, one crossing past the group of Jedi and swinging in at their left side, one drawing up short and landing to their right. The third slid into place between them and the Senate Building, while the fourth settled immediately ahead of them. The maneuver, smooth and seemingly well practiced, left the Jedi and Han within a large, open-cornered box of vehicles. The unhurried and matter-of-fact approach did not alarm the citizens on the plaza, but many were obviously curious about what was going on and began to work their way toward the vehicles.

The sides of the transports facing the Jedi opened. They were large swing-out doors, and from each vehicle issued two full squadrons of men and women in the blue uniforms and helmets of Galactic Alliance Security. They wore black riot armor on chests, forearms, and lower legs, and carried blaster rifles.

There were also civilians aboard each transport—if bounty hunters, as Luke suspected these beings were, counted as civilians. One was a male Quarren in blue-green robes, swinging up onto his shoulder a cylindrical weapon that looked like it carried missiles sufficient to bring down medium-sized buildings; his rubbery skin and facial tentacles were rigid with concentration. Another was a petite woman with long black hair, wearing dark robes deliberately fashioned after those of a Jedi. She carried an unlit lightsaber in her hand. Luke had never seen her before. A third, unusual to see in this day and age, was a Skakoan, his body encased in a round-cornered, brass-colored robotic suit.

There were more bounty hunters, two or three in each transport. Luke noted their positions but did not react.

From the security agents, who spread out into a line encircling the Jedi, Luke felt mixed emotions. A few were expectant, spoiling for a fight. Many were worried, even fearful, and determined not to show it in front of their comrades. A few were very, very frustrated.

Luke glanced among his comrades. "Stay calm. We've known for some time that this was coming."

Which was true. A few weeks earlier, rumors had fallen into the ears of Luke's political allies that the Alliance government was making a legal case against him—a charge of dereliction of duty resulting from his actions during the war with the Confederation. Leading a StealthX unit as part of the Alliance military at a crucial battle, Luke had withdrawn his Jedi from the field and then entirely from the Alliance chain of command, later leading them in assaults against Jacen Solo. Such an action would constitute treason in other circumstances, but no one in the Alliance would make a capital charge stick against someone who had risked all to oppose Colonel Solo. Still, someone in the Alliance government was clearly offended by the desertion and intended to extract some legal satisfaction from Luke.

One of the security officers, a man with captain's insignia on his uniform, his prominent jaw almost ridiculously square, his eyes all but hidden under the partly raised blast visor of his helmet, led a party of four other security personnel toward the Jedi. Luke turned to face them.

"Master Luke Skywalker." The captain's voice was deep and grim. He came to a halt two meters from Luke. The members of his detail, thrown off by his sudden stop, skidded a little to make sure they did not bump into their superior. "I am Captain Savar, Galactic Alliance Security." He held up a black datacard, small in his gloved palm. "This is a warrant for your arrest. I now exercise it. Please do not offer resistance."

Luke could feel Han and Jaina bristling, but the other Jedi remained calm. He could also feel Ben, meters away, agitated and determined.

Luke put on a broad, welcoming smile. "I wouldn't

think of causing you trouble, Captain. May I disarm myself?"

"Carefully." The captain was clearly not put off by Luke's compliance, but Luke sensed disappointment from some of the security troopers and most of the bounty hunters.

And, curiously, from many of the onlookers beyond the circle of troopers. Luke spared them a glance. Many of them, far more than if the plaza crowd had just been random visitors arriving at or leaving the Senate Building, were holding holocam rigs, many of professional quality.

Slowly, Luke took his lightsaber from his belt. But as Savar stepped forward to reach for it, Luke passed it to Leia. She clipped it to her belt alongside her own.

Savar stopped abruptly. His expression turned to one of disapproval. "That, Master Skywalker, does not constitute full cooperation."

Leia turned a scornful look on the captain. "I'll wager you a month's salary—yours, not mine, since I don't receive a salary—that your warrant doesn't mention his lightsaber. Warrants almost never do. You know why? I suspect not. It's because the damage each one does is indistinguishable from the damage of any other, so they are of almost no use as forensic evidence. Now, does your warrant specify his lightsaber?"

Savar looked at her but ignored the question. He returned his attention to Luke. "Please turn around and place your hands behind your back. I have instructions to shackle you."

Luke obliged, turning to face his companions. He kept up his cheerful demeanor. It wouldn't do for any of the holocams to see him looking irritable, for any recordings of such a response would appear on the news broadcasts.

Captain Savar grasped Luke's right wrist and snapped a stun cuff upon it.

Han was not as cordial as Luke. "Are you under orders to treat him like a common criminal, bantha-brain?"

Luke felt Savar stiffen, felt a rush of frustration, anger, and, yes, *guilt* from the officer. It startled Luke; clearly, this was no prosecutorial lackey enjoying the arrest, but someone who regretted it.

"He's resisting!" The voice was muffled and watery. Luke knew it had to be the Quarren speaking. Luke spun, his right arm still in the captain's grasp, in time to see the Quarren bringing his shoulder weapon into line, aiming at Luke.

From that moment, things moved fast. Five lightsabers, Luke's not among them, *snap-hiss*ed into colorful, humming life and were raised against possible attacks. One security agent, who looked to be a boy about Ben's age, twitched and fired, probably inadvertently; the bolt sped toward Luke. He leaned away from it, not feeling threatened, but Kam caught it on his blade and bounced it almost straight down into the permacrete.

Han, a blaster suddenly in hand—a small, powerful civilian model, not his usual DL-44—fired, and the shot sheared through the boy's rifle, throwing the ruined weapon out of his hands.

The Quarren didn't fire. There was now a lightsaber tip poised directly beneath his neck. The blade belonged to none of the Jedi; the dark-haired woman held it, her hand rock-steady, a curious smile on her face. The Quarren's gaze was on her now rather than on Luke.

The security troops brought their weapons up, variously aiming at Han and the Jedi, but, disciplined operatives, they held their fire pending their captain's order.

Savar, his expression ugly, turned toward the Quarren. "Nyz, did you just not understand the words *sup-*

port role? Or are you stupid enough to violate my orders deliberately?"

The Quarren hesitated. "You stiffened. The only reasonable conclusion was that he used a Jedi technique on you."

"The only reasonable conclusion is that you're an idiot. And I don't see you putting your weapon down." At Savar's words, a half squad of operatives aimed at the Quarren, though it was clear the woman with the saber needed no help.

The Quarren, reluctant, lowered the device. He glanced between the woman and the troops covering him. "You shouldn't point weapons at me. It doesn't improve your prospects for survival."

Savar's expression became disdainful. "Now you're on record for threats. Worn-out, petulant, whiny threats, come to think of it." He turned to face Luke again.

The Jedi, at Luke's nod, deactivated and stowed their lightsabers. So did the dark-haired woman. Han tucked his blaster away into a sheath at the small of his back. The troops finally lowered their rifles, though several kept an eye on the Quarren.

"Nice shooting," Luke whispered to Han.

Han's expression was sour. "Short-barreled piece of junk. I was aiming at his nose."

"Sure you were."

Savar led Luke to the personnel carrier that had landed directly in front. Its crew of security troopers, plus the woman in dark Jedi robes and the Skakoan, packed in as well. Leia insisted that someone accompany Luke, and Savar chose Han—"Not a Jedi" were his words.

With Han Solo on one side and an empty seat on the other, Luke waited, listening as Savar, outside, addressed members of his detail. "Bessen, you are the stupidest trooper I've ever had the displeasure to command. Who told you to shoot the prisoner?"

"No one, sir, I didn't—I didn't mean—"

"Good answer. 'I didn't mean to, I'm just incompetent.' Are you competent to do two hundred push-ups for me?"

The boy's tone became one of dejection. "Yes, sir."

"Good. Sergeant Carn, come watch him do two hundred push-ups, then acquire transport and watch him *run* back to the blockhouse on foot."

Han whispered, "To think I originally chose a military career."

"You had a military career. You made the rank of general, then retired."

"Don't rub it in."

"Can you do two hundred push-ups?"

"Shut up."

The troopers watched, eyes wide, as two of the most famous humans in the galaxy, one of them under arrest for a felony, made small talk.

Savar, entering, slammed the transport's side doors shut behind him, leaving them all illuminated by weak blue glow rods. He sat down beside Luke.

As the transport lifted off, Han looked among the troopers. "Who wants to play some sabacc? I'll use my winnings for Master Skywalker's bail."

Chapter Three

LUKE WAS TAKEN TO A GA SECURITY BUILDING, WHERE HE
was separated from Han, who remained in the building's crowded main lobby, already making calls on his
comlink. Troopers hustled Luke into a back chamber
where he was searched and relieved of his personal possessions, then briefly holorecorded for identification
purposes. After that, he was taken to another room, this
one furnished with a bare table and chairs, where Captain Savar asked if he would consent to answer questions without his advocate present. Luke declined.

His next stop was a solitary confinement holding cell,
a special one—beyond the durasteel bars were the glows
of military-grade energy shields. There Luke was un-
shackled and left alone.

A considerable time passed—Luke could not be sure
how long it was, as his chrono was one of the items removed from him—and then a visitor was shown in. The
man was a Twi'lek, green-skinned, broad-shouldered,
richly dressed in black and gray office garments of a
style common on Coruscant. His *lekku*—brain-tails—
were wrapped around his neck. His brow ridge often
cast his red eyes into deep gloom. The anger on his face

and the stiffness with which he held himself made him a forbidding picture.

But Luke was delighted to see him. The Twi'lek, a pilot during the glory years of Wedge Antilles's Rogue Squadron, had lost his right leg below the knee in an engagement and subsequently returned to the practice of law. His limb replaced by a prosthetic one, he had performed as an attorney in numerous places across the galaxy and was now a familiar face in Coruscant litigation, interspersing high-paying cases with advocacy involving pilots or issues of constitutional law.

Luke sprang to his feet as the Twi'lek was shown through the cell door. As the shields reactivated beyond the bars, he held out his hand. "Nawara. It finally happened."

Nawara Ven shook Luke's hand, but his expression did not brighten. "No, it didn't. Not the way we expected."

"What do you mean?"

"Maybe you'd better sit down." He gestured at the cot that constituted half the furniture in the cell.

"I'm fine, thanks."

"They tricked us, Master Skywalker, and I'm feeling rather foolish at being tricked. We didn't look beyond the rumors that this was all about you leading the Jedi out of the Alliance camp and waging a private war on Colonel Solo two years ago."

"It's *not* about that?"

Nawara shook his head. "The government is actually asserting that, in not recognizing Jacen Solo's degenerative moral and ethical changes—the only way they can say 'descent to the dark side' in legalese—you were derelict in your duty as the Jedi Grand Master and were partly responsible for every consequence of his subsequent abuse of power. In other words, a share of every death, every act of torture, every butchered legal right, every military excess performed by the Galactic Alliance in the last war is being laid at your feet."

Luke felt the air go out of his lungs. He sat down. "You're not serious."

"As serious as death." Nawara frowned, deepening the shadow cast by his brow. "I'm certain they're holding back a related charge of treason as a negotiating point. The maximum possible sentence for that is, of course, death."

Luke drew in and then let out a deep breath of hurt. He had to acknowledge that some part of the accusation was valid—he *should* have consciously recognized Jacen's excesses long before he had. That he had not, that almost no one in his immediate circle had done so, was a tribute to the power of self-deception and denial.

Of course, others had recognized Jacen's fall earlier. Ben, whom Luke had not listened to. Luke's wife, Mara, who had kept her own counsel . . . and had died in doing so. If there was any death Luke bore partial blame for due to his refusal to accept reality, it was hers. While his grief had receded from everyday life, the pain still arose at unexpected moments to stab him in the heart. It was almost a physical pain, like a punch to the gut. He took another deep breath.

Nawara dragged the other piece of furniture, a skeletal metal chair, forward and sat backward on it, resting his arms atop the back. "We can beat this charge, too. It will be harder than the fight we were anticipating. It will require a considerable amount of mud slinging. *Everyone* associated with Jacen bears the same responsibility, meaning a lot of people in the wartime government, yet they're not being charged. We can demonstrate that you're being singled out because you're a Jedi. Because you're the face of the Jedi Order."

"Is that the truth? Is that why I'm being charged?"

"As far as I can tell from the hints I've picked up since

your arrest, from the favors I called in while waiting to see you, it is."

"Explain that."

Nawara considered his words. "You must understand, I appreciate the Jedi. What you do, what you risk, what you accomplish. But not everybody does. You're unpredictable. From a military point of view, which I also understand, you're conceivably the most irritating force in the galaxy."

That brought a brief smile to Luke's face. "True." He nodded, unrepentant. "We have a sort of loose alliance with chains of command and legal precedent. Following orders is not as important as achieving goals."

"The Alliance's military and ex-military leaders intensely dislike a resource they know they can't control completely."

"So is the military behind this, or Daala?"

"The Chief of State, but many in the military support her." Nawara paused as if reluctant to continue. "They *can* actually win this legal war even if we stomp them to pieces in some of the battles. If we mount a successful legal defense, so much dirt gets spread around that the Jedi lose a lot of public and government support—compared with what you get if the Jedi and the government suddenly decide to work hand in hand again. Or perhaps they have a case that's too strong for us. On the one hand, they might offer you a bargain: go free and manage the Jedi under their terms. On the other hand, they might just convict. Then you go to prison . . . or do what they'd prefer you to, run off into hiding and prove your unreliability and criminal nature."

Luke leaned back against the bars behind his cot and whistled. "Today just keeps getting better and better."

"They've been putting this together for a while. Some of my sources suggest that the order to make this case came down possibly as long ago as a year, maybe longer."

Luke thought about that. "Then why issue the warrant now? Did it take them all this time to assemble the case?"

"No. The timing, your arrest taking place in a public venue on the first day of the Unification Summit, is obviously no coincidence. It constitutes sending a message."

"To the parties considering rejoining the Alliance."

"Yes."

Luke scratched his jaw and thought about it. "They're saying to the Imperial Remnant, *We're putting a leash on the people who gave you so much trouble over the years. It's safe to come back.*"

"I believe so."

"And they're telling the Confederation, *You and the Jedi had a mutual enemy during the war, but now we control them, which is another good reason to rejoin.*"

"My thinking matches yours."

"Also another good reason to exclude the Hapans this time around. Queen Mother Tenel Ka would not react favorably to the action against me. If she doesn't participate until the next summit, this situation could be resolved by then and she'd have time to cool down." Luke stood and began pacing. His stomach fluttered, either from tension or from the fact that he'd had no meal since his arrest, and he drew on inner reserves of calm to settle it. "Nawara, I'm not sure we can change the way we operate within the Alliance, or should. We serve a higher cause. Life, calm, progress toward a fair and serene future. Self-interest and the kind of pragmatism that sacrifices innocent lives don't motivate us the way they can the civilian and military authorities."

Nawara offered him an unhappy smile. "History, as interpreted by non-Jedi, demonstrates that you're wrong. In the records, Jedi often demonstrate these self-serving and destructive impulses. They just stop calling themselves Jedi. Like Jacen Solo did."

"Ouch."

"Your arraignment's in two hours. I can have a different set of clothes delivered if you'd prefer to appear before the judge in something fresher or more cheerful."

Luke glanced down at his black Grand Master robes. He winced, considering how they might remind a judge of the garments preferred by Jacen Solo. "Send for my white and tan robes, would you?"

"Done."

COURT CHAMBERS, CORUSCANT

At the arraignment, Leia, Han, and Ben waited in the audience, which otherwise seemed to be made up entirely of the press, all with holocams running.

A gray-skinned Duros judge, chosen out of the standard rotation of Alliance judges, turned out to be sympathetic to the Jedi. He listened to the charges, ignored the prosecutor's assertion that Luke was a flight risk, ordered Luke to appear at hearings that would proceed from this event, and released him on his own recognizance. Minutes later, Luke, his family, and Nawara Ven exited the building through a portal Nawara knew but the press did not. They emerged at the fortieth-story walkway level into fresh air and nighttime darkness alleviated by pedestrian lights and traffic streams.

Luke opened the bag Captain Savar had given him at arraignment's end and began pocketing his personal effects. "That was a bad day. I look forward to some meditation."

Grim-faced, Leia handed him his lightsaber. "I don't

think you'll get that chance. Things just keep getting better and better."

JEDI TEMPLE, CORUSCANT

The Jedi Temple's medical center was a complete, if compact, hospital facility—operating theater, private recovery rooms, common ward, bacta chambers, therapy chambers, sealed atmosphere rooms to simulate various planetary environments, laboratories—and Valin Horn was now the centerpiece of the neurology lab. Strapped to a deactivated repulsor gurney that was resting on a platform built to accommodate it, he strained against his restraints, not speaking. There was no one present for him to speak to.

They watched him from an adjacent chamber through a sheet of transparisteel that was reflective on the lab side, transparent on the observer side. Luke stood with Master Cilghal, the Mon Calamari Jedi Master who was the Temple's foremost medical expert. Also on hand were the three other members of the Horn family, Leia, and Ben. Jysella Horn, Valin's sister, a lean woman in her midtwenties, wore a look of resolute calmness appropriate to a Jedi, but redness around her large, expressive eyes suggested that she had been crying. Her mother, Mirax, looked grimly determined and seemed unable to turn away from watching Valin.

Cilghal, her voice as gravelly as that of most Mon Cals, spoke clinically. "The patient is not rational and not cooperative. He continues to insist that everyone he knows, whom he sees now, has been replaced by an imposter. He is paranoid and delusional."

Leia became tight-faced. "Like Seff, only in a different way. Seff was on about Mandos." Not long before, while traveling aboard the *Millennium Falcon,* Leia and

Han had encountered the Jedi Knight Seff Hellin, who had exhibited a mania as pervasive as that which Valin seemed to be experiencing. Seff had left their company before he could be evaluated.

The similarity of their behavior sounded ominously to Luke like something one may have contracted from the other, or something they could have developed from exposure to a common source.

"His blood pressure is high, at a level consistent with his state of anxiety," Cilghal went on, "and there are greater-than-normal levels of stress hormones in his blood. Toxicology, virology, and bacteriology reports are in their preliminary stages but have suggested no answer. Basic neurological tests suggest no damage, but we have not been able to employ more advanced scans."

Luke glanced at her. "Why not?"

"I'll show you." Cilghal moved to a monitor affixed at head height on the wall beside the viewport. Delicately, because her larger-than-human hands were ill suited to the task, she depressed a number of keys beneath the monitor.

The monitor screen snapped into life, showing a series of five jagged lines, like simple graphical representations of extremely precipitous mountain ranges, one above the other. "This," Cilghal explained, "is a brain scan, set to display brain wave forms. It can be set to show many different types of data in different types of graphical representation. This is the scan of a normal being—myself, as a matter of fact.

"Now I will show you Valin's first scan." She clicked another series of buttons.

The image on the screen was wiped away, replaced by bars of jagged peak-and-trough lines so tightly packed, so extreme and savage that Jysella took an involuntary step back from the display. Cilghal continued, "No living member of any species we know could display waveforms like this and survive for very long. A few minutes after we took this, we took another reading. It, and subsequent ones, looked like this."

The monitor image wiped again. Luke thought for a moment that it had not been replaced, for the screen was almost blank. But there were still measuring bars to the right and left of the display. There were simply no lines between—not one.

Cilghal blinked at the image. "This is the brain scan reading of a dead person. Valin Horn is demonstrably not dead. There is no way a reading of Valin could yield a result like this. But it did."

"I've seen this before." Luke stared curiously at the screen, then glanced over at Valin, who was glaring at the viewport. Though unable to see through it, he seemed to be staring at Luke; perhaps he could feel the distinctive presence of the Grand Master. "Years ago."

Cilghal switched the monitor off. "That's true." Her voice sounded reflective. "Perhaps you should explain for the others."

"Jacen could do that. Deliberately, as a Force technique. He did it once during the Killik crisis."

"Is it a technique you know, Master Skywalker?"

Luke shook his head. "I assume it was something he picked up during his wanderings among all the Force groups he visited." He turned his attention to the Horns. "But where did Valin learn it?"

Corran shook his head. "He's never mentioned it. And I'd expect him to, just for fun. 'Look what I can do that my old man can't,' that sort of thing." He glanced at his daughter. "Jysella is more of a confidante. She may know."

Jysella looked from her father to Luke. "Valin and I knew Jacen, of course. But he was a few years older than Valin, and that makes a big difference when you're an adolescent. Jacen was out fighting the war against the

Yuuzhan Vong while Valin and I were stuck in the Maw, at Shelter, for the last half of the war. We didn't see him at all during the years he spent wandering, and not much after that."

Luke frowned. It didn't sound like the sort of relationship in which Jacen would teach Valin an obscure Force technique. "And how about Valin and Seff?"

Jysella shook her head, causing her brown hair to sway. "They weren't close. We all studied together at Shelter and afterward, but once we were apprenticed, following our respective Masters around, hardly ever. Occasionally one or the other of us would encounter him on missions. We were acquaintances, colleagues, but we weren't social buddies."

Luke heaved a sigh. "But the similarities are too striking to be a coincidence. Seff also knew an obscure Force technique we can't account for. Another one that Jacen exhibited, a Force-based paralysis. There's just too much missing in what we know about Jacen's travels, even his thought processes. Whether or not it has any bearing on Valin, at some point we need to fill in as many details as we can about what he was up to in the years prior to the Killik crisis."

Corran caught Cilghal's eye. "Is there anything you can do for him? To snap him out of it?"

"Nothing at the moment. We need psychological experts to evaluate the recordings we have made of him. We need complete toxicological lab work to come back. We need to find a way to complete a brain scan . . . As far as we can tell, whatever he's doing to thwart the scanner works even when he sleeps. I wish he hadn't awakened from Mirax's stun bolt before we tried the scanner the first time."

She pressed another couple of switches on the control board. An opaque panel slid down in front of the window, cutting off their view of the malevolently staring

Valin. Mirax started, then reluctantly turned back toward the others.

"Let's go upstairs," Luke said. "Sit down, get some caf, and figure out what to do about this. And other problems. Ben, I want you to exercise your investigative skills and see what information you can get me on the bounty hunters we encountered today."

"Will do."

"Will he be all right, left alone?" Mirax's tone was soft, full of pain.

"He is being watched constantly on monitors by my staff." Cilghal sounded confident, reassuring. "They will also look in on him personally every half hour to an hour. He is not strong enough to break through his straps, and, as you know, like his father he lacks telekinetic strength—he cannot free himself that way." She led them from the chamber.

Luke patted Corran's back as they departed. "Did you have any trouble with the authorities?"

"We didn't wait for them. Just threw the boy in Mirax's speeder and came straight here . . ."

Valin could sense their departure. Bright lights in the Force, somehow approximating those of his family and respected teachers, grew more distant.

He smiled to himself. They were nowhere near as smart as they thought they were, no matter how much research they may have done. They did not know all his secrets, including the one that was going to free him.

He closed his eyes and looked for other lights in the Force—tiny ones in nearby pockets and streams. Individually they did not hold much life, but their collective biomass exceeded that of all the sapient beings on Coruscant.

They were the insects, and though he had not done so in years, he remembered how to be their friend. Now he needed them to come here. He needed certain species that he could convince to crawl out of gaps in the Temple walls, march up his gurney, and consume just a small portion of one strap holding him down.

One strap, and then when his nurse came on an in-person visit, one lunge. Valin would escape and find his way to where the real people were.

A two-tone musical alarm awakened Luke. He sat up, glancing around his darkened Temple quarters, and saw his monitor lit, Cilghal's face displayed on it. "Master Cilghal. What time is it?"

"Middle of the night. Valin Horn has escaped."

Luke sighed at the inevitability of those words. "This day . . . How long ago?"

"Twenty minutes or so. His night nurse, Apprentice Romor, is not badly hurt but has a concussion."

"Do we have any leads on where Valin went?"

"Better than that. We have the tracking device I planted below his skin in the event of such an occurrence. He will begin to feel it when the local anesthetic I injected there begins to wear off, but that gives us a few hours still. Unfortunately, he seems to be spending a certain amount of time traveling through the undercity, so our signal is intermittent."

Luke rose and began putting on his white tunic. "Alert the other Masters. Assemble all the Jedi Knights present that the Temple can spare. Let Han and Leia know. I'll be in the Great Hall in three minutes."

"And the Horns?"

"They don't need to know."

Chapter Four

SEHA SAT CROSS-LEGGED ON HARD, COLD PERMACRETE IN the darkness at the center of the plaza, glaring at the Senate Building before her. A lean girl in her early twenties, she was dressed as a Jedi, her long red hair held back in a tail by elastic bands.

She glared because nothing was happening. Senatorial aides and office workers were arriving on foot in this predawn hour, a steady trickle, and that added up to nothing. None cast a look out into the darkness where Seha waited. None looked like Valin Horn.

Beside her, stretched out full length on the permacrete, wrapped up against the chill in a full-length hooded robe, lay Master Octa Ramis. A stoutly built, muscular human woman, she lay with her eyes closed as if asleep. The pale skin of her face, surrounded as it was by dark hair and dark cloak, was all that could be seen of her from more than a couple of meters. Now she smiled, not opening her eyes. "You're not calm, Seha."

"I know, Master."

"The less calm you are, the less alert you are."

Seha gestured at the small tracker box that rested on the permacrete before her. "I just have to watch this. It glows the same whether I'm calm or not."

"Spoken like a true, proper, lazy apprentice. Why,

again, did I let you choose where we would have our stakeout?"

"Because I've been on a mission with Valin. I mean, Jedi Horn."

"And you brought us here because?"

Seha frowned, out of confusion rather than irritation. She had already explained her logic once. "Because if he's thinking strangely, maybe he's thinking like an animal. Find a nest, lick his wounds, recover. I led him to the undercity here a couple of years ago. There's more security now, but he can find plenty of places to hide. And if he pops up here, he can use his Jedi powers to steal very good vehicles or maybe kidnap prominent politicians."

"Very good. It's as good a reason for choosing a stakeout as any. You used your mind and your logic to lead us here. And now you're willing to simply abandon them and watch a box because that's just as good as *thinking*?"

Seha sighed. As usual, there was little reward in arguing with her teacher. "No, Master." She tried to quiet her thoughts.

"Do you have a crush on him?"

Seha gave Octa a pained look. It was going to be one of those conversations, no secrets safe. "Yes, Master. Well, I did once."

"Are you embarrassed by it?"

"No. I'm embarrassed that I had a crush on Jacen Solo."

"Don't be. He was a good, thoughtful Jedi for many years. And a nice-looking one. Took after his father. I had a crush on his father once upon a time."

Seha smiled. "You didn't."

"Yes. And just think of the chores you'll find yourself doing if you mention that to anyone."

"I shouldn't allow myself to have crushes, at least on

Jedi. I have a crush on Jacen Solo, he goes dark and dies. I have a crush on Valin Horn, he goes crazy."

Octa's smile faded but did not go away entirely. "Once upon a time, I had more than a crush on a Jedi. He was tortured by the Yuuzhan Vong, then drowned in freezing water fighting them. Should I have stopped loving? Caring? Being attracted?"

"No . . ."

"Then you shouldn't, either."

The device at Seha's feet lit up, the bulb atop it glowing with a faint pulse of amber light. The pulse intensified, faded, and then became steady.

Octa must have felt Seha's excitement. She sat up, eyes opening, and looked at the tracker. "Well done, Seha."

"Thank you, Master."

"Call it in. Then we go looking."

Enneth Holkin, protocol aide to the honorable Denjax Teppler, co–Chief of State of Corellia, dismissed his driver well beyond the vehicle checkpoint that marked the closest approach civilian speeders were allowed to make to the Senate Building. He had a lot to do this morning; a longer walk would settle his mind. For security's sake, he kept his thumb through the panic ring on his topcoat. It wouldn't do for a Corellian functionary to be caught with a weapon at the summit, but the panic ring was perfectly legal and just as likely to save his life in case of kidnapping or a protracted encounter with a criminal.

When he was not far past the checkpoint and beginning to cross the plaza, he heard a faint noise from immediately behind, a scrape of leather on permacrete. He turned and saw the sole of a boot just before it cracked against his jaw.

*   *   *

Valin, rested and calm, looked dispassionately down at the being he'd just assaulted. The man was his own approximate height and coloration, which would prove useful.

He set about relieving the unconscious man of clothes and document bag. He did not bother to take the curious metal ring, with a few centimeters of thin black cord dangling from it, that encircled the man's left thumb.

More than two hundred meters away, in a claustrophobic security office deep within the Senate Building, a security station picked up an automated emergency transmission on the visiting dignitary comm band. The automated programming selected one security officer from the several on duty and threw graphics up on his monitor. Relevant data on Enneth Holkin, including his name, political affiliations, homeworld, and known associates flickered to life on the screen. Next came a holorecording of his face and a copy of his criminal record, which consisted of stealing a dilapidated speeder bike for a joyride when he was a teenager on Corellia. Then came a coordinate listing of his current location, which was, curiously, not far away.

The security agent, a lean, balding man who, after twenty years of street work, was more than happy to earn his living behind a computer terminal, yawned and typed a tracking instruction into his keyboard.

Out on the plaza and on the exterior wall of the Senate Building, holocams traversed from their usual monitoring patterns and aimed themselves toward the tracking coordinate. As the balding agent flipped from view to view, the ultraviolet-enabled holocams all showed the same scene: a pale-skinned human male, lying faceup in one of the darkest portions of the plaza, eyes closed, wearing nothing but underthings. The readings from infrared holocams indicated that his body temperature was more or less stable, suggesting he was still alive.

The agent upped the computer system's threat code from green to yellow, standard to alert. The security system responded by taking control of the external and internal holocam systems, noting the locations of every individual they detected, submitting faces to data banks whose usefulness had been vastly improved during the recent Galactic Alliance Guard years. Every Senator, aide, functionary, visiting politician, hired companion, janitor, driver, bodyguard, and celebrity within the scanning area was suddenly queued for high-priority identification.

Seconds later, cautionary flags began to pop up on the agent's screen. Avedon Tiggs, actor, musician, and frequently arrested libertine, was exiting with the Senator from Commenor. Gerhold Razzik, a member of the Imperial Remnant delegation who had no business being in the Rotunda, was there, gaping like a tourist, probably recording everything he saw with a disguised holocam. Valin Horn, Jedi Knight, was on level 2, moving confidently and steadily through what should have been a secure corridor. Octa Ramis, Jedi Master, in the company of a younger woman also dressed as a Jedi, was approaching the east main entrance.

The security agent had no special instructions concerning wayward musicians or Imperial spies, but he had very new, very specific orders about Jedi.

He activated his comlink and requested the Special Operations office of the Chief of State.

"You have to let us in," Octa said.

The uniformed and helmeted security woman standing in front of the closed east entrance doors shrugged. "Actually, I don't."

"No, really, you do." Octa made a subtle gesture with

one hand and poured soothing feelings of peace and compliance into the security agent. "It's Jedi business, very important."

The woman gave the Jedi Master a smile. Perhaps it would have been a scowl of irritation had Octa not been smothering her with dreamy goodness through the Force. "First, the doors just sealed. It's called a lockdown. Happens all the time, nothing to worry about, nothing to see here. I'm sure the office will tell us in a minute why. Second, no, not only can I not let you in until the lockdown ends, really I don't have to."

Exasperated, Octa turned away and returned to the side of her apprentice a few paces back. "We need another entrance. One with an appropriately weak-willed guard."

Seha's eyes were unfocused as she stared at a blank wall of the building. "He's moving. Looking for something. Ascending, I think."

"A vehicle. He has to be looking for an escape vehicle." Octa turned back toward the guard and raised her voice. "You, where are the hangar exits from this building?"

"That's classified."

"Some of them are public!"

"Everything's classified during a lockdown."

Octa made a strangled noise and turned back to Seha. "I hate good guards. They're the most inconvenient things in the universe."

"Happiness. He's elated."

"Can't he feel you?"

"Maybe. Maybe he doesn't care. He's about to get away."

"Meld with me. Give me a sense of him so I can pick him out."

Seha extended herself through the Force, a tentative expression of power—she was years behind other Jedi students her age, many of whom were already Jedi Knights. But she performed the technique correctly, and Octa could feel her emotions, feel the distinctive characteristics of the living being Seha was trying to track.

It was easier for the Master. "Up about ten meters, this way." She set off at a trot northward, along the wall that would gradually curve around toward the north entrance. Seha followed.

Octa could feel decisions being made—"He's considering two vehicles. No, he's *taking* two vehicles. How can he take two vehicles?"

"One inside the other?"

They found out seconds later. A hundred meters farther, they heard a tremendous shriek of metal from ahead and above. A shuttle with Kuati markings emerged from the building—through a closed portal, the impact hurling slabs of artificial stone and durasteel supports scores of meters. Passing through the non-exit, which was too small for the shuttle's generous girth, caused the vehicle's upraised wings to rip clean off; they fell to either side. The shuttle, angling downward, headed toward the permacrete of the plaza. Octa could neither see nor detect a pilot in the shuttle's cockpit.

The shuttle's repulsors were not the only ones to be heard. Before the building alarms cut in, their howl drowning out all other noises, Octa heard another, more familiar set of repulsors increasing in volume from within the hangar.

She put on a Force-aided burst of speed, then leapt, trying to achieve as much altitude and distance as she could. As she leapt, she shouted, "Push!"

Her apprentice, though underconfident and undertrained, was smart, and telekinesis was something she was good at. Octa felt Seha's effort not as a blow to her back but almost as a short blast of wind, a stream of power that lofted her, propelled her.

As the gray X-wing emerged from the hangar through the ruined door, Octa slammed into the starboard side of the fuselage, her right arm scrabbling at the nose just in front of the canopy. The impact hammered her ribs.

Valin Horn, in the pilot's seat, inappropriately dressed in businessman's garments, looked surprised. He stared at Octa, mouth open.

Unseen, behind Octa in the distance, the ruined shuttle came down on the plaza with a noise like tons of metal and ceramic refuse being dropped by a negligent giant. The noise became a screech and scrape as the shuttle skidded forward, still propelled by its thrusters.

Octa knew Valin's preferred tactics as well as he did. He needed to bank and roll, cause her to drop off. But, halfway emerged through an irregular aperture, he couldn't, not yet—to do so would mangle or even tear free the starfighter's strike foils, turning the X-wing into an expensive, uncomfortable, ugly airspeeder.

Instead, Valin grimaced and eased the yoke forward, emerging two more meters into the predawn air.

Octa got her offhand onto her lightsaber and managed to unclip it. She ignited it and thrust with the weapon at the canopy—not at Valin, but at the point closest to her right arm, where the canopy dogged into place against the fuselage.

The point of her weapon, driven at an awkward angle by her less practiced hand, skidded off the transparisteel and up, inflicting nothing but a scar on the canopy.

She tried again. Valin, timing his action by her attack, punched the thrusters just a little, throwing her off balance. She did not fall off, but the energy blade punched through the canopy centimeters behind the latch. The blade, just above Valin's hands on the yoke, hit the far side of the canopy and burned through there, too.

Now the X-wing was fully extracted from the hangar door. Valin gave Octa a mocking smile, elevated the starfighter's nose, and opened the thrusters full force. The X-wing shot upward at a steep takeoff angle.

Octa felt her right hand slipping across the fuselage. She slid farther down the side of the cockpit, wildly waving her left arm and the lightsaber in it for balance, and then tried another blow. Her attack had no accuracy or leverage; it hit the canopy over Valin's face, well away from her intended point of impact, and again left nothing but a scar.

Valin should have been rolling the X-wing by now, but he did not, and Octa lost a precious second or two trying to figure out why.

Then she understood. *He's taking me as high as he can . . . so I'll die when I hit ground.* She took a moment to look around, but of course there were no speeders below or close by—unauthorized traffic was forbidden this close to the Senate Building, and authorized traffic was rare at this hour.

Valin gave her a last look of triumph. He twitched the yoke and the X-wing shuddered. Octa's hand slipped free and she fell.

She felt a touch of regret. Force techniques to slow falling were of little use in open air at altitudes like this. She was going to be a mess, a dead mess, when she hit.

She deactivated her lightsaber and clipped it to her belt. It wouldn't do to have it shear through some innocent pedestrian running in the wake of the shuttle, which, now burning, had come to a rest against the government building on the far side of the plaza.

Octa prepared herself for impact.

When Octa woke up, she knew only moments had passed. The Senate Building alarms were still howling. Sirens announced the imminent arrival of other official vehicles. There was also a persistent ringing in her head.

She didn't hurt that badly. Quickly, carefully, she

flexed limbs, shifted her body, explored herself in the Force.

Not even a broken bone.

She opened her eyes and Seha, framed by stars, was kneeling over her, looking worried, crestfallen. "Master?"

"I'm all right." Octa struggled to sit up. Well, she wasn't entirely all right. Every muscle hurt and she was certain she had a concussion. "You caught me? With telekinesis?"

"Partly. You still hit hard."

"Not that hard." Octa managed a shaky laugh. "You did very, very well."

"But we lost. He got away."

"We *won*. He's in street clothes and his canopy isn't airtight. So he can't make space. And he's airborne, so his tracking device will give away his location continuously. We flushed him." Standing, she stretched her back, trying to afford it a little relief. "Others will have to run him to ground."

Chapter Five

"COME TO COURSE TWO-SIX-NINE."

Han, following his wife's directions, banked the *Falcon* around and headed toward the government district. Leia, in the copilot's seat, had her personal comlink to her ear.

The *Falcon*'s comm board was alive with Coruscant Security and traffic monitors warning Han to return to designated ship traffic lanes or be subject to arrest. He growled and switched the thing to silent mode. "They found him?"

"They found him. He's in an X-wing with a hole in the cockpit."

"Armed?"

"Fifty-fifty chance. It was in the Senate Building, so it's either a fully functional security vehicle or some Senator's unarmed memories-of-youth vehicle. I'm hoping for the second option."

"Me, too."

"Come to two-five-nine."

"Nah." Han put the *Falcon* into a dive. His stomach fluttered, and the sensor screen filled up with tiny objects getting larger—small-vehicle traffic at and below building-top level. Flashing down at terrifying and illegal speed, he twitched the controls right and left, nimbly dodging the much smaller civilian vehicles.

"Han, what do you think—"

Then he was fully among them, streams of traffic above as well as below. He pulled out of his dive two hundred meters below the average height of the buildings.

"—you're doing?"

"This way, we're off the major sensor boards. Only vehicles with line of sight on us will complain."

"I understand *that*. I mean, why not turn to two-five-nine?"

"His course changes are just to jerk us around, to confuse us. *I* know where he's going."

"Where?"

"The spaceport, right at the edge of the government district. He stole a starfighter; that means he wants to make space. It's damaged, so he can't. He needs another one. Right?"

"Right."

"When it comes to piloting and pilots, I'm all-knowing."

Leia put an artificial sweetness into her voice. "I'll never argue with you again."

Han snorted and increased velocity. A Coruscant Security speeder following in his wake dropped back, left behind as though it were suddenly standing still.

Luke and Ben, in Ben's nimble red airspeeder, received the transmission with Han's guess about the spaceport.

Luke, at the controls, shook his head, not pleased. The spaceport, comparatively flat and built at a much lower altitude than the surrounding residential, business, and government zones, was not, as most supposed, actually situated at bedrock level. Below it were many levels of machinery, repair hangars, Empire-era emergency bunkers, spaceport employee facilities, and repair accesses.

If Han was right and Valin was headed that way, even if he was unsuccessful at stealing another spaceworthy vehicle he might escape into those subterranean regions, making it hard or impossible to find him before he detected his tracking device and destroyed it.

Their speeder emerged from the skytowers and was abruptly out over the flatter region surrounding the spaceport. It was mostly given over to speeder parking, though it had decorative elements, including tree-spotted grassy regions and a small artificial lake.

And sensor stations. Almost immediately, the speeder's comm board began blaring with instructions for them to turn back, to stay away from restricted airspace.

"Tell them who we are." Luke had to raise his voice to a shout to be heard.

"I bet it doesn't work. Who's on the news as a criminal suspect? You are."

"Do it anyway." Luke put the speeder into a holding pattern, keeping close to the ring of skytowers, not approaching the port itself. The authorities might well decide to shoot down a suspicious speeder—piloted by a suspected criminal or not—heading straight toward an invaluable government and civilian transportation resource. Sabotage and terror attacks had taken place as recently as the war, two years earlier.

Ben looked up from the comm board, startled. "We're not the only ones."

"What?" Luke scanned the airspace above the spaceport.

There were a *lot* of small vehicles there now, most of them airspeeders of one size or another. Some were bigger business vehicles, many with lettering and symbols on the sides.

From the utility compartment, Ben pulled out a pair of macrobinoculars and held them to his eyes. "That one's a press vehicle. Turret-mounted holocam on top. That one—hey, that's Jaina. The big green one—oh, kriff."

"Language. What is it?"

"It has an oversized driver's cab and that Skakoan is in it."

Luke frowned. Suddenly everyone knew that Valin was coming here, including press and bounty hunters. That meant open comm channels were being monitored, and people with no business being here were up to date. Daala's people had to be doing this.

Then he saw it, almost at ground level, an X-wing painted in classic First Galactic Civil War grays. Its running lights were off; it was illuminated only by the glows from parking area pole lights—it flew beneath the altitude of the lights themselves.

"Hold on." Luke pushed his control yoke forward, sending the speeder into a precipitous dive.

Ben's lips were drawn back in a grimace—perhaps because no teenager wants anyone else to endanger his vehicle recklessly, that being the teenager's own prerogative—but said, "*Falcon*'s incoming."

"Good." Luke put the speeder on an intercept course, or a collision course if anything went wrong, and switched the autopilot on. He unlatched his seat restraints and slid toward Ben. "Take the controls."

He was gratified to see his son's eyes open wide, but Ben did as he was told; the boy unbuckled, slid under his father, grabbed the controls, disengaged the autopilot.

Luke stood up in the seat, drawing on the Force to keep him pinned in place despite the rush of wind threatening to tear him free.

He counted on Ben to know what to do, and his son did not let him down. Ben leveled off at the same altitude as the X-wing, completing his maneuver just meters behind the starfighter, and drew alongside that vehicle's port side.

Luke sprang across the gap separating his seat from the cockpit. The wind threatened to whip him away, but a boost of Force energy carried him to the fuselage just as Valin Horn was realizing he had a pace vehicle. Luke landed astride the nose, facing astern, staring straight down into Valin's startled features.

Valin yanked up on the X-wing's armrests. The canopy was suddenly open, snapping backward, and gone, and Valin hurtled into the sky, his pilot's chair propelled by a crude one-use rocket.

"Stang! He punched out." Han pounded his steering yoke.

Leia looked as aggravated as Han felt. "Can the cargo tractor beam—"

"Not strong enough. Can't compensate for a fast-moving target."

"We have to go after Valin, then."

Han shook his head. "The ejection won't have left enough controls for Luke to land the X-wing. He may be able to lift it or push it down with the Force . . . but land it with no controls? No. We have to help him." He heeled over, diving toward the X-wing.

"He punched out." Jaina reluctantly turned her attention from Luke, disappearing toward the spaceport on the uncontrolled X-wing, and returned it to Valin, still ascending in his ejection seat. She banked and headed toward the rogue Jedi.

In the passenger seat, Master Kyle Katarn, about Luke's age, dark-haired and dark-bearded, stretched as if coming out of a nap. "You plan to maneuver underneath and catch him?"

"That's right."

Katarn pointed toward another speeder, a large, flatbed cargo hauler with figures standing in the cargo bed. This vehicle rose toward Valin's position from a much nearer position. "So do they."

Valin's seat reached its maximum altitude and began dropping. Immediately the short-term repulsor within the seat activated, slowing his descent.

He felt as though he'd taken a tremendous blow to the top of his head, doing no damage to it but compressing the spine beneath. Ejections were always like that—bad, but better than the alternative.

And he'd always relish the look on Not-Luke's face when he'd ejected. It had been priceless.

A cargo hauler maneuvered itself toward his descent path. Grumbling, he got his lightsaber into one hand, grabbing his seat restraint buckle with the other.

As the hauler came underneath, instead of waiting for the seat to touch down, Valin unbuckled the restraints and flipped forward, landing on his feet moments before the seat landed.

In the cargo bed, three individuals waited—a Quarren with a vastly oversized weapon, a shining droid whose construction bore a slight resemblance to a human skeleton, and a tall blond woman whose black bantha-hide jacket was decorated with a vast number of claws and teeth in different sizes and colors, sewn in place; she carried a Wookiee bowcaster.

Valin smiled at them, but not in a friendly way. "Two maladjusted want-to-be bounty hunters and their dressed-up protocol droid."

"Surrender," the Quarren said. "It will hurt less." He raised his preposterous weapon to his shoulder.

"Jump into a fire." Valin all but ignored the two organic beings. He kept his attention on the droid—a YVH 1 combat droid, one of the most dangerous machines to be found anywhere.

Now even machines were giving him a bad feeling.

And he could detect a life-form heading toward him from straight above—

He glanced upward to see a speeder car passing by overhead, and boot heels, flapping Jedi robes, and an illuminated lightsaber descending toward him at a normal falling rate.

In his lower peripheral vision, he saw the three bounty hunters glance up to spot the descending Jedi. Valin took the opportunity to act: he grabbed his abandoned ejection seat and leapt with it off the rear end of the cargo hauler.

Jaina landed in a crouch just where Valin had been standing. He was gone. She rose to glower at the bounty hunters. "Don't bother."

"We're not here to harm you," the YVH droid said, its tones utterly and confidently human.

Jaina stared at the thing, nonplussed. "Just what have you been programmed for?"

She felt a tickle in the Force, warning of imminent attack, and saw the Quarren's finger tighten on the trigger. She jumped to one side as he fired.

It did her no good. The missile that emerged from the weapon immediately flared out into a haze that wrapped around her, clinging everywhere—it took her a fraction of a second to recognize it as a metal-mesh net trailing some sort of cylindrical package.

Then the first jolt of electrical pain hit her. Startled, suddenly separated from her Force powers, she sailed over the edge of the cargo hauler and dropped into empty space beyond.

Valin clung to the ejection seat and rode it down another twenty meters. The next vehicle to approach him held no ersatz Jedi, no imposters that he could see—it was a boxy blue speeder, the Galaxy 9 News logo painted on its side in yellow. It drew alongside, its pilot skillfully keeping pace with Valin's rate of descent.

A dark-skinned woman leaned out the passenger-side window. "Jedi Horn! Is it true you're on a destructive rampage?"

Valin leapt from his seat, slamming into the side of the speeder, holding on to the woman's door to keep from falling. She drew back, startled, but he gave her a friendly smile. "Get me out of here, away from these people, and I'll give you the greatest scoop you've ever had."

The woman's eyes widened. She turned to issue a brief command to her pilot, then turned back, all smiles. "Let me help you in . . ."

"I'll hang on here, thanks." The news speeder banked, sluggish, and headed toward the business district. "How did you know I was Valin Horn?"

"An arrest bulletin issued a little while ago by the office of the Chief of State . . ."

The Quarren watched, startled, as Jaina Solo vanished over the lip.

The woman in the black jacket clapped him on the back. "Nice move, fish-head. She's not—"

Her words were cut off as an airspeeder, painted in a stylish silver-gray, dived past the cargo hauler's cab, missing it by less than a meter.

The hauler's pilot reacted instinctively, veering to starboard and down. The sudden maneuver sharply tilted the cargo bed.

The Quarren staggered to his left and stumbled clean off the edge of the cargo hauler. The blond woman staggered, too, but dropped, rolled with an acrobat's skill, and fetched up safely against the low rail at the side of the cargo bed.

The YVH droid didn't budge.

* * *

Luke flipped into the cockpit and did an involuntary dance for a moment until both feet found nonsuperheated areas on the floor of the still-smoking compartment.

He glanced at the controls and grimaced. Every screen was out of commission. Experimentally, he waggled the yoke and found it unresponsive. This would be tricky, if not downright impossible.

Unless—

He turned. There, in the circular slot behind the cockpit, rested a gray and red R2 astromech.

"Hey, there. Can you pilot this thing?"

The R2 tweetled, ending on a sorrowful note.

"Forget steering. Can you kill the thrusters but leave the repulsors running?"

The R2 offered a series of notes that sounded quizzical. Luke heard starfighter systems dip and rise in power, fluctuations that lasted a fraction of a second each, then the R2 tweetled an affirmative.

"Do so. Execute. Problem solved." Luke turned to port. Ben was still there, a few meters away, pacing him with considerable skill.

Luke leapt back across, settling into the passenger seat. "Did you keep track of Valin?"

"Up thirty degrees, port twenty, three hundred meters."

"Strap in and take us there."

Leia shook her head as she watched Luke abandon the X-wing. "I'm not sure how, but he thinks he has it solved."

"Probably drafted the astromech. Took me a second to think of that myself." Han did not look away from the silver-gray speeder, which had, moments earlier, matched the netted Jaina's precipitous fall; then the pilot had gestured, drawing Jaina into the seat beside him with an exertion through the Force, and pulled out of his dive. Han glanced at his wife, who, watching Luke, hadn't seen any of it.

He shook his head. Jaina must not even have been alarmed, since Leia had not even detected her brief emergency. He put the *Falcon* into a tight curve, aiming it toward the news speeder that now bore Valin away and the lumbering cargo hauler chasing it. "That YVH droid could be bad news. Want to take the belly lasers?"

"I do." Leia was unstrapped and up in an instant, headed aft toward the laser turret access shaft.

Jaina, helpless, spasmed again as another electrical shock coursed through her. "Get this thing off me."

"I'm driving here, and that's *Get this thing off me, please, Master Katarn.*"

She offered a very Han Solo–ish growl in response.

Dropping almost to parked-speeder level, Kyle set his vessel in pursuit of Valin's conveyance and the cargo hauler. The hauler now seemed to be towing something at the end of a cable. It took him a moment to recognize the Quarren. A cable stretched between his weapon and the tail of the hauler, and the Quarren held on to his weapon with both arms as if to save his life. As the hauler picked up speed, the Quarren was towed along behind at a more shallow angle.

Absently, barely looking, Kyle took his lightsaber from his belt, lit it, and lashed out against the metal cylinder attached to Jaina's net where it lay bouncing on the back of the speeder. His blow sheared through the object without scarring the speeder's paint beneath. "Better?"

"Actually, yes." Jaina lay there a few more moments, then began struggling with the net. It had relaxed, no longer constricting or clinging to itself, and she was able to unwrap it within moments. "Electrical shocks."

"Interfering with your control over the Force. Which turns you from a Jedi into a rather weak gymnast with a spasming problem."

"That's one way to put it."

The Galaxy 9 News speeder reached the edge of the business district before any of the vehicles pursuing it caught up. It shot through the cleft between skytowers that constituted the end of the spaceport zone and dropped toward lower traffic lanes.

The bounty hunter cargo hauler followed, descending at an angle not recommended for such a big, ungainly vehicle, still trailing the Quarren, who looked increasingly frantic. Then came Jaina and Kyle in their speeder, the *Falcon,* Luke and Ben, and finally a stream of speeders with Jedi, spaceport security, press, and more bounty hunters intermixed.

"Whoa." Kyle put the speeder into a side-to-side evasive maneuver an instant before the YVH droid in the cargo hauler opened fire. Streams of blasterfire flashed beside his door, then just above Jaina's head, then immediately under the fuselage.

A pulse of laserfire, four brilliant red streams converging so closely that they seemed to be one, crossed from above and behind the speeder to hit the YVH droid dead center in the chest. The droid was catapulted off its feet and smashed through the rear of the hauler's control cab, disappearing completely.

Smoke poured out of the cab, and the hauler began to nose forward into a shallow dive.

Jaina craned her neck back to see the *Falcon,* pacing the speeder at a higher altitude. She waved at her mother, clearly visible in the underside turret. "Thanks, Mom."

"Most mothers just pack a lunch." Kyle put on a burst of speed, accelerating toward the news speeder. "You want to try another jump?"

"I guess." Jaina checked her lightsaber, then clipped it to her belt.

Another speeder, black with arrow-tipped white stripes on the sides, open-topped, raced past Kyle's. It was no civilian vehicle; the roar from its engines was similar to that of a Podracer. It was a two-seater, and the pilot was the bounty hunter who dressed as a Jedi. Beside her was a man Jaina had barely glimpsed at Luke's arrest, a Rodian holding an unusually long blaster rifle, scoped, in his hands. As they roared past, the woman gave Kyle and Jaina a wave.

The striped racer dipped low and passed the news speeder moments later. Jaina saw the passenger turn, raise his weapon, and fire at the news vehicle.

It was not a destructive shot—it was surgical. Smoke began issuing from the news speeder. It wobbled, probably from a fright reflex on the part of the pilot. Moments later, viewports all over the vehicle opened, allowing smoke to pour out everywhere.

Luke took a moment to assess the vista before him. The news speeder was clearly doomed, so Valin would be abandoning it as soon as possible. "Take me over it, just to one side."

Ben nodded and put on more speed. Crowding the edge of the traffic lane, he passed below the *Falcon,* then above Master Katarn and Jaina. Drawing near the news speeder, he maintained his higher altitude but sideslipped to port, putting Luke directly above the speeder's roof.

Once again Luke looked down into the face of Valin

Horn. He flipped over the side and landed at the rear of the speeder's roof, stabilizing himself through the Force.

Valin flipped up to the roof. "Wish you'd taken longer with that X-wing."

Luke gestured at the lightsaber Valin carried—not Valin's own, it was a very simple cylinder of shining steel. "Did that belong to your nurse?"

"Yes." Valin switched it on. "It's not very stylish, but—"

"That's enough." Luke advanced, activating his own lightsaber. Valin raised his in a preliminary block. Luke struck, twitching his blade out of the most obvious line of attack, and the blade sheared the hilt of Valin's weapon in two, not harming him.

Valin's blade switched off as the weapon's lower half dropped into the darkened urban chasm below. Valin took a step back, the last step he could afford before dropping off the front of the speeder, but Luke's advance was near instantaneous. The Grand Master slammed the butt of his own weapon into Valin's temple.

Valin Horn dropped like a slaughterhouse bantha. Luke caught his topcoat lapel, keeping him from following the lightsaber wreckage into the depths.

Chapter Six

THE PILOT OF THE NEWS SPEEDER NEEDED NO URGING FROM Luke. He picked the nearest plausible landing spot, a portion of a twentieth-story-altitude pedestrian walkway broad enough for two starfighters to land abreast, and set down. Immediately, all the pursuit vehicles set down on one side or the other of it—all but the *Falcon,* which rose, looking for a broader landing area.

Jaina, Kyle, and Ben joined Luke. At his instant order, they stood at the four corners of the news speeder, lightsabers unlit but in hand, and waved the oncoming security troopers, press, and onlookers back. The security troopers, no ranking officer present, hesitated in the face of unthreatening but armed Jedi resistance and simply formed up lines, keeping the press and observers at bay, barring the exit paths of the Jedi.

Kyp Durron and Jedi Knight Doran Tainer arrived moments later, filling in the Jedi line, and Luke could see other Jedi speeders moving in for agile, illegal landings. Luke shook his head. "This is going to be a real mess."

"Going to be?" Kyp looked amazed. "Are you trying for some galactic record in the understatement event?"

The dark-haired female bounty hunter and her Rodian companion arrived, showed identification to the spaceport security officers, and moved through their line, confronting Luke. The woman smiled with what seemed like genuine good cheer. "Care to surrender the prisoner? It will save everybody trouble."

Luke shook his head. "We'll manage this. *You* can save everyone a lot of trouble by convincing the security forces to fall back and leave us to our business."

She shook her head. "The Chief of State has ordered us to take the rogue Jedi into custody. Surely you've heard of her. Natasi Daala."

"I have, but I haven't heard of *you*. Who are you?"

She offered him a slight bow. "Zilaash Kuh. Not, I am afraid, at your service."

"You're not a Jedi."

She nodded. "And may I present Kaddit."

The Rodian offered a minimal glance in Luke's direction, but he clearly had his eye on the growing numbers of Jedi and GA Security personnel.

The noise was incredible—the *Falcon*'s repulsors howling, people shouting.

"Stand back! Stand back! GA Security has jurisdiction here!"

"Hand over the prisoner; this is not your jurisdiction."

"Take one more step and you'll be picking your nose with a prosthetic!"

"Luke! Luke! When did you first realize you were a criminal?"

Master Cilghal was among the later Jedi arrivals. The security troopers let her enter, and she injected Valin with enough sedatives to keep a wampa unconscious for a couple of days. But the security troopers and bounty hunters clearly would not open ranks to permit the Jedi to carry Valin out. Zilaash and Kaddit took the opportunity to retreat to the security lines.

Han and Leia forced their way into the Jedi circle. Han stared out at the thickening lines of security troopers and shook his head. "This is getting way out of control, old buddy."

Luke nodded. "GA Security has legal jurisdiction, those others have a profit motive, and all we have is the fact that we're right. No one's going to back down until someone gets hurt."

Ben gestured toward someone in the security ranks. "There's a familiar face."

Luke peered in that direction. Captain Savar stood there, waving the security men and women around him to silence. "This could help," Luke said.

Leia's expression was one of irritation. "It certainly couldn't hurt."

Luke calculated odds and resources. He now had twenty Jedi here, including six Masters. If violence erupted, the security troopers would be slaughtered—or perhaps not, depending on how well their two bounty hunter allies fared.

Luke gestured until he got Captain Savar's attention. The officer headed his way, ignoring the guns at his back and lightsabers ahead of him, until he stood before Luke. "Quite a mess you Jedi have made here."

Luke shook his head. "It would have been a lot worse without us here. Is there any way you can pack those bounty hunters into a spent fuel drum or something?"

"I wish. That's not on the list of options."

Luke felt as glum as the man looked. "Well, we've got to figure something out. One twitch like your boy had yesterday, and we're going to have blaster bolts, arms and legs, and who knows what else flying everywhere."

"So hand Valin Horn over."

"How do you know his name?"

"He was caught on holocam and identified when he stole a classic starfighter and crashed a Kuati shuttle at the Senate Building."

"Tell you what, you conduct us all to the Jedi Temple

and we'll let you have an observer on hand while we study Jedi Horn to see what's wrong."

"Why would we want *you* to study *our* prisoner?"

Han and Leia, breaking from a bout of hurried consultation, stepped forward. Leia's voice was at her most diplomatic; this was the voice she'd used for all her Chief of State speeches. "Grand Master, Captain, I believe my husband and I can offer a solution that will defuse the immediate situation."

Captain Savar gave her a not entirely hopeful look. "Please."

"Mon Mothma Memorial Medical Center is pretty close to equidistant between the Temple and the Senate Building. That makes it a sort of halfway point for respective jurisdictions. Let's take Jedi Horn there. It's a secure facility and an enclosed space, so we can limit the number of people with access to the situation—say, six Jedi and six security agents."

Han nodded. "And no bounty hunters or press. None living, anyway."

Savar considered, took a look at the growing number of press and onlookers arriving, and nodded. He looked back over his shoulder. "Carn! Commandeer a civilian vehicle suitable for carrying fifteen or more. With a civilian driver. We need it here, *now.*"

"Yes, sir!" A broad-shouldered male trooper pushed his way through the ranks of security troopers and onlookers, then set off at a dead run.

It was almost a re-creation of the previous day's events in the Temple medical center, but with a bigger and more diverse cast. Jedi, troopers, and the Horns waited for the doctors' reports while Valin lay unconscious. News of the rampage spread like a tenement fire through the newsnets. And the Jedi had little to do but watch the news coverage for the first several hours.

It wasn't good. Amateur recordings showed Valin's dressing-robe paranoia outside the hostel the previous morning. Commentators asked why the Jedi had not surrendered him to the authorities then, which would have prevented today's outrage. Luke's arrest was briefly covered, with many angles on the Jedi, lightsabers lit, looking menacing. There were security recordings of Valin performing overrides on the X-wing and shuttle security, followed by gloriously detailed scenes of the shuttle smashing out of the Senate Building and crashing nearby.

And then Valin's final rampage, covered in exacting detail by high-quality holorecorders and far too many members of the press.

Analysts cast the Jedi Order in the guise of un-governed, unprincipled superhumans content to gratify themselves whatever the cost might be to the common population—every Jedi a potential Jacen Solo. No such stigma was attached to Luke Skywalker; his benevolence was too well known, too ingrained in the public con-sciousness. Instead, he was cast as an out-of-touch auto-crat, kindly but dangerously clueless, dedicated to a culture of entitlement that was decades behind the times.

After the ninth news cycle, Leia heaved a sigh. "I can feel the public turning against us from here. Minds are slamming shut like malfunctioning turbolift doors."

Luke gave her a glum look of agreement. "Any rec-ommendations?"

"Daala's masters of reinterpretation already have the public half convinced that the only way to save civiliza-tion is to muzzle the Jedi. You need to prepare yourself for a fight."

The civilian doctors studying Valin reported just what Cilghal had: high stress levels, no physical abnormalities, no evidence of poisoning or drugs, no way to test his neurological functions—Jacen's scanner-scrambling technique stayed in effect even as Valin remained under heavy sedation. By the next day, Luke and Captain Savar had agreed on a reduced number of observers from each camp, the Horns not to count against the Jedi total. Luke returned to his duties.

The government prepared a case against Valin Horn and cleared dockets to advance Luke's first hearing. Nawara Ven confirmed that the prosecutors were exploiting Valin's actions for all they were worth. The situation was very, very bad for Luke's case.

As Nawara explained it, "The public is still hurting from a war where everybody suffered and nobody gained—a war worsened by a Jedi. They're pretty worked up. They want *someone* to take responsibility for Jacen Solo. They want a change they can point to, a change that means problems like Jacen Solo and Valin Horn will never happen again. You can tell them all you want that muzzling the Jedi won't fix things. It's what they want, and they're turning against you."

It was true. Jedi on ordinary missions were booed. Ordinary people they dealt with were suddenly unhelpful, stalling investigations, and not just on Coruscant—the news, spreading throughout Alliance space, caused anti-Jedi sentiment to swell like a pond ripple that never seemed to weaken. Jaina, assigned at her own request to be the Imperial Remnant–Jedi liaison, suffered catcalls and was even thrown filth while in Jag's company. Public speaking engagements for which Jedi had been solicited months earlier were canceled. A years-old academic thesis proposing that interacting with the Force contributed to a tendency toward madness was uncovered and redistributed, and its author, now an obscure philosophy professor on Corellia, was suddenly the darling of interview shows.

Valin slept through it all, fruitlessly studied by doctors and chronicled by the press.

The Unification Summit moved on, relegated to second-tier news coverage. Perhaps the sudden absence of spotlights was a boon; political analysts reported promising responses from the Imperial Remnant and the Confederation.

A week after Valin's rampage, Luke went to bed, lay sleepless for three hours, then rose and dressed again. He walked the Temple halls for the next several hours. The Jedi he passed sensed his deep immersion in his thoughts and did not trouble him. Ben watched him during the hour he paced the Great Hall; then, distressed but unable to help, he went to his quarters to spend his own sleepless night.

Two hours before dawn, Luke used the comlink in his quarters to make a series of quick calls.

Not long thereafter, on foot, he approached the Senate Building. In a few hours, participants in the Unification Summit would collect again, but for now it was a still office building.

He was greeted with courtesy at the main entrance and escorted to the floor where the Chief of State's offices were located. Outside those offices, another set of guards offered equal courtesy but required him to hand over his lightsaber and submit to a brief full-body scan, which he did.

Then, finally, he was conducted into a large inner office, one darkened and unoccupied in this predawn hour. An aide activated the overhead lighting and offered him caf. He declined, and the aide left.

The office showed that this Chief of State had different aesthetic sensibilities than Jacen Solo or Cha Niathal, who had preceded Daala in the position. Jacen had preferred natural woods and landscape tones, though his taste had graduated toward even darker décor in his last months. Niathal, a Mon Calamari, had preferred militaristic themes in blues and greens.

Daala, it seemed, chose to surround herself with the trappings of the old Empire. Her personal office gleamed white, with desks, chairs, and computer equipment that could all have been recently transferred from the bridge of a Star Destroyer.

The door behind him hissed open, and Luke turned to see Daala enter. The Chief of State was once again in admiral's whites. Guards waited in the hall outside, their forbidding expressions, directed at Luke, vanishing as the door closed.

Daala extended her hand. "Master Skywalker."

Luke rose and shook it. "Chief Daala."

She moved around him to sit at the main desk. "Please, sit."

He did. It was a little odd—he had expected to feel something from her, anger or resentment or a desire for vengeance, but he could detect no strong emotions, no aggression.

"Something to drink?"

He shook his head.

The Chief of State propped her elbows on her desk and rested her chin atop interlaced fingers. "When my staff tells me that the Jedi Grand Master wishes to see me, I take it as a serious matter, even if we *are* locked in legal battle. And I assume, when the message does not indicate a purpose for the meeting, that it is one best expressed face-to-face. So here we are, face-to-face. What can I do for you—or you for us?"

"I'm actually not one hundred percent sure. Earlier this evening, I had a feeling that we should meet. A presentiment in the Force."

"What did it mean?"

"I'm not certain, but I *suspect* it means that, somewhere, I now have the argument that will convince you to drop the case. Whether that's true or not, I have to be here. It might actually mean that I need to be in your presence when someone makes an attack on you."

"Perhaps the Force was telling you that you need to be here to suddenly discover that I'm just an imposter with Daala's face, and that you need to cut me down."

"No."

"Well, then, let's wait and find out."

"Yes."

"You will let me know if you change your mind about caf."

"Yes."

"Or sweetcakes."

Luke sighed. The impulse that had brought him here seemed no closer to revealing itself, and Daala clearly thought he was wasting her time.

"While we're waiting for the Force to announce its presence," she said, "I did want to say something. I want you to understand, this suit is not personal. Even when we were on opposite sides, representing enemy forces, I had every respect for you. In reviewing your records, it became clear to me that you have had a significant and beneficial effect on the galaxy."

Luke raised an eyebrow. "But you still need so very much to make the Jedi a mindlessly obedient branch of the government that you're pursuing the trial."

"It's not about obedience."

"Oh, that's right. It's about not detecting a Jedi turning to evil. Which we should be able to do far more easily than, say, noticing an Imperial leader growing so callous that he'd obliterate an entire innocent world to convince other worlds to obey."

Daala became very still. Her face gave away no emotion, but Luke could feel, just for a moment, the pain she had experienced long ago as her love, respect, and even understanding for Grand Moff Wilhuff Tarkin withered and faded in the wake of the atrocities he had committed in the Emperor's name.

Luke was sorry to make her relive that. But she clearly wanted to exchange blows, and Luke was not unarmed in this match.

She regained her composure a moment later. "It's not about that, either. You're as guilty of not detecting Jacen Solo's turn to evil as others were of not checking the excesses of Imperial officers. But that's not why you're being tried. It's just the argument that will allow us to convict you."

"Why am I being tried, then? Give me the next layer of truth. Or the next layer below that."

"It has to do with fairness, and responsibility, and the rule of law."

"Things the Jedi have always supported."

"Things the Jedi have always subverted, at least under your leadership."

Luke couldn't keep his astonishment from his face or voice. "That's ridiculous."

"Let me give you a hypothetical example. A Coruscant bar in seedy sublevels. Two patrons decide they don't like the looks of a third. They assault him. A Jedi intervenes, out come blaster pistols and a lightsaber, *whoosh, whoosh,* severed arms litter the barroom floor. Law enforcement officers are called, the Jedi gives them a terse statement and then flits off to his next adventure."

Luke nodded. "That's a simplistic and overly colorful way of putting it, but, yes, it happens." It had, in fact, happened almost exactly that way to him, with Luke in the role of the patron about to be assaulted, back before he was a Jedi himself, many years before.

"Do you not see anything wrong with the way the situation was resolved?"

"Not really."

"First, there's the maiming of the suspects. Would it have been possible for the Jedi to have defeated them without cutting off their arms?"

Luke nodded. "Possibly. Probably. But once the blasters came out of their holsters, the situation became a lot more dangerous for everybody, patrons and Jedi included."

"Could the Jedi have disarmed them with some use of the Force?"

"That does happen. But we know the Jedi in your example made the correct choice."

"How so?"

"He was not just reacting to what he saw with his eyes and knew from his experience. He was in tune with the Force. The Force alerted him to the true level of danger and he responded appropriately."

"Sad that the Force can never be sworn in to testify about the suggestions it offers to the Jedi."

"True."

"Or to the Sith. The Force talks to the Sith, too, doesn't it?"

Luke blinked. "The dark side of the Force, yes."

"You didn't say your Jedi was only listening to the bright side—"

"Light side."

"Yes, thank you. You just said the Force. But let's stipulate that the good Force is the only one our hypothetical Jedi listens to. It still suggests maiming an awful lot of the time."

"Hardly a life sentence of disfigurement and handicap. Modern prosthetics are indistinguishable from flesh and bone." He held up his own prosthetic hand, waggling its fingers at her, as evidence.

"Though they have to be paid for by someone—often the state, when the amputee is of the lower classes—and then maintained, at a cost in credits and technical skill in excess of the upkeep of an ordinary flesh-and-blood arm."

"Granted." Luke suppressed an impatient sigh. "Is that what the suit is about, then? A perception that arms are being cut off at a higher rate than the government recommends?"

"No, it's about the Jedi giving a cursory statement to law enforcement and then leaving. Or dashing off without giving one at all. Or just refusing to answer one crucial question the investigating officer asks. And, in every case, getting away with it."

"I still don't understand, then."

"I'll walk you through it. The officers show up and ask questions, the Jedi gives a fifty-word statement, the officers say, 'Thanks, now we need to go back to the neighborhood station for a full statement,' the Jedi says, 'Sorry, I have places to be,' and he's gone. Did the Jedi respond with appropriate force? You think so, but at the government level we never learn, because a short while later he's on Commenor dealing with an organized crime family, then in the Hapes Cluster . . ."

"Usually the Jedi does make a full statement. Does co-operate to whatever degree the local authorities require."

"Usually, yes. I have a report here of a Jedi Knight named Seff Hellin who assaulted law officers just a few weeks ago. Whatever he needed to rush off to do, he never came back to offer full cooperation to the authorities. Did he?"

Luke suppressed the urge to fidget. He found himself wishing that Nawara Ven were here, though Daala was herself not being backed up by an advocate. "I can see how incomplete reports and investigations would be frustrating to the government. But you have to trust that we made the right choice at the right time. It's what we're trained to do."

The smile she turned on him was as frosty as anything Luke had seen in the snowy outback of Hoth. "I do, do I? We'll get back to that. Grand Master, the hypothetical incident I described shows at a very minor, very frequent level that the Jedi are *above the law*."

"Not true. Anyone in the bar situation you described could have intervened with lethal force to save the victim from his beating."

"And then would have been obliged to make a full report, and stay in contact until the investigation was resolved. The Jedi don't respect that law, or any law they find inconvenient. And the choice to sever the arms comes dangerously close to a judicial sentence being enacted at the time of the intervention. Judge, jury, executioner: Jedi."

"I'm sorry you have that impression." Luke frowned. "I'd come here hoping that I could persuade you to drop the case. But now I'm wondering whether I should go through the whole trial just to demonstrate to the public that we *do* cooperate with the authorities. That we don't consider ourselves above the law."

Daala nodded, her expression agreeable. "Let's talk about Kyp Durron."

"Master Durron is a fine, responsible Jedi."

"I'm not talking about the Jedi he is now. I'm talking about the teenager who destroyed most of the life in the Carida system all those years ago."

Luke, his composure no longer entirely intact, shifted uncomfortably. "He was under the influence of the dark side of the Force at that time, affected by the mental sendings of a long-dead Sith Lord. And in the years since, he has proven himself to be courageous, a defender of life—"

"Yes, he has. I'm not questioning that. But I want to

take you back a little over thirty years to shortly after he killed everyone who hadn't yet managed to evacuate Carida in the two hours he generously gave the population. Of course, the solar system he destroyed was an Imperial system, your enemy at the time, which does mitigate his crime in your eyes. Is that why you protected him, shielded him from legal ramifications, trained him?"

"No."

"Why did you?"

"Because I could look into his heart and see that he had cast the shadow of Exar Kun out, that he was no longer an agent of the dark side, that he had repented."

"He said he was sorry, and he meant it, and that was sufficient justice for the millions who died on Carida."

"You're oversimplifying. I *knew* that he was on the right path again."

"Because you have the power to see that. Because that's what Jedi are trained to do."

"Yes."

Daala sighed. "And because they're trained to do that, to see into people's hearts, sort truth from lies, see into the future where the criminal has reformed and turned to a life of picking flowers, they can decide who should be thanked and who should be cut down, who should be forgiven and who should be left for the ordinary officers of the law to convict. They protect the common citizen but do not answer to him. They do not pay for their mistakes. They obey government orders when those orders conform to their moral code and not when they don't. *And that's wrong.* Any other group exhibiting that degree of arrogance, that unconcern for the rule of law, would be classified as a criminal organization. That, ultimately, is what this case is about."

She was wrong. And yet she was chiefly wrong from the Jedi perspective. Remove the Force from the equation, and she suddenly became right. That was jarring to Luke. It was so hard for him now to remember what it was like not to have the Force always contributing to his decision making.

It was then that he detected it: the evil that the Force had brought him here to see. He did not see it as a person or an object, but as a process, a trend—one that he was a part of.

Understanding things as much as he could through Daala's perspective, through the perspective of the common citizen, the one truth he could discern was that if the galaxy thought that the Jedi were above the law, abuses were sure to spring up from that notion as toxic weeds growing rapidly from a pile of manure.

Young Jedi, seeing the ease with which their Masters slid out from underneath common but inconvenient civic responsibilities, *would* come to think that such behavior was their right. A few, on the fringes of the border between the light side and the dark side, *would* discern that Kyp Durron had escaped any visible consequence of his actions at Carida . . . *would* accept Luke's assertion that Darth Vader had been redeemed, had died a Jedi instead of a Sith despite his many murders, and would not understand the true meaning of the story.

The answer settled across Luke like a leaden shroud. To prevent this evil from growing, he had to lose this case, to be punished. That was what the Force had brought him here to understand.

He met Daala's gaze again. "Will you be prosecuting Master Durron next?"

"*I* will not. But I could authorize extradition for him to the Imperial Remnant to face their charge of planetary genocide. Head of State Jagged Fel has rather reluctantly presented me with a proposal from the Moff Council on that very subject. But such a thing could be

avoided, of course, if we had already set another decisive example."

Luke gave her a slow nod. "I came here hoping that,
face-to-face, without advocates whispering in our ears,
we could negotiate a deal. Now, having heard what you
have to say, I am certain we can."

"Tell me."

Chapter Seven

THIS REALLY WAS A COURTROOM, A PLACE WHERE JUSTICE was dispensed, and, during regimes like Jacen Solo's, injustice as well. The walls were somber wood panel; the tables and the judge's elevated bench were a dark, beautiful caf-colored antique marble from Ithor.

Luke watched the proceedings from a slight state of detachment, brought on by his lack of sleep and the air of unreality his own decision had created.

The judge, a severe-looking Falleen woman, her pale green skin contrasting sharply with her dark judicial robes, sat at her bench, studying the documents Nawara Ven and the government prosecutor had given her upon her arrival. The audience at the back of the chamber buzzed with a little conversation, and Luke could feel expectation from them far in excess of the level of noise. It was here, the first action in Luke Skywalker's trial, and they were on hand to see blood spilled—metaphorically speaking.

Finally, the judge looked up, glanced at Luke and the two attorneys, and spoke. "In Alliance case why-oh-oh-four-three-dash-seventeen thousand fourteen, *The Galactic Federation of Free Alliances versus Luke Skywalker,* we have a negotiated conclusion, agreed to this day by the prosecution, the defense, and myself."

A faint moan arose from portions of the audience. Luke could sense the source of their dismay. Weeks of court hearings, stories of Jacen Solo's murderous actions, embarrassing revelations, were all about to be headed off before they could take place in all their exploitation-news glory—wiped away by a plea bargain.

It should have been funny. But Luke didn't feel in the least humorous.

"The defendant will stand."

Luke and Nawara got to their feet.

"On the revised list of charges, now consisting of one charge, reckless endangerment of a population, how do you plead?"

Luke cleared his throat. "Guilty, Your Honor."

"You are found guilty as charged. Please sit." Once Luke and Nawara were seated, she continued, "Thus ends the trial phase of these proceedings. We now move on to the sentencing phase.

"For a period of time, beginning tomorrow at one hour before midnight in the current time zone and continuing for not less than ten Coruscant years, you are exiled from Coruscant. You will maintain a distance of not less than five light-years from this world.

"During that same time period, you will not act as Grand Master of the Jedi Order, nor in any position of authority or consultation within the Order.

"During that same time, you will not visit or approach any closer than one light-year to any world upon which there exists a Jedi Order Temple, Jedi Order school, or any other Jedi Temple facility.

"During that same time, you will refrain from establishing any new Jedi Order Temple, Jedi Order school, or any other Jedi Temple facility, or any business that structurally or organizationally resembles those concerns and thus might readily be converted to such a concern after your sentence is fulfilled.

"You will appoint Jedi Master Kenth Hamner to perform the duties of leader of the Jedi Order, and will subsequently exercise no influence over him for the duration of your sentence.

"Any violation of the above restrictions incurs a more severe penalty: incarceration in an Alliance maximum-security prison facility for the remainder of the ten-year period.

"By the provisions of this arrangement, your sentence can be commuted or a pardon issued if you can convince a board of inquiry that you have determined the nature of the events and other causes that led to the aberrant and destructive behaviors of Colonel Jacen Solo leading up to and during the Second Galactic Civil War, the board of inquiry to be made up of one prominent member of each of the following: the Galactic Alliance Judiciary Branch, Galactic Alliance Medical Association, and Galactic Alliance Armed Forces, each of these individual members to be chosen by the Office of the Galactic Alliance Chief of State.

"Do you understand these terms?"

Luke nodded. "Yes, Your Honor." He understood them very well. He and Daala had negotiated them, point for point, only hours before. But though he had played a part in selecting them, Luke still felt as though the situation were a dream that was sad and tiring.

"It is so ordered. The sentencing phase is complete, and, by my order, this case is concluded." The judge stood, and all others in the chamber did as well to watch her leave by her private exit behind the bench.

When she was gone, the courtroom erupted into conversation, shouts, pleas from the members of the press for Luke to spare them a few words.

He kept his back to that portion of the chamber. Security troopers admitted members of the Jedi and Luke's family into the area of the chamber reserved for advocates and their clients, and suddenly Luke was being embraced by Leia, Han, Ben, and Jaina, while other Jedi positioned themselves as a living wall between Luke and the audience.

"Ten *years*," Ben said. He looked as though he'd been hit in the head by a speeder bike.

"We'll fight this," Leia told him.

"*Kenth Hamner?*" That was Han, looking confounded. "Was he chosen because he's the dullest Jedi ever? He says two sentences and it puts Kowakian monkey-lizards to sleep."

Luke addressed his sister's comment first. "We won't fight this. I negotiated it. I agreed to it."

"Without benefit of counsel." That was Nawara Ven, speaking under his breath, just loud enough for the Jedi to hear.

"And it won't be the full ten years," Luke told Ben. "You heard the conditions for commutation at the end."

Han shook his head. "Buddy boy, Daala gets to appoint your tribunal. If they were still alive, she'd pick Palpatine, Lumiya, and Shimrra Jamaane to be your judges."

Luke waved the objection away.

Captain Savar approached. He was in the GA Security dress uniform, his expression somber, perhaps even sad. "Judge Zudan left word that you could leave the courtroom by her door and the back corridors if you'd like to avoid the press."

Luke nodded. "Please."

"This way."

That evening, Luke called a conference of the Jedi Masters' Council.

"I'll keep this brief," he told them, "as I have a lot of preparations to make before tomorrow night, and in the interest of not drawing out an unpleasant event.

"First, I withdraw from my duties as Grand Master of the Jedi Order until such time as my sentence has been served, commuted, or struck down in the court. This is effective as of my departure from Coruscant."

Kyp Durron smiled. "For the first time in this whole mess, you've given me some hope."

Luke looked at him, curious. "How so?"

"You didn't *resign* as Grand Master. Clearly, you plan to come back and resume your position."

"I do. I *hope* to. So while I'm gone, there will be no wild parties in the Masters' Chamber." It felt good to be able to make a joke, even a stale one. "Second, I appoint Master Kenth Hamner as governing Master of the Order."

Hamner, a tall, fair-haired man with features that spoke of generations of family wealth and rule, his posture military-perfect, offered Luke a wan smile. "And I did not even have the opportunity to negotiate before sentence was passed on *me*."

"Chief of State Daala and the military have faith in you." Luke gave him a sympathetic look. "Your own fault for leading a lifetime of military experience."

"I will serve as best I can, Grand Master."

Master Octa Ramis, recovered from the minor injuries she had sustained during Valin's rampage, asked, "What are you going to do while you're gone, Master Skywalker?"

"I plan to do what I negotiated with the Chief of State. To understand what brought Jacen to the dark side, and then set up protocols to anticipate the same thing happening in other Jedi. If we're lucky, this may also have some bearing on what has happened to Valin and Seff. I'll start by retracing, as much as I can, the travels Jacen undertook prior to the Killik crisis. I'm hoping that the answer lies somewhere along his journey."

Master Hamner placed his hands together and peered

over them at Luke. "Since that is distinctly to the Jedi Order's benefit—even though you can't advise us in any significant way until your sentence is concluded—and since the terms of your sentence do not come into effect for another day, I feel no guilt in offering you whatever resources you need to accomplish your mission. We just have to get them all transferred within a day."

"I'll be using Mara's yacht as my main transportation and home. So travel is not an issue. But operating funds are; I don't exactly have savings."

Hamner nodded. "I'll set up an account for you. Not a drawing account, as that would be proof of Jedi Order support after your sentence begins. A sum constituting forty-three standard years' of back pay, I think."

Luke smiled, amused. "And please, bank it out of some world that is not part of the Galactic Alliance, or likely to join it anytime soon."

"Consider it done. You'll have all the details in hand by breakfast."

"That's all I have to say." Luke looked among the Masters. Sadness threatened to descend on him, to constrict his heart, but he kept it at bay by an act of will. "Any issues I need to address as Grand Master, you need to bring to me as soon as possible."

Kyp Durron nodded. "We'll sort it out."

Cilghal was the first to rise. As she approached Luke, her action acted as a signal to the others, who all got to their feet. She enfolded Luke for a brief moment in her rubbery arms. "We will keep your home for your return," she told him. "May the Force be with you, always and everywhere."

Walking with Luke back to their quarters, Ben said, "I'm going with you."

Luke managed another smile. "I don't think so."

"Why not?"

"Well, first, you're not a convicted felon and don't need to serve the sentence of one. Second, no teenager I ever knew, myself included, could survive being in the constant company of a parent for ten years."

"I have you on a point of logic." Ben raised a finger, looking ridiculously like a Jedi Master addressing a roomful of younglings. "No teenager can remain one for ten years."

"Conceded. Still, Ben, I think you should stay here."

Ben's jaw set. Now, as was often the case whenever his tendency toward stubbornness hit him, he truly resembled his mother. "You're my Master, I'm your student."

"You're a full Jedi Knight now, even if there are plenty of places in the galaxy where you can't legally vote or drink. Surely you didn't forget your promotion. You only talked about it for two years."

"I wasn't *that* bad. And you're a rank above Master, so you should have a student a rank above apprentice."

"Interesting logic."

"Dad, this is my mission, too." Ben's voice was suddenly no longer that of a wheedling teen. "I was Jacen's apprentice. In the end, he tortured me, tried to make me a Sith. He killed Mom. Do you think I'm going to be able to rest, *ever,* without understanding why?"

Luke fell silent as he considered Ben's words. Not speaking, they rode the turbolift down to the upper residential level. As they reached their door, Luke came to a decision. "You're right. Pack up and make your farewells."

Ben sagged in relief. "Thank you, Dad."

The next morning, Luke reflected that one of the virtues of living as a Jedi was that packing was really easy. A lightsaber, a bag for a few changes of clothes, his kit of tools, parts, and meters for maintaining his artificial hand, a datapad stuffed with data and popular literature, and not only was he packed but his quarters were almost empty as well. He looked around his bedchamber and found it nearly bare; all that remained were shelf items, holos of his life with Mara, knickknacks acquired during his years of travel or sent to him by admirers, a few articles of clothing he had decided to leave behind.

The thought that the room might remain empty, unchanged, for the entirety of his sentence—or that the room might be needed and reassigned, with the remainder of his things swept into a small bag and stored, scrubbing his presence out of the Temple like one last stain—was depressing. He had to go, and soon, and that fact alone was enough to make him want to stay.

His door chimed. He called, "Enter," and moved into the small living chamber.

The main door slid open, revealing Cilghal. The Mon Cal Master nodded her respects. She entered, allowing the door to shut behind her. "When not studying Valin's test results, I have spent time in the last few days looking for references to odd behavior matching Valin's or Seff's. And I have found something." She tilted her head as if recollecting, and her next words were in a different tone of voice; Luke suspected she was quoting. "Though I have lived among humans for many years, some of the differences between our ways choose not to fade into irrelevance. The electroencephaloscan, for example, would be considered a grave and very personal intrusion by my kind. Fortunately, my order knows of a means to keep even it at bay. Unfortunately, when utilizing it, we cannot demonstrate that we have functioning brains."

Luke snorted, amused. "Who were you quoting?"

"Jedi Master Plo Koon."

Luke considered. Plo Koon had been a Jedi in the last years of the Old Republic—had died, in fact, about the time Luke was being born, one of the many victims of

Emperor Palpatine's Order 66. He was a Kel Dor, a member of a species that was not often seen out in the galaxy at large; they were not oxygen breathers and had to wear special breathing masks when visiting most other inhabited worlds. "Why was that quotation so difficult to find?" With anyone else, he'd be worried that his question sounded like a criticism, but Cilghal had no human neuroses that made her prone to interpret offhand remarks as complaint.

"It was not transcribed as searchable data in our archives. It was a recording of an interview between Plo Koon and a Jedi Knight who was assembling a documentary project on the species represented within the Order. He, too, was a victim of the purge, his project unfinished. I have been using automated vocal translation software against holorecorded materials, searching for a list of keywords related to Valin's situation, and this morning's pass flagged the word *electroencephaloscan* in this entry."

"Good work. Was there anything else useful in that interview?"

Cilghal twisted her body from side to side, a Mon Cal simulation of a human shaking of the head. "That appears to have been, for Plo Koon, a humorous aside, and the subject was not further explored."

"He said, 'My order knows of a means.' Who was he referring to? It couldn't have been the Jedi Order, since we've found no other reference to the technique, and since he was talking to another Jedi . . ."

"He would have said *our Order*." Cilghal tilted her head. Familiar with her ways, Luke took it as a gesture of self-appreciation. Some human nuances of speech were still difficult for her, even after all her years among them.

"Yes." Luke pulled his datapad from his belt pouch and flipped it open. As he used it to access the Temple computer archives, he realized, with a pang, that this might be the last time he would do so—for many years, or perhaps ever.

He scanned Plo Koon's service file. He knew many of its details already. His own studies had made him very familiar with the career of his own first Master, Obi-Wan Kenobi, and Obi-Wan's teachers and confidants; Obi-Wan's Master, Qui-Gon Jinn, had been a close friend of Plo Koon. But Plo Koon's record offered few leads. It mentioned no other order to which the long-dead Master might have belonged, though Luke knew there was one prospect more likely than any other.

Luke snapped the datapad shut. "I'm guessing he was referring to the Baran Do Sages. He might have studied with them before joining the Order, which means that's a trail eighty or a hundred years cold. I might as well make the sages the first stop on my grand tour." He frowned. "There's no record of Jacen visiting them, but his travels are badly documented. I'm going to hope for the best. I just wish I had time to trace all of Valin's movements to see if he's had any contact with the sages."

"I have time. And I have access to the full Order archives."

"I couldn't ask you to do that. And as an exile, I'm not supposed to have access to Order resources."

"You did not ask. *I* decide for whom *I* am a resource. And your sentence said you cannot advise, not that you cannot be advised."

Thrown off for a moment by Cilghal's resolute tone, her unhesitating rejection of Galactic Alliance government wishes, Luke stepped forward and took one of Cilghal's broad hands between his own. "I sometimes forget, with our very orderly system of ranks and duties, that I have friends."

"You established this Order with logic, and you made

your friends with your heart. The Order acts according to your commands. Your friends act according to your needs."

The door slid open, revealing Ben, dressed in his customary black, a cylindrical bag in dark green on a strap over his shoulder. "I'm sorry. I didn't mean to interrupt."

Luke shook his head. "You didn't. We were just finishing up some business. Is the speeder ready?"

"It's ready."

"Then let's head down."

"Up."

Luke raised an eyebrow at his son. "I thought I said to get us a speeder and have it ready in the lower hangar."

"You did, but I got new orders in the meantime."

"From whom?"

"Master Hamner."

Luke sighed. Kenth could have waited until Luke was out of the building before beginning to countermand his orders. "Let's go, then."

The turbolift took them up, and to Luke's surprise— for, engaged again in conversation with Cilghal, he had not paid attention to what Ben said into the turbolift's controller—opened at the Great Hall level.

The three of them stepped out into a crowded hall, and conversation, which had been expectant in tone, died.

It looked as though every Jedi on Coruscant, and perhaps some currently stationed in nearby star systems, was present, as well as many non-Jedi. Some faces were sad, a few even tear-streaked, and even among those maintaining a proper Jedi calm there was an atmosphere of sadness, of resignation.

Ben's next comment came as a dry whisper: "I don't think I've ever seen so many brown robes together in one place. It's like a showroom for the world's dullest textile factory."

Luke repressed a snort. "Quiet."

Master Hamner approached, so Luke stepped forward, extending his hand. "Kenth, was this your idea?"

"Leia's, mine, every member of the Council's, and many others' besides. Many had messages, messages they'll deliver personally as you make your way to the front of the hall, but all of them had a message in common." Kenth put one arm across Luke's shoulders and turned him toward the distant main entrance, then gestured with his free hand across the expanse of Jedi Masters, Jedi Knights, apprentices, and friends. "Forty years ago, there was one practicing Jedi in all the galaxy, and the Order and the Temple were just ill-formed notions taken from suppressed rumors. Today, what you see before you—this is your doing, Master Skywalker."

Despite himself, Luke felt his throat trying to close. "Not alone." His words were just a touch hoarse.

Kenth nodded. "Not alone. But remove any other contributor from the processes and the end result looks only a little different. Remove you, and it all goes away, like a holodrama switched off in midscene." Gently, he took Luke's bag from his hand. Then he gave Luke a little push forward. "I'll have this put in your speeder."

That was the signal for the others in the hall, who pressed forward singly or in small groups, shaking Luke's hand, offering him embraces or kisses of farewell, some of them with tears glistening on their cheeks. Ben, also relieved of his bag, received these attentions as well, always present in the periphery of Luke's awareness.

There were Kyp and Octa, Kam and Tionne, Saba Sebatyne in all her reptilian majesty, Kyle Katarn, the doubly sad Horn family, visitors such as Jag Fel and Talon Karrde. There was a who's who of the Red Squadron and Rogue Squadron veterans Luke had flown with so many years before and since—Wedge Antilles foremost among them. There were Jedi Knights and apprentices he barely knew, such a change from years before when he had personally trained every member of the Jedi Order, a change both satisfying and a little disquieting.

Leia, Han, and Jaina were among the last to intercept him, and held him the longest. "You'll be home soon," Leia told him, forcing a cheerful tone to conceal the misery she was clearly feeling.

Luke smiled at her. "Define *soon*."

She shook her head. "Informative answers are not the Jedi way."

"Hey." Ben, wrapped up in the embrace of his cousin Jaina, sounded miffed. "You stole that line from me."

"I first said it twenty years before you were *born*. Before *I* was even a Jedi."

Han took Luke's hand and pulled him into a wampa-like hug. "You know, anywhere you are in the galaxy, give me a shout on the holocomm, or give Leia a squawk through the Force, and the *Falcon* will be right there."

"I know. You'll take care of Artoo-Detoo for me while I'm gone?"

Han grinned. "Are you kidding? Having Artoo with us means See-Threepio only talks to us *half* as much. I should be paying you."

Jaina tucked herself under Luke's arm for the last few steps out of the Great Hall. "Daala's going to be sorry she did this."

Luke frowned at her. "That sounds suspiciously like a thought of revenge."

"It's not. I just know how things work. Inevitably some mess will arise that she can't solve, that no other Jedi can solve, and she'll know what a mistake she made."

"Be charitable." On the steps outside the hall, in the

afternoon sunlight descending in brilliant, steeply slant-
ing shafts through the uneven cloud cover overhead,
Luke paused to give Jaina one last hug. "She's trying to
do the best she can for the Alliance, the only way she
knows how."

"Well, she's not very bright."

"That's not 'charitable.' "

"Oh. I thought you meant 'honest.' "

The airspeeder that had been acquired for Luke and
Ben's departure was not the Grand Master's usual one or
Ben's red speedster. It was a big white air barge, a model
with a built-in droid brain that would return the vehicle
to its home when its current users were done with it.
Luke let Ben take the controls for the trip out to the
spaceport while he took in what might be his final view
of Coruscant. In this late-afternoon hour, shadows in the
canyons between mountain-high buildings were already
dark as night, the thousands upon thousands of streams of
airspeeder traffic were already putting on their nighttime cruising lights, and the sun, its lower edge peeking
out below the layer of clouds in the west, seemed larger
and more orange than at any other time of day. He
burned it all into his memory, knowing he would miss it.

They spent their trip to the spaceport in near silence
until they moved out of the high-rise districts and into
one of the traffic lanes heading into the hangar portion
of the spaceport. "Think they'll turn us back?" asked
Ben.

Luke gave him a curious look. "Why would they?"

"Because we nearly wrecked the place a few days
ago."

"You exaggerate. The fight didn't even spill over into
the secure zones."

"True."

Soon enough, they set down outside the hangar where *Jade Shadow* was berthed.

Luke entered the lengthy access code in the security console beside the main doors, then peered into its optic sensor to give it a retinal reading. Finally the great doors slid aside, admitting a wash of stale air, allowing Luke to look upon his dead wife's ship.

It had started its career as a *Horizon*-class star yacht from premier shipmakers SoroSuub, but had, over the years, been modified by Mara, family, and friends to become a combat vehicle that was fast and powerful for its size. Low and broad in the beam, with sleek, curving lines, it had a top-mounted airfoil that swept down toward both sides and ended in external ion engine pods. Forward of those, outrigger-style plates stretched from the fuselage and curved down to hold external weapons emplacements. The ship's organic lines gave it the appearance of some nautical shelled beast, and its nonreflective gray surface made its name an apt one.

It did not suggest Mara's appearance so much as her manner when she was on the hunt. It was practical and implacable. It scarcely seemed the sort of ship to become home to a middle-aged widower and his teenage son, but it was what he had.

Luke remotely activated its loading ramp and life-support systems, letting it open and expel stale atmosphere while he and Ben removed their possessions from the airspeeder. Luke gave the speeder's droid brain an all-clear order and it lifted off, accelerating away into the darkening sky, its shiny white coating making it visible for a considerable distance.

It didn't take Luke and Ben long to complete a pre-flight check; the *Jade Shadow*'s self-diagnostics circuitry and software were first-rate, as were the Skywalkers' technical skills. The engines had lost only a little stored power in the many months the yacht had sat unused.

The various compartments within the yacht were a little dusty but otherwise clean. Mara's personal craft, her Z95 Headhunter, an old but reliable predecessor to the X-wing, rested in its tiny launch bay; though it was smaller and slower than its more famous descendant, Mara's Z95, like her yacht, it had been modified and optimized to within a centimeter of its life, and was a far more dangerous starfighter than others of its make and age.

While the preflight check was under way, a delivery speeder arrived. Its crew off-loaded two large crates full of supplies—fresh and preserved foods, water and bottled beverages, replacement battery packs and glow rods. Ben signed for the goods and set about loading them into the *Shadow*'s storage lockers.

And then it was all done. They had no more reason, no additional excuse to wait. It was time to leave Coruscant.

Solemnly, Luke strapped into the pilot's seat, Ben into the copilot's. After a brief comm exchange with the spaceport's flight-control center, Luke eased the yacht out of its berth. Many meters from the hangar, out over open permacrete, he raised it on repulsors, then aimed it toward the stars and punched the thrusters.

The yacht's inertial compensators kept the acceleration from being a crushing experience, but Luke raced upward fast enough to press the two of them far back into their cushioned seats. Behind, in the rear-facing holocam view, the light glaring from Mara's hangar clicked off and its doors slowly rolled shut.

Moments later, they were up past the cloud layer and bound for the stars.

Chapter Eight

THINGS HAPPENED QUICKLY AFTER LUKE'S DEPARTURE.

Valin was released from Mon Mothma Memorial Medical Center and returned to Jedi custody. Cilghal installed him in her own medical facility again, in a more secure chamber, and let him recover from sedation; though not anxious to face the escape attempts she had every reason to believe would come, she knew that endless sedation would have a damaging effect on Valin's health.

The bounty hunters were mentioned in newscasts, not as bounty hunters, but as a special-missions force answering to the Office of the Chief of State, officially part of her security detail. Their names were not mentioned. Jaina, who had inherited Ben's task of assembling data on them, noted those details and copied that broadcast for her own reference.

The morning after Luke's departure, Master Hamner called a meeting of the Jedi Masters. He also invited several Jedi who were not Masters but who were influential in the Order, including Leia and Jaina. They met in the Masters' Chamber, sitting among the circle of chairs once used by the old Jedi Council. Additional seating had been brought in for the assembly—there were, in the face of the Unification Summit and Luke's farewell, more Masters on Coruscant than could be routinely accommodated.

Master Hamner began without preamble. "It seems clear that some of our recent trouble, the public reaction that gave the government so much of its leverage in its action against the Grand Master, arises because of the general public's state of ignorance concerning the Jedi Order."

There was some nodding among the Masters at this statement.

"It is my intent to demystify the Jedi Order to the public as much as is reasonable—without impairing our effectiveness.

"I'd like for one Master to volunteer to be the subject of documentary coverage. That Master and his or her apprentice will be accompanied on an assignment or two by a documentary crew. The story they produce will be broadcast with, I hope, the result of making the Jedi more sympathetic in the public eye. Volunteers?"

No hand raised. Saba Sebatyne said, "Thiz one is perhapz too ferocious for a documentary children will watch."

"I think perhaps you are correct, Master Sebatyne. No one? Ah, Master Ramis. Thank you." Master Hamner consulted his datapad. "An independent producer has contacted us about his plan to create a holodrama about the Jedi. It sounds like mindless, swashbuckling adventure, which ordinarily would stir me to some midpoint between apathy and contempt, but in our current situation I think it will work in our favor. I have denied his rather naïve requests to consult our Archives and record certain sequences in the Temple"—there were sighs of relief from among the Masters—"but I have promised to put forth the request that a Jedi Master serve as technical consultant, and will give my permission to one who does. Here, too, do we have a volunteer? I will not insist . . . Ah, Master Durron. You just won me fifty credits. Thank you."

Sitting in one of the chamber's permanent chairs, Kam Solusar, obviously the loser of the bet, scowled.

Now Master Hamner's manner became more grave. "Finally, we have some bad news to face. We have been informed by the Office of the Chief of State that, effective immediately, Jedi will be accompanied by government observers."

Several Masters, as well as both the Solos, raised voices in protest. Leia said, "Are they trying to cripple our effectiveness?"

Hamner waved them down. "One observer will be assigned to each Master–apprentice pairing, and one to each Jedi operating solo—my apologies, Leia, Jaina, I mean each Jedi operating unpartnered. Their stated objective is to act as a gentle reminder to their Jedi of Alliance and local laws. They will not have access to the secure areas of the Temple, but will otherwise be able to accompany their Jedi most of the time, particularly outside the Temple."

Kyp Durron heaved a sigh. "There goes my social life."

Jaina's expression was a fixed frown. "Please tell me that we're not going to do this."

Hamner shrugged. "Actually, we are. For the time being. But I have retained the firm of the Grand Master's advocate, Nawara Ven, to initiate a legal suit, intended to strike down this government measure. Until we have some progress there, though, we simply have to endure this inconvenience. Observers will be assigned in stages over the next several days, Masters first, beginning tomorrow."

As the assembly left the chamber, Jaina was still wearing her frown. "I'm too young to begin harping about the good old days."

Leia ruffled her daughter's hair. "You're getting there.

Just wait, you'll be talking about those blasted kids next."

"Mom . . ."

SOLO FAMILY QUARTERS, CORUSCANT

"I say, Master Han, Mistress Leia, I am so *terribly* sorry."

Han opened one eye. Though he was being awakened before his alarm had gone off, meaning it was too early by anyone's standards, he had not yet decided to shoot the tormenter awakening him, C-3PO, and therefore he did not need both eyes yet.

Directly beside him was Leia, rousing just as reluctantly from sleep, her hair a tangled mess splayed across her face and pillow.

Han's voice emerged as a hoarse rumble. "Where's my blaster?"

"Under your pillow, as usual." Leia's voice was almost as rough.

"Sir, no." C-3PO, standing by Leia's side of the bed, framed by the curtained viewport that, when bared, offered a vista of Coruscant aerial traffic and skytower tops, waved awkwardly as if to placate Han. "You have a call from Master Calrissian."

Han rubbed between his eyes. "I'll listen to the message in the morning."

"Sir, it's a live holocomm transmission from offworld."

That got Han's attention. He sat up; Leia did as well.

Lando Calrissian was a rich man and a generous one, but he did not waste credits on stunts like holocomm calls just to show off his wealth. As far as Han knew, Lando was nowhere near Coruscant. This had to be important. "Tell him we'll be right there."

"Yes, sir. Thank you, sir. For not shooting me at this time of the morning, sir."

Moments later, wrapped in white robes but not yet fortified by caf, Han and Leia seated themselves at their quarters' comm console and took the main display off hold. The picture snapped from grayness to full-color clarity. Lando sat in a high-backed office seat, industrial gray walls and a closed door behind him.

Dark-skinned and well dressed—the image showed him wearing a maroon dress tunic and a black, sparkling hip cloak—Lando was, Han grudgingly admitted, aging nearly as well as Han himself. His hair had thinned and receded a bit but remained dark, and his features, though more lined, were still handsome and elegant— and still ideally suited to wear expressions of suave self-confidence or comic dismay.

Looking to one side as the picture went live, Lando snapped his attention back to the holoscreen and smiled. "Han! Leia! Good to see you. Oh—is it morning there?"

Leia, binding her hair back with an elastic band, glowered at him. "I'm not a gambler, but I'll bet a thousand credits that you knew exactly what time it was before you called."

"And I *am* a gambler, so I won't take that bet. You'd be right." Lando gave her a look of apology. "I need help. Jedi help, I think, as well as friend help. That adds up to you and Han. And about the hour, after the last . . . *event,* we decided that there was no time to waste."

"What sort of event?" Han turned to C-3PO, standing attentively off to the side, and mouthed the word *caf.* Then he turned back to Lando. "And who's *we?*"

"Nien Nunb and Tendra and me. Here, let me show you." Lando reached forward, his hands disappearing to either side of the picture view, as he evidently grabbed his monitor. He turned it, swinging its holocam view off him. Han expected it to focus on Tendra, Lando's wife, or Nien Nunb, his Sullustan manager, but instead it settled on a view of another gray wall, this one decorated with a holo of a shiny, skeletal YVH1 combat droid, which was manufactured by one of Lando's companies, Tendrando Arms.

But it was not the three-dimensional picture of the menacing droid that drew Han's attention. It was the jagged crack in the wall behind it, stretching from upper right to lower left, passing beyond the holocomm's field of view in either direction.

Leia snorted. "What caused that? A Hutt sat on your roof?"

Lando swung the monitor back to face him. "Quakes. Groundquakes, nasty ones. They're increasing in strength and frequency, and the scientists I've brought in can't figure out why."

Han frowned. Nien Nunb was the manager of Lando's glitterstim spice mines, which strongly suggested where Lando must be now. "You're on Kessel?"

Lando nodded. "I'm in the auxiliary comm center of my main office building. The primary comm center was destroyed in the last quake."

Han grimaced. "Lando, let it go. Kessel is a doomed world." Kessel, an undersized planet near the Maw, was notorious for many things. It was the origin of glitterstim, a drug with just as many illegal applications as legal ones, and the source of a great deal of smuggling activity. Its spice mines were infamous, having been operated by convict labor for so long that, decades after the system had changed, "going to the spice mines of Kessel" was still a fate promised to children to convince them to behave. The planet was also one of the marker points on the smuggler and race route that bore its name, the Kessel Run.

Over time, the low-gravity planet was bleeding atmosphere into space. Ancient atmosphere generation plants increasingly struggled to keep up with the loss, but they were gradually failing. The world would eventually become a lifeless environment.

Lando shook his head. "It's still a profitable operation, and the only source of glitterstim anywhere. Efforts to transplant colonies of the energy spiders that produce the stuff haven't been very successful."

Han sat upright. "You're trying to get them to survive on other planets?"

"Yes, but they just stop feeding and die—"

"Good!"

Lando waved his outburst away. "We need more time to work on the problem. Lots more time."

Han repressed a shudder. Once, back in his smuggler days, before he'd ever met Luke or Leia, he had dumped a load of glitterstim rather than be caught with it by Imperial investigators, a decision that had resulted in him being hunted for years by hirelings of the spice's owner, Jabba the Hutt. Much later, he had spent time in those mines, among the convicts, and had been one of the first to survive an attack by an energy spider and reveal the species' existence to the galaxy. The experience had left him with bad memories. "You do need a Jedi." He gave Lando a helpful nod. "You need Kyp Durron. He's a Master, he spent a lot more time in those mines than I did . . ."

Lando mimicked his tone. "He's impossible to deal with, he hates Kessel more than you do, he's not my friend . . ."

"Of course we'll help," Leia said.

Han looked at her. "No, no, no. Wait until you've had some caf. Your reasoning centers will kick in—"

"Hush." She returned her attention to Lando. "We'll launch today."

Lando sighed, relieved. In his impossibly smooth and

gracious manner, he said, "Bless you, Leia. And you, too, Han."

Han managed to keep his teeth from clenching. "Think nothing of it. We'll let you know when we're en route, old buddy." He switched off the holocomm connection.

Then he turned to glare at his wife.

She gave him a look that was all innocence. "What?"

"Don't you have to clear things like this through the Temple before you rush off?"

"Theoretically, yes. But not this time. It's better to help a friend and take your punishment than be refused permission and not be able to help."

"All right, how about this: *Kessel?*"

"Innocent beings live on Kessel. Even the energy spiders don't deserve to die just because they spooked you."

"Nothing spooks me."

"Then you won't mind going back."

"I do mind. Did you forget about Allana?"

From the way Leia froze, it was clear that she *had* forgotten Allana, perhaps only because Leia was sleepfogged. Allana—known to everyone but Han and Leia as Amelia and never referred to by her real name except in the utmost privacy—was the daughter of Jacen Solo and Tenel Ka, conceived before Jacen's recent efforts to gain mastery over the galaxy. She was Han and Leia's granddaughter, raised for her first five years by Tenel Ka, Queen Mother of the Hapes Consortium. At the end of the war between the Alliance and the Confederation, Tenel Ka falsely announced Allana's death to protect her from those who might kill her to gain the Hapan throne. Tenel Ka had sorrowfully given the care of her daughter to Han and Leia. The girl, now seven, lived these days under the guise of Amelia, adopted daughter of the Solos.

If Han and Leia raced off to Kessel, they'd have to take her along or leave her behind with near strangers. Allana's aunt Jaina was no stranger, but her life as a Jedi was an active and dangerous one. Luke and Ben were gone. There was no one else left whom they could entrust with Allana.

"We take her with us." Leia's voice was decisive.

"Don't get mad at me to cover up the fact that you forgot." Han pointed an accusing finger at her. "We agreed to settle down—as much as possible—for her sake. We agreed that we couldn't drag a little girl around the galaxy as we stupidly try to fix other stupid people's stupid problems."

"That's just it." There was a note of desperation in Leia's voice. "We weren't able to do *anything* for Luke. We can't do anything to stop the bureaucratic catastrophe that's descending on the Jedi Order right now. But we might be able to help a friend."

Han considered. When she put it like that . . . he'd never regretted marrying a woman who could out-argue him on just about every issue, but he was often inconvenienced by it. "Of course, if we just take off this morning without telling anyone where, you won't get assigned your own government spy."

"Observer. And you're right. We wouldn't be accompanied by a nosy intruder who inconveniences you as much as me."

"And Allana wouldn't have to put up with a stranger."

"Also correct."

"We already lose a lot of private time raising a little girl. Add a government spy and we lose the rest."

Leia nodded, encouraging him to continue down that line of reasoning.

"And it could be put off even longer if the *Falcon*'s hyperdrive were to fail somewhere out there—"

"It's happened before."

"Sabotage, always sabotage." He grinned at her. "You're going to be in such trouble with Kenth Hamner when you get back."

"That's what I keep you around for. To drag me into trouble."

"Uh-huh. Whatever you say." Han leaned forward for a kiss.

"Master Han, your caf. Master Han? Mistress Leia? Oh, dear."

RESIDENTIAL DISTRICT NEAR THE JEDI TEMPLE, CORUSCANT

"How did you manage to get free of your Head of State duties? And bodyguards?" Jaina asked.

Jag leaned against the door frame where they'd just arrived. This was one hallway of a residential high-rise; the passageway, its walls decorated with brown rhombuses against a tan background, spoke of a decorative style several years old, but was meticulously clean. Even now, a mouse droid affixed atop a circular cleaning attachment was gliding down the hallway, buffing dirt up out of the carpet and sending a faint, sweet smell of cleanser into the air.

"Most of what my delegation does is negotiate insanely minute points." Jag looked as though he found that prospect about as attractive as a bowlful of worms. "I let my advisers and advocates do that, and at the end of the day I veto every decision they've made. Thus is the balance of power between ruler and bureaucrat maintained. In the meantime, I get to spend my day with *you*. And I tell my bodyguard that you're protecting me. That's where your ferocious Jedi reputation helps me."

Jaina shook her head. "The system is unimaginably

broken." She pressed the button beside the door. Beyond the door, a chime faintly sounded.

"But fun," Jag said.

The door slid open but no one stood there. There was only a short green hallway beyond, a door open and brightly illuminated at the far end. Jaina caught the scent of freshly cut grass, if her nose did not deceive her. She gave Jag a quizzical look and preceded him in. The door slid shut behind them.

The hallway opened into a large chamber that had probably been intended as a living or family room. But where overhead glow rods would normally shine comfortably and placidly, there were brighter light fixtures, emitting, Jaina suspected, the exact frequencies of sunlight. Where comfortable, padded furniture should sit, instead rested weatherproof outdoor furnishings of light, foamed durasteel supports and colorful strapping—there were chairs, lounges, even a patio table with a large umbrella overhead. One picture viewport, as tall as an adult human and twice as long, admitted light and a view of buildings fifty meters away, stretching upward and downward as far as the eye could see from Jaina's position; streams of airspeeder traffic at just the altitude of this apartment added a dash of fast-moving color.

Tahiri Veila, former Jedi, former Sith apprentice, stood up from a piece of lounging furniture as they entered. Blond and attractive, she wore a simple, tight-fitting jumpsuit in gray. She was, as usual, barefoot. Her lightsaber was not at hand but lay nearby, on the patio table. Her expression was just a touch uncertain. The scars on her forehead, earned during the Yuuzhan Vong War, were not visible; Jaina doubted that they could have faded in just the few months since she had last seen Tahiri, so they were probably concealed by makeup.

Tahiri nodded to them. "Jedi Solo, Colonel—I mean, Head of State Fel."

Jag spoke, his manner brusque: "Tahiri."

"Please, sit down. Can I get you anything? Caf, water—"

"No, thank you." Jaina took one of the lightweight chairs and sat facing Tahiri; Jag did likewise. Tahiri settled again on her lounger.

Jaina gestured at the grass. "Please tell me that your refresher doesn't have a dirt floor."

That broke through Tahiri's discomfort and she grinned. "No, perfectly normal tile." She looked over her living green carpet. "I've always preferred being barefoot to wearing shoes . . . but most places just aren't that comfortable. Overheated permacrete, carpets where they glare at you for tracking in dirt . . . Now that I have some credits to spend, I decided I wanted a home where I could be comfortable. And this is much nicer than Tatooine desert sand."

"Now that you have credits and aren't living by anyone else's rules," Jaina amended.

"That's right."

Jag leaned forward. "We're here to ask you a few questions about Jacen Solo."

Tahiri's uncertain look returned. "You really don't need to say Jacen *Solo*. When his sister comes to talk to his former apprentice and Jacen is mentioned, I'm not going to suppose you mean some Jacen who waits tables."

"Of course." Jag gave Jaina a pained look. "In informal circumstances, I really am redundant and stuffy, aren't I?"

Jaina nodded. "Yes, but you're pretty." She returned her attention to Tahiri. "You've heard about the Grand Master and his sentence."

Tahiri nodded. "I heard about his farewell. I thought about going, but I was pretty sure I wouldn't be welcome."

"Not by everyone . . . We're trying to get a better handle on Jacen's thought processes. What made him turn. *When* he turned. It's all part of an effort to help the Grand Master—to help Uncle Luke—make his case for his return to Coruscant."

"People have been trying to understand Jacen for two years." Tahiri shrugged as if the task were hopeless. "No, people have been trying to understand him since we were apprentices. Since you two and Anakin were children together. They've been coming to me since he died. Jedi and government investigators and doctors and the press."

Jaina gave her a sympathetic look. "Any friends among them?"

Tahiri hesitated, then shook her head. "I'm not sure I have any friends. Not that I blame anyone for that. Anyone but Jacen and myself."

Jaina resisted the urge to join in with Tahiri's critics and give the younger woman a verbal beating. It wouldn't help in this situation. "You're not likely to make any, either, as a bounty hunter. You need to come back to the Order, Tahiri."

"Not until I know who I am. *What* I am." Tahiri smoothed an errant strand of blond hair back from her cheek. "I've been more things than I can count. Tatooine girl, adopted Tusken Raider, Jedi, Yuuzhan Vong hybrid, Sith apprentice, addict . . . I've got to get rid of all of them for a while. Learn how to hear myself think."

Jag nodded. "So think about Jacen. What have you figured out about him that you haven't told anyone? Details too subtle or seemingly inconsequential, information that nobody ever asked about."

"I can't tell you when he became a Sith." Tahiri's expression became unfocused. "Only that it might not be important when he did, or even *that* he did. I think Sith was just another thing, another set of armor and

weapons and disguises, that he put on top of Jacen. Like
'Jedi,' or 'Solo.' He was always Jacen . . . until he rejected that, too, and became Caedus."

Jaina shook her head, not comprehending. "You're
saying that it didn't *matter* when he became a Sith?"

"Something like that." Tahiri snapped back to the
here and now. "I think it matters more when Jacen
broke. Maybe he broke when Vergere tortured him for
all that time. Maybe he broke when he was a kid, when
he and you and Anakin kept being handed off to nannies
and protectors while your mother and father were off
doing other things." Tahiri raised a hand to forestall a
biting response from Jaina. "I'm not criticizing. They
were being pulled in too many directions at once, by too
many responsibilities, and when that happens, something gives." She frowned, trying to puzzle something
out. "I think maybe he broke at some other time, whenever it was he decided that the galaxy was a huge, nasty
place that had to be tamed. Whatever gave him that
idea, it made such an awful impression that he had to
become even more awful to confront it."

Jag looked dubious. "You don't think Lumiya broke
him."

"I think she *shaped* him." Now Tahiri looked vulnerable, far more open than when Jaina and Jag had first
entered her presence. "I've been broken. I was broken
by the Yuuzhan Vong. I broke when Anakin died. And
again when I learned that I could be with him again, in
little moments. Every time you break, outside forces can
shape you, and you can't do anything to stop them. No,
I don't think it matters when Jacen became a Sith. I
think it matters when he broke."

Jaina and Jag exchanged a glance. Jaina said, "That's
an interesting theory."

Tahiri managed a bitter little laugh. "Solo-speak for
That's the stupidest thing I've ever heard."

"No, I'm serious. I'll pass it on to the Grand Master. Right or wrong, it suggests some avenues of investigation we haven't considered."

"Oh." Mollified, Tahiri relaxed. "Thank you."

As they were departing, Jaina, seized by a sudden impulse, embraced Tahiri, something she had not done in years, and Tahiri held her in turn.

On the walk to the turbolift, Jag said, "I'm afraid I can't find a way to forgive her so readily. She assassinated a man I respected very highly."

Jaina nodded. "I had a lot of respect for Admiral Pellaeon, too. But who really killed him? The woman we just talked to, who's trying to find her way back from a very dark place, or the woman of two years ago?"

"One descends from the other. They're inextricably linked." Stopping before the turbolift, Jag pressed the button to summon the car. "Does someone shed all responsibility for what she's done when she suddenly decides it was wrong?"

"Neither one of us has ever been broken the way she has." Jaina found her voice was unusually gentle. "Maybe we're too hardheaded, or too stupid, or we've just never run into anything that could damage our core selves the way it happened to her. How do you know what we'd be capable of doing in her situation?"

Jag thought about it and merely shrugged. "The Jedi have more faith in redemption than I do. I'm not saying my way is best. Just that I'm not sure I could do what you do. Forgive something that monstrous."

"I hope I never make a really big mistake in your presence, then."

Chapter Nine

As a senior Jedi Knight—one who, it was said, was under consideration for the rank of Master—Jaina warranted private quarters when staying in the Temple. They were small and bare, but offered her more peace than the dormitories reserved for younger Jedi Knights and apprentices.

At her desk, she studied preliminary information assembled on her behalf about the Chief of State's bounty hunters.

The Quarren was almost certainly Dhidal Nyz, an inventor specializing in imprisonment and capture technologies. He had made some of his fortune capturing high-value fugitives, some from patents and military contracts.

The dark-haired woman had given her name as Zilaash Kul to both Luke and the press. There was no mention of her in Jedi files, and she had no criminal record. Holos that showed her lightsaber had been magnified and strenuously analyzed, only to reveal that its hilt seemed to have been modeled on that of Obi-Wan Kenobi's last lightsaber, the one the legendary Jedi had carried aboard the *Death Star* on his final mission—a weapon reasonably thought to have been lost when that asteroid-sized spacecraft had been destroyed.

The Skakoan was a known quantity. Hrym Mawaar was a bounty hunter with decades of experience, known for returning to his home system and spending years as an elected member of law enforcement between bouts as a bounty hunter.

The YVH 1 droid, fourth on Jaina's list, was the one who caused her the most concern. It was not a droid at all. Vrannin Vaxx, a human mercenary from Dorvalla, had distinguished himself during the Yuuzhan Vong War but had been horribly burned and maimed during a personnel shuttle crash late in the war. He chose not to replace with prosthetics the two-thirds of his body that had been irreparably destroyed. Instead, his family, a wealthy mining clan, had somehow acquired a black-market YVH 1 droid and had it repurposed as a cybernetic body for Vaxx. All that remained of his human self was packed into the droid torso.

Only because there wasn't as much room within Vaxx's carapace as there was in genuine YVH 1 droids was he less formidably armed than a true Hunter droid, and he more than made up for it with human experience and ingenuity. Jaina had received a report that he had survived Leia's laser attack on him and was already repaired and back on duty.

Jaina brought up the file of the next bounty hunter, the Rodian sniper, but her door chimed. Absently, she said, "Come."

The door hissed open and her brother Anakin, dead these sixteen years, walked in.

Jaina froze, a chill running down her spine. This wasn't Anakin as she remembered him, sixteen and dressed in Jedi garments. He was older, fully adult, and taller, perhaps even a centimeter taller than Jacen had been. He wore street clothes in black and crimson and had a professional-quality holorecorder on a strap around his neck.

He also wore Anakin's smile as he advanced on her, hand outstretched. "Jedi Solo."

"Uh." She stood and automatically took his hand. When their palms came together she realized, with distracted embarrassment, that hers was sweating.

"You probably don't remember me. It's been more than fifteen years." He absently wiped his palm on his tunic. "My name is Dab Hantaq."

"Dab Hantaq." Some familiar element in the name kick-started Jaina's brain. "I know that name."

"During the war, the Yuuzhan Vong War I mean, I was kidnapped by Senator Viqi Shesh—"

Jaina sagged just a little in relief, the mystery solved. "—and you were used in her plot to try to kidnap my cousin Ben."

"That's right. You might remember me better as Tarc, the name she gave me."

"Right, right, little Tarc." Jaina sat and made an effort to reassemble her shattered Jedi calm. "Have a seat."

Dab glanced around. There was no other chair. He smiled again. "I'll stand, thanks."

"What can I—what are you—"

"I've been assigned to you." From his belt, he unclipped a small identification folder and opened it. On the left side was the circular shield of an Alliance marshal. On the right was an identicard with a holo of his face, name, and vital statistics. "I'm really a documentarian, but also a licensed investigator because that helps, and there was just a mad hiring scramble for people with certain skill sets and any experience with the Jedi—"

"You're my *observer?*"

He nodded and reattached the identity folder to his belt. "The whole Alliance marshal thing is a matter of convenience, really. They gave it to me so I could bully my way through all sorts of obstacles when following you around. I'm really more about capturing the moment—"

"This will never work. Never, never."

He gave her a look of sympathy. "Because of my resemblance to your brother. I knew when your name came up for me in the random rotation that it was going to create trouble. Since it's going to cause you distress, I'll have myself put back in the pool."

"Yes. I mean, no. I didn't mean it would cause me distress." She clamped down on herself, uneasily aware that it had already caused her much more distress than she would ever admit. "I meant, this whole observer thing will never work. In general."

"Oh." He fingered the holorecorder on the strap. "Would you let me record a reaction from you on this whole observer program, something expressing your thoughts?"

"No! That's not part of your observer role, is it?"

"Well, no."

"You aren't recording anything for personal or professional use, are you? Everything you record has to be turned over to the government, right?"

"Uh, sure."

She glowered at him. "Look, I'm in the middle of some record keeping here . . ."

"I understand. Master Hamner has set up a waiting room for us observers in a chamber off the Great Hall. The old youngling lecture hall, he called it. Did he mean old younglings, or old hall? Never mind. I'll be there. You need to check in with me if you decide to leave the Temple so I can accompany you. And I have to check in with you at intervals to make sure you haven't, you know, wandered off. Sorry."

Stunned, she just nodded. Dab waited a few moments to make sure no further words were going to issue forth, then retreated. The door slid closed behind him, leaving Jaina in merciful silence.

Until she spoke again. "Random rotation, my eye. This is somebody's idea of a joke, and whoever it is will find himself dumped in a garbage compactor."

RESIDENTIAL DISTRICT NEAR THE JEDI TEMPLE, CORUSCANT

Tahiri hit the button to open her apartment door. It slid aside, revealing a tall, very old man standing outside. His hair was white and thin, his eyes a surprisingly clear blue. He wore a loose white tunic belted at the waist, along with black trousers and boots. Oddly, although his left arm was prosthetic, no attempt had been made to disguise the fact; it was an ancient replacement, three-quarters of a century old at least, distinctly mechanical despite its graceful, human lines. It was the color of brushed durasteel from the fingertips to where the white sleeve covered it.

He gave Tahiri a brief, cordial smile. "Tahiri Veila?"

"Yes."

"I'm Commander Trinnolt Makken, Imperial Navy, retired. I'm your government-appointed observer."

She laughed. Then she thumbed the door closed.

The bell chimed again, and she could hear the commander's muffled voice. "This is not a joke. I have legal identification."

She opened the door again. "I heard from friends, I mean contacts, about this observer thing. Commander, I'm not a Jedi."

"It applies to Sith, too, when they can be identified."

"I'm not a Sith, either."

He held up a datacard with his flesh-and-blood hand. "Regardless, your name is on the document."

She glanced at the card. It rose up a couple of centimeters into the air. It strained as if struggling, then snapped in two. The pieces dropped into his palm.

She fixed him with a look that was no longer friendly. "Not Jedi," she explained, as if to someone who spoke only a few words of Basic. "Not Sith. Do you fly? Thrusters from metal arm, thrusters from nostrils?"

Grim, he shook his head.

"Then don't come back until you do, because you may find yourself dropping two hundred stories out a viewport." She slid the door shut.

This time, the commander did not activate the chime.

JEDI TEMPLE, CORUSCANT

Jaina and Master Hamner encountered each other outside the Masters' Chamber. They both frowned.

"Have you seen my new observer?" Jaina asked.

"Can you tell me where your mother is?"

"Come down to the old youngling lecture hall, which he seems to think is a schoolroom for old younglings."

Master Hamner fell into step beside her. "Is that where your mother is?"

"No, that's where he is," Jaina said. "And you know, he's not to blame."

"Perhaps you know where your *father* is, and could tell me, and he would know where your mother is."

"He's not to blame for looking like my brother Anakin."

"Your father? Of course he's to blame for looking like your brother. I would have thought it would relieve him. It does, most fathers."

"Master Hamner, please *concentrate*. Having an observer who looks like my brother can't be a coincidence.

It's a cruel joke or an insult, and if my mother and father see him, it's going to make them feel very bad."

"Ah. Excellent. Where might your mother and father be, that they might see him?"

They came to a stop at the doorway of the former youngling lecture hall. The doorway was double-wide and open. Inside, the chamber was mostly unoccupied; round tables had replaced some of the old side-by-side lecture seating. At some of the tables were men and women, many of them older and ex-military by the look of them, the others a mix of ages, all of them apparently very fit.

She pointed to her new observer, who sat with two others, eating a salad and talking. "That one. Tarc."

Master Hamner looked and tilted his head. "He *does* look like Anakin Solo."

"So you think it's a coincidence?"

"You'd have to ask your father about that, too."

"No, no, that he was assigned to me."

"Oh." He shrugged. "Really, I couldn't tell. The assignments are handled out of the Chief of State's office."

"Well, I want him swapped out for someone else."

"Then you shall have to contact the Chief of State's office. I am certain she will be receptive to the suggestion. The Jedi *are* among her favorite people."

Jaina bristled. "Do you have any dead relatives you'd like to be followed around by?"

He took her arm and led her away from the door at a sedate pace. "You know, you have your mother's mouth. By which I do not mean that the configuration of your chin and lips resemble hers, though they do at certain angles, but that the things that come leaping out of your mouth—words, invective, insults—have a distinctive Organa family flavor to them."

"Thank you. What were you asking about Mom?"

"Where she is."

"At home, I suspect."

Hamner shook his head. "It appears that the *Millennium Falcon* took off for space at just past dawn this morning, with your father, your mother, and your adopted sister aboard."

"Oh. Well, perhaps they wanted to take Amelia out for a field trip."

"Into space."

"Pretty normal for my family."

"The comm recorder at their quarters, responding to my code, said to make requests for direct contact to the office of Lando Calrissian, Tendrando Arms."

"Well, there's your answer."

"And the office of Tendrando Arms says they do not know where Lando Calrissian is, but they will pass the message along. So I was wondering if you had any other means to get in touch with your mother, any back-door method."

"No, I'm afraid not." That was a bald lie, but one she had practiced so well and for so many years that she doubted Master Hamner would be able to detect the deception in the Force.

He seemed satisfied. "Very well."

"I apologize, Master Hamner. Parents like mine, they stay out all hours, they never tell you where they're going, they keep secrets . . . They're making me old before my time."

The Master blinked, and Jaina sensed that, somewhere deep beneath his Jedi calm, he was resisting the urge to throttle her. But all he said was, "*Very* like your mother."

"I need to go off and contact the Chief of State's office. Can I help you with anything else?"

"No, thank you, I've had all the help I can endure."

Chapter Ten

KESSEL

EVEN FROM A HIGH ALTITUDE, IT WAS CLEAR THAT LANDO'S Kessel mineworks had changed substantially in the decades since Han had been an involuntary worker within them—before Lando had owned them. When he and Chewbacca had been captured and pressed into service here, the main mine entrance had been a huge open pit surrounded by broad salt plains and a few administrative buildings. Now the pit was covered, a low, square gray building in place over it, and the buildings immediately around it were far more numerous—though no more attractive; Lando's personal sense of style had clearly been no influence in the motley collection of prefabricated gray, off-white, and tan enclosures.

A couple of the larger buildings and several of the smaller ones now lay in ruined heaps, testimony to the power of recent groundquakes in the area.

Following Lando's navigational beacon, Han found himself staring at a *Falcon*-sized circle of a bare white salt plain surrounded by irregular chunks of brown synthstone probably scavenged from some of the felled buildings. He set down with the speed of confidence, absently adjusting the length of the *Falcon*'s landing gear extensions so that the transport would be perfectly level on the irregular ground. Adjusting thrusters and repulsors to zero, allowing the *Falcon* to settle fully onto her landing gear, he smiled—he might be on Kessel again, but at least his landing had been perfect.

Beside him, sitting on Leia's lap on the copilot's seat, Allana asked, "When can *I* do it?"

"Do what? A landing?"

She nodded, wide-eyed. "Uh-huh."

"When I think my heart will survive the experience." Han gave Leia a look as if to say, *Or maybe I'll be lucky and die before then.*

Leia gave him a smile that was part amused malice. She looked down at her granddaughter. "Soon, I think he means."

By the time Han got the boarding ramp lowered, Lando and Nien Nunb were at its base, waiting, wearing the breath masks required to survive Kessel's thin atmosphere for more than a few minutes. Nunb, Lando's manager in this enterprise, was Sullustan, with a head that looked oddly as though it had settled in melted layers upon his shoulders; unlike most of his species, he was only slightly shorter and rounder than the average adult human.

Lando sprang up onto the ramp with the vigor of a man half his age. "Han! You made great time."

Han gave him a quick embrace. "We were chased off Coruscant by bureaucracy. You were the lesser of two evils."

"I usually am." Lando offered one of his rakish smiles, obviously pleased still to be considered a bad influence. "C'mon inside. Tendra and Chance are there." He glanced up at the top of the ramp. "Hey, Artoo! Long time."

The conference room was laid out with a light lunch and drinks. The chamber did not seem as though it belonged on this dingy, slowly dying world; the oval table in the center was topped with the finest blue-white marble, the chairs were covered in flawless dark leather, and the whole atmosphere conveyed a sense of doing business in the heights of Coruscant's business district.

But the oversized display viewport in the longest wall showed the unpromising grounds of the mineworks, powdery, sterile whiteness from which nothing could grow. In the near distance was the parked *Falcon*. Farther away was a dark building with featureless brown walls; every few minutes, a gout of gas erupted from it, sending much-needed oxygen and nitrogen into the unhealthy-looking pink sky. In the far distance on artificial slopes was a building of tremendous size, gray and tan, its outer walls steeply slanted backward with rows of gleaming durasteel and transparisteel; that, Han knew, was the old Imperial Correctional Facility, the prison from which the former masters of Kessel had drawn the workers for the mines.

Han, Leia, Lando, Tendra, and Nien Nunb sat at the table. In an adjoining chamber, the door left open so sound would carry, Allana and Chance played in the company of the droids—not just C-3PO and R2-D2 but also the little boy's nanny droid. The four-armed automaton with its round, beaming face and almost-human female voice looked identical to Nanna, the ferocious defensive droid fabricated from a nanny droid and a YVH 1 combat droid to nurse and protect Ben Skywalker in his early years; Leia idly wondered if this was the same one.

Tendra, Lando's wife—a lean woman, dark-haired, many years the junior of her husband—was dressed in a pearlescent blue jacket-like top that suggested a world of distant sands and arena duels between animals and men. The blouse beneath it was an iridescent gray, and her long skirt alternated layers of those two colors. Tendra waited until the catching-up chitchat had completely died away before getting to business. "I guess I ought to offer some context."

Han nodded ruefully as he ate a strip of grilled bantha steak from a skewer. "That's definitely the businesswoman's approach. Do you have a printed agenda to give us?"

She smiled. "Quiet, you. Lando has owned these mines for about thirty years now. I bought in when we married. Nien Nunb, who manages the facility, and very well, I might add, gradually acquired shares as part of his contract. The three of us own the business outright."

Leia nodded. "And since Kessel's government basically consists of whatever the major business owners want it to be, there's no one to bail you out if disaster wrecks the business."

Lando looked unhappy. "That's right. And while on the one hand the only thing we stand to lose is money, it's a *lot* of money. And on the other hand, if this business becomes unviable, for us or anyone else, the amount of glitterstim available in the galaxy drops to zero. All the legitimate medical uses of the drug go away."

Nien Nunb spoke in the rapid, singsong language of his people; he understood Basic, but had a hard time articulating it.

Lando translated: "And, yeah, there'll be a negative reaction on the illicit side of things. Glitbiters, glitterstim addicts, will cause a lot of trouble as they fight over the last remaining stores, and there will be a scramble for a new drug to appease them. They'll probably end up with more dangerous ones, like one of the synthetic ryll replacements."

Finished with his skewer, Han set it down. "I thought Kessel was just a rock. An ugly, cold rock shaped like a ground tuber, spinning peacefully through space. No tectonic or volcanic activity at all."

"It is." Lando frowned.

"That's what we thought, too, until the quakes started," Tendra said. "This was about two standard years ago, at the height of the war. Actually, I remember exactly when. I got Nien Nunb's report about the first quake the same day the news broke about the destruction of Centerpoint Station. The first few quakes were very minor, but they've gotten worse over time. The scientists don't know what's causing them, so they can't make any useful predictions, but they have no reason to believe they won't continue to worsen until they wreck everything, collapsing all the mines and destroying the atmosphere plants, which would make the planet uninhabitable."

Nien Nunb spoke again. Lando said, "Yeah, I left that out. Sorry." He returned his attention to the Solos. "He's reminding me that the seismologists we brought in detected a system of natural caverns, really big ones, much deeper than our mineworks. Seismic scanners have detected them, and also revealed that some have collapsed between readings, which may be part of the whole disaster."

"Why are there caverns in the first place?" Leia asked.

Lando looked confused by the change of subject. "Huh?"

"Caverns are usually caused by water moving through soft rock, eroding pockets out of it, correct?"

"I guess."

Han grinned at Lando. "Science hurts, doesn't it, pal?"

"Economics is my science."

Leia continued, "But Kessel has never had that kind of water."

Lando shrugged. "Maybe the energy spiders dug them. To have a place to spin their webs where light wouldn't hit them."

Leia gave him a scornful look. "You're saying the spiders evolved on the surface with photoreactive webs then, figuring out that light destroyed their webs, dug out elaborate cavern systems to live in and waited for prey species to begin wandering down there to be eaten?" She shook her head. "The photoreactive nature of the webs is clearly a later adaptation, something that happened once they'd been down in the caverns for thousands or millions of years."

Lando held up his hands, signifying surrender. "I don't know."

"Lando, there are too many mysteries on Kessel. I spent my time on the trip here doing research. You have tombs on the surface no qualified archaeologist has ever opened. You have avian creatures the size of humans on the surface who have a weird attachment to those ruins. You have caverns that shouldn't exist and groundquakes that can't happen. You've brought us here to solve your problem, but I think it would be half solved already if you'd put some money into answering those questions years ago."

During Leia's rant, Lando gradually hunched down, comically drawing his head closer to his shoulders like a shelled marine reptile trying to withdraw for defense. "Not many of the avians around anymore," he said. "They're a dying species."

"Which is all right with you, because they don't bring any money into the company."

Lando cast imploring eyes on his wife. "Help."

Tendra smiled at him. "Sorry, darling. You're on your own."

"Oh." Lando straightened, resuming a normal pose. He turned to Nien Nunb. "All right. We need a complete archaeological team here to investigate the tombs. Not big, but fully funded for at least one Galactic Standard year, with a tentative extension of two more years if we like their work. We also need a complete xenobiology lab setup and team here, same terms, to study indigenous life-forms other than the energy spiders. Roll the expenses into our losses from the interruption of mining operations." Finished, he looked expectantly at Leia.

She nodded, mollified.

Han snorted. "Well surrendered, General. So lay it out on the table. What exactly do you want from us?"

"I'd like you to go down there. Use your skills and Leia's Jedi abilities to figure out what the scientific teams I've sent down haven't been able to. Figure out why this is happening."

Han had suspected this would be the request, but foreknowledge didn't keep it from turning his stomach sour. To go into those tunnels again . . . Yet Lando was his friend, a friend in need, a friend who had helped them in very bad times. He glanced at Leia, saw her nod. "Yeah, sure." He hoped his voice didn't sound as ungracious as he felt.

"Great," Lando said. "So . . . what do you need?"

"A vehicle," Han said. "Very small, no bigger than your repulsorlift mine cars, so we can navigate wherever they go. Packed with sensors. Active, passive, as broad a range as possible. And weapons. No energy weapons— I'm talking fragmentation explosives, slug-throwers, whatever you can manage, since the energy spiders can gobble up pretty much any energy output from handheld or small vehicle weapons. Hand weapons, too, in case Leia gets it in her head that she needs to step out of the vehicle."

"Done," Lando said.

"When can you have it ready?"

"It's waiting at the mine main entrance." At Han's upraised eyebrows, Lando smiled. "I know your ways, old buddy."

"I guess you do."

"Can I go?" That was Allana, standing at the doorway to the other room—just on the other side of it, half concealed by the doorjamb.

Han and Leia exchanged a look. Leia turned her attention to Allana. "Were you listening at the door?"

Allana hesitated, then nodded. She stepped forward, her movement tentative. "Threepio started telling a story and I got sleepy, but I didn't want to nap so I moved to where I could listen to you, because you're more interesting."

"I'm sorry, sweetie." Han gave Allana a look that he hoped was both affectionate and sternly parental. "It's dangerous. No place for a little girl. You'll need to stay with Threepio and Artoo and Chance."

"I'd rather be with you."

"I know, Amelia. But it's not going to happen this time. On a mission, sometimes people serve best by remaining where others know they're safe. That's a contribution, too." Han turned back to the others, and the amused, knowing looks on all their faces eloquently said, *Not that anyone is ever willing to do that.*

The vehicle Lando had prepared, resting on the white, dusty soil in front of the mine entrance building, had apparently started its existence as an airspeeder; it had the same low, rectangular frame with a central passenger compartment that was ubiquitous to that class of vehicle.

But this was a hard-top model, and emerging from the center of the roof was a small turret. Protruding from that were twin barrels, one no wider in diameter than Han's thumb, one wide enough nearly to fit his fist. He recognized them as a slugthrowing blaster and a grenade launcher, ancient designs seldom seen toward the Galactic Core but more prevalent in Outer Rim worlds and less-developed planets. The turret looked like a recent patch job; there were signs of new welding around it and the turret, a dull metallic gray, had not been painted tan like the rest of the vehicle. On the metal surfaces over the engine compartment and cargo compartment were other recent additions, blue transparisteel bubbles that housed sensor equipment; they were on patches of metal where paint had been burned away and leads punched through so wiring and connectors could pass from the sensors into the vehicle's interior.

Han experimentally rapped on the speeder's frame and viewports with his knuckles. Both areas returned reassuringly deep *thump*s.

"Armored?" Leia asked.

Tendra nodded. "Used to be a speeder for shuttling visiting dignitaries between the prison and the landing field. It's old but sturdy. Sort of like Lando." She winked in her husband's direction.

Lando shot her a dirty look but addressed Han instead. "The grenade launcher has two modes—two sorts of ammunition. The switch is on the weapons-control yoke. One mode is fragmentation explosives, very nasty. Be at least fifty meters away from one of those when it goes off, even if you're inside the vehicle. The other is a decoy we came up with for dealing with the spiders in a nonviolent way. Fires a flying drone with a very powerful heat package in it, gives off an energy signature brighter than a squad of miners. It automatically steers to avoid walls and has a flight duration of about a minute. Fire it off, let the spider chase after it, and go the other way."

"Well, it's no *Falcon*," Han said. "But it'll have to do."

Inside, piled on the rear seat, were thermal suits, in-

frared goggles, spare breath masks with numerous replacement oxygen canisters and batteries, extra energy
packs for the thermal suits, cases of food and water, and
backpack weapons firing ammunition similar to the vehicle's turret systems.

Han caught Lando's eye. "How long do you actually
expect us to stay down there?"

"As long as you want or need to. I actually packed the
vehicle for myself. Over the last couple of weeks, Nien,
Tendra, and I have all taken her down there, looking for
a cause for the trouble and planting sensors for the seismologists. With no luck."

"Fair enough." Han took a deep breath, trying to dis-
pel memories of the desperate flight he, Chewbacca, and
Kyp Durron had taken through those shafts and tunnels
more than thirty years before. It didn't help. "Let's go."

Clad in thermal suits—pallid yellow jumpsuits of a slick,
heat-retentive cloth, further warmed by a network of
tubes laced through the surface—and breath masks,
Han and Leia boarded the speeder, Han at the controls.
In moments, the passenger compartment pressurized
and they could remove their breath masks. They gave
one last wave to the Calrissians and Nien Nunb; then
Han started the vehicle's motivators and set it into forward motion.

Ahead was the building surrounding the main mine
entrance. Han followed its old rail tracks to the door,
which obligingly rolled open before them. Once
through, Han activated the speeder's external lights.

They illuminated a vast single chamber, its ceiling
crisscrossed with metal beams with mobile winches
hanging from them. There was no floor, just a crater, a
gigantic bowl cut out of the gray-white stone, vanishing
into darkness at its deepest point, the exact center. The
rail tracks led straight down the hole.

His shoulders riding up and going rigid with tension, Han followed the rails. In moments, the angled bowl dropped out from beneath them and they descended on repulsors alone down a vertical shaft that seemed endless.

Chapter Eleven

As KENTH HAMNER SETTLED MORE AND MORE INTO THE role of Interim Master of the Jedi Order, he began rearranging things to suit himself, to increase his comfort and efficiency in the position.

For example, morning briefings. Each day after breakfast was served and consumed, he stood in the Great Hall and allowed the Jedi to gather so he could catch them up on all the news he felt he could distribute. Perhaps sending files to all their datapads would have been more efficient, but he liked to see reactions and get immediate responses. Of course, the observers now stood among the Jedi, an odd contrast in their mix of dress—some civilian, some in day wear comfortably resembling their old military uniforms, some in the current uniforms of Galactic Alliance Security or Intelligence divisions.

This day, Master Hamner began, "As you may have heard on this morning's HoloNet News broadcast, there are rumors that the government is preparing a case against Jedi Valin Horn for criminal actions and damages caused by recent events. We will, of course, resist these proceedings, as it is clear that Jedi Horn was, and remains, of diminished capacity. Both the government and the Jedi Order agree that qualified analysts of mental disorders must be allowed to examine Jedi Horn to evaluate the relevance of his mental state; we are in the process of deciding on specialists agreeable to both sides."

He consulted his datapad, then looked around, his manner more stern. "On another matter, I will not single out anyone for direct disapprobation, but it is clear that some of the Jedi Knights have been indulging in behavior that makes it more difficult for their observers to do their jobs. Though the Order approves of passive resistance in circumstances of civic unrest, it is not appropriate for Jedi themselves to perform passive resistance against rules agreed to by the Order itself. This will be my last warning unaccompanied by corrective measures.

"Speaking of observers, former Jedi Tahiri Veila has flatly refused to allow her observer to accompany her. Veila's unusual legal status makes her opposition to the government regulation an interesting one, and the Temple's own lead counsel has accepted her case as she and the government countersue each other.

"Master Sebatyne, Jedi Sarkin, Jedi Tekli, please report to me for new assignments. That is all."

As the assembly broke up, Jaina ducked around a column, the better to remain unseen by her observer, and made her way stealthily to a back set of stairs. Moments later, she was two levels down and entering a conference room little-used because of its low ceiling and uninvitingly dark wall color.

Jag, inside, waited until the door was sealed behind her before taking her in his arms. "You've shaken your pursuit."

"He's so . . . friendly. It would be a shame to kill him." It was a joke, but even in jest, the notion of cutting down Dab, who so resembled her brother Anakin, of killing in a sense a second brother, sent a shudder through her. "This has got to end."

"The sneaking around?"

"Oh, I'm fine with the sneaking around." She smiled, her humor restored. "But to actually be followed *while* I'm sneaking around, I hate it."

"You could always resign from the Order, come away with me to the Empire, and set up that rival Jedi school."

"Stop saying that. It's beginning to tempt me." She spoke in a more serious tone. "Jag, I'm the Sword of the Jedi. I'm the defender of this Order, not of some rival Order, some start-up school. My fate is here."

"Your fate was that you would live a restless life and never know peace. How can you accept that for yourself?"

"What if I didn't? What if I had rejected it, retired as a Jedi, decided to enjoy myself after the Dark Nest mess? I'd have been off on a vacation world when Jacen became the force he turned into. What if I was the only thing that could stop him, and I never did?"

"It didn't happen that way."

"No, but the next one might. If I just shed my responsibilities and run off to the Remnant to play schoolteacher, what happens when the Sword is needed next?" Something occurred to her. "You want to spend more time with me? Over the years, instead of just the next few days or weeks?"

"You know I do."

"Then resign as the Head of State of the Empire. There are plenty of men and women eager to take *that* position."

He was silent a long moment. "I . . . can't."

"Because it's *your* responsibility."

His "Yes" was almost inaudible.

"So don't try to convince me to abandon mine."

"All right."

"We'll try to make this work. If we can't . . . well, at least we'll have this time."

He leaned down to kiss her, but her comlink beeped, a distinctive pattern of two-then-two tones. Jaina sagged and she let her forehead thud down into his chest.

"What is it?"

"Dab. The observers all have to run checks on their Jedi twice a day, at random times, to make sure we're where we're supposed to be. I have to run upstairs and show him I'm still here."

"I could kill him *for* you."

"I said it before—don't tempt me."

ABOARD <u>JADE SHADOW</u>, DORIN SPACE

Ben decided that Dorin was just about the ugliest inhabited planet he could remember, and he had seen quite a lot of them. It was also one of the strangest star systems in his experience. Even after having read up on it in advance of arrival, he found that foreknowledge did not reduce the effect of seeing the system through *Jade Shadow*'s viewports.

The Dorin sun was a small, orange thing, and it was situated directly between two large and proximate black holes. The net effect, looking at the system from a stopping point less than a light-year away, was of seeing a dim and distant light illuminating a precarious path with bottomless cliffs on either side. Except Ben, smoothing down the hair on the back of his neck, did not perceive the black holes as dangerous drops, but as lifeless eyes staring at him. "Kind of gets to you, doesn't it?"

His father looked up from the task of inputting the last hyperspace jump. Calculations here had to be very precise. Situated between two such powerful gravity wells, the Dorin system was very complex, and any mathematical error was even more likely than usual to endanger a ship.

Luke nodded. "Black holes are an interesting astronomical phenomenon to scientists, and a vaguely unsettling image for most other people . . . but Force-users and Force-sensitives have a real dislike or dread of them."

"Why?"

His father shrugged. "The Force derives from life. Even death is not all that disturbing to a Force-user, since it is a part, a necessary consequence, of life. Black holes are something else. A cessation outside of life. Maybe the way they draw in all energy and trap it forever runs against our instincts. I'm not sure. I do know that the Force-sensitive children we hid at Shelter during the Yuuzhan Vong War did *not* like being in the Maw, surrounded on all sides by black holes. You're too young to remember, but the Jedi caretakers at Shelter said there was a lot of crying."

"Did I do a lot of crying?"

"I don't think so. You were pretty much shut off from the Force in those days."

"Well, good."

Luke grinned and returned his attention to his calculations. "Ready to jump in ten seconds . . . five, four . . ."

When space untwisted around them, they were well within the Dorin system. The sun ahead was bigger but no more cheerful, and its dull hue seemed almost dirty. Ben could see stars above and below the sun, but looking rightward and leftward through the yacht's ports, there was nothingness, no welcoming gleam of stars. He suppressed a shudder.

It took a few minutes for Luke to raise Dorin starship control on the comm. The distant officer spoke Basic with an odd, slightly muffled accent, but she rapidly authorized Luke to land his craft at the spaceport in the capital city of Dor'shan and assured him that replacement air bottles for his breath masks were readily available for purchase.

As Dorin grew in the forward viewport, it became no more appealing to Ben. Dark and mottled, it had a gloomy aspect to it. But he reached out with the Force and felt no such emotion emanating from it. In fact, it was as alive as any low-population world he had visited, and far cheerier under the surface than the malevolent Ziost. He relaxed. Dorin was not a place of hidden dread and evil intent.

They slid through a murky atmosphere and descended toward a twilight city of buildings that were small and isolated by Coruscant standards. Many were domes, ziggurats, trapezoids—all forms much wider at the base than at the summit, and Ben was reminded of what he had read of this world, that its architecture and even, to some extent, the abilities of the Baran Do Sages had developed in response to the ferocious storms that frequently swept across the planet's surface. Ben decided that these squat, unlovely buildings were ideally suited to a population that needed to hunker down and wait out bad weather.

And perhaps they weren't so unlovely after all. Even from a great altitude, he had seen the city as a sea of lights blazing in many colors, and as they got low enough to glimpse details on the face of the buildings illuminated by those lights, Ben saw the Kel Dor geometric and organic patterns painted onto those buildings, disguising their rudimentary shapes with patterns of well-matched colors. Some structures bore tawny browns and golds in color waves that suggested sandstorms, while others were in dappled aquatic hues that would probably half convince someone standing beside them that he was resting at the bottom of a shallow bay.

Then they were over the spaceport. Each building had a domed terminal or hangar, with simple arrows on the roofs pointing to a specific landing circle or set of circles. Luke set the *Jade Shadow* down on a circle of permacrete next to a smaller white and tan dome. Then he taxied slowly on repulsorlifts, following blinking lights embedded in the permacrete surface, into the adjacent domed hangar, whose doors slid closed and sealed once the yacht was settled. Inside, the hangar was well lit but bare.

Ben unbuckled and rose. "This place isn't as ugly as I thought at first."

"No, it isn't." Luke pointed at Ben's seat. "Sit."

"Huh?"

"Postflight checklist."

"Oh." Exasperated, Ben sat again and brought up his checklist on the monitor. "Engines cooling within standard rates. I notice there's no one here."

"No one here, check."

"Running engine diagnostics now. And the hangar doors are . . ." Ben bounced a comm query from his control board to the hangar's. "Locked. We're locked in."

"Locked in, check."

"Stop that."

Luke smiled. "We're supposed to stay here until they complete a routine inspection."

"*Inspection.*" Ben felt a touch of outrage. "You're the Grand Master of the Jedi Order."

"And the brother-in-law of a smuggler."

"Well, your rank should count for something. Uh, prelim diagnostics run checks out in the green."

"Full diagnostics on all systems, please."

Ben initiated the program. As he did so, he saw an oval section of wall stretch itself toward them, elongating slowly toward a side coupling ring. "Here they come."

* * *

Ben and Luke met them at the air lock. It cycled open to reveal two humanoids, lean to the point of emaciation, dressed in black robes decorated in vertical black and sky-blue striping patterns. They were bald, with intelligent eyes that seemed very human, but their lower faces were obscured by breath masks. One carried an apparatus in a black backpack; a metal cable ran from it to a wandlike device, numerous sensor intakes along its length, which he held in his hand. The other had only a small card reader.

The one with the card reader extended a hand, palm up. "Identicards, please." His Basic was unaccented.

Ben handed his card to the Kel Dor an instant after his father. The inspector slid each one for a moment into his reader. "I am Lieutenant Dorss, customs. This is Sergeant Vult. He will conduct a brief inspection of your craft. Are all compartments accessible?"

Luke nodded. "They are."

Again Ben felt the urge to protest, to tell them, *Don't you understand, this is Luke Skywalker. Why are you bothering?* But his father seemed unperturbed, so he pretended to be as well. Still, he wondered what good it would do to travel under a name as famous as his father's if it didn't at least lubricate the wheels of bureaucracy.

The second Kel Dor disappeared aft, waving his sensor wand.

Now Dorss began his ritual interrogation. "Purpose of visit to Dorin?"

"Research," Luke said. "We seek an audience with the Baran Do Sages."

"Information brokerage, then?"

Luke frowned, perplexed. "I don't think so. I didn't plan to offer any credits for the information I'm looking for. Nor would I charge any for information I provide."

"No trade goods?"

Both Jedi shook their heads.

The Kel Dor hesitated, then handed back the identi-cards. "Tourism, then." There was an air of finality to his decision. "Will you require accommodations?"

"No, for convenience's sake, we'll be keeping quarters aboard the yacht."

The Kel Dor nodded knowingly. There was something in the gesture, as if he had concluded long before that celebrities were tight with their credits and was happy for Luke Skywalker to reinforce the stereotype, that irritated Ben further.

The sergeant returned and spoke a few words to Dorss in what must have been the native tongue of Dorin. Dorss nodded. "All personal effects within categorical limits. Enjoy your stay on Dorin."

"Thank you." Luke waved agreeably as they reentered the air lock.

Ben frowned. "This is worse than traveling incognito. They acted like they'd never heard of you."

Luke smiled, and there was just a touch of taunt to it. "You've been around, Ben. Wasn't that much nicer than arriving somewhere and finding that everyone is trying to shoot you?"

"Well . . . yes."

"Don't get too used to the benefits of fame, son. You'll find yourself making mistakes in order to regain them when they're taken away from you."

"I guess."

"Now get on the planetary data grid and find us city maps, city directories, the location of the Baran Do headquarters, contact names, for our datapads. I'll check out our own breath masks to make sure they're up to the job."

"Right." Ben returned to the cockpit, wondering if, in

deciding to accompany his father, he had somehow con-
signed himself to ten years of dullness.

No, that was a child's perspective. He had to continue
thinking like an adult. Like a Jedi.

Even a Jedi in exile.

Chapter Twelve

"THE PIT," HAN said, "IS WHAT HAPPENS WHEN AN AT-mosphere plant sits on one spot for a few years. It digs up stones that have oxygen and nitrogen in them. It cracks the stone, spitting the dust out through the hole onto an ever-growing sand hill and spewing the gases up into the sky. Meanwhile, the hole underneath gets bigger and bigger until they have to dismantle the facility and move it. On Kessel, sometimes those pits punch their way into cavern systems."

"And if explorers find spice, a mine is born," Leia said.

Han nodded, gloomy.

Below, the shaft was ringed by a set of lights indicating a specific mine level. Descending past it, their vehicle lights revealed a large metal door in the side of the shaft just above the illuminating ring, suggesting that a side tunnel continued beyond the door. Many meters farther down, they could see another such ring.

On the passenger-side monitor, Leia brought up a schematic map of the mine complex. "So let me get this straight. The energy spiders feed on energy. Drain it right out of living things."

"Uh-huh."

"And they also spin webs to trap their prey."

"Well, mostly they sort of spit the webs up on rock surfaces. They don't usually spin them in the open air. Though they sometimes spin lines to climb."

"Where does the mass for the webs come from? And the mass to let the spiders grow? Not from matter–energy conversion. They couldn't be absorbing that much energy."

Han shook his head. "They eat a certain amount of stone. Kessel is laced with veins of ryll, and ryll is one of the major components of glitterstim." Neither as effective nor as rare a spice as glitterstim, ryll was a mineral found on several worlds, notably Ryloth, home planet of the Twi'leks. As information about the energy spiders had been released over the years by Lando's mining company, Han had kept up with it, out of a sense of horrified fascination.

They passed another two light rings during that exchange. Leia tracked their progress on her diagram. "How low are we going to go?"

"All the way to the bottom, or until you feel something."

"Nothing yet."

"We could just go back up again, grab Allana, and go home."

"I feel something!"

"What?"

"Irritation. Stop trying to slither out of this mission."

Han sighed.

They descended in silence for a while. Eventually the speeder's lights illuminated rough stone all around and below: the end of the shaft, and there were no tunnels, artificial or natural, branching from it. Han increased power to the repulsors and they rose toward the next light ring up, the lowest tunnel entrance.

As they hovered outside the metal door, Leia touched

a control on the board before her. The door slid open, revealing a dark tile-floored chamber beyond.

"Still," Han said, "it's much better than the first time I was down here. Doors open when you want them to, and the mine manager gives you drinks and weapons instead of sending someone to kill you."

"That's progress."

The tile-floored chamber was a ready room. Banks of lockers held equipment the miners would use in their work. There was no one present—Lando had said he was keeping all personnel out of the mine until the situation was resolved—and for some reason Han found the lack of people additionally unsettling. If he and Leia had to run from a monster they couldn't kill, there would be no nasty guards to distract the beasts. Han preferred to have slower-moving people behind him in situations like that.

They moved out of the ready room into a chamber where mine cars waited. The little train of six open-top cars sat on the dusty stone floor but if activated, they would rise on repulsorlifts, resembling a flying centipede. The cars looked like original equipment from Han's first visit to Kessel.

Another large metal door at the far end of the chamber slid open at Leia's transmitted signal, giving them access to the mine tunnels themselves.

"Don't worry," Leia said. "This isn't one of the feeding regions. Reduces the odds that we'll run into a spider here."

"*Feeding regions.*" The last door slid shut behind them. Now only the speeder's lights kept total darkness at bay. Hair tried to stand up on the back of Han's neck; he smoothed it down.

"To help control the movements of the energy spiders and give the miners some predictable sites to look for spice, Lando and Nien Nunb send processed ryll and incendiary devices into specific shafts in rotation. While the spiders are eating in one area and spinning new webs there, the miners go to areas where they were before and get fresh spice. This"—Leia gestured, indicating their surroundings—"is not one of the tunnels in rotation."

"All that's on the map?"

"No, the map just says where the feeding zones are right now. I looked up what it meant in the prospectus Tendra gave me."

"Prospectus."

"You know, a business plan document. Used, among other things, to persuade people to invest."

Han looked at her, alarmed. "Did you want to invest in *this?*"

Leia sighed. "No. It was a convenient source of information, and that's why Tendra gave it to me. But I suppose I could invest in all the businesses that have brought you so much happiness over the years. For instance, Jabba the Hutt's trade empire."

"He's dead. You killed him."

"Yes, but his business lives on. Or how about some of the Death Star manufacturing subcontractors."

"Stop it."

"Maybe just the folk who make trash compactors. Everyone needs trash compactors. Oh, and frozen-in-carbonite dream vacations."

Han just gritted his teeth, determined to wait her out.

Ahead, the tunnel forked. Leia consulted her map, tracing the two routes with a fingertip. "This one, the lower one, Lando has marked as one of the places Tendra and Nien planted sensors. This other one, which doesn't go as deep but heads off westward at an odd angle, hasn't been recently explored. Let's try that one."

"Is that just random interest, or a presentiment in the Force?"

"Random—" She paused, and a look of mild surprise crossed her face. "Both, maybe."

Han turned left, into the tunnel she indicated.

CITY OF DOR'SHAN, DORIN

Ben did not often feel like a complete outsider, but this world seemed bent on convincing him that he was.

It started with his breath mask, a full-face rig that kept the planetary atmosphere, mostly helium with some other gases in the mix, at bay. It was attached to a backpack rig that included canisters of oxygen–nitrogen mix and a converter that broke a proportion of the carbon dioxide emerging from human lungs back into its component elements, reintroducing the oxygen into the breathing mix. A human could go for most of a day on a planet like this on only one charge, but Ben wasn't impressed with the rig's convenience. It was like being chained to his luggage.

Then there were the people. Luke had decided that he and Ben would walk to the Baran Do Sages' temple, as the map showed it to be not too far for a leg-stretching hike, and so Ben had the opportunity to see hundreds of the Kel Dors in the spaceport terminal building and on the streets.

Like the two who had performed the inspection, most were tall and angular. Unlike the inspectors, they were bare-faced . . . and what faces they had! Round bald heads, sunken eyes, narrow ridge-like noses that looked to Ben like failed attempts at becoming birds' beaks, and large, toothless mouths that looked like they belonged on very old humans . . . Ben tried not to stare at every face he passed, but he couldn't help himself, and did not like himself for the conclusion he reached.

When he and his father arrived at the street where the

temple was to be found, a street almost free of speeders but still trafficked by pedestrians, and they were no longer near any crowds of natives, he said, "Dad, these are not a pretty people."

Luke considered. "From a certain point of view, perhaps."

"It sort of bothers me that I see them that way."

"Well, you know the answer to that. What's one of the first things you learned in training to be a Jedi?"

"Don't cut off your own head with your lightsaber."

"After that."

"Your eyes can deceive you. Be mindful of your feelings. Girls are fun but dangerous. Lando has extra cards up his sleeve."

"Well, the truth is in there somewhere . . . Tell you what, if you think it's wrong for you to think of them as ugly, just think of how *you* look to *them*." Luke made a sweeping gesture, taking in his son from head to foot. "Short, squat, unlined skin, a nose that puffs up like a rodent, tiny little mouth with jagged white things in it, a horrible shrublike growth on your head."

Ben laughed. "This, from the man who's worn a bowl-cut hairstyle almost all his adult life."

"You're young, Ben. You'll learn to see with wiser eyes. And if you deliberately set out to do that, it'll be faster."

The stretch of the city between the spaceport and their destination had been thick with smaller buildings, the exterior signs in the Kel Dor language suggesting that most were businesses. Now the buildings were larger, some set within walled enclosures. Ben checked his data-pad, using a comfortingly familiar planetary positioning system to compare their location with the maps, and found they were only forty meters from their objective. He pointed ahead and across the street. "There."

What he was looking at was clearly an estate—one

large ziggurat-shaped building, each of its four levels darker than the ones below it, graduating from thunder-cloud gray-black down to sky blue, surrounded by two-story outbuildings in similar colors, all within a wall made up of black wrought-durasteel posts with transparisteel sheets laid across them. The transparisteel was smooth and a little uneven, and Ben could visualize, perhaps as a tiny vision in the Force, Baran Do apprentices polishing it over the years, removing minute scratches, that had caused the transparent material to become slightly worn and misshapen. Through it, as he and Luke advanced, the buildings seemed to distort and sway.

They stopped before the gates, which were ajar and undefended. A path of red-orange flagstones led from there to the steps rising into the main building. The double front doors were also open, with light streaming out from the interior.

Luke looked at the approach and grinned.

"What's so funny?"

"Tradition. You'll see. C'mon." Luke put on his serene Grand Master face, made sure his robes were smoothed into presentability, and headed in. With a quick check of his own hair, Ben followed, a pace back and to the right.

The entrance chamber of the temple of the Baran Do Sages was large and imposing. Black stone walls reached up more than six meters. White stone columns against those walls, rounded and slightly narrower at the base than the top, not only suggested that the ceiling would be kept at a distance but helped offset the darkness of the décor. The ceiling was of a blue-black stone and sparkled like a starry sky, while the floor was a brown permacrete polished smooth, perhaps even waxed. It was all dimly lit by blue glow rods at floor level against the walls.

Ben nodded, instantly grasping the intent of the decorative style. Sky above, ground below, darkness of the black holes to either side, columns suggesting the constructions or intents of living beings keeping those nightmarish celestial anomalies at bay.

Immediately opposite the main entrance was a raised platform with steps leading up to it. It was only a meter higher than the floor itself, and there was no furniture on it. Ben had half expected a throne of some sort, or a circle of seats like in the Masters' Chamber at the Jedi Temple. There was a Kel Dor woman standing on the platform, her robes white with curved dotted-line decorations in red and black; she was staring off at the left wall as Luke and Ben entered, and did not react to their arrival.

No other doors or hallways seemed to exit this chamber, but the square sheets of black stone on the walls, fitting together almost seamlessly, could hide a dozen exits.

Luke drew to a halt two meters from the platform steps and waited. Ben stood silently beside him.

The Kel Dor woman turned toward them. She spoke, her Basic lightly flavored with a lilting accent: "Who comes to us?"

"I am Luke Skywalker, a Jedi. This is my companion, Jedi Ben Skywalker."

"Ah. Famous names." The woman tilted her head as she studied them. "My name is not so famous. I am Tistura Paan."

Luke nodded a greeting. "I am pleased to meet you."

"What is the business you bring before us?"

"I am investigating the travels of a former student of mine. I am trying to determine whether he came here and what he might have learned."

"Your student's name?"

"Jacen Solo."

"Also a famous name." Tistura Paan scratched at her

nasal ridge. "I think these are questions for the Mistress of our order, Tila Mong."

Luke nodded. "Then I wish to speak with your Mistress at her convenience."

"And whom shall I say wishes to see her?"

Luke hesitated so briefly that Ben suspected only he detected it. "As I said before, Jedi Luke Skywalker and Jedi Ben Skywalker."

"Ah. There is a puzzlement. How can I go before my Mistress and say that the famous Luke Skywalker is here, when I cannot prove that you are indeed he?"

The faintest trace of a smile appeared on Luke's face. "You could take my word for it."

"A word that is beyond price if you are indeed Luke Skywalker, and without measurable worth if you are not."

"I do resemble my holos. Somewhat. If my family is to be believed."

"As would any truly skillful imposter." She spread her arms, palms upraised, a very human gesture of helplessness. "I fear we are at an impasse. Unless . . ."

"Yes?"

"Well, I would stand no chance in combat with the true Luke Skywalker."

Luke smiled outright. "Or any sufficiently well-trained imposter."

"That is not a given. Regardless, were you to defeat me, I would acknowledge that your claim to be Luke Skywalker was possibly true, and convey your message to my mistress."

Luke nodded. "A useful solution. But impractical."

"Why?"

"Because you are not worthy to face me."

Ben felt his eyes widen. He forced himself to resume an impassive, sabacc-playing expression. But his father's words baffled him. They sounded so agreeable in tone, yet were more arrogant than anything he had ever heard his father say.

Luke continued, "Still, if a former apprentice of mine can best you, then the same conditions apply." He turned to Ben. "Son, go beat her up."

Ben froze as if his father's gaze were that of some paralytic monster from myth. After a moment, he was able to clear his throat, covering his confusion, and said, "Sir?"

"Go on up there and knock her down a few times."

"Yes, sir." His mind reeling, Ben strode up the steps to stand before Tistura Paan. And he wondered for a moment if Valin Horn had been right, if the Jedi he knew were suddenly being replaced by impersonators.

Tistura Paan gave Luke a look Ben interpreted as scornful. "I hope you have another child, so that a healthy one can be in rotation while this one lies bruised and crying."

Luke turned his back on them. "Just fight. Let me know when it's over."

Tistura Paan lashed out at Ben, a left-handed, flat-fisted blow straight toward his face. She did not look at him beforehand, gave him no visual warning of her intent. But feeling her channeling her power through the Force, he swayed out of the way, the blow snapping into place just to the side of his nose. He trapped her wrist with his left hand and struck at her elbow with his right—a hard blow but not a savage one, it hyperextended her joint but did not break it. She gave a sudden yank and was instantly meters away, shaking her arm as if to cast the pain free.

Ben sidestepped to take the center of the platform and dropped into a defensive posture. He wouldn't make the same mistake Tistura Paan had. If her role here was to challenge every visitor, or just every visitor claiming to be a famous Jedi, she'd probably be good at her job.

She charged him, arms flailing. He sidestepped, reaching out for her right hand, intending to give it a twist and push to launch her past him out of control, but the wildness of her attack was all show—leaping past, she kicked at his midsection, a fast, hard blow. He continued his own maneuver into a spin; when the Kel Dor connected, the force of the blow was reduced. It still hurt, her skinny leg striking home like a cane, but he was merely forced to step back, his gut stinging where she'd hit him; he did not fall.

Tistura Paan hit the platform in a practiced roll and came up on her feet at its edge; she spun, ready again.

Ben spared a glance at his father. Luke still had his back to the fight and looked as though he were digging dirt out from under a fingernail.

Tistura Paan advanced more carefully, short steps, her left side forward, hands up and ready in a classic martial posture. Ben mimicked it. He wasn't sure how long he should go on letting her demonstrate her skills and tactics as the fight's aggressor—the longer he did so, gauging her skill, the longer he gave her to develop a successful strategy. But neither did he want to rush blindly into an attack for which she had a ready, practiced defense.

She stopped well short of him and gestured as if shooing children before her, but the move was more sudden, more forceful. And Force-ful: Ben felt a surge in the Force, and then suddenly wind was shoving him backward toward the platform's edge, tugging at his garments, pushing at his breath mask.

He knew instinctively that going over the edge would mean losing the match. He got his feet behind him, bracing him against the Force wind, and drew on his own powers to root him in place.

He stopped, his tactical sense telling him that his rear

foot was mere centimeters from the platform edge. But he held where he was.

Then Tistura Paan's attack tore the breath mask from his face. It flew behind him; a sudden yank against his back told him it had reached the end of the cable by which it was attached to the canisters in his backpack.

This was bad. If he devoted any effort to getting the breath mask on, she'd be able to assault him, perhaps successfully. If he did nothing, he would be limited to the endurance the air still in his lungs gave him—less than a minute, considering his exertions. But he had to do one or the other . . .

No, he didn't. His father had always taught him to look for the third of two options. He shucked the backpack, letting Tistura Paan's Force assault carry it away from his body. He heard it clank against the stone wall.

Tistura Paan's eyes grew wide. She smiled. "Thank you for handing me the victory. Well, in a few moments." The Force wind stopped.

Ben wasted no breath on a retort. He advanced and threw a rapid punch–kick–punch combination, not quite at full speed or strength. The Kel Dor blocked the maneuvers with a smooth, defensive style.

Ben settled into an aggressive pattern, one he'd practiced so often with Jacen and at the Temple that it was almost second nature to him. It *was* second nature, which meant that it occupied very little of his mental faculties.

In his mind, he focused on his discarded breath mask and canister pack. He could feel them against the wall, almost see them. He exerted his will against the rig through the Force, lifting the whole mass a few centimeters, bringing it forward to the base of the platform.

Tistura Paan's fist hit him in the ribs, an attack he'd failed to anticipate because of his inattentiveness. The rock-hard blow drove the air from his lungs and forced him to take a step back.

The Kel Dor's smile grew wider. It was an unattractive smile, lips pulled back over hard upper and lower palates that Ben supposed must take the place of teeth. "Wake up, Jedi boy, whoever you are."

Ben felt a twinge of panic, but he knew it was just a physiological reaction to not being able to breathe. He suppressed the emotion and divided his attention more equally between what his body was doing and what he was up to with his manipulation of the Force.

Tistura Paan struck; he parried. The breath mask rig floated another few meters along the base of the platform and rounded a corner. Tistura Paan threw a flurry of feints and punches; Ben blocked each, exerting himself as little as possible, but could feel his energy starting to wane. Still, the breath mask rig floated and rounded another corner. Now it was at floor level behind Tistura Paan.

She stopped for a moment and backed away a step. "Would you like to rest?" Though voiced as if in all seriousness, the question was a taunt, since Ben could not recover without breathing.

Ben glowered as if angered by the question. He sprang at her as if ready to begin one last, futile flurry of blows, then yanked with the Force.

The breath mask rig sailed up over the lip of the platform and caught Tistura Paan behind the knees. Suddenly falling backward, she flailed her arms. Ben spun on one foot, placing the other precisely past her now vanished guard, and hitting her in the center of her chest.

Tistura Paan sailed off the platform and hit the floor beyond, only a few steps from Luke. She did a backward somersault and came up on her feet, eyes flashing. "You failed. You brought outside objects into play."

Ben stooped to pick up his breath mask. He fitted it over his face, not bothering yet to strap on the canister pack, and took a couple of deep breaths. "*You* brought it into play," he said. "You yanked it off me and therefore made an attack of it. I merely followed your lead. Logically, I would have left it right where it was if you hadn't meddled with it."

Tistura Paan glowered, then turned her head as if looking into the distance well beyond the walls. Finally, she turned her attention to Luke. "I will communicate your request."

He looked at her blankly, then turned to Ben. "Are you all done?"

"Yes, sir." Ben donned the canister pack.

"Did you win?"

"Yes, sir. I only knocked her down once. But it was off the platform."

"Well, that will have to do." Luke turned back to the Kel Dor. "Yes, please, and convey my compliments."

Tistura Paan turned and strode, her steps rapid and her upper body a bit stiff, toward a blank section of side wall; a segment of stone, two meters high and two wide, withdrew about a handspan, then slid to one side to allow her entry. Once she was through, it closed.

Ben hopped down to stand beside his father. Keeping his tone down, he asked, "What was that all about?"

Luke gave him a slight, private smile. "Rival school traditions."

"Huh?"

"In many martial schools, such as rival lightsaber training academies in ancient times, or military academies outside the Old Republic, someone visiting a rival school would generally be denied any aid or information until he'd proved his worth. Which meant proving it to a Master of the school in one-on-one combat. As we arrived, I could sense Tistura Paan's presence within and what her role was. And that she knew we were coming."

"But you didn't fight her."

"Correct. If I had agreed to fight Tistura Paan, someone beneath my rank, I would be acknowledging that I was not the equal of her Master, so I'd never see the leader of the Baran Do Sages."

A light flared into luminescence in Ben's head. "Ah, so your student had to beat *her* student."

"And you did, and very well. You turned your mistake into her mistake and your weakness into your strength."

"And you got clean nails in the bargain. A win all around."

The wall panel slid open again. Tistura Paan moved out, her face impassive, and gestured for them to precede her through that entrance. "Mistress Tila Mong will receive you now."

Chapter Thirteen

CALRISSIAN-NUNB MINES, KESSEL

THEY GLIDED FORWARD IN NEAR DARKNESS NOW. THE only lights to be seen were the dim bluish readouts on the control console. The whine of the vehicle's repulsors and the occasional pinging of the sensor board were almost the only sounds to be heard.

"Have we passed any spice yet?" Leia asked. She glanced between the various sensor readouts, each occupying one-eighth of one of the console monitors. Her face was ghostly in the faint light from the instruments.

Han shook his head, then realized Leia might not be able to see the motion. He tapped the lower right readout on her screen. "That's the spice sniffer. A chemical sensor. Also detects ryll, and distinguishes between the two. These things are so sensitive that they'd pick up even very old, activated spice within a hundred meters. What are *you* detecting?"

"Just what you see here. Mostly air currents caused by our repulsors. They return short, false movement positives."

"No, I mean *you*. Through the Force."

"Ah." She shook her head. "Not much. There's life all around us, mostly very faint—lower life-forms like insects, I think. Nothing as bright or vital as a humanoid or a giant arachnid."

"Would the spiders show up in the Force?" Han asked.

"We'll see. They'll show up in the motion detectors." Leia tilted her head, her eyes narrowing in concentration. "Wait, there's something."

Han gulped and looked all around. "Where?"

"Below us. Strong, but distant."

"What's under us on the map?" Han gave the speeder a little more altitude, but this tunnel was only five meters tall; he could bring the speeder as close as possible to the irregular ceiling and a Wookiee standing on the floor could still reach up and touch it.

Leia switched her attention to the monitor where she kept the map. "Nothing," she said. "This isn't the deepest point in the mine, but there's no part of the mine beneath us."

"Uncharted tunnels, then."

Leia turned her head this way and that as if listening to something whose location she couldn't quite gauge. "It's coming this way."

"Straight up?"

"Yes."

Han nudged the thrusters. It wouldn't do to build up too much speed in these twisting tunnels, but he also didn't want to be directly over something when it came crashing up through the floor.

"It's adjusting to follow."

Han blinked. "That's no spice spider, then." He put on more speed.

"Coming up closer. Pacing us, directly beneath."

Han glanced at the sensor board. It showed nothing but their own air displacement manifesting on the movement detector readout. "Pacing us in the rock?" Then realization hit him. "Hey, I know what that has to be."

"What?"

It burst up from the rock below and ahead of the speeder, a swirling ball of colored lights, just large enough to fit an astromech like R2-D2 completely within it. It leapt up directly into Han's path, its comparative brilliance all but blinding him. He twitched the speeder to port, the barest of maneuvers, intended to return the speeder to its original course instantly after it avoided the obstacle . . .

But the speeder plowed right through the ball of light. Han felt hair standing on end all over his body. Instantly, the repulsors quit, and every monitor and readout on the control console crackled and went black.

Han yanked back on the yoke, knowing the attempt was futile. The speeder dropped three meters and plowed nose-first into the tunnel floor. It skidded forward, its contact with the bare stone sending up sparks, then fetched up against the right-hand tunnel wall and was still.

Leia leaned over him. "Are you all right?"

"No problem." Han turned to stare back the way they'd come. The swirling ball of luminescence hovered there, thirty meters away, unmoving, as if watching them.

Leia put her hand on her lightsaber. "Very pretty. And destructive. What is it?"

"The miners here call them bogeys. Some sort of indigenous life-form—"

Leia extended her free hand toward the thing and closed her eyes.

"—and the spiders eat them, so, you know, if one is here, the odds improve that a spider is coming—"

"I don't think it's alive. I can't detect it in the Force as life, just as energy. Energy and intent." Leia opened her eyes again. "I'm going to give it a look." She donned her breath mask, then opened the door. Han felt the air pressure diminish; he grabbed and put on his own mask. Leia stepped out of the speeder.

"Leia, no, get back in the speeder, it just may mean that no Kessel life-form shows up in the Force, you know, like the Yuuzhan Vong, meaning that the spiders might not, either—"

She wasn't listening. Muttering a swear word that would have caused other smugglers to raise an eyebrow, Han grabbed a grenade launcher from the backseat and stepped out. "Leia . . ."

His wife walked straight toward the bogey, her free hand upraised. The bogey hovered there, decorative and unmenacing, making a curious clacking and chattering noise, until she was a meter from touching it. Then it plunged straight down into the stone below, vanishing from sight.

And taking every trace of illumination with it.

Suddenly Han was thrust into the past, into the absolute darkness of these tunnels, when he, Chewbacca, and Kyp Durron had run for their lives with a monster in pursuit. Now, again, he was kilometers deep within Kessel, insufficiently armed or mobile to deal with the dangers of the place.

He forced himself to slow his breathing. Now wasn't then. More than thirty years had gone by. He was in a section of the mine where there was no sign of spice, and therefore no sign of spiders.

But if one came, he'd be just as helpless before it.

"My lightsaber doesn't work."

Han let out a slow breath. "How do you know?"

"Tried to turn it on to give us a little light."

"Let me know if you hear anything like skittering. Clattering. Clicking." Well, maybe he wasn't entirely as helpless as he'd been the last time. The grenade launcher in his hands was reassuringly heavy, and perhaps, given its antiquity and simplicity of construction, it hadn't been disrupted as the speeder and lightsaber had.

Perhaps. He kept his voice under tight control. "Want to get back in the speeder, sweetie?"

"No, I'll just keep my ears open until you get it started up."

Han fought the urge to grit his teeth. "All right."

CITY OF DOR'SHAN, DORIN

The chamber where they met Mistress Tila Mong was far less ceremonial and ostentatious than the one in which Ben had fought. Though it was circular, with smooth black walls of stone, its furnishings of tan wood proclaimed it to be an office.

Tila Mong, seated behind one of three desks when the Skywalkers entered, rose to shake their hands. She was, to Ben's unpracticed eye, perhaps a bit older than the other Kel Dors he had seen, more wrinkles to her face and even less flesh on her bones, but she moved gracefully enough. She wore simple, undecorated robes in a shell-like off-white that seemed oddly detached from the colors around her.

Once her guests were seated and the door had slid shut behind Tistura, she began. "We heard with sympathy and misgivings the news of your recent unpleasantness."

"Thank you." Luke gave her a little nod of appreciation. "Because of those events, it would be inappropriate to refer to me as or accord me any of the benefits that would come to me as Grand Master of the Jedi Order."

"Then we shall limit ourselves to the benefits due the man who refounded the Jedi and helped break the hold the Empire had on the galaxy."

Ben decided that he liked her.

"My recent unpleasantness is related to the Second Galactic Civil War. The war was, in part, due to the actions of Jacen Solo. I am trying to retrace the steps he took throughout the galaxy prior to the war, to find out more about what made him the way he was. Some time back, he demonstrated a Force technique that makes me think he may have been here during his travels—here, studying among the Baran Do Sages."

Tila Mong nodded. "He was here. Some nine years ago. He came seeking knowledge of our ways with the Force."

Ben did a quick mental calculation. That would have put Jacen's visit close to the end of his wanderings, just prior to the Dark Nest crisis.

Neither Luke's face nor any sign in the Force betrayed his reaction. "May I ask, what did you teach him?"

"I, nothing. I was not Mistress at that time. Master of the Baran Do was then Koro Ziil, who has since accepted death."

Luke looked a little puzzled. "I'm sorry. I'm not sure I understand. In most dialects of Basic, one 'accepts death' as a consequence of an act or as an alternative to some other fate. Is that what the phrase means as you use it?"

"Oh. No." Tila Mong shook her head. "To accept death among the Baran Do is to decide that your time has come, to make preparations, to say farewell, and to die. It is a peaceful end."

"If it is not too personal a question, what is the mechanism of death? The actual means by which the body becomes lifeless?"

"We simply offer up the life within us to merge with the Force. Life flees, the body perishes. It is a technique known to the Masters of our Order. The body is then cremated. This is a sign of great respect, as combustible materials are rarer here than on oxygen-rich worlds."

Luke nodded. "Was this one of the techniques Jacen learned?"

"I think not. He was more interested in the areas of our specialty—extension of the senses, detection of danger, detection of evil intent. Also of keeping himself *from* detection." Tila Mong lowered her gaze to the desktop, clearly casting back in her memory. "We thought he was a good man. We hesitated not at all to teach him our methods."

"I think he *was* a good man then." Luke, reflecting, was silent for a moment. "Would it be possible for me to learn the techniques Jacen learned?"

Tila Mong looked up at him—a hard, direct stare. "Would it be safe?"

"I'm not sure what you mean."

"Our observation, thankfully distant, has been that Jacen Solo became a *nryghat*—a monster of nightmares, the sort that haunts the dreams of children. But he was not always so. Could it be that the methods we taught him, Force techniques developed by our species for our own use, could affect the mind of a human in a bad way, a damaging way?"

"It's . . . possible."

"Then you should not be subjected to the same danger. If Jacen Solo, a very powerful Jedi, were transformed by what we taught him, and did all that he did, what might Luke Skywalker, the most famous, most powerful, and most experienced living Jedi, do if he were similarly affected?"

Luke met her gaze steadily. "And yet I have to know."

"Teach me instead," Ben heard himself saying.

Both his father and Tila Mong looked at him, surprised, as if they'd forgotten Ben was not a droid with a restraining bolt keeping its vocabulators from being activated.

Ben continued, "If I change the way Jacen did, well, I'm not as powerful as he was or my father is. I'm no danger. Well, less of a danger. My father could find a way to cure me."

Luke shook his head. "I'm sorry, Ben. It needs to be someone as educated in as many subtleties of the Force as possible, and that means me."

"But if you do turn the way Jacen did—"

Luke gave him a wan smile. "It took Jacen years to become Darth Caedus, and in that time he exhibited signs that we missed or ignored . . . signs that I believe we are very much attuned to now. Yes?"

"Well, yes."

"If something happens to my thinking processes, to the way I feel about people and my duties, I suspect I'll notice the change and seek help. Even if I don't, you will."

"No, Dad. What if it's sudden and total? What if you're Luke Skywalker today and Darth Starkiller tomorrow?"

Luke hesitated. "Then it would be your job to find a way to stop me. Even kill me."

"No."

"Ben, I don't think anything like that will happen. But if it does, you need to be a Jedi first. To put personal loyalties behind your responsibility to the innocent, to the Force. If you can't promise me you can do that, you may need to return to Coruscant."

Ben just stared, stunned by the implacability of that statement. But he knew his father meant it.

There it was again, attachment. The things Jacen and Darth Vader had been attached to had meant more than all the innocent lives in the galaxy, and they had become monsters.

He could not let his own father become a monster.

"All right, Dad."

"Promise me, Ben."

"You have my word. As a Jedi." Every one of those words was a twist on what felt like a clamp around his heart.

Luke sat back, satisfied, and returned his attention to the Mistress of the Baran Do.

She, too, nodded. "Very well. Return tomorrow at dawn. You may want to bring food of your own choice, as humans do not much care for ours. There is a shop catering to human needs near the street market."

Luke smiled. "We'll be here."

On their walk back to the spaceport, Ben kicked a rock lying at the side of the street and watched it bounce off an estate wall. "I think I'd rather be tortured again than go through another conversation like that."

Luke nodded. "Me, too."

"You seemed to take it well enough. Making me promise to kill you."

"Only under certain circumstances. Not just because I insist you eat your vegetables."

Ben snorted, his humor partly restored. "If you start to feel evil, tell me as soon as possible. Don't wait and cut my hand off first."

"Did you notice that she was lying?"

Ben frowned at the sudden change of subject. "The Mistress? About what?"

"I'm not sure. It wasn't as though I had a little spike of perception saying, *Ah, she's just lied about her name.* It was a conviction that grew throughout the conversation, like she was hiding some fact, sitting on it and smothering it so we wouldn't notice it."

"Sort of like trying to not think about the pink bantha in the corner."

"Exactly."

"Nah, you're imagining things. Masters of ancient orders who study the Force never have secrets. Never have shameful events in their families . . ."

"Ben, I think your words alone might turn me evil."

Chapter Fourteen

"THE PROBLEM WITH VENOMOUS REPTILES," MASTER CIL-ghal said, "is that when you use them to harm others, you stand a chance of being bitten yourself."

Surrounded by many other Jedi in the eating hall of the Temple, she thought she was speaking to herself, and that her words were being drowned out by the words blaring from the news monitor mounted on swing-out armatures on one wall. Master Durron had rushed in and gestured at the monitor; it had come to life, show-ing the soaring exterior of the Galactic Courts of Justice Building. Though it was generally against the rules to have broadcasts running during meals, teaching ses-sions, or anytime the Jedi and students needed peace of mind, nobody argued with a Master who had something to show.

And so there on the monitor screen, framed by the Courts of Justice Building in the background and brack-eted by small boxes of scrolling data on either side, had stood Wolam Tser, who had been well respected as a newscaster and documentarian before anyone in the Tem-ple had been born, offering news about them: ". . . rush to accelerate all legal issues concerning the Jedi Order seems to have worked against the intent of the Chief of State's office. Today, in a landmark nine-to-three deci-

sion, the highest court in the Galactic Alliance has over-
turned the so-called Guilty by Association rider to the
recent executive order limiting the powers of the Jedi
Order. Though the restrictions remain in place on the
Jedi, former members and Alliance citizens with training
in Jedi-like arts remain free of those limitations. Chief
Justice Uved Pledesin of Lorrd, in the majority-opinion
document, states unequivocally that possession of a skill
or specific knowledge cannot in and of itself be sufficient
to curtail an individual's rights. Legal analysts point out,
however, that individuals in possession of sensitive information can still be declared a danger to the Alliance,
a measure that allows for person-by-person imposition
of limitations such as those recently levied against the
Jedi.

"Alvida Suar is standing by with the instigators of this
case. Alvida?"

As the monitor picture shifted to that of an attractive
woman with a yellowish tint to her skin, the very well-
dressed Nawara Ven and Tahiri Veila behind her, the
Jedi in the dining hall applauded and raised their voices
in discussion of the decision.

But Cilghal had a feeling of foreboding about it. She
did not think the Force was speaking to her; it was simply experience with galactic politics . . . and the sentient
tendency to exact revenge for offenses both great and
small, real and imagined.

"Master?" The voice was soft and high, immature,
and Cilghal looked down to see, sitting below her peripheral vision, a Jedi youngling, a platter of food before
her. The human girl, who could scarcely have been eight,
looked confused.

"Yes, child?"

"I don't understand what you meant by poisonous
reptile."

Cilghal considered her words. "I meant that the

strength of every blow you strike can be turned against you. The energy in your lunge can be made to propel you in a direction you do not wish to go."

"So the court thing is bad for us?"

"It doesn't improve our situation at all, but it suggests to the government that we are defying them."

"So it's like getting in trouble for what your friend does."

"Very much so." Cilghal's comlink pinged, the signal of the Jedi guarding the main Temple entrance; it was a request from them that a Master come out to deal with some situation. Cilghal gave the little girl a reassuring look and headed out of the dining hall.

Master Durron caught up with her a few meters short of the main entrance. He was smiling, elated. "That was good news."

"For Tahiri Veila."

"Cilghal, it's the first chink in the wall of the government's position against us. The High Court is going to review the entire executive order. It could fall, too."

"It's not the only thing."

They swept out through the huge, open doors at the start of the Great Hall. Beyond was the breadth of Coruscant in late-morning sun.

Much closer were several official speeders hovering over and to the sides of the entryway. One was an ambulance, its rear doors open. The others were mostly Galactic Alliance Security vehicles, their operatives standing with a few medical personnel, and among them were the bounty hunters—Zilaash Kuh, the dark-haired ersatz Jedi, and Vrannin Vaxx, the human-turned-YVH-droid.

As Cilghal and Kyp arrived, a security captain turned from speaking with the Jedi guarding the entryway. He moved to stand before the two Masters. He was in full combat gear and his face, beneath his upraised helmet visor, was flushed red. "You'd better tell these two idiots to begin cooperating or they're going to spend five years in jail."

Kyp's expression darkened. "*You'd* better—"

"Their job is to prevent unauthorized entry, just as it is the job of guards outside your blockhouse to do the same," Cilghal interrupted, as smoothly as she could.

"I *am* authorized to enter." The man held up a data-card. "This is a warrant. My authorization."

"Which the guards, being very young, would not know what to do with." Cilghal reached out to pluck the card from the captain's grasp, moving so swiftly that he stared at his palm for a second as if wondering how it had become suddenly empty.

Cilghal slid the card into her datapad. On the screen appeared the opening lines of a legal document—a warrant for the arrest of Jedi Valin Horn. "Ah. Of course. I must point out that the government and the Order have not yet come to terms on the question of who is to evaluate Jedi Horn's mental state."

"We'll decide that. The Jedi no longer have a say in the matter."

Cilghal felt very un-Jedi-like irritation bubbling up within her. "By the way, where is Captain Savar? The intelligent one who stands a chance of promotion sometime in his career?"

"Out cuddling Ewoks, I expect. Now, it's time for you to hand over Valin."

"Not quite."

The captain took another step forward, putting him face-to-face with Cilghal. She could feel tension rising in the captain's companions. Several of them made sure their weapons were at hand. The two bounty hunters surreptitiously stepped away from each other as if to define separate but overlapping fields of fire. "What," the captain asked, "did you say?"

"You have left out a necessary step. You have failed to identify yourself." Cilghal's palm itched as her sense of the moment told her it would be a very good idea to have her lightsaber in hand. But she couldn't reach for it, not in this situation. She would have to rely on her unarmed skills, and on the actions of Kyp Durron, if things went sour.

The captain hesitated, then drew an identicard from one of his pockets. He held it up directly in front of one of her bulbous eyes. "Captain Oric Harfard, Galactic Alliance Security." The holo on the card matched his face, except that it was not as red. "Now get out of my way, fish-head."

"Two things. First, my name is not Fish-Head. It is Master Cilghal." If Cilghal's tone had been an actual temperature, her words would have given the captain a bad case of facial frostbite. "Second, I am not in your way. That is a logistical impossibility. I am less than a meter wide. The entryway where we stand and the doorway behind me are several meters wide. I now leave it as an exercise of your alleged intelligence to find a way into the Temple. If you do a very good job, perhaps we will name the test after you." She poured her disdain for the man through the Force.

Stupid or not, the captain was not weak-willed enough to be overtly affected. He pocketed his identicard, then waved his troops forward. Slowly they filed past him and entered the Temple. As Zilaash Kuh and Vrannin Vaxx passed, Cilghal felt Kyp leave her side, following them.

The captain remained where he was. "If you're Cilghal, then the perpetrator is your patient. I'm surprised that you don't want to be there when we take your patient into custody."

Cilghal did want that, but she could not bear for this sorry excuse of a human to win any victories she could prevent. "No, I'm going to stand here, enjoy the morning air, and transmit this document to Master Kenth Hamner, leader of the Order, a man who actually had a distinguished military career. Jedi Tekli can prepare Jedi Horn for transportation."

Well, if the captain could not be compelled to leave, perhaps he could be made to suffer for his impudence. As she transmitted the warrant file and added a brief message to Master Hamner, Cilghal altered the nature of the impulses she was issuing into the Force. Instead of encouraging an emotional urge, she began promoting a biological one—the notion that the captain needed to visit the refresher. To her compulsion she added visual aids, including images of flowing streams, beautiful waterfalls, and steady, drenching rainfalls.

The red suffusing the captain's face drained away, to be replaced by something like pallor. "Done with my warrant card yet?"

"No, no. I'm having some trouble with the message I'm adding. Typing on these things is difficult for a fish-head, you know. By the way, do you call Dhidal Nyz a fish-head? Is it a sign of affection, a nickname? What is *your* nickname? Is it Orry—may I call you Orry? Can I get you something to drink, Orry? A tall, cool glass of water, perhaps?"

Even as she parked her airspeeder in a low-level hangar at the Jedi Temple, Jaina could feel agitation from above, a sort of atmosphere of un-Jedi-like worry and anger that filtered down through permacrete and dura-steel like water filtering through coarse cloth. With her observer Dab beside her, obliviously talking about the High Court decision, she rode the turbolift up. The agitation did not feel like a call to arms, did not seem like a physical emergency unfolding, so she forced herself not to reach for her lightsaber. It bothered her that her first impulse was to ready herself for combat. Despite their role in popular entertainment, that was not the way of the Jedi, even for their Sword.

She and Dab emerged into a darkened corner of the Great Hall, finding it full of Jedi who stood in small groups, talking in quiet tones.

Jaina strode up to a nearby group of three Jedi, including Master Katarn. "Master, what's happened?"

Kyle's expression was unperturbed, though he radiated a little anger. "They've come for Valin."

Jaina frowned. "I hadn't heard that we'd come to terms with the government about his evaluation—"

"We haven't. This is unilateral on the government's part. It's in retaliation for this morning's High Court decision."

"But we didn't have anything to do with that!"

"Of course we did. If we had put pressure on Tahiri Veila to withdraw her appeal, all the pressure the Order could bring to bear, would she have continued?"

"Probably not."

"Well, now we know what the government considers cooperation on our part. Unthinking acceptance of their decisions, silent obedience, preemptive groveling."

From behind them came the sound of a turbolift arriving. Jaina turned as everyone else did. From one of the lifts emerged Master Kenth Hamner at the head of a short processional. He marched before a floating medical bed, its repulsorlifts quiet and unobtrusive compared with those of airspeeders. Valin lay on the bed, conscious, covered to his neck by a sheet, and strapped in place. Flanking the bed were Jedi Tekli, Master Durron, and the bounty hunters Kuh and Vaxx. A Jedi apprentice guided the floating bed from the rear.

Valin was not a silent, immobile patient. He twisted and strained against his bonds, loudly talking all the while: "Look at you, all of you. You think you have everyone fooled. But you'll make a mistake. They'll see through your deception as I have. What have you done with the real Jedi? What have you done with the real Horns? Did you kill them? Bring them back alive and unhurt or I'll make you suffer. You'll suffer like you were swallowed by a sarlacc, forever and ever, once I get my hands on you . . ."

Another lift opened, disgorging a squadron of GA Security troopers, who swarmed forward and rapidly formed up around the procession.

Dab recorded the progress of the bed and its guard. "They made a very public event of this," he said, so quietly that Jaina barely heard him. "Not nice."

"You have no room to talk." Jaina's tone was angry. "You're part of the problem."

Unperturbed, he continued recording. "I'm qualified and even sympathetic. If I quit, who replaces me? Maybe a one-armed convict with a grudge against the Jedi, released from prison just for this job? Would you prefer that?"

She didn't answer. Instead, like many of the Jedi present, she followed the procession.

It reached the end of the hall and exited, passing Master Cilghal and a human security captain who looked as though this assignment was making him miserable. Valin, still haranguing the onlookers, was loaded into the ambulance. The security operatives, medical personnel, and bounty hunters took their places in their vehicles.

The captain, pallid and sweating, raised a hand to prevent Master Cilghal and Jedi Tekli from boarding the ambulance. Then the caravan of official vehicles got into motion and was gone.

As Master Hamner reentered the hall and passed her, Jaina caught his eye. She whispered, "This is going to get worse and worse as long as we let it."

He nodded, somber. "And yet I have to stay on this course. I need to be able to look Chief of State Daala in the eye and say, *There is no resistance in the Order to your measures. Just ask me. Ask any Master.*" He continued on his way.

Jaina felt a rush of elation. As stuffy as Master Hamner was, as creased and starched in his personality as any of his old dress uniforms, he did know what was needed. He wasn't just a stooge for the government.

"You look suddenly happy," Dab told her.

"Ever been given permission to do what you planned to do anyway?"

"Sure. What were you given permission to do?"

"Have lunch," she lied.

Chapter Fifteen

CALRISSIAN-NUNB MINES, KESSEL

HALF AN HOUR LATER—A TIME THAT WAS MERCIFULLY UN-interrupted by energy spiders—the bogey's residual energies that had crippled their electronics began to dissipate. The monitors in the speeder came up with patches of static; Leia tested her lightsaber and it came on, fitfully in the first few seconds and then reassuringly steady. Han got behind the speeder's controls and tried to coax the vehicle into life; a few minutes later, its repulsors kicked in and lifted the vehicle off the floor.

As Leia climbed in, Han mopped imaginary sweat from his brow. "Ready to go back up?"

"No, we haven't really found anything."

"I was afraid you were going to say that."

"While we were waiting, I felt more of them in the Force."

"Bogeys?"

She nodded. "Deep, deep down. Maybe they're somehow related to the groundquake phenomenon. I've also traced paths of lower life-forms that I think correspond to tunnels."

"Going down, I assume."

"That's the direction I was looking."

He sighed and put the speeder into motion. "Point the way."

* * *

Kilometers up and to the southeast, in the surface buildings of the Calrissian-Nunb Mines, Allana sat in a secondary conference room that had been pressed into service as a playroom. Chance was gone, having been bundled off by Nanna for a nap. Allana was alone with C-3PO and R2-D2.

She wanted to glare at them, but that would be showing her true feelings, and her mother—her real mother—had always said that only loved ones deserved or needed to see your true emotions. And not even them, if you needed to convince them of something.

"I'm tired of waiting," she told the droids. "I want to do something."

C-3PO looked down at her where she sat on the carpeted floor. "Why, you *are* doing something. You're reading on your datapad."

She closed the electronic device with a definitive *snap*. "No, I want to do something good. Something nobody's ever done before."

"I have done things that no one has ever done before, and I can assure you, it is usually a dangerous and alarming sort of activity. Not suited to little girls."

"What have *you* done?"

"Well, I have been mistaken for a golden god, and in so doing helped strike down the Galactic Empire. Let me tell you that story—"

"*No.*" She grapped her backpack, tossed in her datapad, and dragged out her breath mask. "Let's go outside."

"Not advisable, young miss. Every new world is a place of new, uncataloged dangers—"

R2-D2 interrupted him with a series of notes.

"What did he say?" Allana asked.

"He asserted that we could protect you in the unlikely event of danger. In short, he undermined my already precarious authority. Oh, very well. The outside offers no comfort, you know."

"Maybe, but I like to bounce." Kessel's gravity, lower than that of most worlds where humans settled, had given her the opportunity to make some extraordinarily high leaps on the short walk from the *Falcon* to this building.

Not that bounding had anything to do with her desire to go outside.

Quietly, so as not to alert the Calrissians, Nien Nunb, or any of the occasionally glimpsed members of the skeleton crew Lando had on duty in the building, Allana led the droids down corridors that were so echoingly empty and dimly lit that they all but had signs pointing out that they were off-limits to little girls. Eventually, she found a hatch exit to the exterior, and moments later she stepped out into the bracing chill of Kessel's atmosphere. "Time to bounce," she announced.

"As we are rather ill suited to bouncing, and even more poorly engineered to land in a nondamaging fashion, I believe that Artoo and I will simply watch from a safe distance."

Allana shrugged. She began moving in a straight line away from the main building, sometimes running with long steps, sometimes jumping for the fun of it, always heading away from the perceptions of adults. Soon her shoes and the lower parts of her pant legs were covered in the white powder that seemed to be everywhere.

Now it was time to do as Leia had begun to teach her, to open her mind and feelings. It was hard for her, because she had always had reason and usually encouragement to stay bottled up. Sometimes her life had depended on it. Scary people were less likely to sense weakness or fear if you remained bottled up.

The ground ahead and to the left was darker. She

changed direction to head that way, and soon found herself at the edge of what looked like a series of stone outcroppings, jagged brown rocks protruding from the white dust. The ground was jumbled, rising and falling.

This area wasn't pretty, but it was better than more white sand. Cautiously, she moved out among the broken stones.

"Miss Ameeeeeelia . . ." she heard C-3PO cry plaintively. She turned and saw the golden droid, R2-D2 beside him, a couple of hundred meters back. She waved to them, as though she welcomed their presence and had absolutely no intention of keeping clear of them, then headed farther into the outcroppings, picking up her pace.

Deeper in, the rocks were taller, some as tall as she was. She gracefully moved among them and soon was completely out of sight of the droids. Occasionally she would hear C-3PO calling or R2-D2 tweetling, and she would extend a hand above the level of the rocks, wave, and shout—then immediately head off to some other spot.

After a few minutes, she became aware of something not too far away. It felt different from people and animals; it was a stillness, unlike anything she had felt before. Cautious, she headed toward it, moving as quietly as she could.

A few dozen meters later, the ground became white and flat again. She moved out into an oval clearing surrounding a building. It was not tall, barely twice her height, and since the clearing was in a depression in the ground, she doubted that its slightly peaked roof would poke up above the surrounding rocks.

It was made of gray-white stone. It had four walls and was not large enough to be a house—perhaps more the size of a storage shed. She circled it and found that there were no viewports, just beveled depressions in the stone suggesting where viewports might someday be cut out, and no door, though on the west face the outlines of a door had been incised in the solid stone. The edges of the bevels and incisions, the corners of the walls and roof were worn and rounded, giving the building the impression of tremendous age.

Allana took a deep breath. This was a storage shed of a sort—a storage shed for dead people. A tomb. It did not need a working door or viewports, but whoever had constructed it had given it the semblance of such things, as if the dead needed them.

Dead things did not worry her, but she had seen, when she was not supposed to be awake, parts of many holo-dramas in which dead things in tombs turned out not to be dead after all, and it took brave, roguish heroes with big blasters to save the day. She shrugged. Grandpa Han was a brave, roguish hero with a big blaster, but he wasn't here, so she had to make sure she didn't cause any trouble she couldn't handle herself.

Why had she felt this place? Grandma Leia said the Force was an energy of living things, and there would be nothing living in the tomb. She reached out toward it with her senses, again feeling that oppressive stillness.

And then the stillness was no longer still. She felt something stirring within. Not life, just motion—energy. She froze in place, willing herself to become as small and as still as possible.

It waited, whatever it was, on the other side of that wall, waited with a stillness that matched hers. In the distance, Allana could hear C-3PO calling for her, and she desperately wished that she was with the droids.

She took a slow step backward. The thing in the tomb did not react. She took another, and another, and bumped into the rough surface of a rock outcropping, and still nothing came bursting out of the tomb. Barely breathing, she moved into the outcroppings, not even beginning to relax until the tomb was out of sight.

I can feel you.

The words crept quietly into her mind. Allana almost shrieked.

They were not from the tomb. She stared up into the pinkish sky, seeing only the distant sun and a sliver of the former garrison moon. The thought came from *there.*

Who is there? I felt you. Please . . . please . . . There was such a yearning desperation to the words, such a hunger, that Allana wanted to reply, wanted to reassure whoever was there. But caution and fear and a hundred lessons she had learned at her mother's knee kept her from doing so.

What is your name? The question sent a tingle of dread down Allana's spine. She had the eerie sensation that if she responded, if she offered her name, it would be snatched away and never returned, leaving her to wander forever not knowing who she was. She hugged herself for warmth and, keeping her head low, reined her senses in.

The voice did not return, and a couple of minutes later Allana no longer felt any hint of it. She breathed a sigh of relief.

She almost bumped into C-3PO. As she rounded a particularly wide stone rise, he was suddenly there, splendidly metallic and modern, R2-D2 beside him. The astromech whistled a musical greeting, sounding not at all perturbed.

"Miss Amelia! You really mustn't go off alone."

She nodded and, not slowing, began heading back toward where she thought the mine buildings must be. "I know, I know."

C-3PO hurried to keep up, the faint whining sound of his arm and leg servos increasing as he did so. "Thank the maker you're unhurt. If I'd had to report to Master Han and Mistress Leia that you had come to some harm, I'm sure I'd find myself doomed to an eternity of opening ale bottles in the filthiest taproom in Coruscant's sublevels—"

"You keep talking about a maker. Who made you?"

"Actually, I don't quite recall. But I was made, so the existence of my maker is beyond question. And since I consider my existence to be a good thing, he was without a doubt benevolent and forward thinking."

"I guess."

In a large natural cave, one with several tunnels splitting off at various angles, Leia studied the sensor board, considered their options, and shook her head. She pointed straight up. "That way."

Han looked up as though he could see through both the speeder's opaque roof and the impenetrable darkness, then turned his attention to the sensors. They showed a recess in the ceiling, one that could easily be interpreted just as a natural depression in the rock. But Leia had sensed otherwise. Han put the speeder into a careful vertical ascent.

The cleft was easily wide enough to accommodate the speeder at its base, but it narrowed, becoming a not-quite-straight chimney of sorts. As they rose, something bumped onto the roof, then scrambled free with a skittering noise. Han froze for a moment, then realized it could not have been one of the energy spiders—a spider would have attacked rather than fled.

Twenty meters up, the chimney widened into a broad cave, one that sloped downward to the southwest. At Leia's nod, he put the speeder on a slow, gentle course down that decline.

Leia returned her attention to the sensor board, where topographic lines, constantly changing, showed the irregularities of the channel they were following. "I swear, this is all natural caves and tunnels. Worn by water."

"Do you think Kessel had more water once upon a time?"

She shook her head. "I think Kessel used to be a chunk of some other planet, a much bigger one, with seas and a thicker atmosphere. The life-forms we know of here, the spiders and the avians, must have developed at that time—can you imagine a big avian developing on this world, with an atmosphere so thin they can barely fly? But then some calamity destroyed that world, and the chunk that became Kessel is all that remains of it."

"Maybe the rest of the debris fell into the Maw."

The tunnel they followed continued laterally and downward for several kilometers. It was a winding course but remained broad, clearly the remains of a long-dead underground river. Eventually, Leia spotted signs on the sensor screen of fissures, vertical cracks in the rock. They shone the speeder headlights on those spots and saw that the breaks in the rock were far more recent than the surrounding stone. "Groundquakes," Han said.

As if in response, an ominous vibration filled the air. Small rocks dislodged themselves from the tunnel roof overhead and began clattering down all around the speeder and onto its roof. The rumbling, like the galaxy's largest giant tucking into a big bowl full of boulders for his breakfast, did not diminish—it intensified, the rocks crashing down onto the speeder growing from pebble-sized to fist-sized to head-sized. Han kept his hands tight on the yoke, knuckles white, ready to duck one way or another if he had enough warning of disaster.

The flooring beneath them gave way. The speeder's repulsors, set to maintain an altitude of a meter above the ground, were not strong enough. Han, Leia, and their vehicle dropped into pitch blackness, with more stones and boulders following them.

CITY OF DOR'SHAN, DORIN

Luke could tell that Ben was finding the temple of the Baran Do both alien and comfortably familiar. The décor was characteristic of the Kel Dors, a constant barrage of symbols and metaphors stylistically representing their natural surroundings and forces of nature, but the chambers had obvious purposes he instantly understood. Training halls. Classrooms. Meditation rooms. Dining halls. It all operated on a much smaller scale than the Jedi Temple; Luke did not ask Tistura Paan, their student guide, but estimated that there were perhaps six Masters here and no more than twenty students of various ranks.

The combat training hall was comparatively small and very lightly equipped. Staves rested on weapon racks; padded body armor hung on wall hooks. There were padded mats on the floor for practice. The hall could accommodate perhaps two sets of sparring pairs at a time.

Ben asked Tistura Paan, "Don't all your students train in combat?"

"No. The Baran Do are not a militant order like the Jedi."

"We're not *that* militant."

She offered him a smile, showing her grinding palates. "You all study fighting. That's militant. Our role is one of advice and advance warning. The first Baran Do were village seers who had a heightened weather sense and could warn their fellows of impending storms. Over the centuries, they and their descendants corresponded with one another, exchanging techniques and philosophies. The best became personal advisers to the rulers of our kind. Eventually the order became a scholarly one, collecting and cataloging knowledge of the arts and sciences, as well as of the ways of the Force."

They passed through an angled archway into a meditation chamber furnished only with small circular mats on the floor. The chamber had no viewports and the walls were a soothing, rough-textured gray-white, like the inside of a cloud.

Luke asked, "I've been assuming, but did not ask yesterday, that Master Plo Koon was once a member of your order."

Tistura Paan nodded. She sat on one of the foam circles and, by gesture, invited Luke and Ben to do likewise. They complied. She said, "Over the centuries, many of the Koon family have been Baran Do. The Force runs strong in that line, as, it is said, in the Skywalker line. It is said of Plo Koon that he never grew weary of living among oxygen breathers, of having to cope with claustrophobic masks and strange faces. Me, I would grow weary of it within weeks or months."

Ben tapped the transparisteel mask over his own face. "I know how you feel."

"Your father will be instructed by Master Tila Mong in the *hassat-durr* technique, which I understand you are not learning. Would you like to get in some fighting practice?"

"You promise not to yank my mask off this time?"

"No promises."

"Oh, well. Sure."

Once the two were gone, Luke did not have long to wait. Tila Mong entered, gestured for Luke not to rise, and sat on a pad opposite his. "One Master to another," she said. "You will not object to an accelerated course, devoid of learning rituals and training artifacts?"

"That would be most agreeable."

"Well, then. The technique you asked to learn is the

ayna-seff technique of the *hassat-durr* family. In our language, the term *hassat-durr* means 'lightning rod.' "

"Why do you call it that?"

"Because if you are not absolutely perfect in your mastery of the technique and perform *hassat-durr* during a storm, you will be repeatedly struck by lightning and killed."

Despite himself, Luke laughed. "You're kidding. Right?"

She shook her head. "The *hassat-durr* techniques suffuse your body with a very low level of electromagnetic radiation. You produce the radiation as an interaction between the Force and your own mental influence over your central nervous system. The energies a student produces early in his study of the technique attract lightning much like a lightning rod. It is for this reason that this skill, like that of dismantling high explosives, is best perfected before it is ever attempted in the field."

"Other than scrambling brain scans and permitting a rather difficult-to-solve form of suicide by lightning, what do the other *hassat-durr* techniques do?"

"They can disable one's own prosthetics and electronic implants, can interfere with shock shackles, can cause one to be perceived by animal senses as something terrible or something inoffensive, and can allow one to act as a very effective range-boosting antenna for comlinks. And there are other uses."

From a pocket in her robes, she drew out two objects. One looked like an ordinary sphere of durasteel-gray metal about four centimeters in diameter. The other was a flat plate of the same material; it had a rimmed depression that was clearly intended to accommodate the ball. An insulated cable was attached to the edge of the plate. About a meter long, it ended in an elastic strap with an electrical lead embedded in it.

She set the plate down in front of Luke, put the ball in

the depression, and handed him the elastic band. "Please attach that to your hand, placing the lead in your palm."

Luke began to comply, then thought better of it and put the strap on his flesh hand instead of the prosthetic one.

"This device," Tila Mong said, "is a simple teaching tool. It is attuned to the precise intensities and frequencies of electromagnetic energy produced by someone correctly practicing the *ayna-seff* technique."

"How, by the way, does *ayna-seff* translate?"

"Dead brain."

Luke grinned. "You Baran Do have very practical naming conventions."

"Our artistic senses lean toward the tactile and visual, not verbal. For us, learning Basic is always a ritual of discovery of colorful adjectives and breathtaking arrays of synonyms. Anyway, your first step is to learn to channel energies that will cause the ball to lift off the plate."

Luke looked at the ball. He allowed himself to sink into a meditative state. He resisted the urge to push at the ball with the Force; he could certainly lift it telekinetically, but that would not benefit his training. Instead, one by one, he cycled through all the Force techniques he had learned, not utilizing them but putting himself in the mental state required by each.

Half a minute later, as he prepared for a technique that caused holocams briefly to go to static, a method by which Jedi could bypass many security setups, the ball sprang up and began spinning, bobbing up and down between ten and twenty centimeters above the plate.

Tila Mong nodded. "Well, that's about eight weeks of apprentice training bypassed."

"But that's only the first stage. What are the others?"

"You learn to stop the ball from spinning. That means you have found the exact form of energy necessary for the dead brain technique. You learn to maintain the ball at an altitude of about one centimeter. That means you have found the correct amount of energy to exert, an amount that makes it hard for any but the most delicate and most correctly attuned devices to discover that there is any anomaly in your electromagnetic energy output. And you learn to sustain the output without tiring yourself—for days, weeks, or even longer."

"Is this how Jacen Solo learned the technique from Koro Ziil?"

Immediately, something shut down in Tila Mong's mind.

Luke wasn't sure whether someone who was not a Jedi Master would have noticed it. He wasn't even sure most Masters would have detected it. But something, the equivalent of a durasteel vault door, slid shut within Tila Mong's consciousness.

Her face and manner betrayed no sign of it. She just said, "Yes."

"How long did it take him?"

"As I recall, about three days."

Luke smiled. "It's very un-Jedi-like of me, but I want to break his record."

Chapter Sixteen

CALRISSIAN-NUNB MINES, KESSEL

"WHERE'S UNCLE HAN?" CHANCE, SITTING BESIDE ALLANA at the gleaming white cafeteria table, rhythmically kicked the underside of the tabletop.

"Not back yet." Allana paid him no attention. Her gaze was on Tendra and Lando, who sat alone at an adjacent table, whispering urgently to each other.

She glared at them. While Nanna prepared dinner in the adjoining, cavernously empty personnel kitchen, Nien Nunb waited in the communications room for a call from Han and Leia, and Chance was busy being a toddler. The Calrissians, it was clear, were discussing the Solos' fate but not doing anything about it.

Allana spoke in tones so low they couldn't hear her. "They're not dead, you know. I'd have felt it."

"Where's Aunt Leia?"

"Not back yet."

Chance's kicks grew more energetic. Allana felt like joining him in punishing the table. Finally, she raised her voice. "Why don't we go looking for them?"

Lando and Tendra looked her way. Lando flashed her a smile she knew was supposed to be reassuring. She resented him for it.

"We're not sure that it would do any good at the moment, sweetie," he told her. "We're trying to figure out what to do next."

"We should just go down there and look. I'm really good at looking."

She saw Lando suppress a shudder. "Amelia, do you know what a transceiver is?"

She nodded. "It's like a comlink, except you talk into comlinks, and you don't talk into all transceivers."

"Right. Your mommy and daddy are carrying several transceivers, some of which they don't even know about. In their speeder, in their equipment."

"I know about tracking devices, too." She shot him a suspicious look. "You put tracking devices on them."

"Of course! Comm signals don't go very far in the mines. They don't go through stone. So I had special transceivers put in their gear that communicate with the seismic sensors we've got all over the tunnels. A while ago, after we stopped receiving signals and we had that groundshake, your aunt Tendra and I did go down to look."

"Why didn't you tell me? I would have gone with you."

"Yeah . . . Anyway, there's a lot of fallen stone between us and Han and Leia right now. We have to dig through to them."

"And none of our miners are here right now," Tendra added. "Most of them are away on paid leave. We've sent out word asking for volunteers."

"Well, until they get here, *we* can—"

"We can stay here," Lando said, sounding stern for the first time in the conversation. He fixed her with a stare, and when she did not reply, he turned back to Tendra.

"I could find them," Allana whispered.

"What's that, Miss Amelia?" C-3PO, dithering beside

R2-D2 on the other side of the table, leaned forward as if it would help his audioreceptors to pick up her words.

She gave the droid a resentful look. "Nothing."

R2-D2 tweetled, a lengthy statement for him. Allana glanced at C-3PO for a translation.

The protocol droid leaned toward her again. "He says he approves very highly of adventuresome young girls being adventuresome young girls. But not this time."

Allana sighed.

NINTH HALL OF JUSTICE, CORUSCANT

She was the same Falleen judge who had handed down Luke Skywalker's sentence, and she was identically impassive now. "It is the determination of this court that Jedi Valin Horn is not competent to stand trial for his actions in the above-named suit."

At the back of the chamber, standing among the handful of Jedi who had been allowed into the packed courtroom, Jaina heaved a sigh of relief. This was good news. Valin would not be going to trial after all.

The judge's next words shattered her misapprehension. "This court has further determined that the defendant, because of the extraordinarily dangerous nature of his abilities and the overt criminality of his mental illness, is too dangerous to be confined in any conventional facility. For this reason, he will be detained through carbonite imprisonment until such time as—"

Her words might as well have been an unexpected reversal in a crucial bolo-ball game. Suddenly half the observers in the court were on their feet, the Jedi and friends of the Jedi among them shouting protests, the press standing tall or even getting up on benches the better to holorecord the proceedings. Nawara Ven, alone at the defendant's table, was roaring to make himself be heard above the crowd: "Your Honor, this is an outrageous violation of my client's rights, of the rights of all citizens—"

The judge pressed a button on her bench. A musical note like a nautical ship's warning bell sounded through the chamber; it was just loud enough to be painful to those with normal hearing. As the shouts continued, she pressed it again and again, each time creating a louder tone, until all the chamber was silent, most of those present covering their ears or tympanic membranes.

The judge glanced around the chamber, her expression cool. "Would everyone who desires a month in jail on a charge of contempt of court please speak up?"

No one spoke. Few were even daring enough to lower their hands from their ears.

The judge gestured for everyone to sit. All did except those who, like Jaina, had found no empty seats.

"To continue, he will be detained through carbonite imprisonment until such time as a treatment for his condition, based on evaluation of his test data, can be determined. He will be brought out of carbonite stasis at intervals, as new and relevant tests, as well as periodic mental evaluations, are ordered. He will be brought out not less often than twice per standard year regardless of test and evaluation concerns.

"That concludes this hearing." Her movements brisk, perhaps irritated, she rose. The advocates and onlookers did, as well. When she was gone, voices erupted again, this time the press hurling questions at the advocates, the Jedi, and the Horns.

Jaina ignored the heartfelt but irrelevant complaints of the Jedi around her. She watched Corran and Mirax Horn embracing in their shared misery, watched as the forbidding stare of Master Saba Sebatyne kept the members of the press from approaching them, watched as

Nawara Ven sat again at his table, slumped in temporary defeat, shoulders knotted in frustration and anger.

And she was struck by a sense of foreboding. *They're all killers,* she thought. *Jedi and combat pilots and smugglers, killers all, who waged war for the New Republic or who killed to stop the Yuuzhan Vong. The government is turning this situation into a war, and the people they're offending, beneath the surface, are killers. Myself included. This can't end well.*

UNEXPLORED DEPTHS, KESSEL

The speeder plummeted into darkness. The underside almost immediately slammed into a slab of rock angled at about forty-five degrees to their descent. The repulsors, overrevving themselves to compensate, bounced the speeder away from the slab and flipped it. In the beams of the headlights, Han saw rocks seemingly spin around him as the speeder rolled.

He clicked the repulsors off the standard setting and brought them up toward full strength, trying to slow the speeder's descent and eventually hover. Then Leia shouted something he didn't understand. She was staring upward and he could feel more than see the immense shelf of rock falling into the shaft after them.

He killed the repulsors and fired the thrusters, rocketing the speeder straight down the shaft. In the spare second he had before further action was required, he flipped the repulsors to collision reduction, a forward projection that would reduce the severity of the crash when they hit.

They entered a huge cavern—or perhaps a tunnel, for it was of an almost constant diameter, more than a hundred meters, and there were faint glows to the right and left. He flipped over to normal flight mode and rolled to starboard. The sensors screamed that a collision with the floor was imminent—

He'd almost managed to pull out of the dive when the front portions of the speeder smashed into the stone floor. They hit at an oblique angle, a lifesaving circumstance. The impact was powerful, slamming the two of them forward in their restraints, but the speeder continued forward, bouncing like a flat stone being skipped across a pond.

The repulsors kicked off. The speeder hit again, jarring Han's spine, and bounced up again in Kessel's low gravity. Then it hit a third time and stayed down, skidding forward for another forty meters or more.

They stopped, but the thundering noise of descending stone didn't. Well behind them, an avalanche of rocks, boulders, and billowing dust poured out of the ceiling, creating an enormous hill directly beneath the hole through which they had fallen.

Hurried but detached, Han went through his emergency checklist. Leia: unhurt, unstrapping herself, checking for her lightsaber. Himself: minor pains in neck and arms, nothing significant. Control board: dark. Sensors: off. Odors: recycled air, nothing toxic. No sign that the recyclers were still functioning.

He let out his breath for the first time since the floor had dropped away. He unstrapped. "Be ready to run in case more of the ceiling drops."

She gave him a look no other person could have interpreted—half appreciation for his concern, half aggravation that he was telling her things she was already prepared to do.

The air around them dimmed as the outer edges of the dust cloud rolled over them. But the noise of the avalanche diminished. A few moments later, it was reduced to the sound of an occasional rock tumbling onto the mound, and stony grumbling as the mound itself settled.

Carefully, quietly, Han and Leia emerged from the speeder. There was no pop of the atmosphere seal breaking as they did so; the speeder's frame must have twisted, ruining seal integrity, during their crash.

Leia found a powerful glow lamp in the jumble of equipment in the backseat. She snapped it on and played it toward the cavern ceiling. Though weak at this range, the beam showed that the hole in the ceiling was no more; it was plugged by jagged chunks of stone, some of them weighing dozens or hundreds of tons.

"Great," Han said. He moved to the front of the speeder and opened the engine compartment.

"Hey, any landing you can walk away from is a good one," Leia said.

He offered a derisive snort. "That's survivor talk. A pilot says, any landing you can't *fly* away from is a failure."

"You did all right."

"I know I did. It was this archaic piece of junk that let us down." He shook his head over the state of the engine and slammed the compartment closed. Then he gave the side of the speeder a savage kick.

"That good."

"Yeah. I hope you like walking, lady."

"Han, you may have noticed, in the distance, some light sources?"

"Probably phosphorescent lures of an infinite number of giant carnivorous tunnel beetles."

She laughed at him, then began pulling equipment from the backseat. "Let's gear up for a hike."

Half an hour later, they looked out over a new and different world.

It was the source of the light they had seen down the tunnel past the mound of fallen stone; Leia had judged it to be closer, so they had headed in that direction. The walk had been easy. Though they had all but emptied the gear from the speeder and Han had taken turret gun grenades besides, in Kessel's gravity the sixty or so kilos of gear he was packing was a comparatively comfortable load.

The approach to the point where lofting tunnel met vast cavern was a rise; Han and Leia had to clamber up a steep climb of stone some three meters high before they could look into the cavern beyond.

The size of a city, the cavern was lined with great blocks of manufactured equipment, each block the size of a human habitation; some were as large as three-level houses, some the size of ten-story apartment buildings, and all were thick with colored lights, some constant, some blinking regularly or intermittently. The faces of the equipment blocks were broken down into rectangles of different colors of metal, but at this distance Han could not tell whether they were merely decorative touches or if the rectangles were access hatches.

In addition to the indicators on the equipment, there was light from above and below. The ceiling of the chamber had patches of greenish material, possibly organic, that exuded a soft blue-green glow. The floor was bare of equipment and was littered, though not thickly, with greenish round-capped fungi, some of which stood taller than Han. Light from all these sources blended together into the dim, pale glow Han and Leia had seen from so far away.

The vista of machinery, fungi, and cavern walls went on as far as the eye could see—kilometers at least.

Leia reached over and gently pressed up on Han's jaw under his breath mask, closing his mouth. "Lando has no idea what he's sitting on, does he?"

Han shook his head. "If all of this shut down tomorrow, just the scrap value would make him a richer man. But what's it for?"

"Let's find out." Hitching up her pack, she walked down into the cavern.

They divided their duties naturally and without discussion. Leia investigated the machinery. Han kept his eye out for predatory life-forms.

Within a few minutes' walk, they reached the first bank of machinery on the right-hand sloping wall of the cavern. First in their path was a cabinet-like structure the size of a warehouse. Its panels, mostly black, gleamed with what looked like thousands of small rectangular lights.

Leia put her hands on her hips and stared up at the thing. "Where to start?"

"Something's powering it. If it doesn't have some sort of internal reactor, there's probably a series of cables entering it somewhere. And unless it's doing whatever it does in isolation, it's receiving or sending data—by cable, by broadcast, somehow."

At nearly ground level, a bogey emerged from the face of the machine. It hovered there, a few meters from Han and Leia, and emitted a faint chittering noise, like a whole colony of curious insects.

"Or maybe I have no idea what I'm talking about," Han said.

CITY OF DOR'SHAN, DORIN

Fresh from the *Jade Shadow*'s sanisteam and dressed in a clean robe, Ben joined his father in the main cabin. Dinner consisted of prepackaged meals heated in the yacht's tiny pulse oven, but Ben was all right with that; the nerf loaf, tuber mash, and seasoned greens in the individual compartments of the tray reminded him of food from home—bad food from home.

"So," his father said. "What did you learn today?"

"A little bit about the difference between the way skinny limbs with dense, leather muscles move compared with human arms and legs. That's about it. Oh, and you know that thing where the sages decide that it's time to die, and they just will themselves to do it?"

Luke nodded.

"One of the Baran Do Masters has decided to do that. Charsae Saal, the senior combat instructor. He worked with Tistura Paan and me today."

"Did you talk to him about it?"

Ben nodded. "I didn't, you know, just blurt it out, *Why have you decided to die?* or anything like that. But Tistura Paan had some questions about his ceremony tomorrow. She was pretty sad. She was his special student. He gave her a datacard with his memoirs and instruction manuals on it. He'd just finished it."

"What did you ask him?"

"Well, I said that from the human perspective, it was always sad when a good person died, when he took his knowledge with him. He said he was leaving his knowledge behind. I asked if he had family, and he said he would be seeing them again someday, by which I took it he meant they were already dead."

"He plans to die *tomorrow.*"

Ben nodded.

Luke frowned.

"What?"

"Turn of phrase." But Luke said no more on the subject.

"What did you learn today, Dad?"

"I learned to make a ball float at a constant altitude, but not to make it be still."

"You had an exciting day."

"I also learned that there's something about Jacen's visit here, or about the former Master of the sages, that

Tila Mong doesn't want me to know. That was probably the hidden thought I kept feeling last night."

"Once you've figured out the scanner-blanking technique and you've pried all of Tila Mong's secrets out, where are we going next?"

Luke shrugged. "We'll have to take that as we come to it."

Chapter Seventeen

HAN WATCHED LEIA AS, UNAFRAID, SHE APPROACHED THE bogey. Unlike the previous one, this creature did not retreat at her approach, but hung in the air as if watching her.

She came within a meter of it and still it did not move, though its chittering grew louder and the lights within it swirled even faster.

"Leia, be *careful* . . ." Torn between a need to know what was happening with his wife and an equally strong need to know they were not being crept up on, Han kept switching his attention from the tableau with the bogey to the surrounding machinery and field of fungi.

"I don't sense any hostile intent. Or, for that matter, any life." Leia raised a hand as if to touch the bogey.

Her hand penetrated its outer boundaries. Colorful lights swirled around her fingers as if they were the center of some new maelstrom. Leia's hair rose, standing on end, and a crackling noise joined the chittering Han heard. "Leia, keep talking."

"It's all right, I'm not hurt." There was some strain to her voice, as if she were making an effort of exertion or concentration. "It's . . . it's . . ."

"What?" Han heard a note that was almost a yelp in his voice.

"A datacard." She swayed backward, almost falling, and the action broke her contact with the bogey. Abruptly, it zoomed away, straight up.

Han put a hand on Leia's shoulder to steady her. He watched the bogey ascend. Several moments later, it hit the ceiling and vanished into the rock there. Han breathed a sigh of relief.

Leia straightened, shaking her head to clear it. "That was . . . interesting."

"What did you mean, it was a datacard?"

"That was what it reminded me of. I think that was something like its function. I could sense a reservoir of energy within it, and the ability to communicate, and a big store of data . . . fresh data. From this device, I think." She gestured at the building-sized cabinet. "I saw a three-dimensional pattern of, I don't know what to call them, *intensities*. Thousands. Millions. It had a mission, an intent to go somewhere and deliver the data. There was something else, too. A sense of futility."

"You got a lot out of that contact."

"Its whole purpose is communication. Not with me, not with anything like us. It helped a lot that I was trying to do what it was meant to do. I need to find another one. A lot more of them. Learn more from each one." Energetic again, she set off at a brisk walk along the row of immense cabinets, holding her right arm out as she did as if to wave more bogeys out of the machines she passed.

Han shook his head and followed.

Han saw things on that walk, some of which were fascinating and some of which he'd prefer not to have seen.

There was animal life in the cavern, moving among the fungi. He cataloged at least two different species of centipede-like creatures, one about a meter long and green, the other about two meters long and a dangerous-looking red and yellow. Both species had vicious-looking stingers at their tail ends. He saw the larger centipedes attack, sting, and eat the smaller ones.

He also saw small avian things, like miniature hawk-bats, swoop upon both species of centipedes and snatch things from their backs. Only when he drew out his macrobinoculars and trained them on one of those flying attacks did he realize that the avian was taking young centipedes riding on the backs of the older ones.

The fungi were also prey to animal life. Some looked chewed on around the periphery of their caps. But others had defenses. When a green centipede went crawling across the cap of one of the fungi, the cap collapsed, rolling up on itself and trapping the centipede within. That fungus did not unroll in all the time it took Han to walk out of sight of it, and he did not care to think about the digestive processes now going on within it. He just vowed not to touch any fungus caps as he passed them.

Two kilometers into the hike, he saw the energy spider. He stopped abruptly, the air leaving his lungs. Leia must have sensed his distress; she turned to look at him, then followed his gaze.

Seventy meters away, its body the size of an airspeeder, it rose from within a tall clump of fungi, glassy and transparent, at least fifteen legs on a side, formidable pincers up front.

Its head swiveled as it surveyed its surroundings. Slowly, so as not to attract attention, Han slid the slugthrowing rifle off his shoulder strap, lowering it to the ground, and put his hands on the grenade launcher. He'd start with a decoy grenade; if that didn't work, he'd switch to high explosives, then go to the rifle if the spider got nearer.

The spider took a couple of steps in Han's direction,

clambering up on an especially large fungus as if to get some altitude to see better.

Then it settled down on the fungus cap. The skin of the fungus beneath its body began to turn black, withering away.

"It's eating fungus," Leia said. "That's not very aggressive. *You* do that."

"It's different." Now that his initial burst of panic was subsiding, Han could see that there were differences between this creature and the energy spider he had seen, the ones he had read about in Nien Nunb's communiqués. Instead of being blue, with little flares of light glistening within its transparisteel-like skin, this one was more of a crimson color. Its legs were not festooned with all the claws and blades the spice spiders possessed.

And, of course, it was not charging at him.

"A related species. Maybe herbivorous." Leia remained irritatingly unafraid.

"Maybe *omnivorous,* and willing to add a couple of humans to its snack list." Han reshouldered his rifle. "C'mon, let's get out of here. Maybe it's an out-of-sight, out-of-mind predator."

"All right."

They moved on, Han keeping a sharp eye on the spider. But it never rose from the perch it was feeding upon, never turned their way. It did not even pay attention to the centipedes moving across the tops of adjacent fungi, and realizing that, only then was Han half certain the thing had to be disinterested in animal life.

Another kilometer farther on, Leia made a noise of surprise. Another bogey emerged, this one from a silver-gray structure the size of the building where the Solos kept their quarters on Coruscant. It had a darker color scheme, its lights a more muted arrangement of violets and reds. The noise it made was quite musical, like a harp being played by a Kowakian monkey-lizard.

Leia did not hesitate, but approached it and brushed her hand across its outer nimbus. Again she crackled with static electricity; again her hair stood out in a display that suggested electrocution.

"Start talking, Princess. I need to know you're not unconscious on your feet."

"Looking," she said, her tone distant. "Variables. Unimaginable numbers of them. Maintaining."

"Maintaining what?" Reluctantly, Han turned his back on Leia and the bogey, once again keeping guard against the sea of fungi and the life-forms within it.

"I don't know . . . The data will be lost. Cycle ending, cycle winding down."

That had an ominous sound to it. But Han was distracted by something in the distance. If they were following a north–south wall—and he had no reason to believe they were, for the speeder's sensors were long gone, but he called it north–south because he had to call it *something* of his own—then off at an angle, maybe a kilometer away due northwest, there was something in the middle of the fungus field. It looked like a mound of—he wasn't sure. Steel barrels, lashed together, like an improvised fuel dump in a wartime encampment.

"Centerpoint . . . *Oh.*" Leia gasped. Han turned to see her staggering back, the musical bogey disappearing into the stone at their feet.

Han grabbed her, held her upright while she recovered. "Why did you say *Centerpoint*?"

"I saw Centerpoint Station! As clear as a holo." Her eyes darted back and forth as she reviewed what she'd just experienced. "Han, that image I had before, the millions of random intensities?"

"Yeah?"

"Gravity wells, I'm sure of it. A galaxy's worth of gravity wells."

"Huh. Is this thing one gigantic astronomical observatory?"

"Maybe." She straightened, recovered, but did not break his embrace. "But for what purpose?"

"Centerpoint Station was all about gravity. Its super-tractor-beam was gravitic in nature." Han glanced along the seemingly endless row of machinery. "Could this be from the same makers? The so-called Celestials? It doesn't look that old."

"Neither did Centerpoint."

Han gestured at the distant mound of barrels. "Something different to look at."

"Let's eat first. Communing with energy blobs is hard work."

Half an hour later, fortified by travel rations, they reached the mound.

Traveling through the fungus forest to get there had not been safe. Most of the life-forms fled at their approach, but the red-and-yellow centipedes were aggressive and fast moving. Fortunately, they were also loud, skittering forward with all the subtlety of a two-year-old flying a speeder bike. Han shot two before they approached closer than ten meters, and Leia cut one in half with her lightsaber when it reared up over the fungus ahead of them.

And then they were there, at the foot of the apparatus Han had seen.

It rested on a disk of something like durasteel, six meters in diameter and a meter thick. Rising from that was a central pole with something like a broad sensor antenna stretching out from it. The antenna was curved like a dish; given the way it was situated, Han was certain it was meant to rotate. Piled up against the back of the dish, strapped to it by metal cabling, were the numerous barrel-like objects he had seen, each large enough to hold a full-grown bantha. The whole structure towered some fifteen meters into the air.

Leia looked at him. He shrugged. "You got me."

"I—hey!" Leia's deactivated lightsaber suddenly stretched out toward the apparatus, as if leaping toward it, and she staggered in that direction.

So did Han. It was as though his weapons and backpack were suddenly caught in a tractor beam, dragging him along.

Then the pull ceased. Resisting it, Han and Leia were abruptly stumbling in the other direction.

Leia straightened. "Magnetic pulse. Why don't we, um—"

"Move back a ways, yeah."

They did so, observing the apparatus from what they felt was a safer distance: thirty meters.

Han was unsurprised when a bogey emerged from the base of the apparatus. "Call for you, sweetie," he said.

Leia shot him a half-amused look and approached the bogey.

"Ask it what the gizmo is for and if there are any good bars or clubs around here."

"Your sense of humor is returning—*ah*." She offered a little gasp as her hand came in contact with the bogey. Again her hair whipped up into an electrocuted nimbus.

"Draw in," she said. "Push out. Deactivate. Next. Next. Next. Acceleration. Interaction." Clearly pained, Leia kept up the contact.

"Leia—"

"Not now, Han. I can see the sequence. They're everywhere, it's *huge*. Evaluations almost complete, then terminus." Finally, she staggered back. This time she did fall, sprawling on the mulchy cavern floor, eyes open but glazed.

"Leia!" Han knelt over her, torn between making sure she was unhurt and keeping a wary eye out for centipedes. He decided to rely on his ears for the latter danger and bent over his wife.

She was panting, the meter on her breath mask indicating the increased demands on its processing, but her vision was clearing. She sat up almost as abruptly as she had fallen. "We've got to go."

"Where?"

"The surface."

"*I* knew that already." A cold suspicion formed in Han's gut. "Why?"

"This cavern is going to blow up, and then another few, and then the rest all at once, and that's the end for Kessel."

As they ran, she explained. "That antenna-thing is an electromagnet. A super-electromagnet. When it starts spinning, it will yank the machinery off the walls and drag it all to itself."

"Not a chance. Across all those kilometers?"

"Han, the makers of this place might also have built Centerpoint Station. Remember how powerful *it* was?" Centerpoint's gravitic tractor could, in theory, move planets and suns; could collapse and destroy whole solar systems. Han didn't miss its presence in the universe.

"Point taken. Super-destructive."

"No, that's only the start." They charged through the fungi toward the nearest wall, almost heedless of the dangers. Leia had her lightsaber in hand, and twice had to cleave red-and-yellow centipedes as they struck at her. Once they raced by a fungus with a crimson spider atop; they were ten meters past before the adrenaline hit Han and gave him a burst of speed, but the spider did not follow.

"Those barrels are explosives," Leia continued. "I didn't get a sense of how they functioned, whether they're protonic or nuclear or something we don't even understand, but when all the machinery is encrusted onto the antenna, they blow up and incinerate it all . . . and collapse the cavern."

"Making getting out of here an *especially* good idea." They reached the cavern wall and the banks of machinery they had already passed on the way in, and ran toward the entrance, still kilometers away. "How long before it happens?"

"I don't know. Minutes?" Leia put on a burst of speed.

From long experience, Han knew that when a Jedi was running for her life, normal folk needed to try very hard to keep up.

The antenna, not visible until Han used his macrobinoculars, was already spinning by the time they reached the cavern entrance. As he watched, a piece of machinery the size of a small refueling station shivered, tore itself off the cavern wall, trailing cables and a field of debris, and rolled across the fungus forest, finally fetching up, deformed, against the antenna.

The antenna was not slowed by the gigantic apparatus now obscuring it. The thing kept spinning, the huge machine spinning atop it. A moment later, when Han imagined that the antenna was pointing toward the cavern mouth, he lurched forward, pulled by his backpack and metal gear. The pull wasn't strong enough to drag him back into the cavern, but it was exerting considerable force.

Then the sensation passed as the antenna kept turning. "Got any ideas, lady?"

"Yes." Leia shucked her backpack. From within it, she drew out a small holocam, one that Lando had provided them. "Got any strapper tape in your bag?"

"Leia, you're joking."

She shook her head. "I'm going to set it to record and

transmit. If we can get any visual images from this to take back to the surface, it might help persuade Lando what's going on down here."

Han set his pack down and began rummaging through it. "What *is* going on down here?"

"Something caused the complex—and Han, the complex is planetwide—to end its sensor operations. Systematically, caverns have been self-destructing. These explosions are tests, sort of proofs of concept, making sure that the ancient program is still achievable."

"You got all that from kissing a glowing ball of light?"

She glared but nodded. "Because I asked direct, specific questions this time, I think. And because I'd gotten better at communicating with them through practice. Anyway, there are going to be a few more caverns blowing up as the tests come to an end. Then they'll blow all the remaining caverns in a sequence that will crack the world into pieces."

"You're kidding, right?"

"Han, Kessel has less than a week to live."

Leia got the holocam strapped into place on the stone wall, oriented more or less toward the center of the cavern and set to maximum zoom. She set it to broadcast. Han confirmed that he was receiving its signal on the holocam in his own bag.

Then they ran, their great bounding, low-gravity steps carrying them rapidly away from the source of the explosion to come.

"Got any idea how to get out of here?" Han asked between breaths.

Leia nodded. "Sensor leads up to the surface. Shafts concealed topside, but I know what to look for down here. If we survive."

They passed the mound of rocks and then the wreckage of their speeder.

Han suddenly felt warmth on his back. He saw the tunnel walls all around and ahead of him illuminated, the shadow of the rock mound cleaving the light into two halves. He grabbed Leia's hand and hauled her back, crashing with her to the stone floor just in front of the speeder.

A thunder like he had never known, and a howling wind driving stone and metal roared past, rocking the wrecked vehicle.

Allana awoke, frightened out of a dream she couldn't remember. She pulled her covers tighter around her and looked out the viewport. It showed only the sky above Kessel: a glittering starfield, a sliver of a moon, an empty patch where the Maw was.

R2-D2, at the foot of her bed, offered a questioning tweetle. She wasn't sure exactly what he said, but she had a sense of it. "I don't know," she said. "But it isn't good."

Three minutes later, after she lay down and tried to go back to sleep, the groundquake hit.

At first it was just a low rumbling and a sense of dread. She distinctly heard C-3PO say "Oh, dear" from an adjoining room.

Then there were crashes from throughout the building as items fell off shelves and furniture toppled. The walls shook; dust filtered down from the tiles overhead. Allana drew the covers over her head and clamped her hands over her ears, willing it all to go away. She desperately wanted to be in her own little bunk on the *Falcon*. She'd be safe there, even with Han and Leia gone. She liked Lando and Tendra, but they were almost strangers. She wanted to be with her family.

Before the rumbling had quite subsided, the door to

her room crashed open and light sprang up, visible at the edges of and through her cover. She flipped her blanket down and saw Lando, groggy and disheveled, wearing only sleep pants decorated with the insignia of Tendrando Arms. His voice was not as smooth as usual. "Are you all right?"

She nodded. "Can I sleep on the *Falcon* from now on?"

He thought about it. "Yes, you can. In fact, I wish *I* could." He began to draw the door closed.

"Good night, Uncle Lando."

"Good night, sweetie."

Chapter Eighteen

CITY OF DOR'SHAN, DORIN

THE CITY WAS OVERCAST AND VERY WINDY ON THE MORN-
ing of Luke's second day of training. Ben could see that
the Kel Dors on the streets were agitated; they walked
briskly, said little to one another, and all but ignored the
humans.

As they came within a block of the Baran Do temple,
Ben learned why. A wail, mechanical and unsettling,
rose in the distance from several points in the city. Kel
Dors immediately ran for nearby doorways and gate-
ways. As far as Ben could tell, they were rushing to
homes that were not their own; no one ran farther than
two buildings from his or her current position, and residents of those buildings were opening the outer doors
and urging them in as they arrived. Some waved for
Luke and Ben to enter. A general announcement in the
Kel Dor language sounded across both the Skywalkers'
comlinks.

Luke and Ben put on a burst of speed and rushed to
the temple. Curiously, the walls there were retracting
into slots in the ground, leaving the estate seemingly undefended. Luke and Ben made it into the main building's
antechamber, running past Tistura Paan, who was on
front-door duty, peering outside and urging pedestrians in.

The general announcement switched to Basic, recited

by a woman with a pronounced Corellian accent. "This is a general announcement. A force-four storm front is approaching the city of Dor'shan. All residents and visitors should seek shelter immediately. The storm is approaching from the south and will be at the outskirts of Dor'shan within seven standard minutes. All spaceport traffic is suspended for the duration of the storm event. A force-four storm is characterized by winds of up to one hundred eighty kilometers per hour, periodic funnel clouds in clusters, and rapid lightning strikes."

She hadn't mentioned rain, but outside the doors the sky was now almost black, and sheeting rain descended as rapidly and unexpectedly as a giant foot. One minute it was dry; the next, rain was hitting the pathway and street beyond so hard that drops seemed to explode upon contact. As Ben watched, the roof of a landspeeder went spinning by as if hurled by a rancor.

Ben whistled. "You don't mess around with your storms, do you?"

Tistura Paan shook her head. "In the old days, the people only had the sages to warn them of storms. Today there are weather stations and satellites, but a storm can still coalesce in moments. Sometimes a sage will know in advance of the most modern instruments."

"Did you lower the wall to keep it from blowing away?"

"Yes. Most of the time it's up to keep people from wandering around on the grounds, but at times like this we want people to be able to rush in. Besides, a wall is nothing but a big wind sail. One good gust, no matter how strong your welding is, and a section of wall could go flying. And nobody wants to be where it lands."

She had her attention on the outdoors through her entire speech, constantly scanning for travelers in need of immediate shelter. But the street, now dimly illuminated by lights, was empty of traffic.

The side passage through which they had been conducted on their first night now opened for the Skywalkers. Luke headed through it to his lesson. Ben found a lounge area, packed with Baran Do and a few trapped pedestrians, where a large wall monitor alternated between satellite views of the storm front and holorecordings of the effects of weather around the capital city.

It was a spectacular show, and one that went on for hours. Lightning descended from the clouds, mostly striking harmlessly against lightning rods and shielded antennas, but occasionally hitting the tall, leafy plants that served the Kel Dors as trees; such a strike superheated the fluids within the plant, causing it to explode and spray burning cellulose in all directions. Funnel clouds touched down at several points, twisting and dancing their way along streets or across rooftops, often damaging but not destroying the buildings; but on one occasion an especially vicious funnel swept across a large theater, grinding it into unrelated chunks of permacrete, shredding lengths of tapestries and recognizable padded seats, spraying all the debris out across the surrounding few blocks. One of the non-sage Kel Dor present said something in his own language, then, for Ben's benefit, translated: "I hope they were in their basement levels."

Ben nodded. "Me, too."

By midafternoon, the storm front had passed. Several injuries were reported, but no deaths. The visitors to the Baran Do temple thanked their hosts and returned to their lives.

Luke found Ben lingering in the lounge. "All done," he said.

"You've mastered the technique?"

"And I'm making inroads into the other 'lightning-rod' techniques. By the way, we've been invited to Charsae Saal's farewell ceremony. Care to attend?"

"Yeah." Ben frowned. "It was mentioned a few times here while everyone was watching the storm coverage. I got a strange sense about it."

"What do you mean?"

"His students, like Tistura Paan, were sad about it. So were the Baran Do Masters, but it was different."

"Of course it was. Masters tend to have a greater depth of philosophy and understanding about such things—"

"Dad, they were even sadder."

That got Luke's attention. "What's that again?"

"I got the impression that the Masters had an even deeper regret."

"Interesting." Luke frowned as he thought about it. "Now I'm certain that we need to attend."

It happened at nightfall. Behind the main temple, on a broad paved area, stood a raised hearth surrounded by a bronze-colored metal rim. On the hearth, a pyre had been built. It was not made of wood, for wood did not burn in Dorin's oxygen-free atmosphere; instead, it comprised planks made of a self-contained solid fuel already enriched with oxygen.

For the first hour, as the sun went down and Baran Do and friends gathered, Charsae Saal circulated, greeting guests. He was, by Kel Dor standards, short and burly, meaning that to Ben he looked somewhat less scrawny than the others. He might have been old by Kel Dor standards, but he moved energetically and easily; he had certainly shown considerable combat skill when working with Ben the previous day. He wore a simple draping robe in black. A hood hung partway down his back.

Drinks and tidbits of food were served. Luke and Ben, the only non–Kel Dor present, did not partake.

Eventually, Charsae Saal stood up on a benchlike platform, also made of the combustible material, and addressed those who were gathered. He spoke in the Kel Dor language, but Tistura Paan, standing near the Skywalkers, translated into Basic. "Thank you all for attending. There is no lonelier thought than the idea that you might die alone; there is no more comforting thought than that you may die gently, among friends. I now take that step, moving aside so that others may succeed me. I pray that I will be remembered fondly. I will remember all of you fondly."

So saying, he flipped his hood up so that it shrouded his eyes. He lay down on the platform upon which he had been standing. He placed his hands together, fingers laced, over his chest.

As the others watched in silence, his breathing slowed. Ben could feel him in the Force, a strong, vital presence.

Then the Force presence that was Charsae Saal faded, became smaller. In moments, it was completely gone, though his body still lay on the platform.

Four Kel Dors approached the platform. They carried what looked like a casket made of the same combustible material. Two poles were slid through hoops along the casket's sides; one Kel Dor held each end of each pole. They maneuvered the casket over the body of Charsae Saal and lowered it, carefully settling it into place. A moment later, they lifted it clear of the platform. The top layer of the platform adhered to the casket's underside. The bearers carried the casket and placed it atop the pyre, then withdrew the poles and stepped back.

Mistress Tila Mong approached the pyre. From the distance of a meter, she extended her hand. A crackle of lightning leapt from the end of her fingers to strike the base of the pyre. Instantly the combustible material caught fire, an odd, purplish flame that rapidly spread across all the surfaces of pyre and casket.

The flame became very fierce, very fast. Soon the Kel Dors and the two humans had to stand farther back so as not to be burned themselves. Purple flames leapt into the sky, rising nearly to the height of the temple roof. The onlookers spoke little, but soberly watched the fire consume the body of their friend.

Not long after, the pyre collapsed. Remains of the casket fell into the center of the burning mass. The flames were still fierce, but dying. One by one, the Kel Dors began turning away, taking their leave.

At an appropriate time, before the last of the Baran Do had left, Luke thanked Tila Mong and led Ben around the building toward the front gates.

"Kind of sad," Ben said. "He was pretty nice. A good fighter, though he didn't have a lot of weapons experience. Staff, mostly."

Luke's tone was equally soft. "It always annoys me to be lied to."

"I wasn't lying to you, Dad."

"What?" Luke looked startled. "No, not you. Them."

"What do you mean?"

They passed through the gates. Instead of turning south, toward the spaceport, Luke led them north, toward the mercantile district. "They lied. About Charsae Saal. He didn't die, and they didn't cremate him."

"Are you kidding? I felt him die."

"You felt him vanish in the Force, as I did. A graduated diminishment that was not much different, in the way it felt to Force-sensitive onlookers, from death. Ben, have you ever met anyone who could conceal himself in the Force?"

Ben grinned. "Other than myself? And Jacen? And you? And—"

"They put an empty casket on that pyre and burned it. And ordinarily I don't need to pry into other people's secrets. But this one may have something to do with what Jacen learned here, so we have to root out the truth. We're going to find a restaurant for oxygen breathers, have a good meal with our masks off, and then we're going to come back here. And find the truth."

Two hours later they returned, but not as official visitors this time. Instead of walking up the street, they moved as Jedi knew how to, darting from dark place to dark place, sending tiny distractions into the minds of pedestrians so that they might pass unnoticed. Their dark garments helped, as did the lateness of the hour and the still-ominous cloud cover, which blocked out starlight and moonlight.

Soon enough they found themselves at the base of the durasteel-and-transparisteel walls of the temple. Luke gauged the height and sprang upward. He came to rest atop, one haunch on the transparisteel lip, balancing there. He extended his hand down for his son.

Ben leapt up, letting the Force enhance his jump. He landed beside Luke in a crouch, both boot heels on the transparisteel lip, and grinned at his father. Together they leapt down into the grounds of the temple.

Moments later, they stood by the hearth where Charsae Saal had theoretically burned. The remains of the fire had been mopped up; no ashes remained.

Luke turned his attention to the platform where the Kel Dor had stood for his speech, had lain down to die. "If we assume that this was the means by which he disappeared, there's probably a mechanism here."

"Or a sensor," Ben said. "From which they're watching us right now, and plotting our demise."

"You watch too many holodramas." Luke stroked the platform along its top.

"No, it doesn't take that many before you learn all the rules."

Luke paused over one spot. "If he triggered the mechanism himself, it was with use of the Force."

"We would have felt that."

"Good point. So it was done by a confederate." Luke snapped his fingers, and a portion of the top of the platform swung downward, leaving a gap easily large enough for a good-sized human or a Kel Dor to fit through. "Shall we?"

"Masters first."

They used Luke's hook and grapnel, no longer worn on his primary belt but still in his customary gear, to descend. Ten meters down, their boots touched a stone floor. Luke pointed a finger up and the hook dislodged, dropping into his other hand; he gestured again, and the rectangular opening above their heads closed.

They were in a storage chamber of some sort. There were many metal shelves here, loaded with crates marked in the Kel Dor language. There were also several large containers that themselves looked like coffins—but silvery, lozenge-shaped, high-tech coffins. It was all dimly lit by low-intensity glow rods.

They stood on some sort of hydraulic platform that, retracted as it was now, was almost at floor level, but when raised should take it up to the ceiling and the hidden entrance above.

"Pretty simple," Ben whispered.

Luke tucked his grapnel and line away, nodding. He gestured toward the one door out of the chamber.

They waited by the door, extending their perceptions through it. In the Force, Ben could feel living beings beyond, but not close by.

Luke activated the door. It slid open quietly, but the hiss was loud enough to make Ben cringe. Sneaking around was so much more difficult when you had to rely on other people's machinery, he decided.

He followed his father into a plain, permacrete-lined

corridor. There was a large rolling cart against the hall-way wall opposite; other doors lined the hall. The Force presences Ben had detected were beyond the one at the end of the hall to the left.

Luke had come to the same conclusion. Together they approached the door. It was sturdy durasteel, too thick for sound to carry through.

Luke looked at Ben and shrugged. "Might as well barge in," he whispered.

"They're Baran Do Sages. They're not going to try to kill people for prowling through their basement, I hope."

Luke smiled. He activated the door, and it slid up.

The chamber beyond was not large. Two shining metal rails at waist height led into a round hole, a meter in diameter, in the wall; one of the lozenge-coffin containers rested on those rails. Beside the container stood Mistress Tila Mong, Master Charsae Saal, and two other Masters whose names Ben had not learned. All four turned in surprise at their entry.

"I apologize for the intrusion," Luke said. "Master Charsae Saal, you look very good for one who is recently deceased."

Tila Mong looked decidedly unhappy. "This is unforgivably rude of you."

"Unfortunately, my need—which I expressed to you, a need involving all possible knowledge about Jacen Solo—forces me to do some uncomfortable things. Such as intrude on your rituals. The problem is, when I realized that Charsae Saal was not dead, it occurred to me that your predecessor, Koro Ziil, might not be dead, either. True?"

Tila Mong, tight-lipped, did not immediately answer.

Charsae Saal spoke up. "In a moment, I will climb into that transport." He indicated the silver lozenge. "I will be swept away, never again to see sunlight, the temple, or my family. Then Charsae Saal will truly be dead."

"Charsae Saal will," Luke said. "But *you* won't."

Charsae Saal hesitated, then nodded. "I will take a new name. Charsae Saal will be dead."

"So Koro Ziil also took a new name?"

Tila Mong interrupted: "We cannot answer that. It is forbidden."

"And yet I need to speak to Koro Ziil, or whoever he is now."

Tila Mong looked at them, considering. "This could be arranged. If you are willing to do what Charsae Saal is about to do."

That alarmed Ben. "Fake our deaths?"

"No. Climb into a transport and ride to where Charsae Saal is going."

"I will go," Luke said. "Ben can stay here."

"It is both or neither," Tila Mong said. "Answers for both or answers for none."

Luke frowned, but Ben nodded. "I'm in."

His father turned to him. "Ben—"

"*Dad.* Jacen. Coruscant. *Answers.*"

Luke scowled. "I don't like it that you can win an argument without using verbs."

Ben just smiled at him.

Charsae Saal climbed into his transport. The lid was lowered over him. Tila Mong shoved the transport along the rails until it fully entered the hole in the wall. Then gravity, magnetic propulsion, or some other motivator Ben couldn't detect took over. The transport disappeared, clattering its way down into the depths of the planet.

The other two Baran Do Masters returned with transports on rolling carts. They lifted one onto the rails. Luke climbed in and gave Ben one final, encouraging look. Then the Masters lowered the lid on him, too, and shoved him into the railed tunnel.

As they positioned his transport on the rails, Ben wondered what he was getting into this time—and whether he would soon consider his time on the surface of Dorin to have been a vacation spot in comparison.

CALRISSIAN-NUNB MINES, KESSEL

They had breakfast in the conference room where Lando, Tendra, and Nien Nunb had first talked to Han and Leia, but none of the adults were there now. Nanna served, C-3PO chattered, Chance treated his food as though it were as much a toy as a meal, and Allana moped, scarcely tasting her food.

Lando's wild yell of victory jolted her. She stared wide-eyed as he burst into the conference room, his hip cloak askew, his face all smiles.

"Get your breath mask," he told her. "We're going on the *Lady Luck,* my yacht. To pick up your parents."

Ten minutes later, Lando, Tendra, Allana, and Nien Nunb, all crowded into the cockpit of the *Lady Luck,* came in for a landing on a salt plain many kilometers from the mine. Han and Leia stood there in the middle of nowhere, breath masks not concealing the smiles on their faces. They looked dirty, scuffed, tired, and cold, but they had never looked better to Allana.

"That's the way it is with your folks," Lando told Allana. "Everything's fine now."

Chapter Nineteen

THINGS HAPPENED FAST AFTER THE SOLOS' RETURN.

Mere minutes after Lando, Tendra, and Nien Nunb heard the Solos' story, they placed a rush order to Trang Robotics for dozens of small flying sensor drones, a type used in military operations for reconnaissance over a large area. Two days later, a first shipment of ten drones arrived. Tendra already had their programming worked up and ready to be installed; then Han and Lando used the *Falcon* to take the drones to the sensor access tunnel by which Han and Leia had escaped the underworld. They released the drones into the shaft, planted a data relay unit there, and returned to the mineworks.

Hours later, the drones had transmitted enough visual and sensor recordings that the data could begin to be integrated. In the conference room now being used as the Calrissian-Nunb-Solo base of operations, Tendra brought up a schematic of the planet, a green wire frame of the entire world.

"All right, start your Podracers." Tendra pressed a button on her console, and an elaborate webwork of yellow lines appeared on the diagram; the yellow web spread hundreds of kilometers from the site of the mineworks, straight lines intersecting at larger bulbous spots.

Leia leaned in close, peering at the design. "Where were we?"

Tendra tapped a spot on the diagram, a yellow line between two closely situated yellow blotches. "This is where you escaped the complex." She tapped one of the two yellow zones, which was dotted with blackness. "This is the cavern that blew up."

Han whistled. "Every one of those yellow things is a cavern?"

Tendra nodded. "Every one. All part of the same ecosphere, with pretty much the same sorts of life-forms. A lot of the caverns were destroyed already, though, apparently due to magnetics-and-explosives devices like the one you saw at the center of yours. Sometimes they caused complete cavern collapses, sometimes not."

"And if Leia's interpretation of her contact with the bogeys is correct"—Lando raised a hand to forestall an objection from Leia—"and I'm certain it is, then we have a limited amount of time to figure out how to disarm the rest of those devices before they all blow up and crack Kessel into pieces." He nodded to his wife. "Show them the rest."

"Oh, good," Han muttered. "There's more."

Tendra keyed in another command, and more wireframe data superimposed itself on the schematic of Kessel. Red tracings, complicated but small, appeared in several spots on the planet's surface, and a series of thick orange lines, jagged and wandering, seemed to meander their way through the center of the planet from pole to pole.

"Red is mineworks," Lando explained, and he tapped the one closest to where Tendra had indicated a moment earlier. "You are here. The orange thing is an enormous fault system. The seismologists made us aware of it as they've been investigating the groundquake phenomena. We had them run some numbers, and it's pretty clear that if enough of these caverns blow up at the same time, it'll cause the fault to crack, basically shaking Kessel to pieces."

Nien Nunb offered a comment in his own language, and Lando translated: "He says for Han not even to talk about just evacuating. We want to save this planet."

Han grimaced. "I hate it when I'm the only sensible one—it's a bad precedent for me—but it's even worse when *no one* gets to be the only sensible one."

Leia waved away his objection and turned back to Lando and Tendra. "So how do we visit, investigate, analyze, and then defuse all those detonation devices in the time we have available?"

Lando looked unhappy. "That's where I'm stumped. We're already losing drones to the bogeys. They get too close, the bogeys come out to investigate, there's contact, and the bogeys go down the way your speeder did that first time. We've had six of the ten drones go down like that already, and only two have recovered sufficiently to continue their missions. I'm not sure how to get a crew of demolition experts and scientists down there, keep them safe, give them enough time to figure out how to defuse the explosives . . . It sounds pretty close to impossible."

Han opened his mouth to speak, then closed it again.

Leia glanced his way. "I felt that."

"No, you didn't."

"You had an idea."

"I was just yawning."

She grinned at him. "I know you think the galaxy would be a better place without Kessel in it. But not everyone agrees."

"Come on, old buddy." There was a genuine plea in Lando's tone. "If you've got an idea, let's hear it."

Han sighed. "All right. My idea is this. You don't even try to defuse those things. Instead, you set them off."

Lando's brows rose. "We're not even waiting for them to blow up my world? We're doing it ourselves?"

"No." Han pointed at the yellow patches on the monitor screen. "It's not just that they're blowing up. It's that they're blowing up all at once. Right? But if you set them off in some sort of random order, some sequence that will keep the strain from cracking that big fault . . ."

Lando's face cleared. "Han, you just earned yourself some shares in Calrissian-Nunb."

"Thanks, but I'd rather have shares in a firm that makes space-station trash compactors."

"I can arrange that." Lando turned back to the map. "We get one of the big tunnel grinders, one that's not cracking minerals anymore, and dig a shaft straight down to the tunnel nearest the surface. That'll give us a straight in-and-out big enough for small transports. We'll need teams of demolition experts who can figure out how to set off those explosives mounds reliably."

"The Jedi can help," Leia said. "I'll—"

"Noooo," Han said, and the others echoed his sentiment.

"Why not?"

"The Jedi have government watchers now, remember?" Han said. "This world represents big, scary technology like Centerpoint Station did. Things the government could study. As soon as the government hears about what's here—"

Leia nodded ruefully. "That's true. They'll put a halt on all proceedings until they've sorted out what they think should be done, and *that* decision will be slowed to a standstill by the promise of new technology. Then it'll stay deadlocked until everything blows up and Kessel becomes a cloud of asteroids."

"So no Jedi," Lando said. "Other than you, of course."

Leia sighed. "Agreed."

Tendra looked thoughtful. "So Step One, I guess, is to figure out what we can do to set off those explosives mounds at the times of our choosing."

DEEP BENEATH THE SURFACE OF DORIN

Though he had expected the trip to take only seconds or, at most, minutes, Ben rode in his unlit coffin for what seemed like forever. He checked his chrono from time to time—fortunately, its tiny screen was lit—and watched ten minutes trickle by, then twenty, then an hour . . .

The only thing he heard was occasional clattering as the container's grippers traveled over debris or coupler-joined sections of rail. He shouted on two occasions for his father, but Luke was clearly too far away to hear. Ben could feel Luke out there, though, calm and unalarmed, so Ben himself had no reason to fret.

He was just bored.

Two hours and five minutes into his trip, the container slowed. Ben breathed a sigh of relief. The container continued to decelerate, and within a minute it came to a complete stop. Ben could see light glimmering along the edges of the lid. Then he heard voices speaking in the Kel Dor tongue and the lid opened. The sudden light blinded him.

Blind or not, he was ready for trouble, using senses beyond sight, but he detected no hostile intent in the three nearest beings, even as they reached for him. He let one take his hand and guide him up and out of the container. Warm, humid air washed across him—all but his face, still enclosed in the breath mask—and he dropped to his feet on a rocky surface.

As his vision cleared, Ben found himself in a stone tunnel, one obviously burned out of the stone rather than a natural formation; the walls were heat-fused rock, clear sign of tunneling devices that used a high-temperature mechanism such as laser drills. One end of the tunnel narrowed into a diameter just large enough to accommodate the containers, and rails issued from it. The rails continued the length of this sixty-meter tunnel and ended in an upraised loop.

Charsae Saal's container was stopped at the loop, and beyond it, five meters away, was a blast-door exit. Charsae Saal stood beside his container, speaking rapidly with two men and one woman, all Kel Dors, dressed as he was. They cast glances back to Luke, who was halfway between them and Ben, standing beside his container, nonchalantly leaning against it. One Kel Dor stood beside him.

Two of Ben's greeters left his side to walk to Charsae Saal's group; the third, a woman, remained behind, eyeing Ben cautiously.

Luke looked toward his son. "Restful trip?"

"The minutes flew by like hours." Ben stretched, then looked at his Kel Dor companion. "You speak Basic?"

She looked mildly offended. "Of course."

"I'm Ben Skywalker."

"You were. Now you are not."

Ben gave her a puzzled frown. "Come again?"

"You will have to choose a new name here."

"Why?"

"Because Ben Skywalker is dead."

After conferring, the black-robed Kel Dors, including Charsae Saal, led Luke and Ben through the blast door. The chamber in which they found themselves was roughly circular, some twenty meters in diameter, with blast doors set in the walls at regular intervals and a black stone support pillar in the center. The Kel Dors did not treat the Jedi as if they were prisoners; their manner was civil but uncertain.

One of the blast doors opened into a tunnel that led to a much larger chamber—forty meters or more in diameter, ten meters high at the center, with eight support columns arranged in a circle midway between the walls and the center of the room. Against the far wall was what Ben had looked for in vain in the Baran Do temple: a raised platform with a large, imposing chair upon it. The chair appeared to have been carved from white stone and had white cushions on the seat and back.

Settling into it was a Kel Dor male, taller than many of the others. He had more wrinkles around his eyes and the corners of his mouth than most Kel Dors that Ben had seen. Other than his placement on the throne, there was no sign of rank about him; his robes were as simple and as dark as everyone else's. Luke and Ben were led to stand before him.

He looked down upon them, his expression quizzical. His voice was reedy but not infirm. "Why are you here?"

Luke gave him a nod of greeting. "We are here in search of answers."

"Ah." The enthroned Kel Dor nodded as if satisfied. "A worthy goal at the end of one's life."

Luke frowned. "You intend to kill us? For what?"

"No, certainly not. You have come here. This is the place after life. The world below, the world after. You are already dead."

Ben spared a look at the other Kel Dors present. None of them reacted to the statement.

Luke clearly decided not to pursue that subject further for the moment. "May I assume you are Master Koro Ziil?"

"I was, in life. Now I am *hu'aac-du'ul-staranjan*."

Luke frowned, considering. "That does not sound like a name, especially a Kel Dor name."

It didn't to Ben, either. Kel Dor names tended to follow a pattern similar to that found among Coruscanti humans—personal name first, clan name second, with both names tending to be short, usually one or two syllables; three or more was a rarity. The Kel Dors whom Ben had met always referred to themselves and one another by their full names or by a title and a clan name.

"It means 'the one who dwells in darkness' in our language. Or 'the hidden one.' It is my title, for I have no name at all. I have transcended not only life but identity. You, too, will have to choose new names now that you are among us."

Luke gave him a look that suggested he regretted being displeasing. "We won't be staying."

The former Koro Ziil smiled. It was not a cruel smile, but a sympathetic one. "There is no way to leave. You are with us forever. Seek your answers among us, but become reconciled to the fact that you will never take those answers away from here."

JEDI TEMPLE, CORUSCANT

Swearing under her breath, Jaina pulled on a robe and moved to the door of her quarters. She nearly tripped over a waste receptacle in the darkness, and decided that it was good her observer hadn't seen that; it wouldn't do for word to spread that the Jedi could be klutzes like anyone else.

In the outer chamber, at the door to the hall, she hit the button to turn on the lights and another to open the door. It slid up, revealing Jedi Tekli in the act of pressing the door-chime button for the third time.

Not waiting for an invitation, the Chadra-Fan Jedi—

fur-covered, with big ears and gnawing upper incisors that gave her a cute, pet-like appearance that caused her no end of trouble with children—rushed in. "Darkmeld, darkmeld," she said.

The word sent a thrill of coldness through Jaina's insides. *Darkmeld* was a word of Jaina's own invention, part of a plan she'd put into motion after her last conversation with Master Hamner. Only a few Jedi whom Jaina trusted, and who were not Masters, knew the term—knew that it referred to Jaina's new circle of conspirators. An even smaller number of non-Jedi knew it.

Jaina hit the button again to slide the door shut. She found herself whispering without meaning to. "What is it?"

Tekli stood before Jaina's desk, putting her weight first on one foot, then the other, an unconscious dance of agitation. "I saw him."

"Who?"

"I was at the prison. Master Cilghal has a plan to keep pressure up on the authorities to let us examine Valin. She visits once per day, staying for an hour or two to annoy them, and I do so in the evenings."

"So you saw Valin."

"No, *Jedi Hellin.*"

Jaina blinked. "Seff Hellin? He's in prison?"

"No, he's outside it. Dressed as a workman, entering the underground through a workers' access hatch."

Jaina whistled. "He has to be evaluating the prison defenses. So he can break Valin out."

"That was my thought. He didn't see me. I don't think he even felt me. I wasn't using any Force abilities. I felt surprise when I saw him, but I suppressed it pretty quickly. He made no reaction suggesting he felt anything. I think I got away with it cold. I came straight here, straight to you." Tekli began pacing, gesturing as she talked. "We have to have him. We can't study Valin, but if we can get Seff, study him without the government knowing we have him . . ."

"Wait, wait." Jaina's mind raced. "We need to be sure he has the same condition Valin does."

"All evidence suggests it. What's more, he came back to Coruscant without notifying the Temple he was here, and now he's staking out the facility where the only other Jedi who behaves like him is being held. Besides, if we're wrong, we can let him go."

"Right." Jaina checked her chrono. It had been only two hours since Dab had awakened her with one of his random checks of her whereabouts. This meant that, in all probability, she had several hours to act before he'd check again. She should be able to sneak out for a while. "All right. I'm going to mobilize some people I've contacted about our little Darkmeld conspiracy. You need to set things up here so that when we bring Seff in, whether it's tonight or later, we have a secret place to hold and evaluate him."

"Understood, understood." Tekli nodded so fast it made her fur sway, and Jaina wondered what would happen if the Chadra-Fan were to drink a couple of cups of caf while in this state.

Tekli moved to the door and reached up to slap the button. "Sorry to cost you sleep."

"Don't worry. It's worth it."

All of them dressed in inconspicuous garments of the sort favored by the middle class when traveling, they met in a tapcaf a kilometer from Valin's prison—Jaina, Jag, Tahiri, and a lean woman with white hair and elegant, ageless features. Jaina introduced the last: "Jag, this is Winter Celchu, my former babysitter. Winter, this is Jagged Fel, Head of State of the Imperial Remnant."

"Galactic Empire," Jag corrected absently. "You're married to General Tycho Celchu?"

Winter nodded.

"And you're ex-Intelligence. In addition to ex-babysitter."

She gave him a faint smile. "I hate it that people have heard of me."

"Well, your husband and my uncle are best friends. It makes some secrets hard to keep."

Jaina waved to get their attention. "I'll make this short. I've got the Jedi resources and ways in and out of the Temple, but I'm going to be hobbled by having an observer. Jag, you have unlimited financial resources, at least by our standards."

Jag nodded. "I can't really be a despot if I'm not wasting the Empire's money."

"Tahiri, you have the full range of Jedi abilities, which we'll need in order to handle Seff, and no observer hanging around your neck." Jaina did not voice her next thought: that Tahiri had been very easy to convince to help on this mission. Tahiri hadn't been able to repair much of the damage she'd done in Jacen's service. It apparently meant a lot to her to be able to help with another Jedi's mess. "Winter, you have Intelligence skills and contacts. Between the four of us, we're the core of this operation. We need to set up an observation of Seff, secretly grab him at our earliest opportunity, and get him into the Temple for Tekli to evaluate."

The others nodded.

Tahiri looked doubtful. "And we have to do it without him being alerted to us. He's a Jedi Knight. This is not going to be like doing surveillance on a bail jumper."

"Not a problem." Winter held her datapad up. "On this is a shopping list. High on the list are holocam droids and security holocams. If it's mostly holocams watching him, he won't feel it in the Force."

Tahiri shook her head. "Problem. He may know the

technique that allows him to fuzz out holocam feeds for a moment or two as he passes in front of them."

Jaina gave her a reassuring smile. "*Not* a problem. We still have the software we used to track Alema Rar when she was using that technique, back when she was sneaking around on the *Errant Venture*. We can plot Seff's movements even if he does that."

Jag slid a credcard across the table; it fetched up against Winter's forearm. "There should be enough there for your shopping trip. Let me know if you need more."

Winter pocketed the card. "This can't be traced back to you?"

He shook his head. "I made sure it was clean. It's supposedly for gifts and surprises for Jaina, things that *shouldn't* be traced back to a Head of State's expense account."

Jaina looked crestfallen. "I'm not getting my presents?"

The others looked at her. Unable to maintain the pose, she laughed. "You're just lucky I'm a low-maintenance woman," she told Jag.

"That I already knew."

Chapter Twenty

CALRISSIAN-NUNB MINES, KESSEL

In two days, the Solos, Calrissians, and Nien Nunb had much more data and a little more useful information.

The drones, reinforced by a second shipment, continued tracing the webwork of the tunnels and caverns deep within Kessel and confirmed that the complex encircled the entire world.

Six YVH 1 combat droids, fresh from the Tendrando Arms assembly plant, arrived and were immediately put into service. Transported into the cavern system through connections with the mines discovered by the sensor drones, they began investigation of the demolition mounds.

Deployed in two-droid teams, the first thing they discovered was that anytime they approached the mounds, bogeys arrived to investigate them. The bogeys invariably flew through them, crashing the droids' systems. The automata, unlike the sensor drones, eventually recovered from this electronic mistreatment, but when they continued their approach toward the mounds, the bogeys returned. Unable ever to reach the demolition mounds, the YVH droids retreated to a safe distance.

One YVH pair, assigned to a cavern chosen as safe to destroy, utilized a long-distance military-grade missile launcher to fire on its mound from the comparatively safe distance of the cavern entrance. On Tendra's monitor back at the mines, the Solos, Calrissians, and Nien Nunb watched the first explosives package, a concussion missile, roar from the weapon barrel barely visible at the bottom of the screen. The bright flare of its thruster dwindled in the distance as it arced down to hit the ground mere meters from the mound.

The missile exploded. Viewing the scene through the high magnification of the YVH droids' visual sensors, the humans and Sullustan saw the explosion kick up soil and shredded fungi from the ground. The antenna-shaped device did not even rock. The barrels in the explosives mound shifted a little but did not otherwise react.

Lando looked dour. "Not very promising."

Tendra keyed the comlink on her control board. "Next package, please." She switched the microphone off and leaned back. "This will be a thermal detonator, one of the smaller ones YVH droids have as a basic option."

"You sound like a speeder salesman," Han muttered.

The monitor showed the arms of the droid loading a different, miniature missile into the launcher, then taking aim. Again the missile flew on its ballistic trajectory from the weapon and arced down to land meters from the demolitions mound. It, too, detonated—

The monitor blanked, going to whiteness. Tendra and the others leaned forward, expectant, hoping that this wasn't just a comm glitch. For long moments, the screen remained white and silent; then gradually holocam transmissions of sight and audio began to resume, first as bursts of static and then as full-resolution sound and visuals. The images showed a cavern whose center raged on fire, a fungus-shaped cloud of black smoke rising from a scorched crater at its base, a corresponding burned area on the ceiling above. As the YVH droid turned its head for a panoramic view, the onlookers saw machinery against the cavern walls shattered into junk, some of it burning . . . but the destruction was nowhere near as total as it had been in the cavern whose destruction Han and Leia had witnessed.

Lando whistled. "Frankly, I didn't expect that to work."

"Some difference in the explosive characteristics of thermal detonators." Han's voice came as a distant murmur. "Temperature, probably."

"This is good." Tendra breathed a sigh of relief. "If we'd had to go to proton torpedoes—I don't know how many we could have gotten in time. But we manufacture these thermal detonators. We can get all we need, and fast."

Leia bent close to the monitor. "There, in the distance. Look at the bogeys." Fifteen or twenty of them were swarming in the vicinity of the crater. Then, as a swirling cloud, they began flying toward the holocam view, toward the YVH droids.

"Uh-oh." Lando picked up the comm board's microphone. "Five and Six, pull out. Immediate full-speed retreat. Return to pickup zone."

The droids complied. The holocam view swung around, showing stony tunnel rocking as the droids ran from the cavern entrance.

Thirty seconds went by, and then the monitor went mostly dark. Diagnostics boxes along the sides began flashing red malfunction indicators.

Tendra's expression turned unhappy. "Both offline."

"Still, sweetie, it's a successful test." Lando rubbed his hands together. "Get enough combat droids down there, and we can do it."

Han, solemn, shook his head. "How many is enough,

old buddy? A hundred? A thousand? How many can you get here in a day or two?"

"Not that many."

"What we can do, though . . ." Han frowned, concentrating. He moved to the monitor and entered the command to bring up the schematic of Kessel and its tunnels. "Here's what we do. We refit the *Falcon* and the *Lady Luck* to launch thermals instead of concussion missiles—"

Nien Nunb spoke a few words, sounding indignant.

Han didn't need Lando to translate. "Yeah, and the *Half a Star*. I also think we know some crotchety retirees who own their own starfighters and can get here on short notice."

Tendra's face brightened into a smile. "Right. We plot out the best paths through the tunnels."

"Won't work," Leia said. "As the starfighters fly through and launch their detonators, the explosions will be taking place in just the sort of progressions we don't want them to." Then her expression brightened. "Unless we rig the thermal detonators so they don't blow up on impact, but on timer."

"Yeah, yeah." Lando's eyes scanned back and forth, obviously seeing something other than what was actually in front of him. "Mechanical timers, I think, not electronic. We don't want the bogeys disrupting them. It can work." Then his expression turned sad.

"What is it, honey?" Tendra asked.

"Time to spend a lot more credits."

CAVERNS OF THE HIDDEN ONE, DORIN

They did call him the Hidden One, these other Baran Do living in the caverns deep beneath Dorin's surface, and they did not refer to him in hushed tones, which Ben took as a good sign—an indication that they did not fear him as a god or a tyrant. But because the Hidden One was currently too busy administering this tiny subterranean kingdom to bother with time-consuming, mundane tasks, the job of shepherding the Skywalkers around fell to the sage who had accompanied them to these caverns, combat instructor Charsae Saal. His first exploration of the cavern became the Skywalkers', as well.

Of course, he was now the *former* Charsae Saal. He called himself Chara and insisted that the Skywalkers do likewise.

The three of them walked from chamber to chamber, exploring, unhindered by the other Kel Dors present. Ben thought he had counted twenty different Kel Dors in ten chambers and tunnels so far, but as they were all dressed alike it was hard for him to tell. In addition to the arrival tunnel and the Hidden One's grand chamber, they had walked along a gallery tunnel with holes leading into private quarters, a large chamber where vegetables and grains of all sorts were grown in circular hydroponics vats, and a storeroom where primitive digging tools such as pickaxes and shovels were hung. Now they moved through a large chamber loaded with recycling equipment—waste and water recyclers, polymer decomposers, tiny foundries for durasteel and transparisteel.

"Obviously," Luke said, "you've known about this place for some time before coming here."

"I have." Chara nodded. "It was nearly twenty years ago when Master Koro Ziil, sensing that I might someday be suited to this existence, came to me. He swore me to secrecy and told me of the Hidden One, who then was the former Tokra Hazz."

Ben snorted. It caused a touch of condensation to form on the inside of his breath mask, but the film quickly evaporated. "And the idea of living in a hole in the ground and pretending to be dead was just irresistible to you."

Luke gave Ben a *now's not the time to mock* look.

Chara did not seem offended. "It's not an issue of pleasing ourselves. It's an issue of service. Service to the Baran Do, and to the cause of knowledge." Having completed the tour of this chamber, he led them back through the blast door and out into the hallway beyond. "And in a sense, you Jedi are responsible for it."

Luke smiled. "I don't recall sending out a communication asking for arrangements like this."

"Not you personally. Before your time. I was just a child when it happened. The day the Jedi disappeared from the galaxy."

"Oh." Luke sobered. "The purge."

"Yes." The next chamber was not behind a blast door; the entryway was merely curtained. Chara brushed the black cloth aside and entered. He fumbled against the wall on one side and then the other before he found the glow rod activator switch. Light sprang up along the ceiling, revealing racks of depressingly identical black robes. "Ah. You'll want some of these, though they'll have to be adjusted for your diminutive height."

Ben grimaced. "*Diminutive.*"

Chara switched the light off and led them back into the access tunnel. "Anyway, Master Tokra Hazz was horrified by this. All the Baran Do were, so the story goes, but Tokra Hazz was profoundly affected. Perhaps he felt the deaths of the Jedi through the Force. Tokra Hazz was not so much distraught at the loss of individual life as at the loss of knowledge. Remember, at the time it was believed that all Jedi everywhere had died— that the Jedi Order had completely winked out. Fearing that the new Emperor would extend the same genocidal impulse to other Force-sensitive orders, Tokra Hazz sent many of the Baran Do Masters into hiding and thought about what to do next."

Ben looked around dubiously. "And *what to do* was to dig a hole in the ground."

"Yes." The next chamber, also behind curtains, proved to be a storehouse of preserved foods, all in bottles or cans. Ben recognized brand names from Dorin manufacturers. Chara continued, "As a repository of knowledge. If the Empire were to come and destroy the sages, a cell would survive, deep in the ground, and would be able to . . . communicate its learning to others on the surface."

Luke frowned. "Communicate how?"

"The rails that brought us here are also direct comlink connections with the surface. Not just with the temple, but other places. And should the rails be destroyed, the Hidden One knows a Force technique of mind-to-mind communication."

"Telepathy." Luke sounded dubious.

"Yes."

"Interesting. I've experienced communications through the Force from loved ones light-years away, but they tend to be emotional surges, perhaps a few words, perhaps a vision . . . Exchanges of anything but emotions and general impressions are impossible to maintain for any useful length of time. That's not the sort of communication through which you can teach all your techniques."

Chara shrugged. "This technique is known only to the High Masters of the Baran Do."

Luke looked thoughtful. "I'd love to learn it. I'll have to speak to Koro Ziil."

"Koro Ziil is dead. You will have to speak to the Hidden One."

"Yes, yes."

Ben tried to steer the conversation back to Chara's

story. "So the old Master, Tokra Hazz, eventually decided on making this underground shelter."

Chara nodded. "He used tunneling equipment to dig the tunnel by which we entered. It's very long, some two hundred kilometers, circling and winding. It eventually reached natural caverns that he decided to use as the center point for his complex. The first tunnel took years to dig, and the caverns took more years to modify."

They reached and passed by a communal sanisteam chamber. The next chamber beyond seemed to be a sort of sauna, not currently in use.

"Why such a long tunnel?" Luke asked.

"A practical choice. Tokra Hazz's intent was to recruit only those Baran Do and servants who were fully dedicated to the cause. But in case someone changed his mind . . . well, it is impossible for any Kel Dor, or human, to leave by that tunnel. To crawl two hundred kilometers—you couldn't carry enough food or drink and would die in the attempt. Should someone put together a viable means to ascend through the tunnel, like the little rail vehicles they used during the construction days to go back and forth, the Hidden One can, at the touch of a switch or issuance of a special command through the Force, trigger a series of explosions along the tunnel's length, sealing it forever."

Ben felt a little trickle of worry. "So how do Dad and I get out?"

"You've already been told. You don't." Chara looked serene but sympathetic. "Like the rest of us, you are here forever. For your own sanity, you must resign yourselves to the idea that you are already dead—that you now exist only to preserve knowledge."

NOT FAR FROM THE ARMAND ISARD
CORRECTIONAL FACILITY, CORUSCANT

Under an assumed name, Winter rented quarters in the
residential building nearest the prison in which Valin
was being held—in which Valin was *stored,* since someone frozen in carbonite needed only monitoring, not a
cell and sustenance.

The prison itself was an artifact of early-Imperial-era
architecture. Surrounded by a comparatively narrow
plaza, which would serve as a kill zone for guards
should prisoners escape, it consisted of a tall, tiered single building within an exercise yard surrounded by
fifteen-meter walls, all made of black synthstone. Synthstone towers with snipers' nests rose from the corners;
spotlights, bright enough to give a sunburn to a target
fifty meters away, were mounted atop the towers and at
intervals along the walls. Otherwise the only bright
points to be seen were on the upper reaches of the building, where lit viewports indicated the quarters of the
warden and senior officers. It was a place of gloom and
oppression, and the Darkmeld conspirators' new quarters looked down upon it from a distance of half a kilometer.

In those viewports, Jaina's team placed holocams with
powerful zoom functions. On nearby desks and tables
were banks of monitors for the holocams deployed to
watch Seff Hellin.

Monitoring had been reasonably successful. Using
holocam-equipped mouse droids, holocams surreptitiously mounted on government buildings surrounding
the prison, and even data feeds stolen from surveillance
satellites, the team had not only watched Seff perform
his workman deception but had used a mouse droid to

follow the rogue Jedi to his temporary quarters a kilo-meter from their own stakeout. All the darkmeld conspirators took shifts at the stakeout quarters—even Jaina, when she felt she was safe in sneaking away from Dab for a few hours.

She had done so this night, and she and Jag shared duty at the monitors.

Jaina looked up from the screen displaying the notes the others had been keeping. "His timing is as steady as public transportation on Kuat."

Jag, leaning back in his chair with his eyes closed, nodded. "Seems to be. The eight hours prior to dawn, he's in his workman disguise, mostly underground in front of the prison. The next eight hours he's at his quarters, presumably asleep. The next eight hours we can't reliably track yet, but he seems to use them to acquire gear and maybe get in touch with contacts."

"We need to find out what he's doing in front of the prison. Digging a tunnel? Planting high explosives? Surely he's not that crazy."

"We do." Jag rubbed his eyes and then looked at Jaina. "Armand Isard. Any relation to Ysanne Isard?"

"Her father. She sent him to prison. Not this prison." Ysanne Isard was one of the officers who had acted as temporary rulers of the Empire after Palpatine had died. Earlier in her career, she had won a private power struggle with her equally treacherous father. He had been executed; she had replaced him as director of Imperial Intelligence. "I think it was some sort of act of malicious humor rather than contrition on her part to name a prison after him. Bureaucratic inertia has kept it from being renamed. Or repainted. Or torn down."

"Well, the New Republic only conquered Coruscant, what, thirty-six years ago? The century's still young." He waved the subject away. "At dawn, when Seff leaves,

Winter and I are going to do just what you said. See what he's been doing down there."

"Good."

"Got a question for you."

"All right."

"What do you think about bringing Mirax into this?"

Jaina sat back and considered. "Well, she has skills, useful contacts, some funds, and plenty of motivation."

"Right."

"But she'd need to keep it a secret from Corran. He's her husband, a former security investigator, and a Jedi Master. A hard man to keep secrets from."

"Also right."

"And she and Corran are very, very busy right now." That was an understatement. Each of the senior Horns was doing everything possible to free Valin from his car-bonite imprisonment and return him to the Jedi Order for evaluation. Corran was calling in favors from his ca-reers before joining the Jedi—from veterans of Corellian Security and Starfighter Command. The latter offered more possibility of success, because many of his col-leagues from his piloting days were now senior officers in the Galactic Alliance military, but so far they had demonstrated little effectiveness in this task, as the mili-tary officers and other government leaders supporting Valin's sentence were even more powerful. Mirax, simi-larly, was cashing in favors she had accumulated over the years, but her contacts—chiefly traders and smugglers—were having even less luck than Corran's. Jaina had seen Corran several times at the Temple since Valin's sentenc-ing, and it was clear that, as much as he tried to spare his fellow Jedi the pain he felt, he was suffering. Mirax had to be in similar shape.

That decided matters for Jaina. "Let's designate her an in-case-of-emergency resource. Maybe get Winter to ap-proach her on a preliminary basis."

Jag nodded.

Jaina's comlink beeped, a familiar, unwelcome series of notes—two musical tones, a pause, and two more.

Jaina froze. "Oh, no."

"Didn't you say he checked up on you only an hour ago?"

"Yes." She looked stricken. "That should have given me three or four hours more at least. I haven't heard of any of the observers doing their checks an hour apart." She pulled out her comlink and glared at it.

"How fast can you get to the Temple and sneak back in?"

"Nowhere near fast enough. He's going to beep again—"

The comlink did beep again, the same notes.

Jaina winced. "And then he's going to assume I'm too deeply asleep to hear him. He'll go down to my quarters, which takes only a minute, and start ringing the chimes."

"If he doesn't get an answer then?"

"He'll comm the Master on duty and they'll force the door. But I have one chance." She scrabbled around in her pouch and brought out a second comlink. "I rewired the door intercom with a comlink matched to this one. I can talk to him as if I'm just inside my quarters. Maybe I can bluff him. Maybe I can convince him he doesn't actually have to see me." She knew she didn't sound hopeful. She wasn't.

"What happens if you can't?"

She sighed. "I get found out having sneaked out of the Temple without my observer. Master Hamner will be obliged to punish me somehow. Teaching basic telekinesis to the younglings out in the Transitory Mists, for example. That's assuming the government doesn't prosecute me, which they might."

"Which they *will*. They're not showing any mercy to the Jedi right now."

She glared at him. "Thanks. You're making me feel *much* better."

The second comlink sounded, this one with a chime identical to the one at Jaina's Temple quarters. She took a deep breath, then pressed the button. She made her voice sound sleepy. "What is it?"

"Hello, Jedi Solo. It's Dab. Routine location check."

"Weren't you—what time is it?"

"I'm sorry. Yes, it was just an hour ago. My randomizer went off again."

"Dab, just go away. I'm tired, I'm in bed, you *know* I'm here."

"I have to see you in person, Jedi Solo. You know the rules."

Jaina switched off the comlink and mouthed a curse. She glanced at Jag. "I'm sunk."

"Maybe not. Maybe the Empire can rescue a Jedi." He reached over and plucked the comlink from her fingers, and smiled at her startled expression. He thumbed the comlink on. "Who's out there?" He made his own voice hoarse, sleepy.

Jaina stared at him.

"It's Dab. Dab Hantaq," Dab said.

"Where's my blaster?"

Jaina caught on and suppressed a laugh. As she'd heard her mother say many times over the years, she said, "It's under your pillow. Where it always is."

"Give me just a second. All right, let him in. I'm going to burn a hole right between his eyes."

"Jag, he's only doing his duty—"

"Vape his duty. Come to think of it, vape the neat little hole between his eyes. I'm going to burn his face clean off. Closed-casket funeral for him, diplomatic immunity for me. Let him in."

Dab's voice emerged from the comlink: "Um, Jedi Solo, I'm satisfied that you're here. I'm just going to mark this one as confirmed."

Jaina breathed a silent sigh of relief. "Thank you, Dab. Good night."

"Good night."

She took the comlink back and switched it off. "Staying ahead of the Moffs is keeping you sharp."

Wearing workmen's jumpsuits similar to Seff's, Jag and Winter clambered down through the street-level access hole into the underground just in front of Valin's prison. Jag pulled the hatch closed above them.

This was a well-maintained maze of permacrete tunnels, metal pipes, access hatches, and machinery, some of it ancient. None of the tunnels headed in the direction of the prison.

"Which is as it should be," Winter said. "Tunnels to and from the prison would mean a higher rate of escapes."

Jag looked up and down the passageways leading from the access. "So what has Seff been doing? We haven't seen any sign that he's been removing debris."

"Let's find out."

Half an hour's exploration revealed some of what Seff had been up to. An electronics junction box that was suspiciously free of grime held an oversized, very powerful datapad recently patched into the box's electronic components. Winter activated it, spent a few minutes bypassing its simple security, and then flipped through the presets in its programming. Each showed a length of permacrete tunnel, walls at right angles to an almost blemish-free floor, dim glow rods in a line across the ceiling. One preset displayed a simple diagram of the underground area, showing the leading edge of the prison and a spot a quarter kilometer away joined by some sort of access tunnel.

"Got it," Winter said. "It's a riot raid tunnel."

"Which is what, exactly?"

"It's a tunnel with only two accesses. One is at the prison, and it can't be opened from the prison side. It's probably not even detectable as a door on the prison side—it'd be disguised as a permacrete wall, maybe in a storage area. The other end goes straight to a law enforcement station of some sort and can only be opened from inside the station. If there's a prison riot or mass breakout and the prisoners take over, the authorities have a fast, secret way to get into the prison."

Jag considered. "So he's sliced into the holocams observing the tunnel and probably subverted them—and he may have already drilled an access into the tunnel itself. He'll be working on a bypass for the prison-end door next."

"That's it. He goes into the prison from this access, thaws Valin, brings him out the same way. Minimal fuss. But how does he find Valin?"

"Through the Force. Jaina says she can feel him, even in his present comatose state. More significantly, how did he find out about this tunnel?"

Winter shook her head. "I'm not sure. Back in the days of the Old Republic, Jedi sometimes helped the authorities in suppressing riots like this. Perhaps he found a reference to such an event in the Jedi Archives?"

"I'll ask Jaina to look into that . . . Can you keep Seff's holocams from recording? If there's an access into that tunnel, we need to go down there."

"I can."

Seff's access was easy to find. A sheet of durasteel with weld marks all along its edges appeared to be a wall-damage patch, but turned out to be simply held in place by four large blobs of a gluelike substance. Behind the metal sheet was a ragged circular hole, clearly cut by a lightsaber, into the tunnel shown on Seff's monitor.

Jag and Winter entered the tunnel and walked its length, finding no sign of sabotage at the security station end. Seff had clearly been at work at the prison end, however.

Sophisticated bypass gear had been attached to the access console beside the blast door. Winter activated it and ran through its memory, determining that it had been testing thousands of possible activation codes at a rate designed to prevent the security station's central computer from flagging the events as intrusion attempts. "It shouldn't take him much longer," she told Jag. "A few hours, a day, maybe two."

In silent response, he pointed up. She looked that way and saw what he had found: two small thermal detonators, one affixed to the ceiling above the blast-door controls, one in the ceiling twenty meters down the tunnel.

"He brings Valin out, shuts the door if he can, and if there's pursuit, he triggers the detonators," Jag explained, "bringing the roof down and preventing further pursuit. There's another one, past the hole he cut, that will keep security station personnel from following."

Winter nodded. "So that's his plan. What's ours?"

"This tunnel is a perfect trap. We follow him in here— the two of us and Tahiri. We confront him, capture him, and spirit him back to the Jedi Temple."

"Which is simple and brilliant as long as everything goes right. Now let's get out of here and start planning for everything that might go wrong."

Jag signed. "I really thought that when I got out of flying for my living, I'd also get out of mission planning."

"You aren't that lucky."

Chapter Twenty-one

CALRISSIAN-NUNB MINES, KESSEL

SEATED AROUND THE TABLE WAS A WHO'S WHO OF NEW
Republic–era piloting history, and Leia was so cheered
to see them all that she could not stop smiling.

Wedge Antilles sat to Han's right. More relaxed now
since his retirement was proving to have some staying
power, he had his feet up on the table before him—
scuffed, ancient boots on the elegant stone top, much to
Lando's unspoken dismay. Wedge sipped from a tumbler
of Corellian brandy. Lean and graying, he still had the
sharp, angular features and piercing gaze of his youth.
He was dressed in the flight uniform of a New Republic
X-wing pilot, orange jumpsuit and mostly white accou-
trements—but then, most of the pilots present had been
dressed in the service uniforms appropriate to their
starfighters when they arrived, and not all had had time
to change into civilian clothes. Not all wanted to.

Next to Wedge was Derek "Hobbie" Klivian, still
somber—some said mournful—of appearance, on a
brief break from his duties as a Coruscant spokesman
for the Zaltin Corporation, the bacta manufacturer.

Beside Hobbie sat Inyri Forge, a former Rogue
Squadron pilot who had been born on Kessel—her parents and surviving siblings were among those who had
been evacuated from the planet as the groundshakes

grew worse. They were temporarily quartered in old Imperial barracks on the garrison moon. Brown-haired and fine-boned, she looked almost too delicate to be a pilot, but her kill record made a lie of that assumption.

At the far end of the table was Kell Tainer. A large man about Leia's age, he was bald on top; he wore his long gray hair in a ponytail and had a drooping mustache. He looked far more like a pirate than a former member of New Republic Starfighter Command, but his experience as a pilot, demolitions expert, and mechanic made him invaluable for the process of converting thermal detonators into warheads for other types of missile systems.

Then there was Cheriss ke Hanadi, an Adumari pilot who was said to be deadlier with her vibroblade than with a starfighter; short, dark-haired, and freckled, she looked like she should be managing a farm goods store.

Next to Cheriss was Nrin Vakil, a Quarren whose watertight flight suit sloshed because it was filled with salt water kept in constant circulation by a backpack processor. Beside him sat Rhysati Ynr, a human woman living on Coruscant; her husband was Nawara Ven, currently Coruscant's best-publicized advocate. She seemed a little uncomfortable sitting beside Maarek Stele, who was still brooding and vital despite the complete loss of his hair; he was an Imperial retiree who had served, among other roles, as an officer on Kessel's garrison moon and later as a TIE fighter pilot in the famous 181st Imperial fighter group.

And, Leia reflected, the pilots sitting with her and Tendra at the head of the table—Han, Lando, and Nien Nunb—weren't exactly slouches themselves.

Lando rapped a shot glass on the table to divert everyone from catching-up talk and bring them back to the subject at hand. "So we have a mixed bag of starfighters—X-wings, A-wings, a Blade-Thirty-six, an Eta-Five acquired under circumstances I won't discuss, and a TIE bomber whose owner wants it kept in the exquisite condition it now enjoys, so don't even think about scratching the paint.

"The next two crews of pilots I'll be briefing in here are the rescue vehicle crews and the subsonics crews—those are the airspeeders you saw lined up outside. Each of you will be paired with one of them. Their job is to precede you into the cavern, activate the monstrous sonic systems we've mounted on their speeders, and drive out the animal life. Sometimes they'll be doing it at the same time as your missile pass, or after, if you're firing detonators on timer. If your detonator's supposed to go off on impact, they'll be preceding you."

Wedge took another sip of his drink. "Who's acting as mission control?"

"Tendra—"

Tendra looked at her husband and shook her head.

Lando continued smoothly, "—or someone else. I'll make sure it's someone with plenty of experience. Nobody's going to be forgotten."

Han stepped in. "The subsonics pilots are going to be doing more flying than the rest of us. They'll fly several passes in each cavern, driving the animal life in one direction. They'll be notifying mission control when each cavern is done."

Cheriss raised a hand. "What if the bogeys knock down a subsonics speeder?"

"That's bound to happen," Leia confirmed. "We have a whole net of sensors set up down there. If any vehicle goes down, it shows as being offline on our computer. We send in a rescue transport. Since the detonators are on mechanical timers we can't abort, we're trying to make sure there's plenty of time between the end of a subsonics run and the scheduled detonation—time to get any stranded pilots out. We're trying to preserve the lives of as many of the animals as we can, but the over-riding goal is to save Kessel and keep our pilots alive."

Wedge offered Lando a slightly malicious smile. "A hundred to one says you weren't able to secure insurance for this little operation."

"True." Lando looked regretful. "I knew better. I didn't even try."

"So if a starfighter goes down and gets blown up, you're paying for it out of pocket, correct?"

Lando's expression went from regretful to mournful. "Dodging the bogeys is better for all of us. I can't stress that enough."

Tendra leaned forward. "Each of you will be responsible for hitting between twenty and thirty of the munitions devices. In most cases, you'll be targeting a spot near the device and your warhead will not be set to explode on contact. It will go off on timer. Sometimes, though, it will be on impact. We'll try to remember to tell you which is which."

"Considerate of you," Hobbie said.

"Also, if one of you goes down," Lando continued, "that is, one of *us* goes down, as I'll be doing what you are in *Lady Luck,* and Han in the *Falcon,* then the uncompleted targets on your list will be assigned to other pilots—the pilots with the nearest routes. Launch time is still holding at oh six hundred local time tomorrow."

Though these veteran pilots were twenty, thirty, or forty years older than green recruits, they groaned just like newly commissioned fliers.

Lando offered them a bright smile. "Suffer. I have a toddler. I'll be up then anyway. We'll see you in the morning. And, again, really: Thanks."

"No," said Allana.

Leia remained firm, at least on the outside. Looking down into Allana's anxious face, she didn't feel anywhere near as decisive. "It'll just be for a few hours. Chance is going to be there. He'll be with Nanna."

Han, standing behind Leia's chair, gave his wife's shoulder a reassuring squeeze. "Leia and I can't keep you safe while we're firing off bombs in the caverns. You need to be on the garrison moon. Especially if there are more groundquakes."

"No."

Leia took a deep breath. Arguing with Allana was so much like arguing with Jacen had been. The child was very bright and she intellectualized, rationalized like someone far beyond her seven years. Sometimes the only thing Leia could use to win was pure willpower. "Allana, this isn't open for discussion. Han and I have decided."

"The garrison moon is up in space. There's something waiting for me up in space."

Leia looked up at Han, but he seemed as baffled as she was. She turned back to Allana. "Something *what*?"

"Something scary."

"Allana." Han's voice was not harsh, but there was a warning tone to it. "You shouldn't try to get out of things you don't want to do by fibbing."

Leia schooled herself to remain absolutely impassive. The number of times Han had gotten out of things he didn't want to do by lying . . . well, not to Leia, but to just about everyone else . . .

"I'm not fibbing! There really is something up there. It talked to me."

Leia frowned. "When?"

"When I—when I was outside the main building the other day. While you were underground."

"What did it say?"

"It wanted to know who I was. It was sad but scary."

"Did anyone else hear this?"

Allana shook her head. She lowered her voice to a

whisper. "It talked through the Force." Searching her grandparents' eyes, she continued, more desperately, "I know the difference between what's real and what's not. This was real."

"Give us a minute." Han gestured for Leia to accompany him outside Allana's temporary bedroom.

Once they were in the hallway with the door shut, Han whispered, "What do you think?"

"She's telling the truth as she understands it. Which means there may actually be something out there." At a loss, Leia shrugged. "With the time we have available, we have three choices, none good. Leave her here in the main building, which means danger if the groundquakes get bad during our operation, which they very well may. Take her on the *Falcon,* where we'll be dealing with high explosives, potentially dangerous animal life, bogeys, and perhaps collapsing caverns. Or send her to the garrison moon, where, if she's right, something may come after her."

Looking unhappy, Han considered. "If we have to choose one of those, I'd choose the one where we can watch after her ourselves."

"Me, too."

Han punched the door button. The door slid aside.

Allana stood just inside, looking up at them, her face shining as though she'd heard the entire exchange. "I can go?"

Han stooped to pick her up. He straightened without even a fake groan or a *you're getting too heavy* comment. "You can," he told her. "If you promise to be a good member of the crew. That means following orders, even the ones you hate."

"I promise."

"All right."

"And we fib all the time. Every time you call me Amelia, that's a fib, isn't it?"

Han scowled at her. "Don't confuse the issue with facts. Leia does that all the time, and I hate it."

ARMAND ISARD CORRECTIONAL FACILITY, CORUSCANT

Seff Hellin stepped through the hole he'd burned in the permacrete mere days before and pulled the metal sheet into place again. With luck, this was the last time he'd have to do that, the last time ever.

He was so close to his goal that he could feel himself trembling. The isolation he'd felt for so long might at last come to an end. He still wasn't sure how he'd recognized Valin over the holorecordings of the man's trial—how he'd instantly realized that it was the *true* Valin, not some imposter—but he had.

Soon he would free his fellow surviving Jedi Knight. And maybe, just maybe, Valin would have answers that Seff lacked.

The tunnel was as he'd left it, the near end still rigged with his bypass equipment. Something was different, though, which he could recognize even at the distance of twenty meters: the main light indicator on the console now glowed green instead of red. It had completed its task; it had cracked the door's access code. He breathed a sigh of relief and headed that way.

Something else was different, too, and he was in mid-stride, halfway between his entrance and the door, when he felt it. This was a faint stirring in the Force, more subtle than most he had felt in recent times. There were presences nearby. They weren't workers in adjacent tunnels or prison personnel beyond the door; he could feel that they were waiting for *him*.

He stopped and slowly turned, unsealing the front of

his workman's jumpsuit, and pulled his lightsaber from beneath its folds.

The metal patch he'd set over his access hole was gone, pulled away so quietly that he hadn't heard it. From this angle, Seff could not see much through the gap, but the intruder wasn't waiting. She stepped through into his view.

He knew her, all right. Tahiri Veila—or, actually, the imposter in her form. She was not dressed as a Jedi; she wore a tight-fitting jumpsuit all in black, almost featureless. Nor was she barefoot. Her lightsaber, unlit, was in her hand. Her expression was grave.

He gave her a look of scorn. "You could do better than that. At least get the footwear, or lack of it, right."

Her answer was almost a whisper: "Just like Valin." She moved sideways, all feline grace, until she was in the center of the tunnel.

"Which is why I have to be stopped, yes?"

"Yes, absolutely."

"Tell your comrades to come on in. I want to see who *they're* impersonating."

The false Tahiri glanced toward the hole and nodded. A man stepped through, but Seff did not recognize him; though not tall, the man was burly, clad in loose-fitting pants and tunic in black, with dull silver gloves protruding from the cuffs of his garment. He wore a black hood that cast his face into shadow. He looked unarmed, though he could have been hiding a multitude of weapons under the tunic.

On second glance, his burliness was not natural. Seff was sure the man wore some sort of breastplate under the cloth. Coming through the gap in the wall, he had not bent properly at the waist; he was stiff in his movements.

That sent a jolt of alarm down Seff's spine. "A *Mando*. Of course, they'd send a Mando against me."

The hooded man said nothing. And whoever else was beyond the gap did not enter, did not come within sight.

With at least three-against-one odds, speed and aggression were of the essence. Not waiting for any irrelevant declaration of intent or repartee from his opponents, Seff threw up a hand, exerting his will through the Force. The false Tahiri merely narrowed her eyes as she used her own powers to adhere to the permacrete beneath her, but the unknown Mando staggered backward and slid for many meters, flailing. Perhaps he wasn't a Mandalorian after all; he seemed too awkward.

The false Tahiri waited only a moment, until Seff's surge flagged, and then ignited her lightsaber and charged forward. Seff lit his own blade.

"Seff, things will be a lot better if you just surrender." She twitched her blade, a feint designed to lure him into a premature attack.

Seff pretended to fall for it, striking down at her, a classic cleaving blow, but he jerked the blow to a halt and redirected it down at an angle against her left side. Halfway into a block against the anticipated blow, Tahiri had to leap frantically back and maneuver her blade into the path of Seff's, a successful block that nevertheless left her off-balance and on the retreat.

"You're lucky," Seff told her. He struck again, throwing a series of attacks to keep her off balance. "Whoever you are, I have far less contempt for you than for the real Tahiri. Murderess, traitor, pathetic slave to her emotions—that's what *she* is."

Seff was surprised to feel a jolt of anger and hurt from his opponent. Could it be that she identified so strongly with the woman whose face she wore? Interesting. He kept up his attack.

He felt the Mando reenter the fight before there was any visual evidence of it. The black-clad man was on one elbow, as if hurt and struggling to rise, and then Seff saw that the man had drawn a blaster pistol, built over-sized to accommodate his crushgaunts, but had con-cealed the action behind the sleeve of his other arm. The Mando swept his obscuring arm out of the way and fired; a blue stun bolt headed toward Seff.

Seff felt a jolt of jubilation. He caught the bolt on his blade and deflected it down into the false Tahiri's leg. Tahiri's eyes widened for a fraction of a second, then rolled up into her head. She fell backward.

Now to take advantage of the situation before his en-emies could regroup. Seff dashed back to the blast door into the prison and hit two buttons—one to open the door, one to trigger the thermal detonator toward the center of the corridor.

Nothing happened. He wasn't too surprised. If his en-emies had found his work here, they could easily have sabotaged his computer.

He glanced back. The Mando was on his feet, headed Seff's way, pistol in hand.

Seff glanced up to where he'd planted the nearest ther-mal detonator. With an exertion of telekinesis, he yanked it free and let it drop to the floor of the tunnel. It made a metallic sound as it hit. He made sure he could visualize the triggering button; then he sent the small canister-shaped weapon rolling toward the fallen Tahiri.

The Mando skidded to a stop beside Tahiri. Stooping, he picked up the unconscious woman then turned and ran, sheltering her with his body.

Grinning, Seff kept the detonator rolling after them, even allowing it to bounce once or twice for additional noise.

But he let the Mando gain on his rolling weapon. His task was not to kill these enemies.

When the detonator was halfway down the tunnel, when the Mando and the unconscious woman were far enough ahead that the blast might not kill them, Seff dropped into a crouch, turned away from the detonator, clamped his hands over his ears, and telekinetically pressed the trigger.

There was a brief pause, then the world flashed red and white. Walls and floor shook, and Seff's ears were hammered as though he'd been cuffed by a rancor. Braced as he was, the shock wave of the explosion still slammed him into the blast door. He was pelted with superheated pieces of permacrete gravel, one of which burned his side and caught his jumpsuit on fire. The lights went out and smoke filled the air.

Shaky, he rose, patting out the burning portion of his garment. He was now in complete darkness—complete until he reignited his lightsaber.

The gleam from his blade showed the tunnel collapsed, rubble filling it to within ten meters of where he stood. His bypass computer was wreckage.

The blast door was unhurt, at least for the moment.

If he'd calculated correctly, there would now be a crater in the bare kill zone above. The prison personnel would be on alert, but guessing either that there had been some sort of fuel mishap outside the prison or, at worst, that someone was trying to stage a prison break from without. His entry was likely to remain a secret for now.

And his enemies, if still alive, were trapped on the other side of the rubble.

He got to work, pressing the tip of his blade against the metal of the blast doors just at the seam, watching the durasteel begin to glow red, then orange, then luminous yellow.

Chapter Twenty-two

JAG YANKED HIS HOOD AND HELMET FREE. HE GASPED FOR air. The explosion had hit him like a metal beam in the chest, driving the air from his lungs. He knew it would have been much worse if he had not been wearing his Mandalorian breastplate.

Rising to his knees, he drew out a glow rod. The blue light it cast showed Tahiri, flat on her face beside him, and a tremendous mound of construction wreckage behind them. His blaster pistol was nowhere to be seen. He pulled off his left crushgaunt and pressed fingers against Tahiri's neck. He could feel her pulse, and saw her lips part in a groan he barely heard.

He became aware that there was a faint noise emerging from his helmet. He raised it to his ear.

"Gaunt, Sand, this is Hoth. Come in." The voice was mechanically distorted and deepened, not clearly recognizable as either human or female, but it was definitely Winter, using the call signs they'd agreed upon for him and Tahiri. "Gaunt, Sand, come in." Even through the distortion, there was an edge of worry to the voice.

"Hoth, this is Gaunt." Talking hurt. Jag paused to draw in a pained breath. "Sand is down but recovering. Mad Nek is separated from us, continuing his mission. Are you intact?"

"Gaunt, Hoth. Not badly hurt."

Jag looked at the debris mound. He switched his glow

rod over to a focused beam, shining it across the top of the mound. There were gaps there. It was a precarious, dangerous thing, but there might be a way across. "Call in the rest of Darkmeld. Bring in whoever you can. Bring them in close and have them stand by. If we're lucky, this won't be a complete foul-up."

"Understood."

"Gaunt out."

"Hoth out."

Tahiri's eyes opened. There was no confusion in them, only anger. She experimentally moved her head, then rolled over onto her back. "Did he have to hit me with a whole cargo ship?" Her voice was almost distinct; Jag's hearing was returning.

Jag pulled his crushgaunt back on. "Turns out that just because he's crazy, he's not inept. Who would have guessed?" He donned his helmet again.

She rose. "Where's my lightsaber?"

He stood as well, looking over the mound. "Somewhere under that, I suspect."

Her expression turned sour. "This just keeps getting better and better."

Seff peered around another sublevel corner, spotted the security holocam down the corridor, and caused it to fuzz for a moment as he ran past.

He'd had no pursuit, nor was there any sign that the prison's internal security forces were alert to him. And now he could feel Valin, a dull, faint light in the Force, very close—one or two levels up, not more than forty meters laterally from his position.

It only took a simple bypass to get this level's turbolift doors open. The prison designers had done him a disservice by making the air shafts far too small for an adult human to crawl through, but air shafts were not the only accesses. Now he stared up the turbolift shaft.

The lift car itself was far above him, not moving—Seff suspected that the state of alert caused by the explosion had resulted in all the turbolifts going to a certain level and locking down. So much the better for him. He leapt across to the ladder rungs on the back of the shaft and began climbing.

The door two levels up would have been even easier to bypass—he was operating from the undefended shaft interior instead of the exterior—except that he had to do the delicate electronics work with one hand while hanging by the other from the top of the access box. But finally it offered up a little spark of defeat and the door slid open.

Three security guards, armed and armored for a riot, stood on the other side. They'd had their backs to the lift door but turned in surprise as the door slid up.

Seff jumped to stand in their midst. "Sorry," he told them, then kneed the one on the left viciously in the stomach while putting an elbow into the temple of the one on the right, cracking the man's helmet.

The one in the center backed away, bringing his blaster rifle into line, and got a shot off. Seff sensed his intent, a chest shot, and twisted out of the way. The blast passed close enough behind him to sear his shoulder blades.

He ignited his lightsaber and cut the blaster rifle in half at the base of the barrel. The guard, wide-eyed, continued his backpedaling and reached for his comlink, but Seff kicked him square in the jaw. The guard fell, unconscious, his jaw disturbingly askew.

Seff took a look around. This level of the prison, still below the surface, was dimly lit and quiet. The high-ceilinged main corridor and its all-metal walls led right and left from the turbolift lobby. It had many doors, some of them oversized, all of them closed. He nodded.

This would be a storage level, and it was reasonable for them to put the harmless Valin Horn here.

There was a holocam mounted at the ceiling corner. It was pointed straight at him—straight at the spot where people entered or left the turbolift. If it was being monitored at this moment, he would be discovered. He fuzzed it, hoping that he had not yet been detected, and left it that way for the seconds it took him to shut the turbolift door and then pull the three unconscious guards to a point outside the holocam's line of sight. Then he let it return to normal operation.

He trotted down the corridor to the left, brushing his fingers across each door as he passed, fuzzing each security holocam as he came within its range of vision.

What he found curious was that the prison was not being flooded by false Jedi. Any force that could infiltrate and replace the Jedi could do so more readily with the government's cooperation, which meant that the government and the Jedi should be hand in hand, which in turn would make it easy for them to send an army of false Jedi down here after him. But only the fake Tahiri had come. Why? Had the government somehow held out against the imposters? He felt a little stirring of hope.

On the other hand, perhaps there were two or more groups of imposters at work—groups that did not cooperate. The Jedi could have been infiltrated by one, the government by another. That would make sense of what was happening here.

He felt a pulse in the Force as he neared one oversized door. Yes, Valin, however diminished, was beyond it. He got to work on the door security. But the security panel was new and of a very sophisticated type, obviously installed because of the important nature of the captive beyond.

Seff ignited his lightsaber and plunged it into the

durasteel door. In less than a minute, for it was not as formidable as a blast door, he cut a large gap into it.

Down the corridor, the turbolift door slid open. The false Tahiri stepped through. Her hood concealed her features. She carried no lightsaber.

She spotted Seff, but instead of rushing toward him, she turned to stare up at the holocam monitoring the turbolift. She began jumping up and down, waving at it.

Seff sighed. Now she was using the prison's resources against him. Things would be more difficult.

He ducked into the chamber beyond the newly ruined door. It was a storehouse, packed high with old furniture, broken exercise equipment, computers dating back to the Old Republic . . . and a huge rolling rack from which hung the carbonite prison of Valin Horn.

Valin had obviously been bound when frozen. He stood, arms behind him, a statue in mottled gray-black with an expression of pain and outrage on his face, sealed in a rectangular plate. A monitoring panel was embedded along the right rim of the carbonite.

Seff moved to it, hurriedly entered a series of commands. The tiny screen read, ERROR. ENTER AUTHORIZATION CODE.

Seff glowered at the apparatus. Now was not the time to face one final layer of security.

A strident *breep-breep-breep* alarm filled the air. Then Seff's ersatz Mando opponent squeezed through the hole in the door.

Seff moved toward him, reigniting his weapon, and slashed to cut this persistent enemy down, but the man took the blow on one skillfully interposed gauntlet. The blow did not penetrate. It was clear that he was wearing true Mandalorian crushgaunts made of *beskar*.

Seff spun, bringing his blade down at the false Mando's shoulder. His target caught the blade on his other gauntlet cuff—clearly, he'd had some training against lightsabers—but Seff maneuvered his hilt up, the blade down, using the gauntlet cuff as a lever point, and the blade slapped against the shoulder, a lighter blow than originally intended.

The false Mando's tunic burned away there and caught fire at the edges. As Seff drew back, he could see that the breastplate beneath, too, was *beskar*.

All right, then. The neck would be his next target. He lunged, arcing his blade in a visually bewildering attack—

The lightsaber hilt was yanked out of his hand. It spun through the air, its blade tip glancing off the false Mando's hood and revealing the black metal helmet beneath, and then the hilt landed in the palm of Not-Tahiri, now stepping through the hole in the door. Immediately she switched the weapon off and then unscrewed the pommel, rendering the weapon temporarily useless.

Seff looked at the carbonite imprisoning his colleague. "Sorry, Valin. Not this time."

"Not ever," the false Tahiri said.

With a gesture, Seff sent Valin's rack hurtling toward his opponents. Not-Tahiri leapt out of the way. The false Mando, too slow, was hammered by the rack and thrown to one side.

As the carbonite reached the door, Seff raised it two meters into the air, letting it slap up against the exit. Seff followed, ducking through the hole he'd cut, then let the rack fall. It slammed to the floor behind him, momentarily sealing the door.

Seff raced down the corridor toward his exit. Ahead, the turbolift door was still open, but he could hear the rushing noise of an oncoming lift car.

There was no time to gauge its distance or travel rate. If he was lucky, he'd live and escape. If he was unlucky, he'd die. He heard Valin's carbonite being shoved out of the way as he put on a burst of Force-augmented speed and leapt into the turbolift shaft, slamming into the rungs at the back. He didn't grab at them; he dropped.

An arriving lift car shuddered to a halt just above his head. He grabbed at rungs a few meters down and held on, listening to the sweet sound of prison guards rushing out of the lift. He smiled; they wouldn't stop a trained Jedi or even a good imposter like the false Tahiri, but they would slow the false Tahiri and her companion long enough for him to get away.

He dropped again, grabbing a new rung five meters down, and continued down the shaft.

"What's the rush?" Dab rubbed sleep from his eyes, then cringed as Jaina brought her speeder up to within centimeters of a fast-moving cargo hauler, sideslipped out of her traffic lane and directly in line with oncoming speeders, bypassed the hauler, and whipped back into the proper lane a handspan in front of the larger vehicle. All around them, other speeders veered and wobbled a bit in nervous anticipation of the next wild maneuver from Jaina's vehicle.

"No hurry," Jaina lied. "This is just revenge."

"Revenge for *what*?"

"For waking me up three times in the dead of night during the last week for your spot checks."

"It's my *job*. I take no pleasure in it."

"Well, I'm taking pleasure in this." Jaina sent the speeder rightward into a narrow thoroughfare. She dived, dropping precipitously and illegally through three different traffic levels before joining the lane nearest the surface.

All around were the lights of pedestrian walkways. In this area, an aging, run-down region where residential edifices gradually gave way to old, poorly maintained government structures, there was little traffic and few pedestrians.

To his credit, Dab didn't shriek or grab at his restraining straps. He just shook his head, resigned to the trip. "So you're going to see Jagged Fel?"

Jaina's eyes snapped wide. Having no idea of her true purpose for being here—supporting Jag, Tahiri, and Winter if they absolutely needed her—Dab thought it was a romantic liaison. And he obviously thought that Jaina must be absolutely desperate for it.

Infuriated, she tromped on the reverse thrusters, sending herself and Dab slamming forward into their restraints, as she made a sharp right-angle turn onto a side throughway.

Thrown back into his seat by normal acceleration, Dab rubbed his chest. "Ow."

"I am *not* going to see Jag—and that's Head of State Fel to you."

"Fine!"

"There's a little rooftop park up here I like."

"Of course. At this hour."

Jaina went into a steep climb, going completely vertical as she approached the wall of a particularly large residential block. Out of the corner of her eye, she could see Dab's features drawn back in a rictus brought on by acceleration.

Then she reached the top of the building. She rolled until she was level with the rooftop. She immediately set her speeder down on a broad bed of grass. It was indeed a park, with carefully arranged ponds, trees, and flower beds, fully occupying this rooftop and those of several surrounding buildings. Open-air, railed turbolifts provided access between the roofs.

Dab breathed a sigh of relief. "I get it."

"You do?"

He nodded. "You come to this run-down neighborhood in the middle of the night, dressed in anonymous brown clothes, and you walk around in the park, hoping someone will attack you so you can beat them up. That way you relieve stress and also get to take dangerous criminals in."

She stared at him. It was a brilliant excuse, and she was embarrassed that she hadn't come up with it. "You're absolutely right."

"Well, it sounds like a good thing for Jedi to be doing."

"It does, doesn't it?" She unstrapped herself and hopped out of the speeder. She gestured toward a spot where the trees were thickest. "I'm going to walk around on the path on the other side of those trees."

He unbuckled his own restraints. "I'll come with you."

"No, I'm less likely to be attacked if there are two of us."

"And I'm more likely to be attacked if there's only one of *me*."

"True." She pointed at a set of bushes away from her trees. "Hide there and wait for me." She raced off toward her trees.

This was not her favorite park, of course. It was the park atop the building where Winter had taken out quarters for the Darkmeld team. From here, she could hear the sirens of public safety vehicles far, far below as they arrived to deal with the crater that had appeared in the plaza minutes before.

Past the trees, she found the roof access to the turbolift and rode down to surface level.

Seff jumped through the hole he'd cut in the blast door and rolled to his feet in the tunnel beyond. There was the mound of debris his thermal detonator had created, and between him and it were six surprised-looking Alliance Security troopers.

Seff sighed. Of *course* they'd opened their end of the tunnel to investigate. Of *course* they'd found their way here.

Of *course* the highest-ranking trooper shouted, "Halt! Hands in the air!"

Seff raised his hands—the backs of his hands rather than his palms facing the troopers. He made a grasping gesture and yanked.

Debris, chunks of metal and permacrete, tore itself from the mound and hurtled toward him.

The troopers in the rear, hearing the noise, turned just in time to catch the sideways rain of punishing detritus in their faces and chests. The blocks of masonry and support durasteel knocked them down and kept on coming, catching the three troopers in front by surprise. One inadvertently fired as he was hit, his blast passing Seff a meter away.

Seff charged forward, kicking two troopers who were still moving. They lay still. He snatched up the blaster rifle from one and the pistol from another. He made sure both were set to stun.

His access hole was not covered by the debris, but the metal patch was back in place over it. Seff reached for it, then hesitated as a sense of unease passed over him.

Again he gestured, this time lofting a big chunk of broken permacrete right into the patch. The impact tore the patch away, folding it around the debris, and there was a crack and sizzle of electricity. A length of electrical cable now dangled in the gap.

Seff smiled. He brushed the cable away with a gesture, then leapt through the hole.

He didn't need to look around. As he straightened, he aimed the blaster rifle and fired, his stun bolt catching his target before he even registered what it looked like.

Another woman, also in close-fitting black garments, a hood concealing her features. She hit the floor with her eyes closed.

He took a moment to get his bearings. In the Force, he could feel the many life-forms out there in the tunnel and more closing from both sides. There were still more above, and those numbers were growing.

He darted for the shaft to the surface, hoping that it had not collapsed.

Chapter Twenty-three

MIRAX HORN, PILOTING A SPEEDER SHE HAD STOLEN MERE minutes before from the parking rails outside Kallad's Dream Vacation Hostel, circled a kilometer out from Armand Isard Correctional Facility, catching occasional glimpses of the flashing lights of official vehicles at the scene, of the crater that dominated the little ground-level plaza in front of the prison.

Winter hadn't told her much. It was imperative that she help the Jedi; check. It was related to her son's condition; check. It was very important that she not be identified; not just a check, but a guideline she'd followed since she was a teenager. She needed to get near and stand by; check. All of this was second nature to her. Though she largely operated on the proper side of the law these days, she was a felon's daughter, a smuggler and rebel herself. She knew how to acquire matériel when she needed it, how not to leave forensic or visual evidence. She was happy to do it, too, when she knew *why*.

"Credcoin, this is Slicer. Do you read?"

Mirax's new call-sign was Credcoin; she frowned at that, wondering if Winter thought she was all about money. The woman had practically raised the three Solo children—she must know how positively frantic Mirax was feeling about Valin, both his illness, if that's what it was, and his horrific imprisonment.

And who was Slicer? The voice, possibly female, was distorted. Mirax raised her comlink. "Slicer, Credcoin. Go."

"Our target is probably coming out of a workers' access hole right in front of the prison. It is imperative, I say again imperative, that we grab him."

"Understood." Mirax angled over to line up on the throughway leading straight to the crater. From this direction, she'd have to come in over the prison, a distinctly illegal approach, and make a steep dive down to surface level. "How do I grab him?"

"No idea. Maybe just harass him. He's armed and very, very dangerous."

"Oh, good. Who's my backup?"

"All of us, when we get there."

"Who's my backup *right now*?"

"No one."

Mirax shut up. She didn't want to ask more questions that yielded bad answers.

An Alliance Security vehicle rose into her path, broadcasting on all channels for civilian traffic to turn away from this zone. Mirax dipped her speeder and flashed by under it so close that she instinctively ducked. She was pretty sure the pilot got a good look at her, which was another thing that would let him know something wasn't right; she was wearing a sheet of transparisteel foil wrapped around her face, concealing everything but eyes and nose, visually distorting her features.

She was over the prison now. Spotlights, rising to illuminate her, almost blinded her. She could distinctly hear the alarms sounding within the structure. She put the speeder into a dive.

There was the crater, looking much like an asteroid-impact site, surrounded by official vehicles. Men and women on the ground were now mostly looking up at her. There was no sign of—

No, there he was, a tousle-haired man in a gray worker's jumpsuit, a blaster rifle in his hands, climbing unnoticed from an access hole. Mirax nodded. Her target was in sight. Now how to *get* him was the question.

Best tactic for the moment: buzz him, force him to flee, keep him moving until her backups arrived. And she'd try not to get shot in the meantime.

Leveling off just above the surface, ignoring the new spotlights being trained on her from several Alliance Security vehicles, she aimed for her target—and then her head banged against the viewport to her left as she was sideswiped from that side. Startled, suddenly dizzy, she angled off to her right, straight toward a government office building, most of its viewports dark.

She vectored hard and found herself roaring along the face of the building at a right angle to the ground, her repulsors barely keeping her from scraping along the building front; their force blew several viewports completely in. Then she was angling away from the building face and leveling off once more, rubbing her temple.

She shook her head and sent the speeder into a tight loop, heading back toward her target. What had happened?

Running toward the security cordon around the prison, now packed with pedestrians and press, Jaina saw the whole event unfold. The big civilian speeder, a garish red so unlikely for a covert operations vehicle, roared toward Seff, who was now out of the access hole. But there was another vehicle, a small, speedy flatbed cargo hauler approaching from the red speeder's port side. The pilot was visible through the front windscreen: Zilaash Kuh, the bounty hunter. Jaina swore to herself.

The cargo hauler sideswiped the speeder, knocking it off course. The hauler continued its sideslip so that it would pass over and to one side of Seff Hellin. The

Quarren, Dhidal Nyz, leaned over the side of the hauler's bed with his oversized weapon and fired at Seff.

Seff sprang to one side with the speed of an experienced Jedi, but the net expanded too wide for him. It wrapped around him as it had Jaina days before. As its connecting cable went taut, the Quarren was nearly pulled over the rail, but he was braced for the impact. Seff was yanked off his feet and hauled into the air behind the vehicle.

Jaina grimaced. Seff would be experiencing the same shocks she had. She decided she intensely disliked that Quarren.

But the cargo hauler came on straight toward her.

The red speeder was getting turned around. Jaina brought out her lightsaber and thumbed on her comlink. "Credcoin, Slicer here. Your package is in the net. Follow the package."

"Understood." Even distorted, Mirax's voice sounded irritated.

As the cargo hauler passed, not quite overhead, Jaina ignited her lightsaber and hurled it, giving it direction and velocity through the Force. Its brilliant blade intersected the metal cable, shearing through it. Jaina positioned herself underneath her plummeting weapon but transferred her telekinetic effort to Seff, slowing his descent.

Slowing his descent *some*. She didn't know how incapacitated he was by the net-weapon's electrical charges. She let him hit the permacrete fairly hard, and could hear a loud grunt from him as he landed. The cargo hauler sped on, Dhidal Nyz staring down at the two of them in surprise; then the Quarren turned and began hammering on the back of the pilot's compartment.

Jaina caught her lightsaber, switched it off, and raced to stand beside Seff, stepping on and crushing the net's power pack as she did so.

Dazed, Seff looked up at her. "Oh, not you, too."

"Sorry." She hammered the side of his head with the lightsaber hilt, a crude, inelegant blow. But it had its intended effect. Seff slumped.

Mirax's speeder settled beside her. Using the Force to augment her strength, Jaina lifted Seff and tossed him into the backseat, then leapt in beside him.

Less than a hundred meters away, official vehicles around the crater were lifting off, turning in their direction. Jaina looked at Mirax. "Is this thing fast?"

"I only steal the best."

"Go, go."

They accelerated away from the scene.

The security officer, standing beside her speeder, watched four of her fellows' vehicles take off in pursuit of the red speeder. But she must have felt some presentiment of danger. She turned, grabbing for her blaster pistol, just as Tahiri's open-palm strike connected with her chin, bypassing her helmet entirely. The trooper slammed back into the side of her speeder, then slumped to the ground.

Behind Tahiri, Jag, with Winter over his shoulder, ducked so the speeder would help conceal him from the gaze of the other security officers, but they were all looking after the fleeing speeder. Over the sound of the alarm and sirens of arriving vehicles, none had heard Tahiri's attack. "I'll drive," Jag said.

"*I'll* drive," Tahiri snapped, sliding into the pilot's seat. "You're about as maneuverable as a nerf in a child seat with all that on. I doubt you can handle the controls."

"I've flown a starfighter in this." Jag opened the back hatch and carefully slid Winter in, then followed. "Go—"

She had the speeder off the ground before he finished

his word, and turned on the lights and siren as she joined the chase. Jag managed to get his hatch shut.

Mirax glanced at Jaina. "You're Slicer?"

"What else would the Sword of the Jedi do but slice?" Jaina gestured at the bounty hunters' vehicle, which had gotten turned around and was headed their way. "Don't give them a clear line of fire at you. There's no telling what the Quarren's weapon can do."

"Right." Whether that was a confirmation or an indication of direction, Jaina didn't know, but Mirax abruptly vectored rightward, down a narrow accessway normally used by waste haulers and maintenance workers. It was a surface-level tunnel, opening to the sky each time it came to a thoroughfare. The violence of the maneuver threw Jaina across Seff's body and against the hatch on the left side. Seff remained unconscious.

Five security speeders and the bounty hunters' vehicle followed, the bounty hunters third in line.

"Running out of time." There was a shrill edge to Tahiri's words. "As soon as they get more pursuit on Jaina, this becomes a chase we can't win."

"Hoth is still out. And now we have to yank this vehicle's recorder. Since you're using real names."

"Right, sorry. If I can get you to the cargo hauler, can you disable it?"

Jag straightened up from looking at Winter. He stared over Tahiri's shoulder. They were now halfway along the accessway and accelerating. Their speeder was last in line, and it did not appear that any of the security troopers in the pursuit had realized that the last security vehicle was occupied by hostiles. "I lost my blaster. I have some knockout grenades—no, wait. Get me within reach of the underside." That was an insane thing to expect of an ordinary pilot, but Jedi tended to be no more ordinary than Jag himself.

Tahiri nodded and accelerated. She passed beneath the fourth security speeder so close to the surface that Jag could feel the repulsors pushing off from permacrete below; he could see debris at road level being kicked in all directions by their thrust wash. The next speeder forward was too low for such a maneuver, so Tahiri climbed, her vehicle's aft grazing the nose of the speeder she'd just passed. She went as high as the tunnel ceiling would allow, climbing over the speeder in front of her.

The unexpected repulsor wash kicked that speeder downward and to the left. Jag heard it scrape along the tunnel wall, and then it was behind them, rolling at surface level, sending out showers of sparks. He winced, hoping that the security troopers inside, innocent of wrongdoing in this mess, would be all right.

The bounty hunters' vehicle was directly ahead now, and the Quarren in the bed only had eyes for Mirax's speeder. Tahiri dipped again, moving up directly beneath the hauler, rising as close to it as she could against its repulsor thrust.

Jag slapped down his helmet's face shield, lowered the transparisteel in his viewport, and reached up for the speeder's underside. Repulsor thrust hammered at his arm, forcing it down. He could overcome that pressure, but still couldn't reach the vehicle's underside; it was centimeters out of his reach.

Cursing, he opened his hatch. Gripping the speeder's roof with one crushgaunt, he half stood, his knees straining as the repulsor thrust from above shoved him down.

There was a sudden flash of light as they and the other vehicles of the caravan crossed a thoroughfare, exposing them momentarily to sky and lights from traffic. Then they were in the next tunnel.

Jag got his left crushgaunt on machinery in the hauler's underbelly. He exerted himself, and the strength-augmenting servos in the gauntlet squeezed the repulsor nozzles out of recognizable shape. Next he grabbed a maneuvering thruster vent, destroying it similarly, and then there was the auxiliary energy cell—

That actually exploded as he squeezed it, a minor detonation that pelted him with little shards of metal. He felt stings in his neck and upper arms. Then smoke billowed from the area he'd damaged.

The cargo hauler slowed, dropping behind Tahiri's speeder. Jag saw the Kuh woman staring at her control console and pounding on the yoke; then she looked up and caught sight of him.

Had he been another man, he would have offered her some flippant gesture, but he was Jagged Fel, known among pilots and Jedi everywhere as the most humorless—

Come to think of it, he wasn't Jag Fel right now. He was a mystery man, and needed for his role in this affair never to be associated with Jag Fel. So he blew a kiss to Zilaash Kuh before resuming his seat and slamming the hatch shut. Kuh's vehicle dropped farther behind until it was lost in the distance.

Mirax had to shout for Jaina to hear her. "Two pursuers down."

"The next to last one is ours," Jaina shouted back. "Tahiri and Jag are in it." She got back to work, bringing out the sedative pack that all the Darkmeld conspirators on this mission were carrying. She injected Seff with its contents. This was slow work; Mirax's aerobatics with the speeder made even the simplest medical procedure next to impossible.

Finally it was done. Making sure her garment hood

was up, concealing her features, she turned away from Seff and back toward the pursuers.

Even for an experienced Jedi Knight, it took concentration to lift a speeder telekinetically, especially when its rapid movements made it a difficult target. But she found it, grasped it, and shoved it sideways—gently but irresistibly. Its right side ground into the tunnel wall, abrading the metal there, filling the vehicle's main compartment with sparks and smoke. Suddenly the pilot was decelerating, descending, in a frantic effort to retain control of his vehicle.

She did the same with the next vehicle, and then, as Tahiri closed, with the last vehicle in the caravan.

Suddenly there was no enemy pursuit. Tahiri switched her lights and siren off.

Jaina, more familiar with Coruscant than most of the others, navigated, guiding Mirax to a shadowy nook off a major thoroughfare. The two speeders settled there in the darkness.

Jag took a moment to yank the security speeder's recording device and crush it beyond any possible retrieval of data. Then the five conspirators gathered. Winter, though groggy, her reflexes shot, was at least awake again.

"All right." Jaina looked at each of the others—confused but resolute Mirax, sweaty but confident Jag, relieved Tahiri, pale but smiling Winter. "We're almost done. Mirax, you'll come with me. We need to steal another speeder, then pick up the rest. Then you'll drop me on a specific rooftop not far from where all that mess took place. Jag, do you need to get back to the Imperial Remnant embassy?"

"Galactic Empire. And yes."

"All right. Drop Jag off near there. Then, Tahiri, I need you to guide Mirax to the Masters' speeder hangar access at the Temple. Tekli will get you in."

While Jaina and Mirax were gone, Winter removed forensic evidence from the security speeder and Mirax's stolen red vehicle. Jag pulled off all his armor, dressing once more in the now ridiculously large black tunic. After Jaina and Mirax returned with the new acquisition, a sturdy yellow hard-top speeder with enough room for two adults, eight younglings, and a Wookiee, Jag stored his armor in its cargo compartment, along with the Quarren's net and incriminating items of clothing. Stripped of armor, he once again became a well-muscled man of normal size.

Jaina gave him one last, worried look. "Not too many non-Mandos have *beskar* breastplates and crushgaunts. The fact that you do isn't well known, but—"

He put a finger on her lips to shush her. "There's nothing to worry about. I have an alibi. Like all sensible Heads of State, I have a double, hard at work pretending to be me back in my quarters."

She moved his finger aside. "My mother didn't use a double."

"Well, she was clearly crazy."

That drew a short laugh from Winter. The others looked at her.

Winter indicated herself, Jaina, and Jag. "That sounds like a toast for all our families. Here's to crazy women, and the pilots who pursue them."

Jag raised an imaginary glass in her direction.

Chapter Twenty-four

BEN WASN'T GLASSY-EYED, BUT HE WANTED TO BE. HOURS of using pickaxes to hack away at living rock had tired and infuriated him. In theory, he and Luke were doing this to carve out their permanent quarters in the residential gallery, a process that would take years; in truth, Ben knew they wouldn't be here anywhere near that long, which meant that every blow with the pickax was a wasted one.

But now, work done for the day, after a sanisteam, dressed in fresh clothes—even if they were the horribly dull robes worn by everyone in these caverns—Ben felt a little better as he and his father walked to their audience with the Hidden One.

Ben glanced at his father. "So, what's your strategy?"

Luke frowned, puzzled. "Strategy?"

"To convince him to let us out of this hole."

"Ben, what's our objective here?"

"To get out!"

"The objective that brought us to Dorin in the first place."

"Oh. To find out about Jacen."

"If we were to march in there and demand our release, and he agreed and somehow magically transported us to the surface, we would have failed in achieving that objective."

"Well, yeah. Ultimately it's the more important one."

"Ultimately, yes. But since we're under no time pressure, let's handle things in a logical order."

Ben let out a sigh.

They left the main corridor and entered the communal dining hall, which was all but empty at this midpoint hour between afternoon and evening servings. It was not that large a chamber; there were fewer than fifty Kel Dors in these caverns, and the hall could accommodate all of them. Tables and benches meticulously cut out of stone and sanded into straight, clean lines were arrayed in neat ranks for the diners, flanked by matched stone benches.

The Hidden One sat alone at the nearest table. He nodded at the Skywalkers as they entered.

The informality bothered Ben. The Hidden One was effectively a king, though his kingdom was tiny, and yet he was not accompanied by advisers for an important meeting with a fellow Master.

Luke seated himself opposite the Hidden One. "Thank you for seeing us."

Ben slid into place beside his father.

The Hidden One offered a toothless smile. "It is no inconvenience. The opportunity to talk with those fresh from the surface world is one of our few pleasures. As I understand it, you wanted to know about Jacen Solo."

"Yes."

"He came here—that is, to the temple in Dor'shan—about nine years ago, very full of life, very sure of himself. He wanted knowledge of the Force, especially as it was understood by those outside his Order."

"Did you see any sign in him . . ." Luke paused to consider his phrasing. "Of what he was to become?"

"I think there were scars on his spirit, but they seemed

to be well healed. From my many conversations with him, I concluded that his childhood had been an unsettled one, and that he had severed himself from much of it, as though it were dead flesh that needed to be cut away lest it endanger his life." He looked at Ben. "You are his cousin, no? Is it the same with you?"

Ben shook his head. "You're not going to have a normal childhood in this family, and I guess I have some things in common with Jacen. Separated from our parents for long stretches. I was tortured, too, but not as long as Jacen was." He saw his father suppress a wince. "I don't know if, when I get to be Jacen's age, I'll want to cast my childhood off, but I don't think so. If only because, if he did, he's a bad example to follow."

"Interesting."

Luke continued, "And you taught him the lightning-rod techniques."

"First, I taught him techniques of weather anticipation and the ability to sense energy piling up in the natural world. You can feel heat in the water in the seas, heat that will become cyclonic storms, for instance. But he heard rumor of the lightning-rod techniques and asked about them."

"Did he teach you anything?"

"I trained against him in combat."

Luke's eyebrows rose. "You're one of the Baran Do with combat training?"

"I am. In life, I was the teacher of Charsae Saal, who is now Chara. The Baran Do who study combat train mostly in unarmed and staff combat, and I was interested in learning to defend against the lightsaber."

"What was your conclusion there?"

"The lightsaber is a weapon of the Force and, if you are not similarly armed, must be countered with the Force."

Luke nodded in agreement. "Did you have any sense

of a problem Jacen might have been dealing with, an overriding fear or concern?"

"No. I think he was a man at peace. I would not say he was *happy*—but he was at peace."

Luke sat back to think.

Ben asked, "When he left Dorin, did he say or give any indication as to where he was going next?"

"No, I believe not." The Hidden One's eyes looked back through the years. "He had been talking about returning to Coruscant. I think his search for knowledge was finished for the time being. But there was something . . . One day he asked me what I knew about places where the energies of the Force concentrate and linger, though there is no indication as to why they do so."

Luke sat forward again. "I trained in one such place. A nexus of Force energy on a small swamp world."

"Late in his stay, he evidenced a sudden interest in such things. I believe he had found something in his studies of written materials, though not ours—perhaps something he had brought along from one of his other stops."

"But he mentioned no names or places."

"No."

Luke glanced at his son. "That's about it for me. Does anything else occur to you?"

"Well, on another subject."

"Go ahead."

Ben looked the Hidden One square in the eye. "Are you going to kill the Jedi who come looking for me and my dad?"

The Hidden One's eyes widened. "*Kill* them? That is not what we do."

"But they will come. And when they don't get answers that help them, they'll send someone like Master Horn, who's trained in investigation. He'll figure things out. So my question is, how many are you going to kill in order to keep your little secret?"

"*This is not a little secret.*" The Hidden One seemed almost embarrassed by his outburst; he looked back and forth to see if anyone had witnessed it, then returned his attention to Ben. He leaned forward. "This is the seed of the Baran Do, the seed that must take root if the Order itself dies. You have never lived in a time when the threat of extinction of an entire way of life was very real—"

Ben laughed outright. "I was born halfway through the Yuuzhan Vong War. Remember that? Maybe, as far out as you are, you didn't hear much about it. Some of my earliest memories are of hiding, surrounded by darkness, knowing that if we were found we'd be wiped out. Here I am again, same situation." He gestured at the gray-black stone walls of the chamber. "People are still afraid of it, afraid of annihilation by some unknown enemy. War trauma. Civilians and soldiers both get it. I think it's what you've got."

"You little larva." The Hidden One was almost spitting in his anger. "Are you too stupid to realize that you Jedi are facing a new purge?"

Ben gave him a scornful look.

"There's the arrogance of youth." The Hidden One turned to Luke. "Surely you know better. You're about to experience another purge. If you're unprepared for it, the Jedi may wink out once again, this time forever."

Luke shook his head. "I don't think so. I've dealt with Chief of State Daala directly. She has no agenda of destruction."

"*She* has none, perhaps. What of her subordinates? What of her military planners, all of whom came to power in the wake of a war made so much more horrible by a *Jedi*? Recent history is not unknown to me; we get the holonews feeds here." The Hidden One began counting off on his fingers. "One, the leader of the Jedi

Order, once immensely popular, is discredited. The Jedi Order is weakened. Two, he is sent off into exile, depriving the Order of his strength and wisdom. The Order is weakened again. Three, each Jedi is accompanied by an observer who tells the government where he or she is at every moment. The Jedi are suddenly more vulnerable to a mass attack, a mass extermination. How soon before the Jedi are wearing tracking devices? How long before they are implanted with explosives? All in the name of Alliance safety?"

Luke gave him a flat, hard stare. "You're wrong."

"*You're* wrong! You have made your own Order vulnerable. The fate of the Jedi now rests with leaders who are weaker and less experienced than you. That decline will continue until the Order is locked in a hopeless struggle with its government and all but helpless. Then it will die again."

Ben smiled at him, a scornful smile. "And do you oppose the destruction of the Jedi Order?"

"Of course I do!"

"Even though you're helping it along by keeping us prisoner."

The Hidden One stood, and Ben thought for a moment that the Kel Dor would attack him. Then the Hidden One stepped away and departed, walking so fast that his robes whirled around him.

When he was gone, Luke gave Ben a look of mild reproach. "You really need to work on your adolescent confrontational impulses."

"That wasn't adolescent, Dad. It was an *investigational* impulse."

Luke looked quizzical. "It's true, you're not demonstrating the emotions I'd expect of a testy sixteen-year-old."

"Questioning can't always be polite and courteous, Dad. I learned that from Lon Shevu. At a certain point, you *push* and you see how they respond." He gestured in the direction the Hidden One had taken. "And what did he react to? Enemies. The Alliance government possibly destroying the Jedi. The Jedi looking for us and possibly finding him. Everyone's out to get him, Dad."

"In other words, he's paranoid."

"At least. He might even be crazier than a piranha-beetle with a pin through its head."

"Possibly. The problem . . ." Luke thought about it. "The problem is, he may also be right. The Jedi Order is vulnerable, and it may be in genuine danger."

"We need to see if we can reach Jaina or Aunt Leia through the Force."

Luke shook his head. "I tried, last night, several times. There's some interference here . . . either the first Hidden One chose this spot very well, because it naturally concealed his followers from searchers using the Force, or the Baran Do have perfected some technique that accomplishes the same thing. Either way, contact seems unlikely. We're on our own."

UNDERGROUND ACCESS SHAFT, KESSEL

"Mission control to Rogue. Report. Over."

Wedge, hovering in his X-wing only a few meters from the new shaft in the chalk-white soil ahead of him, activated his helmet mike. "Rogue here. I'm getting too old for this."

"Copy that, too old." Koyi Komad, Nrin Vakil's Twi'lek wife, acting as mission control, sounded amused. "Begin your decline."

"You mean *descent*." Wedge eased his X-wing forward until he was directly over the shaft. Other starfighters ringed the shaft at the same altitude; their pilots were waiting for similar authorization from Koyi.

Wedge reduced power on his repulsors and began to descend. In moments he was surrounded by stone wall, so recently drilled that his repulsor wash constantly kicked dust and pebbles free. He activated his landing floods so he could lean to either side and see through the canopy into the depths below.

Over his comm board came the next exchange: "Mission control to Homegirl, report."

"Control, Homegirl." Inyri Forge sounded crisp and alert, not affecting the unconcerned drawl that so many retired pilots including Wedge, did. "Everything's in the green."

"Homegirl, start your descent."

It was a quick two kilometers down for Wedge; he spent it listening to the others reporting and being issued their go orders. There was no diminishment of comm signal strength, as Lando's crews had situated communications repeater units in the tunnels. Wedge had been warned that the farther away from the entry point he ventured, the more likely it became that signal strength would periodically wane or be lost; Lando's crews had not had the time or resources to saturate these tunnels with the repeaters.

At the bottom of the shaft, Wedge found himself in a broad, high-vaulted tunnel as straight as a proton torpedo's trajectory. He consulted his navigation screen, brought his X-wing around to starboard, and kicked in the thrusters.

Of course, in this environment, a starfighter would not ridiculously outclass an ordinary speeder in velocity. They couldn't afford full starfighter speed in a place where sudden turns, debris, and even dangerous lifeforms might pop up every kilometer or two. But with high explosives and Han's anecdotal energy spiders around, he'd much prefer to be surrounded by composite armor and shields than a thin durasteel carapace.

He followed the route indicated on his nav board, a dotted line that led him far away from the entry point. Each pilot would be doing the same, heading off to a distant start point widely separated from the others. Then each would begin an even more complicated route back, dropping a lethal demolition package in each cavern he or she visited. Pilots would be making rearming stops, too; Wedge's X-wing could only carry a total of six missiles, so he'd be making one or two such stops.

Wedge felt the old familiar tightening of his gut and shoulders. This wasn't a combat mission, but people could die . . . and if they failed, a world would perish.

Han and Leia, in the cockpit of the *Falcon,* watched the last starfighter, Nrin Vakil's A-wing, begin its descent. The *Falcon* would be up next. Han turned to look over his shoulder at Allana, who was in the rear seat. "All strapped in, kid?"

Allana nodded, solemn.

"As am I," C-3PO assured him from beside Allana. "I assume your failure to ask the same of me means that you assumed I would be properly restrained."

Han turned forward again. "You should always be properly restrained, Goldenrod."

"I'm sorry, sir?"

Leia shot Han a reproachful look. "Han means you should always be safe, Threepio."

"Obviously what I meant." Han tapped a button on his comm board. "You secure, Artoo?"

An affirmative whistle emerged from the speakers. R2-D2 was back in the engineering space, ready to deal with any mechanical problems that might occur.

"*Millennium Falcon,* this is mission control. Report status."

"We're having a party here," Han reported, prompting a giggle from Allana. "How about you?"

"Wishing I were. You are cleared to go."

Han eased forward, then began a careful descent. The hole dug for this purpose, spacious by starfighter standards, barely accommodated the *Falcon* or the two ships to follow. Han cautiously eyed the distance-to-obstacles readouts as he descended.

But soon enough he was at bottom level again and taking a route that would gradually lead the *Falcon* to the southeast.

The first several caverns went without incident for Wedge. He'd hovered in the entryway to a cavern, armed his proton torpedo system, taken careful aim at the explosives mound in the center, and fired. The missile, with its comparatively inexpensive thermal detonator warhead instead of an expensive, ship-crippling proton torpedo, had flashed across the intervening space and buried itself in the ground a few meters from the mound. Within moments, sparkly balls of light, bogeys, had arrived from floor or ceiling or distant banks of machinery. Wedge had turned away and kicked in his thrusters, and that was it.

Approaching his fifth cavern, Wedge saw its entrance tunnel alive with animals—centipedes especially, and one big crimson spider. They were fleeing, some of them attacking one another as they went. He nodded; one of the speeders with a sonic unit had recently been here and accomplished its mission. He approached this cavern cautiously; the speeder's presence might have stirred up bogeys here, and he'd hate to have one knock out his starfighter's systems, even temporarily. But as he reached the cavern entrance, there were no bogeys in sight, and only a couple showing up on the X-wing's sensors; they seemed to be at the cavern's far entrance.

Wedge hovered, fired his payload, and turned away.

There was a *clunk* from immediately above and

Wedge jumped as a green centipede, a meter long, suddenly appeared on the canopy over his face. The creature coiled and struck, its tail-end stinger hammering the transparisteel.

It did not penetrate. Several cubic centimeters of black liquid that had to be venom oozed out over the canopy. The centipede struck again and again, the successive strikes accompanied by decreasing amounts of venom.

"Sorry, little guy." Wedge eased his starfighter forward. "Nothing for you to eat here."

Wedge's astromech tweetled at him from behind, barely audible through the canopy but easy to hear through the X-wing's comm system. Wedge checked the comm board translation output to make sure he'd understood. "That's right, Roll-On. One more missile and we have to rearm."

The centipede, responding to either the R2 unit's noise or the rotation of its head, scrabbled its way aft over the canopy toward the droid. Dividing his attention between the tunnel ahead and what was transpiring behind, Wedge watched its progress.

The creature came within half a meter of Roll-On and stopped there, raising its tail to strike.

A small panel on the astromech's front opened. A probe extended and touched the centipede. There was a faint *zatt* noise and a flash of blue as an electrical charge hit the insect. The centipede spasmed and, stunned, fell off the X-wing. Roll-On retracted its lead and shut the panel.

Wedge grinned. With luck, that would be the most dangerous enemy action he'd have to face today.

Later, at a tunnel intersection broad enough to be considered a cavern itself, Wedge set his X-wing down beside two other vehicles.

One was a cargo speeder with a long bed loaded with

plastic crating. In his career, Wedge had seen more of those crates than he could possibly remember. Each held six or eight proton torpedoes. Unloading one crate were a sandy-haired young man, who spared a smile and a wave for Wedge, and a loader droid half again the height of its human partner, its bulky frame designed for lifting strength and slow movement.

Nearby sat the operation's sole Eta-5 interceptor. Its body was similar to that of an A-wing, sleek and wedge-shaped, but extending port and starboard from the fuse-lage were struts to which inwardly curved solar wing arrays, like those of the old Eta-2, were attached. The starfighter was painted a deep blue but carried no planetary or other service markings.

Leaning against it was its pilot, Rhysati Ynr, a lean, blond woman dressed in a black variation on the A-wing pilot's uniform. She pushed herself away from the hull and walked to the X-wing as soon as Wedge popped his canopy. "Awake yet, General?"

"Reluctantly."

"This'll wake you up." Rhysati turned back toward the young man handling her missile rearmament. "Hey, kid, come over here and introduce yourself."

Obliging, the teenager trotted over. He was compact of frame and wore a tan jumpsuit. He extended a hand up to Wedge. "Good morning, sir. I'm Drathan Forge."

Wedge shook his head and raised an eyebrow. "*Forge.* Inyri's nephew?"

"Great-nephew, actually."

"And you work for Lando?"

"For now. Mostly as a mechanic. But I'm a good flier. I've put in an application to the academy. I have provisional acceptance. I have to keep my grades up for the next year."

"Good luck with that."

The loader droid straightened from the Eta-5 and

turned its inverted-triangle head toward Drathan. "Twelve missiles loaded and reporting online." Its voice rang metallically.

"All right." The young man gestured at the X-wing. "Let's prep six proton formats for this one." With a half salute for Wedge, he headed back to resume his work.

Wedge returned his attention to Rhysati. "How's Nawara?"

"Wishing he were here with me. If he weren't trying to dig the Jedi out of a legal hole, he'd be flying *something* on this operation."

Wedge gestured at her interceptor. "Looks fast."

"You've never flown one?"

He shook his head. "I've done some simulator work, but never actually been in one. My daughter Syal flew them."

"You want to trade for the rest of the operation?"

Wedge blinked. "What, in the middle of a mission?"

"Sure. This isn't the armed forces, Wedge. It's more like a heavily armed bachelor party. What's Lando going to do to us if we trade?"

Wedge scrambled out of his cockpit. He knew it was an unseemly spectacle for a retired officer. On the other hand, it was no longer his job to set a good example.

Chapter Twenty-five

TAHIRI AND MIRAX CARRIED SEFF BETWEEN THEM, HIS arms over their shoulders as though he were a drunk comrade; he was not heavily built and they were strong women, so it was his awkwardness rather than his weight that posed the greatest problem. Tekli preceded them, and Winter followed behind.

They hauled the unconscious Jedi through the darkened speeder hangar, trying to keep themselves as calm and centered as possible; other Jedi, especially the Masters whose hangar this was, were more likely to sense distress. But no one met them in the corridor outside the hangar, and no one approached them as they made their way to the nearest turbolift.

As they neared the lift, it hummed with the sound of an arriving car. Tahiri and Mirax got Seff spun around and made it with Winter and Tekli to a darkened nook before the turbolift door opened.

Tekli peered into the hall and breathed a sigh of relief. She motioned the others forward. They stepped out again and saw that it was Jaina awaiting them at the lift.

"Any problems with your observer?" Tahiri asked. They moved into the lift car.

"No. He sympathized with me for not catching any petty criminals tonight." Jaina blinked, affecting an expression of innocence. "It looks like my night's outing was a complete failure."

Tekli addressed the turbolift controls: "Second medical level."

The lower medical level was a solemn, quiet area of bare walls and windowless doors—not too different, Tahiri reflected, from the prison she'd just visited.

At the back of one medical supplies storage chamber was a door marked RADIOACTIVE MATERIALS. AUTHORIZED ACCESS ONLY. The door had a security pad beside it. Tekli tapped in the access code. "Master Cilghal and I are the only ones authorized to enter. Even Master Hamner must come to us. This is the lesser of two radiation storage chambers. I've moved all the materials that belong here into the primary chamber." The door slid open, and they moved through into a small outer chamber; inset in the right wall was a swing-out door as thick as a blast door. Through it was another chamber, this one set up with a heavy patient bed and a bank of monitoring equipment.

In minutes, they had Seff strapped down to the bed and hooked up to the monitors. Finally Jaina could breathe a sigh of relief; this mission was done, and now the Jedi could begin to benefit from the knowledge Seff might provide. She turned to Tekli. "You're all right here?"

"Fine, fine."

"Everybody, come on up to the main level. You can get cleaned up—plenty of extra clothes around—and grab a cup of caf. Rest for a few minutes."

Mirax shook her head. "Have to get back to our quarters. There's no telling when Corran will be back."

Winter looked regretful, too. "I wish I could."

Jaina sighed. "I'll get you back out through the same hangar you came in by. No worries. Tahiri?"

Tahiri appeared dubious. "I don't know. There are plenty of Jedi who don't remember me fondly—"

"And they should know that you and I are on good terms. It'll make them think about things." Jaina's tone was firm. "Come on."

"All right."

Fresh from a sanisteam and in clean garments, Jaina and Tahiri nursed fresh cups of caf and talked, their voices low. At this hour of night, the common dining hall was all but unoccupied, with the banks of overhead glow rods along the walls switched off, leaving only those in the center of the ceiling still shining. It was a restful place, particularly after the events of less than an hour earlier. Tahiri looked around, her expression wistful.

"You miss it?"

Tahiri nodded.

"Then come back."

Tahiri shook her head. "No. Not yet, anyway . . . Have you suddenly acquired the Luke Skywalker urge to save everybody, one person at a time?"

"Better than the Darth Vader urge to make the galaxy a better place by destroying everything that doesn't behave."

"True. Jacen had enough of that for both of you."

A man entering the dining hall paused in the shadows by the main doorway, then headed their way. As he emerged from the darkness, Jaina saw that it was Dab.

He waved as he approached. "Jedi Solo. You couldn't sleep, either?"

"That's it. Dab, you remember Tahiri Veila."

"Do I ever." Reaching their table, he extended a hand toward Tahiri. "Good to see you again. You probably don't remember me. From Borleias. Dab Hantaq."

From the corner of her eye, Jaina caught Tahiri's sudden stillness. She turned to see Tahiri frozen in place, her caf cup halfway to her lip. Her eyes were wide, her expression as stunned as if she'd just shot herself while cleaning her blaster.

And then Jaina realized why. Inwardly, she cringed. She made her voice very gentle. "Tahiri, you knew him as Tarc. Remember little Tarc?"

"Tarc," Tahiri repeated. "Little Tarc. Yes, of course." Her voice was almost mechanical.

Dab dropped his hand to his side. "Would you two care for company?"

Jaina shook her head. "Girl talk. Sorry."

"Understood. Good night, ladies." Dab turned and headed off in search of the caf cart.

Slowly, Tahiri set her cup down. "He's . . . he's *Anakin*."

Jaina nodded. "Remember, that's why Senator Shesh chose him all those years ago. A distraction because of the way he looked."

"You could have *told* me."

"I had gotten used to it. I wasn't even thinking about it when I put the Darkmeld team together. I forgot. I'm sorry."

"Forgot. I spent months getting myself addicted to seeing him, Anakin, and then a couple of years trying to get over it. And, boom, he's here." Tahiri was pale and she shook as if with cold. "And you want me to come back? With him here every day?"

"The observers won't be here forever. Nawara Ven says that the High Court is leaning toward reviewing the whole executive order about the Jedi. If they do, they're sure to strike down most of its provisions, including the observers—"

"That's not the luck I deserve, and it's not what I'll get." Tahiri's expression turned bleak. "I'll come back, and they'll give me *him* as an observer. That's what will happen."

Desperate to wrench Tahiri's attention from the man who looked like the long-dead love of her life, Jaina flailed through memories of the night's events. "Your lightsaber."

"What?"

"You lost your lightsaber at the prison."

Tahiri nodded, confused.

"If they find it . . ."

"Oh." With a visible act of will, Tahiri yanked her thoughts away from Dab. "I don't think it will be a problem."

"Why not?"

"It's probably crushed under tons of rock. It may never be found. If it is . . . well, it's new. I didn't want to use my old Jedi lightsaber anymore. I just built that one. The hilt design won't have been recorded anywhere. I was wearing gloves tonight, so no fingerprints. And non-conductive gloves when I was assembling it, so no prints inside."

"Good."

"But Jag lost his blaster at the same time—"

"Also not a problem. That model is custom-built for him. Big enough for him to hold with his gauntlets on. Unless he throws a switch on the butt, if it's separated from him for more than a certain number of seconds, it blows up."

"That's strange. Your boyfriend's strange."

"I know."

Tahiri's gaze wandered over to where Dab now sat, alone at one long table, peering into the tiny playback screen of his holocam, doubtless reviewing recent recordings. She stood. "I have to go."

"Tahiri, I don't think you ought to be out on the streets and walkways the way you're—"

"Let me know when he's gone forever." Tahiri whirled away and left the dining hall at a run.

UNDERGROUND COMPLEX, KESSEL

It was hours into the mission, and its organizers could begin to relax.

Demolition mounds all through the gigantic cavern-and-tunnel complex had been detonating on schedule. Mission control, Koyi Komad, monitoring events from low planetary orbit in the Imperial-era mobile command post Lando and Tendra had overhauled for this operation, reported that the resulting tremors were doing what they were supposed to—taking place, waning, and then subsiding, doing only the damage to be expected of individual groundquakes. The precise sequence of detonations was not permitting overlapping ground-shakes to reinforce one another, and sensors in the Great Kessel Fault running along the planetary axis reported no undue motion, no dangerous stress.

The *Falcon,* having fired its last refitted missile into its last target cavern, sat on a tunnel floor only a few kilometers from the exit shaft.

Leia gave Han a curious look. "We really can leave now."

"True."

"Any reason we're not?"

"I'm going to be the last one out." Han knew that he sounded stubborn, maybe even sulky, rather than determined, but he didn't care. He'd demonstrated far too much nervousness about the underworld of Kessel, and he was determined to show himself and the planet that he wasn't driven by fear.

Leia glanced back over her shoulder. "Actually, technically, since Allana's in the seat behind us, *she's* going to be the last one out."

"I *should* be the last one out." Allana's voice was decisive. "I got to be the last one to shoot a missile."

Leia smiled. "You sure did, kid."

"Control to *Falcon,* come in."

"*Falcon* here." This was, Han hoped, the announcement that all other vehicles were out, and that the only thing left to do was stay clear of the planet's surface until the explosion sequence had run its course.

"Rearmament Team Epsilon is offline and not reporting in. Suspected bogey encounter. You're the closest vehicle with rescue capabilities—our last rescue speeder is bringing a stranded subsonics pilot out now. Can you investigate?"

"Absolutely. Let's have the coordinates." As Han watched, both a set of XYZ coordinates based on Kessel's master map and a dotted-line navigational diagram based on the caverns map appeared on his nav console. "Got it, thanks."

"Control out."

Han brought the *Falcon*'s repulsors up and gently lifted the transport from the rocky tunnel floor.

Leia leaned over to give the navigational diagram a look. "Not very far. He must have been on his way out."

"Well, let's make sure he gets there."

Their route led them through the cavern they'd seen destroyed before their original escape from the complex. Most of the life there had been lost by the explosion, so the cavern was dim, very little of the phosphorescent fungi on the ceiling remaining.

Once past the far entrance to the cavern, they progressed barely a kilometer into the connecting tunnel before they saw Epsilon. A human man, young and sandy-haired, he ran toward them as fast as his clearly exhausted legs would carry him, frantically waving at the *Falcon* as he came. He was alone and carried no equipment.

Leia unstrapped from her seat. "I'll get him at the boarding ramp." She hurried aft as Han gently set the *Falcon* down as close to the running man as he dared. While the transport settled, Han heard the whir of the ramp descending. "Hey, Goldenrod, give up your seat for our new passenger. You can join Artoo aft."

"Yes, sir. If I must, sir." C-3PO unstrapped and awkwardly eased past Allana, then hurried aft.

"Rogue to *Falcon,* come in."

"*Falcon* here, Wedge."

"Are you on that rescue call? My exit route takes me out right past that spot, so I'm inbound. I can stand by your retrieval targets until you get there."

"No, thanks, we're already on station." Han heard the ramp lift into position. "Lifting off in about ten seconds."

"No worries, then. Rogue out."

There was a clatter of feet on deck plates, and Leia and their new passenger entered the cockpit. Han spared the young man a look. He was drenched with sweat and gasping so hard for breath that he was almost sobbing. "What happened to you, kid?"

The young man dropped into C-3PO's seat, his chest heaving. "Ran."

"Where's your partner?"

"Destroyed. We need to *go.*"

Suddenly uneasy, Han lifted off and spun the *Falcon* around. "Destroyed by what?"

"Energy spider."

Han's breath caught for a moment. He kicked in the thrusters and accelerated along their exit route. "Tell me you mean one of the new ones, the red ones."

"No, one of the blue ones."

A chill of apprehension climbed Han's spine. "Not good. You said *destroyed,* not *killed.* Your partner was a droid?"

"Loader droid. We'd been hearing this skittering noise at our last station. We took off for our exit, but we ran into a bogey—literally—which killed our speeder and our lights, except for pocket glow lamps. The skittering got closer, and then we saw it." Han couldn't see the young man shudder, but he didn't have to; the reaction carried into the young man's voice. "Jayfor told me to run for it. He charged at the spider. Last I saw, it had him all wrapped up and the lights in his eyes were going dark . . ."

"Yeah." Han put on a bit more speed.

His sensor board alerted him to a new contact. He glanced at it and saw a distant blip behind, rapidly over-taking them. For a moment he had the sudden fear that energy spiders could now outrun the *Falcon,* but the sensor board presented the pursuer's transceiver code as Rogue.

"Wedge, this is Han. You're probably already past it, but there's an energy spider back your way somewhere. Stay alert."

"Haven't seen it. Saw a crashed hauler and a mangled lifter droid. I think it was the same one Drathan Forge was with."

Han glanced back and saw the name FORGE on the breast of the boy's jumpsuit. "It was, but the kid's all right. Just keep your eyes open."

"Will do."

Leia finished buckling herself into the copilot's seat. "You any relation to Inyri Forge?"

"She's my great-aunt."

The *Falcon* roared through the ruined cavern and into the tunnel beyond. As they exited the cavern, in his rear holocam display Han could see Wedge's borrowed Eta-5 entering the cavern at the far end and following.

"Han, this is Wedge. I see your spider."

"Where?"

"On your—"

An insectile leg, like hollow transparisteel filled with a sparkling dark blue beverage, came down onto the cockpit viewport from above and behind.

"—top hull."

Han jumped. The reflex action might have carried him clear out of his seat but for his restraint straps. Allana screamed, a high-pitched peal that went on and on. Drathan said a word that, had Han's entire universe not been focused on the blue leg, he would have wished Allana hadn't heard.

The spider had to have come up on the *Falcon* along the tunnel ceiling. The creatures absorbed energy; they soaked up anything active sensors had to throw at them and could not be detected by such devices. They were nature's perfect predators . . . and now one of them was in reach of his *family*.

Almost numb with shock but operating on years of training, Han flipped on his energy deflectors and scanned his weapons board. Concussion missiles all gone. Lasers at full power—no, the power flow wavered just for a moment, then spiked back to normal. Ground buzzer antipersonnel blaster operational. But nothing could be brought to bear against the spider; the top quad-linked lasers could not depress far enough to hit something clinging to the top hull.

Allana continued screaming, despite Leia's efforts to hush her. Leia's eyes were on the viewport above, and her hand was on her lightsaber. Han wanted to shout, *That won't work, the thing will absorb it and then all of us,* but he was too busy. The deflectors were not coming up, despite the fact that their generators all indicated they were in the green.

Of *course* they weren't coming up. The energy spider was drinking in every bit of energy in its vicinity. And now the thruster engines skipped, a miss of less than half a second's duration, but long enough for Han to feel that his heart had stopped for the same amount of time.

The deflector shields weren't doing a bit of good—

Not true. They were still running: if they hadn't been, the spider would have been draining energy right out of the occupants of the cockpit, or straight from the engines, or both. Han glanced at Leia. "Increase power to the shields. Give them everything you can."

She leaned over her controls. "Tell me you have some plan in addition to 'more power to the shields.' "

"When I do, I'll tell you."

Allana continued to scream.

The spider leg raised, then hammered down again. It was joined by another, this one featuring a ferocious-looking backspike with a serrated edge.

Even over the sounds of Allana's wail, C-3PO's voice carried from the transport's aft sections. "I say, sir, I'm not quite strapped in yet—"

They reached a tunnel intersection. Han vectored to port, a hard turn. Being slammed sideways in her restraints cut off Allana's breath for a moment. Han could hear another cry from the rear: "I sayyyyyy—" followed by a crash of a droid into duralloy bulkhead.

On the sensor board, the blip representing Wedge's interceptor was close, and his voice came across the comm board: "Han, I have a shot."

Those words sent a new kind of chill down Han's spine. A shot from the interceptor's twin lasers, missing the spider and hitting a ship's hull unprotected by shields, could punch straight through. And the spider was on top of the cockpit pod.

On the other hand, Wedge knew that.

"Take your shot."

The tunnel walls lit up red all around them. The *Falcon*'s diagnostics reported no new damage. The energy spider's legs kept hammering—and now it heaved itself

farther forward, its multifaceted eyes at the aft edge of
the viewport, peering down at the living treats within
the cockpit. Allana resumed her screams.

"No effect." Wedge's voice sounded as impressed as it
did annoyed. "Swallowed up the entire blast. It's like firing into a Yuuzhan Vong coralskipper void."

"Great." Ahead, Han could see a shaft of brightness
stretching from floor to ceiling—sunlight entering
through the operation's access shaft. "Going up,
Wedge."

"I'm on your tail."

The *Falcon* took the right-angle turn into the climb
like the finely tuned ship not everyone admitted she was.
Han could see a circle of sunlight, their exit point, far
above. The blows of the energy spider continued to rain
down on the cockpit viewport.

And Han saw, finally, the effect the monstrous creature's attacks were having on his beloved craft.

None.

No cracks had appeared on the transparisteel. The
viewports were not being kicked free of their housing.

Even without the shields operating, the *Falcon* was
sustaining no damage.

Something eased in Han's chest, like a durasteel spring
under tension suddenly snapping free.

The *Millennium Falcon* shot out into sunlight toward
the pallid pink sky above. Han rolled her over upright.

Things were different than they had been three
decades earlier. Han Solo wasn't a prisoner, running for
his life from a creature far larger, far deadlier than he
was. Behind the controls of the *Falcon*, he *was* the *Falcon*. As Han had once been nothing but a bit of food,
the fearsome energy spider was nothing but a bit of
trouble.

Two seconds later, Wedge's interceptor shot up from
the shaft entrance and instantly leveled off in the *Fal-*

con's wake. Wedge brought his starfighter above the *Falcon,* remaining close for further laserfire attempts. The sensor board showed more starfighters and *Lady Luck* headed his way.

Han grinned, happy as a little kid. "Wedge, break off."

"What?"

"Break off. The situation is under control."

"If you say so." The interceptor climbed, dropping behind as it did so. Clearly, to Wedge, *break off* meant "be prepared to return at any moment and open fire."

Han looked back. Drathan Forge had his arms around Allana, shielding her, though his eyes were as big and as frightened as hers, and fixed as hers were on the monster above. "Al—Amelia." Han's voice was now calm and strong enough that not only did the little girl grow quiet, but Leia gave her husband a curious look. Drathan, too, tore his gaze away from the unwanted passenger above.

"Yes?" Allana replied.

"We're going to be all right," Han assured her. His voice was, even to his own ears, oddly calm.

The energy spider heaved itself farther forward, even against the tremendous wind force generated by the *Falcon*'s speedy passage through the air. Now it opened its mandibles. Bluish fluid sprayed from its mouth, splashing across the top part of the viewport.

Han turned forward again. He sent the *Falcon* into a wide, easy loop back toward the shaft. "That's pure spice, Amelia. Notice the way it sparkles in the direct sunlight. It's being activated and used up."

"Its legs are doing the same thing." The little girl still sounded frightened, but she was finding some comfort in being analytical.

"That's right. If it were to stay out in the sunlight for too long, I think it would probably die. Leia, stand by to reverse inertial compensators. Everybody, be prepared to get thrown into your restraints." He raised his voice. "That means you, too, Artoo, Threepio."

"Us too what, sir?"

Han decreased altitude, bringing the *Falcon* down to less than thirty meters above the surface. Range to the shaft closed to one kilometer, half, one-quarter—

Han nodded at Leia, then brought up the repulsors and fired the reverse thrusters at power. The ship's rapid deceleration threw all four of them forward. They slammed into their restraints harder than they should have, Leia's reversal of the inertial compensator causing it to do just the opposite of what it was supposed to. Instead of cushioning their deceleration, easing the effects of delta vee, the compensators increased those effects.

The energy spider flew off the cockpit as though it were a winged insect, arcing down to the dusty ground. It hit, rolling, kicking up a tremendous cloud of dust as it went, its legs thrashing. Then it rolled to a stop and righted itself, turning toward the *Falcon*.

It wasn't unhurt; at least two of its legs were clearly broken, dangling uselessly. But it was obviously capable of continuing the fight.

"*Falcon*, Rogue. I have two missiles left, and I have a shot."

Han indicated, by gesture, for Leia to return the inertial compensator to normal mode. He set the *Falcon* on a slow climb, traveling backward while continuing to face the spider. "Negative on that, old buddy. Just let it go."

"Understood."

The energy spider trotted forward a few meters. The sparkles beneath its glassy skin were bright now, sometimes eye-hurtingly intense. It peered up at the *Millennium Falcon* and rocked back and forth, seeming to gauge the leap. But it must have concluded that the distance was too great.

It turned and, with one last look back, scrambled the two hundred meters to the lip of the shaft. Then it was over the edge and gone into the darkness.

Allana's voice was surprised. "You didn't kill it."

Han felt very tired and unexpectedly relieved. "That's right."

"Why?"

"It was just hungry, sweetie. And, yeah, it wouldn't have been a good thing for it to get us, because it would have killed us . . . but the spider's not *evil*. That's just its nature." He turned the *Falcon* around, orienting toward the muster point for the operation.

"You don't hate it anymore?"

"I guess not. Or Kessel, either. Come on up and sit in my lap. You can have your hands on the controls and help me with the landing."

Chapter Twenty-six

THE RAID ON THE PRISON WAS ONE OF THE LEADING STO-
ries on the holonews the next day.

Recordings taken by security holocams in the prison
and all around the building offered inconclusive visual
information. One intruder, dressed as a routine worker,
was identified as Jedi Seff Hellin. Two black-clad,
masked intruders remained unidentified. The three of
them had managed to penetrate the lower levels of the
prison, though whether they were a team or rivals was
not yet determined.

Their evident objective was the rescue of Jedi Valin
Horn. They managed to enter and leave the prison without taking life or doing permanent harm to any of the
guards on duty, and failed in their efforts to free Horn.
Outside the prison, mercenary units assigned to the
Chief of State's office, having already identified Seff
Hellin as a Jedi, captured him. But Hellin had immediately been rescued by two more confederates, both
women, one probably a Jedi, who escaped with him. A
high-speed pursuit ensued. The last sight security officers had had of the situation was of the black-clad intruders in a stolen security speeder working their way
toward Hellin's two female confederates.

That was the story as the press understood it. It wasn't

a lot of information for a press corps voracious for information. But in interviews on the steps of the Jedi Temple, Master Kenth Hamner, demonstrating dignity and poise, denied the involvement of the Jedi Temple in these crimes.

On the day after the raid, Captain Oric Harfard, now point man for Alliance Security–Jedi Order interactions, made a visit to the Temple. Master Hamner met him at the main entrance. The red-faced Harfard did not wait for them to reach the privacy of Hamner's office to begin his questions and complaints; Jedi along the main hall, including Jaina, heard it all as the two men passed.

"Where is Jedi Hellin?"

Master Hamner gave the captain a cool, indifferent look. "I do not know, and that is the truth."

"Why didn't you tell us that Jedi Hellin had gone rogue, that he would stage a rescue attempt?"

"We told you he had 'gone rogue.' " Hamner's tone was endlessly but not cheerfully patient, as though he were answering the same question from the same hard-headed child for the thirtieth time. "We told you, when we provided you the list of all active Jedi, that he was no longer maintaining contact with the Temple and was pursuing his own agendas. Hence, 'gone rogue.' We don't know his plans."

The two of them walked past a group of Jedi, among them Corran Horn. Jaina winced to see Corran, who looked leaner than she had ever seen him, his expression distant and bleak. But as Harfard passed before him, Jaina saw Corran's expression change. Anger flashed in his eyes. Jaina could feel his anger in the Force; it struck her like a slap and, intense as it was, she would not have been surprised to see him ignite his lightsaber and cut the captain down. Every Jedi in the Hall turned his way, and Master Hamner gave Corran a look of worry and caution.

But Corran did not attack, and Harfard remained oblivious to him—or nearly so: He rubbed the back of his neck nervously as he passed Corran, but he kept talking. "Who was the female Jedi, the one who rescued him from Dhidal Nyz?"

"We don't know her identity. We don't know that she was a Jedi."

"She was using a lightsaber!"

"So does Zilaash Kuh, who works with *you*."

"Kuh's whereabouts last night are very well known."

"My point is that not everybody with a lightsaber is a Jedi. The recordings I saw cannot even prove that the subject you're looking for was either human or a woman. Take a lean man and pad his clothes properly—"

The two men reached the turbolift and waited for a car to arrive. Harfard shook his head, angry and frustrated. "You'll wish you had been more cooperative." His voice suddenly became low enough that Jaina had to strain to hear. "The next step is going to be tracking devices. Implanted in every one of you Jedi."

Master Hamner drew himself up to his full height and said a few words very, very quietly. Captain Harfard stiffened. Then the lift doors opened and the two men entered. They were gone a second later.

Jaina whispered to Kolir, a female Bothan Jedi Knight, "I wonder what the Master said."

Someone right behind Jaina answered. "He said, 'I would be privileged to show you where such a device might be implanted.' "

Jaina turned. The speaker was Dab. He had his miniature holocam to his face and was peering into its tiny screen. Jaina suspected that Dab had listened to the Master's words through the device's microphone. "Good answer. Informative, yet insulting."

Dab grinned and brought his holocam down. He lowered his voice so only Jaina could hear. "You know, I'm not stupid."

"I never said you were."

"They're looking for a female mystery Jedi. And there we were last night, not half a klick from the scene of the crime, and you were out of my sight for, well, quite a while . . . If I had mentioned all that to the captain as he walked by, he'd be pretty sure he knew who the mystery woman was."

His words sent a chill through Jaina. "Then why didn't you?"

Dab looked straight at her. "My job is to tell the authorities what I know about the Jedi. Not what I suspect. My lifelong job as a documentarian is to show the truth and expose lies. If I conclude that the position of my employers—that the Jedi have to be reined in for the sake of society, and anything the government does to rein the Jedi in is justified—is a lie, it sort of puts me in an awkward position." He shrugged. "So I don't speculate. I try to figure out what the right thing to do is, and then do it."

"Very much like a Jedi."

"Maybe."

"Thank you for not speculating, Dab."

"So tell me about Tahiri Veila. After I left you two last night, did she talk about me?"

It took a moment for Dab's intent to click in Jaina's mind. Her jaw dropped for a second. "Dab, you need to stay away from Tahiri."

"Why?"

"Because you look—you look like—"

"I look like your brother Anakin, and they were together just before he died, and since then something about him has messed her up. Not surprising. Young love and tragedy. I've heard the stories. But I'm not

Anakin Solo. I don't feel I should have to bear the burden of all that he did."

"No, you shouldn't. But Tahiri—"

"I won't hurt Tahiri."

"Yes, you will."

"I've liked her ever since I met her on Borleias. She was sixteen and would never have noticed someone four years younger than she was, but I certainly noticed *her*."

Jaina suppressed the urge to strangle him. "Right. Now that she's recently come out of emotional turmoil involving Anakin, here you are, sniffing around, and things should be just fine. Accident or not, you showed up when she least needed to be reminded of Anakin."

"So, to make sure nobody ever experiences a twinge of pain, I should move to Dantooine and live in a cave."

"You could move to Mustafar and jump into a volcano instead." Jaina turned and headed to the turbolift. Other than specific authorized trips to residential levels, observers were not allowed below the Great Hall level, and so Dab could not follow. She heard his exasperated sigh as she left him.

She visited the lower medical level and the chamber housing Seff. She tapped on its door, hoping that Tekli was inside to admit her. A moment later, the door opened . . . revealing Master Cilghal within.

Jaina froze. "Uh . . . Master."

"Well said." The Mon Cal Jedi withdrew a pace so Jaina could enter. "Come in. Best for this door not to remain open."

Numbly, Jaina stepped in, and Cilghal shut the door behind her. Jaina looked around. Through the portal into the inner chamber, everything was as it should be, Seff strapped to his bed, monitoring devices activated . . . except that Cilghal was here instead of Tekli. Jaina took a deep breath. "How did you, um . . ."

"Am I supposed to be stupid?"

"People keep asking me that today."

Cilghal moved to Seff's side and began scrutinizing the monitor readouts of the devices measuring his brainwaves.

Jaina followed. "Of course you're not supposed to be stupid."

"Seff Hellin tries to free Valin Horn. We can correctly gauge his intent and his relationship with the others in the intrusion even if the authorities cannot . . . Jedi end up in possession of Seff. Where is he going to turn up except the Temple? Civil of you to keep Master Hamner in the dark."

"We were trying to keep *all* the Masters out of the loop."

"Also civil, but not wise. You need me for this. Both for my medical expertise and because I'm the only Jedi in regular communication with the Grand Master."

That revelation rocked Jaina back on her heels. "You've talked to him recently?"

"Relatively. He's on Dorin, learning the scannerblanking technique Valin manifested. I haven't heard from him recently."

"You're risking a lot."

"We're often called a militant Order, but do you know one of the principal differences between the military and the Jedi Order? And please, give me no Solo sarcasm."

"I won't. There are a lot of differences. I can only guess at which one you mean."

"The military are expected to follow orders, even when they feel those orders are not what's right. The Jedi are expected to do what's right, even when that course of action runs contrary to orders."

"Well, yes."

Cilghal turned back to Jaina. "Finding out what's

wrong with Valin and Seff, helping the Grand Master . . . that's what's right."

Jaina felt a touch embarrassed. "I'm sorry we didn't include you from the start."

"No harm done. Include me now. I need to know where your mother is. She and your father were the first ones to contact Seff in his current distorted condition. I may want them to come and see him as he is now, to gauge whether there has been any advancement of his dementia."

"They're on Kessel. I'll get you the direct holocomm data you need to contact the *Falcon*."

Cilghal gestured toward the monitor. "Already we have interesting results. Seff does not possess Valin's trick of blanking the electroencephaloscan. The portions of Seff's brain that are active when he dreams have been seeing activity during his waking hours as well, for some considerable time—these stress patterns here so indicate."

"Meaning that he's, what, sleepwalking?"

Cilghal shook her head. "But he is in some small way in a dream-like state. Which may be the first clue toward determining how to restore him and Valin to normal. So . . . well done."

"Thank you, Master Cilghal."

CAVERNS OF THE HIDDEN ONE, DORIN

It had been days now since their audience with the Hidden One, and that audience had not been repeated. Luke and Ben had divided their time among numerous tasks: digging out the chamber the Baran Do intended to be their permanent quarters, exploring the caverns, and talking to the other dwellers in this lonely environment.

Ben grew impatient. Swinging his pickax at a particularly stubborn outcropping of stone, he imagined it was the Hidden One's face, a fantasy that gave him some satisfaction as he worked. "Dad, we need to get out of here."

Luke, shoveling stony debris into a small rolling cart, smiled—the enigmatic, you're-so-young expression that Ben found so annoying. "Is that our objective?"

"Of course it is! We have to get out of here to continue our mission."

"But is it our most immediate goal?"

"Sure, why not?"

"Ben, what is our purpose as Jedi?"

Ben sighed and lowered his pickax. This was going to be one of *those* conversations. "Well . . . to keep the Force in balance and to help people stay in balance with the Force. To detect wrongs and make them right. To serve as models for very attractive lines of boots."

"Let's go back one. Detecting wrongs and righting them. Is there a wrongness going on here?"

"Absolutely. They've kidnapped people. Which we can right by escaping."

"Is that the only wrong?"

Ben lifted his breath mask for a moment, wiped his sweating face with the sleeve of his overlong Kel Dor robe, and lowered the mask into place again. He exhaled, forcing the helium-rich Dorin atmosphere out of the mask, then took a new breath before answering. "I guess not. These Baran Do are wronging themselves, too. Following a paranoid down into this hole, pretending to be dead—"

"There you go. The Force is an energy of life. These Kel Dors, in pretending to be dead, are rejecting life. They're unwittingly *becoming* dead. How much happiness have you seen down here? How much enthusiasm?"

"I'd say it reaches pretty far into the negative numbers. They're all about duty, but not about happiness."

Luke shoveled the last of the larger rocks into his cart. "So if we escape now, what happens to them?"

Ben slumped, defeated. "They continue to live their nasty little lives and nothing gets better."

"Correct."

"They brought it on themselves."

"Spoken with all the sympathy and altruism of a teenager who'd rather be doing something else."

Ben grinned, unabashed. "You've got that right."

In his free time, Ben set out to uncover the cavern's secrets.

First there was the question of the trigger the Hidden One was supposed to have that would collapse the tunnel leading to the surface. It had been said that the Hidden One could activate it through the Force or by physical action. Ben set out to find out where that trigger was.

When the largest hall was empty, he searched the Hidden One's throne and the platform it rested on. It took him mere moments to find what he was looking for. The throne, though seemingly cut from a single block of white stone, was not; close examination showed that it was assembled from several pieces, their seams so fine and patterns so well matched that the deception was undetectable by anyone more than a few centimeters away. The right armrest lifted outward on hinges, and beneath it was a single button—round, black, inset in a red depression. That had to be it.

But Ben frowned at the discovery. Would a paranoid mind be content with one easily disabled trigger for his ultimate act?

Ben restored the armrest to its closed position and sat on the platform next to the throne. He dared not sit on the throne itself; the Hidden One, a Force-user, was even more likely to detect that he had been there if he rested in the seat of power.

Ben relaxed, letting the Force flow through him. He thought of nothing but the trigger beside him, seeking anything related to it—images, flashes of insight about the future—

Up.

Ben looked upward. He saw only shadows in the irregular stone ceiling four meters up, but something there had all but called him. He stood, stepped onto the throne armrest he had so recently closed, and sprang upward, giving himself a little boost in the Force.

In the ceiling directly over the throne, his fingers gripped either side of a hole, about the size of a human head, cut into the stone. He hung there a few moments as his eyes adjusted to the reduced light. Then he saw it: a polished durasteel cylinder protruding twenty centimeters from the rock above.

Ben concentrated on it, trying to obtain through the Force some sense of how it worked. He could feel its length, nearly another meter inset in the stone, and machinery above it—simple mechanical parts made of durable metals.

It was simple, all right. Drive the cylinder home, like a plunger, and contact with something above it would relay the signal to detonate the charges in the entry tunnel. Without being able to look at the device, Ben doubted he would be able to disable it. Thoughtful, he dropped back to the platform.

In the hall where he regularly trained in combat against Chara, he found another such apparatus in the ceiling. And in the dormitory where he, Luke, and four male Kel Dors slept, another. The next day, Ben determined that every chamber of any significant size had one of these triggering devices in it. The Hidden One was clearly determined to be able to seal these caverns if he felt the need.

Later that day, Luke joined the audience for combat training. Not many Kel Dors were in attendance. Chara was on hand; Ithia, the female who had been beside Ben's canister upon his arrival in the caverns, led the proceedings. A Kel Dor male, younger than the others, merely sat and watched.

Ben went a few minutes against Chara, staff against staff. Chara was still far more experienced with the weapon, but Ben was able to defend himself longer and get in more good blows than when he'd first faced Charsae Saal.

Next, Ithia took the combat ring against Chara. They were obviously opponents of many years' acquaintance, for Ithia immediately matched her combat style to Chara's. Ithia was more fluid and evasive, Chara more aggressive and direct; the contrast was a pretty one, and Ben enjoyed watching the proceedings.

Luke spoke to the young Kel Dor observing the sparring. "I'm Luke Skywalker."

The youth glanced at him, uncomfortable. "I am Wyss."

"You're younger than most of the Kel Dor here."

Wyss nodded, his attention back on Ithia and Chara. He unconsciously leaned away from Luke as if hoping the man would just leave him alone.

"Will you be training?"

Wyss shook his head. "I am not a sage. I am a servant."

"But you could still learn. You're obviously interested."

" 'As in life, so in death.' "

That statement, so obviously a quote, so evidently a tolerated rather than a welcome philosophy if Wyss's tone was any indication, drew Ben's attention. He turned to watch his father and the Kel Dor.

Luke frowned. "What does that mean?"

"It means that in death, you should be content with preserving the skills you had in life, but should not worry about acquiring new ones."

"That's the custom here?"

Wyss nodded again.

Luke turned away from the boy, obviously deliberating what he had just heard. Ben returned his attention to the practice.

Ultimately, Chara won each of his three matches against Ithia. When they were done, Ithia laughed. "I *am* out of practice, Charsae—Chara."

Chara gave her what, among the Kel Dors, must have been considered a sympathetic smile. "I think so. In the old days, you would have had at least two of those matches." He turned to Luke. "Will you be sparring?"

Luke shook his head. "Not today. Too sore from shoveling. Tomorrow, perhaps."

"I look forward to it." Moments later, Chara and Ithia departed, headed for the sanisteam, and Wyss followed them out, leaving Luke and Ben alone.

Ben gave his father a suspicious look. *"Too sore from shoveling?"*

"Perhaps *too sick of shoveling* would have been more correct. Ben, they just gave us the answers we needed here."

"Did they? The servant, Wyss?"

"He had one of them, and Ithia the other." Luke stood. "I need to get word to the Hidden One. I'd like for all the Kel Dor in these caverns to be present for our renaming ceremony."

Ben stood. "We're choosing new names?"

"No."

"Oh. That's sad. I was looking forward to being Sparky."

"Sounds like a name for a monkey-lizard."

"And you could be Grand Master Whango Mittphool."

"Not in *this* lifetime."

Chapter Twenty-seven

They gathered in the Hidden One's throne chamber, four dozen Kel Dors and two humans. As the last of the Kel Dors, servants who operated the foundries, arrived, conversation dropped off and all Kel Dors turned toward the Hidden One on his throne.

He gestured toward the Skywalkers, motioning them to approach. As they did, he offered them a benevolent smile. "It is with whole heart that I greet you this day. I understand that you have determined to choose new names, the better to make your way among us, the better to accept your circumstances."

Luke looked surprised. "I'm sorry, great one. There has been some misunderstanding. I did ask for a naming ceremony. I did refer to it as *our* naming ceremony, but I did not mean that Ben and I would be renaming ourselves. It is my hope that we will be renaming some—or all—of *you*."

Exclamations of surprise and disapproval filled the room then. Ben kept his face impassive, but inwardly he was smiling. Much as he liked causing trouble from time to time, it was just as much fun watching his father do it.

The Hidden One's expression darkened. "You have wasted my time."

Luke shrugged. "What do the dead have *except* time? And admit it, as annoying as you find my words, this is the most interesting event you are going to experience all day."

The Hidden One sat back, clearly not amused. "And who were you going to rename first?"

"I thought, great one, that we would start with Chara. Restore his name of Charsae Saal. He was the one most recently named. We could go in reverse order, from the newest one who joined the dead to the oldest."

The Hidden One sagged just a little as if dispirited. "Why are you doing this?"

Luke abandoned all pretense at good cheer. He drew himself up straight and fixed the Hidden One with a forbidding stare. "Because you're wrong. And if you were only wronging yourself, that would not be so bad. But you are wronging every one of them as well." His sweeping gesture took in all the assembled Kel Dors.

"I have accepted their sacrifice as a gift to future generations. They knew what they were doing as they offered their oaths and took their new names. There is no wrongdoing."

"Again, you're wrong." Luke sprang onto the Hidden One's throne platform, eliciting a gasp of outrage from some of the Baran Do. He began pacing as he talked, crossing back and forth in front of the Hidden One, addressing all the Kel Dors before the platform. "Let's answer some simple questions. The Baran Do Sages are a group who study and utilize the Force. Correct?"

The Kel Dors looked between Luke and the Hidden One. Ben saw the Hidden One pause and then nod. One of the Baran Do toward the front of the crowd said, "Yes."

"And the Force is the energy of life."

Another Kel Dor said, "Yes."

Luke spared an admonishing look for the Hidden One as he passed. "Life is risk. Life is energy, vitality. Yet you have rejected these things. In rejecting them, you reject the Force. In rejecting the Force, you deprive yourself of the right to teach its ways to the living. You have brought nothing to these caverns but your own bodies, and even then, you don't have the decency to start moldering like ordinary corpses."

Many of the Kel Dors looked offended, including Chara. He stepped toward the platform, moving to the front of the audience. "Now you're just being insulting."

"Which angers you, because you're approximately still among the living." Luke stared down at him. "The dead don't take offense, Charsae Saal."

"My name is Chara."

Luke hopped down and brushed past Chara. He walked to Ithia. "Here is a woman who used to beat you consistently in combat, Charsae Saal. Now she is no longer your match. What has happened? Has she grown feeble with age?"

Chara shrugged. "Of course not. She does not train as much down here."

"Why not?"

"There is less need."

"Of course there is no need." Luke walked through the crowd; the Kel Dors stood aside to let him pass. "Thinking you're dead, knowing that you have no future, leaches all energy and hope from you. Drains your very life away. Diminishes you in the Force. How can you even feel a need?"

Luke came to a stop in front of Wyss. "And here we have a boy who gave up his life on the surface to serve you in this place. And what do you give him besides food, water, and the opportunity to serve? Not much. No chance to learn, to improve himself, to *grow*. Growth is for living things. Here, it's 'As in life, so in death.' "

One of the Masters, a male Kel Dor even more wizened than the Hidden One, his name Burra, spoke up. "We have debated the philosophy you mention."

Luke turned a cheerful, if mocking, smile on Burra. "Good for you! Debate would seem to be a good thing for dead people to do. It would keep the cemeteries lively. And how did your vote turn out?"

Burra looked uncomfortable. "Here, we do not vote."

"Because your lord of the dead decides everything."

Burra hesitated, then nodded.

"Those of you who debated, did the majority support letting the dead learn new things?"

"Enough." The Hidden One rose to his feet. "This gathering is at an end. Everyone is to return to his duties."

"Your duty is to the living," Luke shot back, "and you've already abandoned that. Why not abandon it for five more minutes?" He gestured toward the exit, and the blast door there slid closed. The Kel Dors already heading toward it hesitated, confused, and turned back toward the throne.

"You want to save the Baran Do teachings," Luke said. "A noble goal. You want to be prepared in case another purge comes. A good thing to do. Koro Ziil, do you know how the Jedi survived the last purge?"

"That is no longer my name."

"Do you know?"

"By luck, two Jedi survived. Your Masters, Obi-Wan Kenobi and Yoda."

"No." Luke shook his head. "Of course, they did survive those events. But there were other Jedi and former Jedi out in the galaxy. There were resources like the Jedi Holocron. The Jedi survived because they were scattered, their knowledge disseminated throughout the galaxy. You Baran Do plan to survive by concentrating. Few of you ever leave Dorin in the first place, and your backup plan, this series of caves, is just one toxic bomb or groundquake away from extinction. I applaud your goal . . . but your execution is bound for inevitable failure."

There was muttering among the Kel Dors present. Ben had the sense that it was not the conversation of people just waking up to a fact, but among people who had voiced these objections many times before, quietly and futilely, in the face of a ruler who opposed their view.

"And those would be lucky ways for you to die," Luke continued. "Fast and decisive. It's more likely that most of you will just wither away. Like Ithia there." Luke turned in a slow circle, making eye contact with as many of the Kel Dors as he could. "Who is your best fighter?"

One said, "Ithia." Two or three, including Ithia, said "Chara."

Luke nodded. "Charsae Saal, because he has decades of experience. And because, having only recently come here, he is not a listless, lifeless reflection of his former self. But he has still been fading for years. He's been preparing himself for death all that time. My bet is that he's a shadow of *his* former self. And that my son, his junior in experience by many, many years, can take him."

Ben froze, trying desperately not to look like a woodland creature caught in the spotlight beams of an oncoming speeder. Aware of numerous Kel Dors now looking at him, he offered them a scowl, a tough-guy posture.

"And what is it that you bet?" The Hidden One was seated on his throne again. His voice was cold.

"If Ben fails, I abandon the subject for as long as I live in these caverns."

"Very well." The Hidden One waved at Chara. "Do it."

Chara nodded, decisive. "Yes, Master."

The Kel Dors drew back from the center of the chamber, leaving the area ringed by columns empty but for Chara, Ben, and Luke.

Ben turned to his father. "You're doing it to me again," he whispered.

"I am, aren't I? I'm a terrible dad." Luke gave him a reassuring smile. "You'll do fine."

"What if I lose?"

"Two things. First, you'll still demonstrate to all these people just what it's like to be alive. Second, I promised that I'd abandon the subject . . . not that *you* would."

"Hey, you *are* sneaky."

"Besides, you won't lose. Unlike them, you have something to fight for."

Ben handed Luke his lightsaber.

Luke looked at the weapon. "Are you sure?"

"I'm not going to convince anybody of the value of life by cutting him in half. Win or lose, I'm doing it without my lightsaber."

Luke nodded and withdrew to the circle of pillars.

Ithia presented Ben with a staff, a meter and a half of hardwood—gnarled, black, and polished. Then she withdrew as well.

Ben and Chara faced each other from opposite sides of the open space.

Luke leaned against the nearest pillar, trying to look relaxed but feeling no more nonchalant this time than during the fight Ben had waged their first night on Dorin.

Ben faced his opponent, features set in the neutral expression he always assumed when he didn't want anyone to know what he was thinking or feeling. Chara's eyes were on the Hidden One.

The Hidden One looked at the two opponents, made a little expression of displeasure, and said, "Go."

Ben and Chara moved toward each other. When about a meter and a half separated them, they began circling.

Chara lashed out, the lower end of his staff flashing up toward Ben's groin. Ben reacted almost too late, parrying awkwardly. Chara responded with reflexive speed, striking down at Ben's collarbone with the other end of his weapon. Ben caught that blow, too, interposing his own staff mere centimeters from his skin; the blow hammered Ben's weapon down into his flesh. It staggered him, and as he stumbled backward, Chara swept with his staff, catching Ben's ankle and hurling him to the stone.

Ben continued the roll into a backward somersault and came up on his feet. He bounced up and down on the balls of his feet like a prizefighter anxious for action. Luke could tell that he was testing his ankle, determining how forcefully it had been struck.

There was more than just vigor to Ben's bounce, though. Luke could feel the boy getting mad—angry with himself for being the first to fall, angry with his father for putting him in this situation, angry at the Kel Dors for forcing Luke's hand. Luke restrained himself from sending calming thoughts through the Force. This was Ben's fight, and the many Baran Do Sages present would be able to detect any interference from Luke.

Ben and Chara came together for another exchange. This time Ben managed to get a grazing shot against Chara's bicep before the more experienced fighter struck him. Chara's riposte connected with Ben's staff, raised in an across-the-body block, and was still strong enough to take Ben off his feet.

Again Ben rolled backward to get up, but this time Chara gestured, an exertion through the Force, and Ben's somersault continued out of control. Ben smacked up against one of the support pillars, his back and head hitting the stone hard enough to make Luke wince.

Groggy, Ben shook his head. As Chara advanced, staff

up and back for a thrusting, spearlike blow, Ben's eyes cleared and snapped into focus.

He shoved off from the pillar, an exertion in the Force allowing him to slide forward as though the surface under him were oil instead of rough stone. Chara's thrust cracked into the pillar where his head had been. Ben's kick unloaded into Chara's gut, taking the Kel Dor clean off his feet.

Ben bounced upright, seemingly unslowed, and Chara was up a fraction of a second later. Luke wanted to cheer. He could feel his son's emotions, feel that Ben was in control, intense but focused. Win or lose, he was fighting like a Jedi, not a furious teenager.

Now the fight was on in earnest. The two combatants moved their staves at such speed that onlookers unused to combat could not possibly follow their movements. Theirs was a dance-like rhythm, now one of them the aggressor and driving the other back, now the other. Chara hammered again at Ben's damaged ankle, hurting it further, and Ben now limped as he moved. The next time Chara tried targeting the same injury, Ben leapt clear over the blow and swung his staff at extension, its end catching Chara full on the crown of his head, knocking the Kel Dor down.

"Chara!" That was one of the Baran Do, a female, shouting encouragement. Another yelled, "Chara, *kaya-mash*!"

Now Luke no longer bothered to conceal his smile. They were feeling it, these long-dead Kel Dors—feeling blood circulate through their veins, feeling adrenaline pump. Suddenly they were sports fans, rooting for a favorite son.

Ben felt it, too. He looked around, clearly realizing that he was the outsider competing with the beloved champion. It seemed to discourage him not a bit; and Luke felt the moment that the meaning of it all clicked into place in Ben's mind. Now the boy had everything: emotion, focus, and purpose. Ben returned his attention to Chara.

Chara was up fast, but obviously woozy. Ben approached again, limping, an aggressor closing in for the decisive blow.

Luke's attention was drawn to the Hidden One. The Kel Dor ruler was leaning forward, whispering intently to a servant, a young woman. He nodded, encouraging her to act. She moved away around the periphery of the crowd and headed toward the main exit. The blast door opened for her. Luke felt a trickle of danger, but he could not leave these events in order to follow the girl.

Ben and Chara exchanged blows and blocks, feints and ploys at lightning speed. They circled, struck, parried, dodged, all to the percussive accompaniment of staves hammering against each other.

Ben took a glancing blow to the side of his left knee. His riposte caught Chara in the ribs. Chara pinned him against a pillar. Ben shoved Chara clear, feinted with a staff blow, and spun into a side kick that caught Chara in the center of the chest, making an audible *crack*. Chara slammed to the stone again and was slow to rise.

The chants of "Chara . . . Chara . . . Chara . . ." continued, but the chanters sounded more uncertain, as if not sure they should encourage their champion to take more damage.

In the Force, Luke could feel the change. Ben, hurting from several blows, remained focused, razor-sharp. Chara was losing the will to win.

They came together again. Ben let Chara get inside his guard and lock up his staff. It was not, as it first looked, a mistake of inexperience. Chara yanked, an attempt to disarm Ben, but Ben offered no resistance. Ben's staff went flying, but Chara stumbled backward, off balance. Ben followed, hammering Chara in the chest and stomach with a boxer's barrage of blows. As Chara tried to rally, bringing his staff up, Ben struck at the weapon itself, breaking it in two. The open-palm blow continued onward to crack against Chara's chin.

Chara went down. This time he did not immediately struggle to rise.

The crowd went mostly quiet. A few Kel Dors offered little groans of disappointment.

Ben limped to where his weapon lay. He picked it up and, impassive, turned to face the Hidden One. Ithia moved up to kneel beside Chara, who was moving at last, attempting to rise; she helped him sit up but did not allow him to stand.

The Hidden One stared at Ben. His expression was unhappy, but Luke suspected he actually felt some measure of grim satisfaction. "You win." The Hidden One's tone was flat, almost emotionless. "Your father may continue his tedious complaints so long as he has breath within his body. But he's still wrong about what we're doing here. About the life within us."

"No, Master." That was Chara, his voice pained. "He may be right."

The Hidden One turned to glare at him. "Not you, too."

Chara struggled to rise. Abandoning her futile attempt to keep him still, Ithia helped him to his feet. "Master," he said, "I am this boy's superior in fighting skill. I am strong in the Force. But he won. He won through the will to win. Through conviction, through strength of purpose. I lost because I lack these things."

"Perhaps you do." The Hidden One sounded scornful. "But it is because you have listened to him." He gestured at Luke. "He has confused you, diverted you from your purpose. Once he is gone, you will return to the correct path."

Luke stepped forward to stand beside his son. "Gone? So we can leave?"

The Hidden One shook his head. "No one leaves. I have made that clear already. No, you are not going to leave. But very soon, things will return to normal." He took a deep breath, assuming a regretful expression as he looked among his people. "I'm sorry. But the Skywalkers are clearly too dangerous to live among us, and they know too much to be free."

Luke returned Ben's lightsaber to the boy. "So you're going to kill us."

Burra, the ancient Kel Dor, shook his head vehemently. "That is not our way, Master."

"I will not do it," Ithia said. Others echoed her sentiment.

The Hidden One glared down at Luke. "Do you see what you've done? Until your arrival, they were satisfied. Obedience to our goal, our destiny, was our first concern. Now you've made them, made them—"

"Alive?" Luke kept his tone quizzical.

The Hidden One glared at him for a moment, then turned his attention to the Kel Dors. "Of course we will not murder them. That is not our way." As a sigh of relief circulated among his followers, he added, "I have informed those above that the Skywalkers died in a collapse of the cave they were excavating. Above, they now know not to send down any more oxygen-nitrogen canisters. We will not kill the Skywalkers . . . but in the matter of a day or two, once their remaining canisters have been depleted, the atmosphere of Dorin will."

Chapter Twenty-eight

ANOTHER MURMUR ROSE. BURRA CALLED OUT, "MASTER, no."

But the Hidden One brushed his hands together as if ridding himself of imaginary dirt. "It is done. No rebellion on this matter will be tolerated. Or effective. I had the comm encryption codes advanced. Should one of you be foolish enough to try to send unauthorized messages to those above, your words will not be understood." He looked at Luke and Ben. "Now, finally, like us, you must resign yourself to death."

Ithia stepped forward. Her voice was soft, a plea. "Master, please. Reverse your decision. And I wish you would consider something that has been troubling me for years now, something that I have tried to bring up with you many times, something you have never been willing to hear."

"Which is what?"

"Our purpose here." She paused for a moment as if trying to gather the right words. "Our lives here only have meaning if the worst occurs—if the Baran Do are wiped out above and must be restored. If that never happens, our lives here are wasted."

"Which is why we choose to be dead before we descend to this place." The Hidden One sounded annoyed. There was no sign on his face that Ithia's words had meant anything to him.

"Master . . ." A look of great sadness crossed Ithia's face. "You're *wrong*. You're wrong in what you're doing to the Skywalkers. And I think it's time for you to understand, and admit, that this experiment is a failure."

"This is no experiment." The Hidden One was suddenly on his feet, his voice raised in a shrill shout, his anger so potent that all present except Luke and Ben took a step backward. "It is our way, and it will continue to be our way, and it is time for you to be silent and obey."

"Like the dead." Sorrowfully, Ithia shook her head. "No, Master."

The Hidden One stood on his platform, breathing hard, and then stepped down to the stone floor. "I see. I cannot let these humans remain among us even for the time it would take them to suffocate. Their influence is too strong." He raised his hands. Little crackles of electricity flickered between them. "*I* will show you life. I will show you the Force."

"Ben," Luke whispered. "Stand back."

It happened all at once: the Hidden One gesturing toward Luke, Ben leaping away, lightning flashing from the Hidden One's hands. It was not the purplish lightning of Emperor Palpatine, which had so nearly cost Luke his life nearly forty years before; it was all brilliant whiteness.

Luke had his lightsaber activated and up in time. The lightning crackled against his glowing blade. The strength behind the attack, of the Hidden One's energy and anger, took Luke off his feet and threw him backward. He slammed into a pillar, feeling jolts of pain in his spine and the back of his head.

But the lightning did not reach him. His blade kept it at bay. And, bracing himself with the Force, Luke took a step forward.

The Hidden One tossed his head. It was not just a gesture of anger; Luke felt the motion as a ripple in the Force. The air in the chamber responded, a wind springing up and roaring around the walls of the chamber, gaining speed and strength. It tattered the robes of the Kel Dors near the walls as it went. It veered from the wall over the throne and howled down at Luke, engulfing him, trying to drive him backward.

Luke gritted his teeth and rooted himself. Then, against the might of both wind and lightning, he took another step forward.

The Hidden One's eyes widened. His head rolled around on his shoulders, and the roar of air across Luke intensified. It tore at his robes, causing them to stand out from his body, shudder, and snap in the wind.

Luke took another step forward. It was slow going, for the Hidden One's power was great, but Luke now felt sure in his footing and in his own strength.

Out of the corner of his eye, he saw Kel Dors retreating, some of them streaming out through the blast door, Ben waving them onward.

The Hidden One's face, flushed fully red, was contorted in a mask of anger. He flicked his fingers and the lightning ceased. He moved his now freed hands in circular gestures. Luke felt the wind increase in ferocity. Most of it still whirled around the chamber before battering at him, but some, a diverted flow, spun in a tight circle directly in front of the Hidden One. As Luke watched, that errant stream of air swallowed up dust from the floor and walls, defining its outlines as a miniature funnel cloud, a few centimeters wide at its base and broadening to two meters at the ceiling. It writhed like a mortally wounded serpent.

With a gesture, the Hidden One sent the whirlwind straight at Luke.

Luke lunged at it, visualizing it, wrenching at it with

the Force. His exertion was like a physical blow as he stepped into it. He felt the wind intensify for a bare moment, and then his telekinetic attack flung the whirlwind free. It rocketed off to the side and hammered into a pillar to Luke's left.

Luke took another step forward. He was more than halfway to the Hidden One now. He deactivated his lightsaber. He could turn it on again swiftly enough if the Hidden One brought forth his lightning a second time.

The whirlwind moved from pillar to pillar as if leaping. When it was directly behind Luke, it lingered there. Luke kept his senses, both the physical ones and that of the Force, alert to its movements. It hammered at the pillar itself, and Luke could hear and feel the permacrete mounting at the summit begin to crack.

The mounting at the base broke, too, and the pillar toppled toward Luke. He heard Ben's warning cry. He raised his left hand backward, using the same exertion he'd made a moment earlier against the whirlwind itself, and the pillar stopped, frozen in midfall. He gestured again and it reversed direction, toppling onto the empty floor.

And Luke took another step forward.

The Hidden One's howl of outrage was like that of his own wind. The stone throne behind him rocked and rattled on its platform.

Luke made a sweeping gesture, bringing his rear hand forward, and with it came the toppled pillar, flying forward like a spear. As the throne launched itself toward him, the pillar met it in midair, shattering the stone seat into a dozen pieces, some smooth-cut and some broken.

Luke let the pillar fall to the floor. With a wave of his hand, he sent it rolling toward the Hidden One, who leapt sideways over it as it neared him.

Luke was already in motion as the Hidden One

jumped. The Kel Dor's concentration was broken, his control over the wind diminished, and Luke was able to race forward three steps in the time it took the Hidden One to clear the rolling pillar. As the Baran Do Master came down again, Luke kicked out, a spinning kick that caught the Kel Dor in the gut, throwing him backward. The Hidden One smashed up against the platform's front, crushing in its wooden front panel.

Remarkably, he stood up from the impact, raised his hands for another attack . . . and collapsed, falling onto his face.

The wind died. The rolling pillar fetched up against one that was still upright and stopped. All sounds died except that of the Hidden One's strained, frantic breathing.

There were still a few other Kel Dors in the chamber, mostly Masters, and they began to move forward.

Ithia ran up to kneel beside the Hidden One. Chara, moving more slowly, joined her. After looking at the Hidden One for a few moments, they cautiously rolled him over onto his back. Ithia sat beside the platform and pulled him up so that he could be partially upright, propped against her.

She looked up at those in the chamber. "He is exhausted," she said. "He will recover."

The Hidden One said something, his voice so low as to constitute a whisper, and then exerted himself to be heard. "I will do as you say."

Ithia looked relieved. "You will free the Skywalkers?"

"I will allow the servants to learn. I will appoint a board of advisers to make recommendations about our purpose . . . and morale." The Hidden One gulped for air for a moment. "I will tell those above that the earlier message was a mistake. They can resume sending air canisters for the humans. And in a year or two, we can review their situation with new eyes . . ."

"*A year or two?*" That was Ben, his voice an expression of pure outrage. "Don't you get that you *lost*? You're not going to be making any more decisions like that."

"He's right, Master." Ithia's voice was softer than Ben's, but just as unrelenting. "It's time for them to go."

The Hidden One shook his head, weary. "I still decide. And no one leaves."

"You're just too crazy to learn." Ben's hand shot up, pointing toward the ceiling above the platform.

Luke, breathing hard as he recovered from his exertions, distinctly heard a metallic *clunk* as something in the ceiling was driven home.

There was a distant *boom* and the tiniest shiver of chamber walls and pillars.

The Hidden One sat upright, away from Ithia. His eyes widened as he turned toward Ben. "What have you done?"

"The same thing you did to us." Ben's tone and expression held contempt. He limped forward until he was only a couple of meters from the Hidden One. "I've taken your choice away. I've activated your bombs and collapsed the entry tunnel. It's gone. You want it open again, prepare to spend a few hundred years with your pickaxes and shovels."

"You have only doomed yourself." The Hidden One looked more stricken than angry. "Now your air cannot come, while we can survive."

"Stop *lying*. I'm sick of your lying. Your whole petty kingdom down here is based on lies, and that's part of the wrong you're doing to all of the people who serve you. It's pathetic."

The Hidden One's jaw moved, but he said nothing.

"What lies?" That was Chara, seating himself on the edge of the platform, pressing a palm against his ribs.

Ben sighed. "Well, let's start with your so-called self-sufficiency. Yes, you have hydroponics. Provides nice fresh vegetables. Good for you. But if they met all your food needs, you wouldn't have storerooms full of food from above. King Paranoia there—"

"Show respect, Ben." Luke's voice was soft, but he let an edge of warning creep into it.

"Yes, sir." Ben took a couple of deep, calming breaths. "Koro Ziil there wouldn't tolerate the risk of those food shipments being detected or traced down here if the food wasn't absolutely necessary. Therefore it is. Therefore, in blowing up the tunnel, I've doomed us all. We suffocate, you starve.

"Except for the other lies. Here's the next one. Look!" He gestured at the exit. Most of the Kel Dors followed his gaze, then looked back at him, confused.

"Blast doors," Ben said, as if explaining to a none-too-bright classroom of younglings. "The lie that these big doors were made here. Your foundries do fine for re-cycling metal containers and making metal parts. But they're not big enough to build blast doors. The big pieces had to come from an industrial-sized metal plant. And they're too big to fit down your little tunnel. So where did they come from?

"There's lie number three, the really big one. That lie says the tunnel you've been using for shipments, two hundred kilometers of pure tedium, is in any way necessary. It's not.

"Here's why. Lie number four. The lie that if the bad thing happens and the Baran Do are wiped out up top, you'll wait for the dust to settle, then begin teaching new sages by telepathy. No, you won't. The technique doesn't exist. If it did, the Hidden One would have issued his orders to the surface by telepathy, not by com-link. Those blast doors came down by bigger tunnels, the first tunnels dug down to this place, and if the bad thing happened, you were going to get back to the surface by those tunnels and spread out to begin your teaching.

"Those are the lies most of you have lived with down here for I don't know how many years. Probably only the Hidden One and the first generation of Baran Do dead sages know where the big tunnel is. But it's here, and now you need it." Ben glared, defiant, at the Hidden One.

The Hidden One tried again to stand. Ithia attempted to hold him in place but then relented, and the aged Kel Dor got to his feet. He faced Ben, unbowed, unrelenting. "Then you have killed us all, not just yourself. I will not give up the secrets of this place. Nor will anyone else."

Undismayed, Ben stared at him. "So your pride is more important than your mission. The fact that you rule here and would be just another retired Master up there means nearly fifty of your followers have to die."

The Hidden One glowered but did not answer.

Burra did. His expression sorrowful, he stepped forward. "The tunnel out is just above the garment storeroom."

The Hidden One turned on him, his eyes eloquent with the betrayal he felt. "Burra, not *you*."

"The ceiling there is synthstone, artfully detailed to match the natural stone around it. A few blows with chisels will reveal a sliding hatch. Above it is a turbolift chamber. Its generator will need maintenance before it can be activated."

The Hidden One just stared at him. Then, with slow, halting steps, he turned toward the exit from the chamber.

The boy, Wyss, came forward to tuck himself under the Hidden One's arm and support him on his walk.

It was as Burra said. A few minutes with mining tools broke away the veneer of synthstone, revealing a door mounted in the ceiling and a control panel beside it. The control panel, a single mechanical switch, had no lights or readouts to indicate whether it was functional, but Burra had no doubts. "It triggers a capacitance charge, which opens the door."

And so it did. Once the switch was flipped, the doors slid open and air, kept contained and musty for some sixty years, flowed down into the caverns of the seed of the Baran Do.

As they waited for Burra and others to get the generator in the chamber above operational, Luke took Ben aside. "You acted, well, unilaterally."

"He wasn't going to change, Dad. The only other thing we could have done would be to make the others turn on him and force the information from him. Would that have been better?"

"No. It would have been shattering for them. But the Hidden One, after a night's sleep, might have reconsidered. You took that choice away from him."

"Yes, I did. It solved the problem. It didn't kill anybody. It spilled out some nasty truths that they all needed to hear. Dad, sometimes you *shouldn't* wait that extra day. Sometimes you have to cut the other guy's arm off."

"Yes, if the Force guides you to do so. Did the Force guide you to do that?"

"I'm . . . not sure." Finally Ben did look a little contrite. "Was it the wrong thing to do?"

"I'm not sure."

"Oh, good. A really useful answer for once."

Luke grinned.

"Dad, you had added it all up, too, hadn't you? The tunnel size, the blast doors, the telepathy . . ."

"Yes."

"So what I did really didn't shock you. You knew I wasn't sealing us in forever."

"Yes. And even if it was the wrong thing, it clearly wasn't *very* wrong. Add it to everything you did right while we were here, and you're still very much ahead of the game." Luke reached over and affectionately mussed Ben's hair.

"Dad, the *hair*."

Chapter Twenty-nine

THE TURBOLIFT CARRIED THE SKYWALKERS AND THE FIRST few exploratory Baran Do one kilometer straight up. It ended in a large chamber packed with cloth-shrouded speeders, most of them seven decades or more old, and a ramp to a surface-level door. The capacitance charge on that door worked as well, and soon they were at the top of the ramp, staring up into the starry sky of Dorin, the black eyes of the neighboring black holes on either side.

Ben's planetary positioning system datapad put them at about thirty kilometers west of Dor'shan. With Ithia's blessing, they unshrouded a speeder, poked at the engine and connections to make sure they were in good working order, and started up the vehicle. Within minutes, they were nearing Dor'shan's outskirts.

"Are we going to stay and offer them any help?" Ben asked.

Luke shook his head. "We may stay for a day or two and actually relax, but they don't need help. Mistress Tila Mong is capable of handling things among the living, and Charsae Saal and Ithia among the formerly dead. And really, I doubt they want our help right now. I suspect they would be happier not seeing us for a while."

"You're probably right. What's going to happen to the Hidden One?"

Luke thought about that for a few moments, searching among his feelings, his knowledge of the way such Force societies operated, his sense of the future. "One of two things, probably. If he gets better, if he finds a new direction for his original goal, he may end up distributing the archives of his Order, or maybe organizing groups of Baran Do to go out into the galaxy the way Master Plo Koon did. If not, if he doesn't get better . . . well, he'll probably stay in those caverns, maintaining them as a hideaway for the Baran Do. The place will just be a bit less secure than it used to be."

"I wish I could feel happy for him."

"Feel happy about the others."

"Hey, there's something I've been meaning to do for you. I've been practicing while you weren't around."

Luke shot his son a suspicious look. "Go ahead."

Ben pulled his breath mask free and took a deep breath of the helium-rich Dorin atmosphere. " 'Where fields once grew, a road runs through, and buildings hide the sun,' " he sang, his voice as high and ridiculous as that of an animated Ewok in a children's broadcast.

"Ben, don't."

" 'Where grass of green could once be seen, are only gray and brown.' "

"I hate that song under *normal* circumstances."

" 'My childhood home, while I did roam, became a place of sadness.' "

"I'll just wait until you pass out."

" 'Now I return, my heart does yearn for times of light and gladness.' "

"You'll make your throat sore."

CALRISSIAN-NUNB MINES, KESSEL

It had been a couple of days since the pilots' expedition into Kessel's caverns, and a day since the last of the caverns not prematurely detonated had self-destructed. Things were different now.

The groundquakes had ceased. Lando's seismologists had concluded that the surface effects of cavern collapse were over for the time being. Mine workers and other inhabitants of Kessel were being returned in stages from the garrison moon.

There were no more bogeys to be seen. It seemed that their continued existence had depended on the functioning of the mysterious machinery that lined those caverns.

Lando and Tendra had filed a report about the whole affair with the Galactic Alliance government, and had been castigated for acting without consulting the authorities. Lando's company was now under strict orders not to blow up anything else on Kessel until government scientists had the opportunity to make a thorough study of the planet's underworld—a task, Han knew, that would require lifetimes just to generate preliminary conclusions.

But at the moment, no one was worried about extinct bogeys, recovering subterranean ecosystems, or the dictates of the GA government. Today a celebration filled the cafeteria of the main building, a chamber that had been little used in recent weeks.

Pilots of the three phases of the operation, seismologists, mechanics, returning miners, a recently arrived archaeological team, spouses, and children filled the room, crowding the tables. Animated, cheerful conversation, for so many years and in recent weeks a rarity on Kessel, rose as a din.

At the first table sat the Calrissians, the Solos, Nien Nunb, and several of their friends. Tendra raised a glass. "Here's to no more groundquakes, *ever*."

The others raised glasses and drank. Leia, her cheeks flushed, set her tumbler down and turned to Lando. "Is that just a hope, or is that the way it is?"

"The way it is." Clearly deeper into his cups than Leia, he leaned toward her and almost lost his balance; he braced himself against the table and sat upright again. "More caverns that have been weakened by the explosives might collapse, but the likelihood of them interacting in any way is basically nil. And the Great Kessel Fault remains stable."

Han gave Lando a nonchalant shrug. "Stable or not, it's all your fault. Yours and Tendra's and Nien Nunb's."

"That's right, old buddy. All our fault. We'll be exploring it next, by the way. You want to earn some easy money?"

"Noooo." Han put an arm around Leia. "It's back to Coruscant for us. We're trying to settle down. Raise a kid." He didn't add, *And we need to do it on a world where she isn't terrified of some specter from space coming after her.* Allana hadn't mentioned any further contact from the mysterious presence that had spoken to her, but just the possibility was keeping the child jittery, costing her sleep.

Lando would not be deterred. "Who knows what you'll find down there? Spiders the size of frigates. Gigantic glow rods that can light an entire solar system. Ancient Sith preserved in blocks of crystal for thousands of years."

Han shook his head, not uneasy, just disinterested. "They're all yours."

"Oh, well." Lando raised his glass, gesturing to old

friends and new. "My final drink of the evening, then, and my final toast for now." Suddenly he sounded much more serious. "Kessel is a homely world without much to commend it. It's a demonstration of your generosity of spirit that you would all come here to save it. You have my respect, and my thanks."

"And your hospitality," Wedge said.

"And my hospitality. Here's to you." Lando drank and set down his emptied glass. He rose and extended a hand to help Tendra up. "I'll see you off as you leave over the next few days. Those leaving tomorrow, we'll cry over our hangovers together." Smiling, the Calrissians departed.

Han drew in one deep, satisfied breath, let it out slowly, and turned to Leia. "Home?"

"Home."

DOR'SHAN SPACEPORT, DORIN

Dressed in fresh clothes and breathing the Coruscant-like atmosphere provided by *Jade Shadow*'s life-support system, Ben and Luke sat in the yacht's small lounge area. Momentarily free of responsibility, they could relax for a bit. Ben sprawled in a reclining chair while Luke sped through several days' worth of holonews recordings and communications.

"What's new in the galaxy, Dad?"

"I had about a dozen queries from Cilghal. The fact that I wasn't replying had her a bit concerned . . . I just asked her to look into reports of Force nexuses Jacen might have heard of while he was here. Not the one on Dagobah or the one walled in at the base of the Jedi Temple. He was already aware of those. Somewhere different."

"Nexuses. Thrilling."

"They caught Seff Hellin. Jaina and some allies did."

"The crazy Jedi that Aunt Leia mentioned?"

"That's the one."

"Good."

"Cilghal reports some abnormalities in his brain scan. A place to start her research. And—oh, excellent."

"What?"

Luke angled the monitor screen so his son could see more clearly. It showed aged newsman Wolam Tser speaking in his usual grave manner; then the image cut to Nawara Ven, well-dressed, standing on the steps before the Courts of Justice Building, surrounded by members of the press. Luke dialed up the volume and Tser's voice could be heard: "—action initiated by advocate Nawara Ven. The High Court's ruling effectively strikes down the Chief of State's executive order, lifting many of the restrictions imposed on the Jedi Order in recent weeks." Nawara Ven raised a fist, triumphant, and shouted silently in answer to someone's question; then the image cut back to Wolam Tser. "Chief of State Natasi Daala has not yet issued a statement about the ruling. Privately, many of the observers assigned to the Jedi, whose mission came to an abrupt end this afternoon with the issuance of the ruling, have expressed dissatisfaction, claiming that the Jedi tendency toward willfulness and disregard of the law make the observers' role a crucial one. Jedi Master Kenth Hamner, asked about—" Luke dialed the volume down again.

Ben raised a fist, mimicking Nawara Ven's gesture. "That's one for us." He saw his father take a breath and hastily added, "Yes, I know. Dangerous forces out there. The Hidden One may have been partly right. Mustn't get cocky. Dad, just for tonight—"

Luke grinned. "Just for tonight, no admonitions. No advice."

"Thanks. Where do we go next?"

"We'll see what Cilghal tells us. Until then, we relax."

Ben put his hands behind his head and closed his eyes. Relax—*that* he could do.

And though he was countless light-years from home, only a few weeks into his father's ten-year exile, sore from physical labor and being beaten by a combat trainer, he decided that things could be a lot worse.

It was good to be alive.

Read on for an excerpt from
Star Wars: Fate of the Jedi: Omen
by Christie Golden
Published by Del Rey

ORBITING ZIOST
TWO STANDARD YEARS AGO

DICIAN FELT THE PLANET EVEN BEFORE IT APPEARED ON THE
main bridge monitor of the *Poison Moon*. She sensed
it had seen her, as she now saw it, this seemingly harmless world of blue and white and green, and she smiled
gently. The pale geometric tattoos on her face, which
stood out in stark contrast with her dark skin tones,
crinkled with the gesture. This was the destination she
had beheld in her mind's eye a short while ago, the un-
voiced answer to the question of what she was hoping to
intercept here. She had ordered the crew of this frigate
to make all speed, and only hoped she was in time.

Where are you going, charming one?

To unopened eyes and dead senses, this planet would
seem a world much as any other: a world with oceans
and landmasses, heavily, practically entirely forested,
with two white, icecapped poles on either end. White
clouds drifted lazily above it.

But it was not a world like any other.

It was Ziost. Homeworld of the Sith.

What was left of the Sith Order now remained silent
and in hiding on Korriban, of course. She would return

there soon, but not without the prize she had come to claim.

Dician realized she was leaning forward slightly in anticipation, and settled back in her command chair. She gently pushed her excitement down lest it interfere with her mission.

"Wayniss, take us in to orbit." In her role as an intelligence gatherer, the light, musical tone of her voice often deceived others into thinking her much, much more harmless than she was. Her crew knew better.

"Aye, Captain," the chief pilot of the *Poison Moon* replied. Wayniss was a laconic man, not at all Forcesensitive, pleased enough to do as he was told in exchange for the generous pay he was receiving. In his own way, the graying ex-pirate was as fair, honorable, and hardworking as many so-called upstanding citizens. He had done well by Dician on this mission already.

"Any sign of the meditation sphere?" she asked Ithila, her sensor officer. Ithila leaned forward, her face, which would have been beautiful in the traditionally Hapan manner if not for the horrific burn scar that marred the right side, furrowed in concentration.

"Negative," Ithila replied as Ziost appeared in the forward viewports and the *Poison Moon* settled into orbit around it. "No indication of it on the planet surface." She turned to regard her captain. "Looks like we beat it here."

Dician smiled again. No mistakes. All that remained was to capture the small vessel itself.

Dician settled in to wait, her dark eyes on the slowly turning planet in front of her. It gazed back at her, and she felt a tug in her heart. She wanted to land the *Poison Moon*, to walk Ziost's forests as other Sith had done in ages past. But that was not why they were here. She must think of the good of the One, the Order, above her own yearnings. One day, perhaps, she would stand upon the surface of this world. But that day would not be today.

They did not have long to wait. Only a few moments later, Ithila said, "Picking it up on long-range sensors, Captain."

Dician sat up straighter in her chair. "You have all served well and brilliantly. Now, as our smuggler pilot might say, it is time to close this deal."

It was time for her, Dician, to be perfect. She could not afford a mistake now.

She felt it even as Ithila transmitted the image to her personal viewscreen. There it was, the Sith meditation sphere. She regarded it for a moment, taking it in—the spherical shape, the orange-yellow-red hue, the twin sets of bat-like wings on either side of it. It resembled an enormous eye.

"Hello again, charming one," she said in her most pleasant voice.

Silence from the sphere.

"As you see, we have anticipated your arrival. Why have you come to Ziost?"

Home.

The voice was inside her head, masculine and intensely focused. A little thrill of exhilaration shivered through Dician. This was not a pet to be coaxed, but a mount to be broken. It respected strength and will.

Dician had plenty of both.

There is a better place for you than on an abandoned world. Dician did not speak the words. Her melodic voice was no asset in this negotiation; the focus and strength of her thoughts were.

The vessel continued its approach to Ziost, not wavering in the slightest, but Dician sensed she had its attention. It would listen.

You are a Sith meditation sphere. Come with me to where the Sith are now. Serve us, as you were designed to do. She let herself visualize Korriban as it was now: with not just two Sith, but many who were One, with apprentices in need of focus and training in the power of the dark side if they were to achieve the glory and power that were rightfully theirs.

"It's slowing its approach," Ithila said. "It's come to a full halt."

Dician didn't bother to tell the Hapan woman that she already knew that; that she was intimately connected with this meditation sphere, this . . . Ship.

It seemed particularly interested in the younglings, and she understood that this had been the focus of its design. To protect and educate apprentices. To prepare them for their destinies.

You will come to Korriban. You will serve me, Dician, and you will teach the younglings. You will fulfill your intended purpose.

This was the moment upon which everything hinged. She sensed scrutiny from the vessel. Dician was unashamed of her strengths and let it see her freely. It sensed her will, her drive, her passions, her desire for perfection.

Perfection, said Ship. It mulled over the word.

Nothing less serves the dark side fully, Dician replied. *You will help me to attain perfection for the Sith.*

Perfection cannot be obtained by hiding.

Dician blinked. This had caught her by surprise. *It is wisdom. We will stay isolated, grow strong, and then claim what is ours.*

Ship considered. Doubt gnawed at the corner of Dician's mind like a gizka. She crushed it utterly, ruthlessly, and poured all her will into the demand.

The Jedi grow strong and numerous. It is not time to hide. I will not serve. I will find a better purpose.

She felt it shut down in her mind, close itself off to her

in what was tantamount to a dismissal. Dician felt her cheeks grow hot. How could it have refused?

"Captain," said Ithila, "the ship has resumed course to Ziost."

"I can see that," Dician snapped, and Ithila stared openly. Ship was a rapidly disappearing sphere on her screen, and as she watched it was lost to sight.

Dician returned her attention to her crew, who, she realized, were all looking at her with confused expressions on their faces. She took a deep, steadying breath.

"The vessel would not have been appropriate for us," she said, her pleasant voice challenging anyone to disagree. "Its programming is antiquated and outdated. Our original message was successful. It is time to pick up the shuttle crews and return home. Plot a course through hyperspace for Omega Three Seven Nine," she instructed Wayniss. He turned around and his fingers flew lightly over the console.

The *Poison Moon*'s original mission had not been to recover Ship, as Dician had begun thinking of the sphere. Dician had initially been sent to track down a Twi'lek woman named Alema Rar and her base of operations. Rar had somehow inherited a lost Force technique that enabled her to project phantoms across space. Dician had been ordered to destroy both the woman and the dark side energy source lest either fall into Jedi hands. And then she had been forced to choose between two unexpected prizes.

When the *Poison Moon* arrived at Alema Rar's base, coming in stealth, Dician had discovered they were not alone. One of the two vessels already at the asteroid was none other than the *Millennium Falcon*. Subsequent observations of her operations revealed that it was more than likely her notorious owner Han Solo was piloting her—and quite possibly his wife, Leia Organa, traitor to the noble name of Skywalker, was with him. Her crews had placed bombs on the asteroid that had been Alema's base, and Dician, not about to let such a victory slip away, was turning her attention to the destruction of the Corellian freighter.

But before Dician could issue the orders to detonate the bombs and attack the *Falcon,* Ship had emerged from the base—without Alema Rar.

Dician had made the decision to follow and attempt to capture Ship, forgoing an attack on the *Falcon.* She had ordered the bombs to detonate and the crews that had placed them to await her return on the largest asteroid in the system, designated Omega 379. No doubt they were anticipating her swift return.

Dician pressed her full lips together. She had chosen tracking Ship over blowing the *Millennium Falcon* out of the skies. She had done exactly what she had threatened her crew not to do—made a mistake. And now she could claim neither victory.

Let Ship remain isolated on Ziost. It would find no one to serve, no one to permit it to do that which it was designed for.

In her irritation, Dician let the thought comfort her.

JYSELLA HORN FELT LIKE A PART OF HER, TOO, WAS EN-cased in carbonite. Frozen and isolated and unable to move. Yet somehow she forced her legs to carry her forward, toward the Jedi Temple that would, she hoped, have some answers for her today.

Ever since the inexplicable and horrifying moment when her older brother, Valin, had turned on their parents, eyes wild, teeth bared, screaming nonsense, part of the youngest Horn had gone with him into the cold prison in which he was now encased.

She had always been the baby of the family, the tag-along, the *me too!* little sister. Ten standard years separated the Horn siblings, and it had only been in recent years that they had begun relating as friends and not just as brother and sister. Jysella had always idolized her easygoing, levelheaded big brother. The lives of her rather famous family had been fraught with danger almost since the day she was born. Often, she and Valin were separated from their parents and even from each other for long periods of time. Three Jedi in a family did not make for much time spent doing traditional fa-milial things. But the challenges and the separation had always brought them closer, not driven wedges between them.

So the sight of her brother coldly staring at them through the one-way transparisteel panel, knowing that he had attacked both their parents and claimed that his beloved sister, father, and mother were "fakes," had somehow been stolen away—

Jysella shivered. Cold, she was cold, he was cold and in carbonite, her kind, grinning brother, the gentle and loved one, whom they said was criminally insane.

Bazel Warv laid a heavy green hand on her narrow shoulder as they climbed up the long ceremonial staircase of the Processional Way toward the Jedi Temple. A series of grunts and squeaks issued from his tusked mouth as he offered reassurances.

"I know, I know," Jysella said to the Gamorrean with a sigh. His small, piggy eyes were full of compassion. "Everyone's doing their best. It doesn't make it any easier."

Bazel, "Barv" as his little circle of close friends called him, considered this and nodded agreement. He squeezed her shoulder, putting all his concern into the gesture, and Jysella forced herself not to wince. Around his fellow Jedi, Bazel tended to forget how strong he was. With little Amelia, the young war orphan who had been adopted by Han and Leia Solo, though, the Gamorrean was gentle to a fault. Amelia often went for piggyback rides on Barv's huge shoulders, laughing and giggling. The little girl was fond of everyone in "the Unit," as Barv, Yaqeel Saavis, Valin, and Jysella called themselves.

"The big guy's right," Yaqeel, walking on Jysella's other side, commented. "Don't underestimate what a group of top Jedi can do when their backs are against the wall."

Jysella had to force herself to again refrain from wincing, this time from the coolness of the Bothan's words.

She'd known both Barv and Yaqeel for a long time now. They had been Valin's friends first, but had drawn Jysella happily into the circle as she grew older.

Yaqeel used words in the same controlled, deadly way she used her lightsaber. Normally the acerbic, cynical comments she was fond of drawling didn't bother Jysella in the slightest. But now she felt . . . raw. Like her emotional skin had been filleted away and even the slightest breeze caused agony.

Barv oinked, annoyed, and Yaqeel's ear twitched slightly. Barv was convinced that the Jedi were working hard to find a cure for Valin's condition not because their own necks were threatened, but because it was the right thing to do. Because that's what Jedi *did*.

Tears of gratitude stung Jysella's eyes as she smiled at her friend. Yaqeel's ears lowered slightly, a sign that Barv's simple faith had gotten to her as well. That wasn't unusual. Everyone—well, everyone except dear, slightly dense Barv himself—knew that Yaqeel had a soft spot for "the big guy," and no one blamed her for it. Barv was uncomplicated and true, with a heart as big as the galaxy and an unshakable sense of right and wrong.

Jysella desperately wanted to believe him in this case, but the fear, fluttering at the back of her throat like a living thing, prevented it.

"Anyway, honey, we know your brother's got his head screwed on right," Yaqeel said in a gentler tone of voice. "Whatever's happening to him, I'm convinced it's only temporary. What you need to do is stop watching newsvids. They're all about reporting whatever sounds juiciest. And that's usually *not* the truth."

They'd reached the Temple entrance. Once, the Jedi Temple had been notable for its five spires, a unique feature of the Coruscant skyline. But much of that had been destroyed during the Yuuzhan Vong War. A great deal of the interior of the Temple had been restored to its former appearances—right down to the marble patterns on the floors in some cases—but the exterior, a collection of several stone and transparisteel pyramids in a variety of sizes, was aggressively modern. Jysella found she missed the familiar statues of four former Masters that once stood guard over the main entrance.

She sighed. She'd just turned around to speak to her friends when she found herself caught up in a nearly crushing hug. A grin curved her lips despite herself and she hugged Barv back.

"Thanks, Barv," she said, using up the last bit of air he'd left in her lungs.

He released her and she gulped oxygen, smiling up at him. Yaqeel embraced her now, all warm, slightly spicy-scented fur and a softness that most people never really got to know. "You'll feel better once you're doing something," Yaqeel said.

Barv allowed that he himself always felt better when he was doing something. Usually that involved attacking bad guys. Yaqeel patted Jysella's cheek. "Sure you don't want us coming in with you?"

"No, it's okay. You two have done enough. I—I don't know what I would have done without you, honestly," Jysella said, the words burbling out of her. "Mom and Dad have been so focused on Valin—and I mean, of course they *should* be focused on him. I am, too. Just—"

"You don't need to say it," Yaqeel interrupted her gently, sensing, as Jysella now did, that if the human girl continued she'd lose what tenuous control she had. "We're the Unit. And the Unit can always rely on each other. You'd have done the same for us."

Barv nodded vigorously. And it was true. Jysella and Valin would have done the same for either of these two friends and fellow Jedi Knights. Done a lot more, as she knew they would have if they had to.

"Well," she said, trying to put a brave face on it, "with you two and the whole Jedi Order, I'm sure we'll have Valin out of that carbonite slab in no time. Though I have to admit, when I was a kid, there were plenty of times when I'd have loved it if he'd been a coffee table that didn't talk back."

It was a feeble attempt at humor, but they all seized it and laughed. *Gotta laugh or I'll cry,* Jysella thought. And Valin wouldn't want her to cry. She'd done altogether too much of it in recent days.

Grinning, Yaqeel slipped her arm through Barv's. "Come on. I'll buy you a caf. We still on for lunch, 'Sella?"

Lunch. She'd forgotten about that. She seemed to be forgetting a lot these days, except the overwhelming longing for everything to be all right again.

"Oh, right. Yes, come back in a few hours. I'm sure Cilghal will want me out of her . . ." She paused and laughed, a genuine laugh this time. "Except Mon Calamari don't have hair, do they?"

It was a good note to end on, and the three remnants of the Unit waved at one another. Jysella watched Barv and Yaqeel walk off, then sighed and turned to enter the Temple. She smiled politely at the five apprentices who were stationed there as guardians.

How many times had she been here before? She had lost count. It had always been a special place, as it was to every Jedi. For long stretches, when she was not out on assignment, it had been home. But now it seemed even more to her to be a bastion of hope. Somewhere within this vast repository of knowledge, some information that could help her brother had to be housed. Some clue as to what had happened to him, and how to put it right.

Barv thought so. She clung to that hope as well.

Jysella's booted feet rang in the vast, open space of the

Temple entrance hall as she headed toward the turbolift that would take her to the First Wing of the archives. She crossed her arms, fidgeting slightly, as the turbolift hummed softly and bore her to the top floor.

She found Cilghal in a small alcove in the depths of the stacks, seated at one of the tables and surrounded by tall piles of glowing blue data tapes and datacards. Her smooth brown head was bent over an ancient text, and her flipper-like hands were encased in gloves to protect the delicate old flimsi. She looked up at Jysella's approach.

"Jysella. Right on time," she said, her gravelly voice warm.

Jysella offered her a weak smile in return and slipped into the seat across from her. Even though this was the arranged time for them to meet, it was clear that Cilghal had been here for a while already. There were piles of datapads on the table beside her and curious objects she had obviously signed out in order to examine.

"I . . ." Jysella sighed and reached out for a datapad, holding it in a limp hand. "I'm sorry, Master Cilghal. I don't even know where to *start* trying to help."

Cilghal regarded her sympathetically, slightly turning her head to fix Jysella with a single large, bulbous eye. "You know everyone is doing everything they can. It is important to us all that your brother recover fully—and that we understand what happened to him. With understanding will, we very much hope, come a cure, and the ability to negotiate his release from the GA."

Jysella winced and brushed back a lock of reddish brown hair that had escaped the haphazard bun she'd pinned up this morning.

"I know. It . . . it's upsetting that this is only serving to damage the Jedi in the eyes of the public. Valin—he would never have wanted that."

"Of course not," Cilghal soothed. "This is no way a

reflection on your family, Jysella. It is simply a tragic and, temporarily I hope, an inexplicable event."

Cilghal sounded utterly earnest, and Jysella believed that the Mon Calamari healer meant every word. She knew that Cilghal was, to some degree, against the idea of Jedi having attachments. And yet she was still so kind and supportive to Jysella. It meant a lot.

Still . . . She wished Master Skywalker were here. Although Luke had done everything he could to make sure the transition of power was smooth, the Jedi Order had been thrown into tumult upon his departure. She knew Master Kenth was doing his best in the thankless role of trying to make everyone happy, but also knew he wasn't succeeding. The last thing the Order needed was a nutso Jedi Knight running around claiming that people weren't who they were.

Jysella closed her eyes for a moment, feeling again the sickening pain as her adored big brother stared at her and demanded in a cold voice, "Where's my sister? Where is she? What have you done with her?"

And now he was encased in carbonite in a GA prison, unable to be with those who loved him, to even comprehend that those who loved him were trying to help him. Sympathetically feeling the cold that enshrouded Valin, Jysella wrapped slim arms around her own body and shivered slightly.

Oh, Valin. If only you could tell us what had happened . . . why you looked at Mom and Dad and thought they weren't them. How could you not know us? Not know me?

Tears leaked past her closed lids, and she brushed them away angrily. *Stop it, 'Sella,* she told herself sternly. Grief and worry would not serve Valin, or the Order, now. Only calmness and knowledge would. She opened her eyes and reached for the discarded datapad.

"That looks like a very old record," she said, lifting her eyes to Cilghal. "Do you have any theories on—"

And felt the blood drain from her face.

The Mon Cal was apparently done with the old flimsi and now was intently studying the information on a datapad. Her large eyes were fastened on it, unblinking in her concentration. The alcove was quiet, save for soft voices talking and the sound of footfalls some distance away. All was as it was just a moment ago.

Except everything—everything—had been turned upside down.

Valin had been right. She saw it now . . .

Jysella inhaled swiftly. It *looked* like Cilghal. Whoever had done this had not missed a detail. It even moved like the Mon Calamari healer. And it had certainly acted and sounded like her. But Jysella suddenly and sickly understood exactly what her brother had meant.

The Not-Cilghal turned her head to regard Jysella, cocking her head curiously. "Jysella? What is it?"

"N-nothing. I . . . you know what?" She gave a shaky laugh. "I think I may be too upset to help you out much," Jysella managed. She rose. She had to get away, and fast, before this doppelgänger realized she was on to its deception. But where would she go? Who could she tell? If Valin had been right, then everyone except for her had been taken and replaced by their doubles. How could she not have seen this earlier? *Oh, Valin, I'm sorry I didn't believe you—*

The imitation Cilghal looked fully away from the datapad she had been studying, turning her head slightly to fix Jysella with one huge, circular eye.

"You've held up very well indeed throughout all this, Jysella," the doppelgänger said gently. "It's not surprising that you might now be finding you cannot carry it all. Do you wish to talk about this? Speaking one's worry and fears can be as healing as bacta tanks, in its own way."

The rough voice was warm and concerned. It only rattled Jysella more. Stang—whoever it was, they were good, they had mastered Cilghal's voice, her inflections, her movements. No wonder it had fooled so many for so long.

But Valin hadn't been fooled, although in his confusion he had mistaken his sister and parents for doppelgängers like the one before her now.

Oh, no . . . what if he'd been right about Mom and—

"I think I had just better go." One hand dropped casually to her waist, resting on the lightsaber hilt that was fastened there. As a full Jedi Knight, she was authorized to carry the weapon throughout the Temple except in a very few restricted areas. She'd almost forgotten it this morning in her stress over Valin. Now she was tremendously glad she had gone back for it.

Not-Cilghal's eye followed the gesture, and she got to her feet. She had her own weapon, of course, but made no move to take it. "Jysella, why don't you come with me and we'll—"

Terror shot through Jysella, and a sob escaped her. She stepped back, her hand gripping the lightsaber hilt so hard her knuckles whitened.

"Get away from me!" she screamed, her voice shaking.

"Jysella—" It reached out to her imploringly.

"I said get *away*!"

Jysella drew the lightsaber in one hand and shoved the other in the false Cilghal's direction. The males in her family were unable to use telekinesis. Jysella was not so hampered, and she used that ability now. She put all her fear, all her focus, in the gesture, and Not-Cilghal was caught unawares as Jysella Force-shoved her back into a stack of datapads.

She didn't pause to watch as Not-Cilghal crashed into the stack. By then Jysella Horn, quite possibly the only real person left on the planet—maybe in the galaxy—except for her brother, was racing down the aisle toward the turbolift as fast as she could go.

Cilghal recovered quickly, using the Force to steady the stack and prevent it from toppling entirely. A few datapads clattered to the floor as she rose and reached for her comlink with one hand and her lightsaber in the other. She'd been utterly taken by surprise and mentally rebuked herself.

"Temple security, this is Master Cilghal," she said even as she began racing after the fleeing human. "Jedi Knight Jysella Horn is to be captured and retained. Do not harm her if at all possible. She is not herself. Notify Master Hamner immediately. Tell him—tell him we've got another one."

"Acknowledged," came a crisp, cool voice. Cilghal clicked the comlink off. Time enough for more details once Jysella was safely apprehended.

It was obvious what had happened. Like her brother, Jysella Horn had lost her reason. But unlike Valin, who had been irrationally angry, Jysella was pouring utter and abject fear into the Force. Whatever her mind might be telling her, it was terrifying her beyond anything Cilghal had experienced from a human before.

Compassion combined with a grim determination to prevent the frightened girl from harming anyone else lent the Mon Calamari speed. One way or another, they would stop her. After all, this was the Jedi Temple, and Jysella, although quite a capable Jedi Knight, was hardly unstoppable, even if fueled by insane fear.

Where could she possibly go?